popCult!

.

popCult!

David Barnett

Pendragon Press

First Published in 2011by
Pendragon Press
Po Box 12, Maesteg, Mid Glamorgan
South Wales, CF34 0XG, UK

ISBN 978 1 906864 24 8

Typeset by Christopher Teague

Printed and Bound by
CPI Antony Rowe, Eastbourne

www.pendragonpress.net

This one's for the Library Boys:

Kev, Phil, John, Chris,
Dave and Tony.

"Have you been to see him?"

"It, Monroe. *It.* Not everything in this world's got a dick for you to tease, you know."

"Okay. Have you been to see *it?*"

"Mmm. It's getting bigger. I think we might have to take another wall down."

"We're already pretty close to the Circle Line as it is..."

"So a couple of thousand commuters go home with ideas for new TV shows every night. That's kind of the point anyway, Monroe. Besides, we can always get the Machine Elves to dampen the walls again."

"I don't know, Tyler. It's all happening so fast..."

"It is growing more quickly than it ever has. I suppose that's only to be expected, though."

"Tyler, what's it like? I don't mean what it looks like, I've seen it, of course, I mean... what's it *like?* Being near it? So many times? For such long periods?"

"Curious, eh, Monroe? You can see it again, if you want, you know. It's like... it's like... it's like everything. All at once. And the ideas you get... millions of them, tumbling around your head. Which reminds me; have you found anyone yet?"

"There's a guy I've got my eye on."

"So what else is new?"

"Tyler."

"Okay, I'm sorry. Go on."

"He's a bit of a loner... a collector. He's writing a book, as far as I can gather. I think we can probably hook him in easily enough."

"Why should we? What's special about him?"

"I'm not sure... I've just got a hunch."

"Brief MacGuffin and get him to cook something up. We're one down since The Waif got herself toasted. That look was so last century, anyway. No great loss."

"Tyler, you're terrible."

"I'll tell you what else I am, as well. Being near it always makes me horny as hell."

"Oh, Tyler..."

"Come on, Monroe. You know you love it... That's it... Maybe I'll take you to see it, sometime... That's it, Monroe... Oh."

One

It must have been a Wednesday when Stuart first saw the astronaut, because he was on his way to the corner shop to buy a lottery ticket. It can't have been a Saturday, because he always put the lottery on at the papershop near the home his mother was in on a Saturday. So it was a Wednesday; raining, he remembers, soft drizzle that soaked him through, the light – such as it was – failing although it was barely four, the cigarette hanging damp and lifeless between his lips. He sucked hard enough to make it glow uselessly at the tip and weighed up the change in his pockets. Enough for his lottery, maybe a packet of ten fags, and perhaps a sausage roll. He'd been working straight through since nine and hadn't eaten a thing. His stomach was raw with hunger and his eyes red–rimmed from staring at the laptop screen in the glum shadows of the flat. Abandoning the cigarette and grinding it underfoot without breaking stride, Stuart wondered how much longer it was until the next tranche of payment from Professor Garrett. He would have to deliver a damn sight more than he'd written so far to get Garrett to dig deep into the university coffers, he thought. In the meantime... a diet of cheap pre–packed savouries and the eternal optimism of the lottery. Blindly sorting his pound coins into a column with his right hand, Stuart turned the corner on to the main road, and ran straight into the astronaut.

"Jesus Christ!" he exclaimed as his own distorted face gaped back at him as though reflected in a giant spoon. The glass of the space helmet was opaque and polished, merging smoothly with the white dome that encased the head of whoever was inside. Stuart took an involuntary step backwards as the astronaut walked towards him with exaggerated slowness, aping a low–gravity moonwalk. From somewhere, static hissed and burbled, stopping abruptly and then starting again. A distant, tinny, American voice said what sounded like "Houston" and "green–to–go".

For a split–second Stuart was horrified by his grotesque reflection, the rain–plastered anti–styled hair that hung in hanks from his head, the stubbly chin, the narrow eyes. He tore his gaze away and looked quickly around. Across the road two women with prams were pointing and laughing at him. No, not at him, surely. At the astronaut.

Stuart squeezed against the damp brick wall to allow the astronaut to lope past. The suit was pretty good, he had to admit. It looked genuine, he thought, although he had to concede that he'd never actually seen a real space–suit. But this one was bulky and solid–looking, white and clean. The astronaut turned his whole upper body so that the helmet was facing him; Stuart didn't like the feeling of being scrutinised from beneath that dreadful black fish–bowl. Then the astronaut moved on, swimming through the heavy air, continuing his pantomime walk down the street, and Stuart could breathe again.

He shook his head, as people do in these situations, and continued on to Moe's shop which perched on the next corner.

The shop was empty apart from Moe, who sat on a small wooden stool behind the counter, watching on a small fuzzy television set a cricket match beamed in from sunnier climes. He was really called Mohammed, Stuart knew, but had liked the name Moe ever since he first saw *The Simpsons*. He felt it gave him some currency with the locals, he once implied, that it made the racists laugh a bit and maybe think twice about stoving in his windows with chair legs.

"Two Lucky Dips for tonight, please, Moe," said Stuart, pausing by the magazine rack and glancing at the cover of some celebrity gossip magazine. *Mikey tells Joey it's off!* screamed the cover line. Stuart felt vaguely distressed that he not only didn't know who Mikey and Joey were, but had no idea either what combination of genders the coupling comprised or that what was now "off" had ever, in fact, been "on". Distressed because his next proper meal and merest hope of paying the bills depended on him being one of the country's leading authorities on popular culture. Or at least, that was how he'd sold himself to Professor Garrett. He weighed up the pros and cons of ditching the fags and buying the magazine instead, then decided against it. He needed fags to get through the night; he could always find out who Mikey and Joey were later on, if they were important.

"Did you see the spaceman?" asked Moe, without taking his eyes off the TV screen, sucking in his cheeks as a wicket was lost, or won. Stuart felt unaccountably relieved. Not that he thought he'd imagined the astronaut, but it felt good that someone as grounded in stark reality as the proprietor of the corner shop had seen him too.

"Who is he?" said Stuart, stuffing the magazine back in the rack and perusing the contents of the refrigerator. "Some kind of mime artist?"

Moe shrugged, still transfixed on the cricket. "I thought he was advertising something, a nightclub maybe. Perhaps you should put him in your book."

Stuart selected a cold, waxy–looking Cornish pasty and put it on the counter next to the lottery ticket. "And ten Marlboro Lights, Moe," he said.

Moe reached for the cigarettes. "Not allowed to call them Lights any more, Mr Balfour," he clucked. "Makes them sound as though they are not going to kill you. So how is the book, then?"

Stuart surveyed his purchases and pulled from his pocket the column of pound coins he had palmed . "Oh, good," he said absently. Maybe Moe was right and he should put the spaceman in the book. He made a mental note to include a chapter on urban attention seekers, and was thinking about the others he'd seen, the pretend statue people in Covent Garden, the stilt–walker who abused the orators at Hyde Park Corner, the tramp he'd seen in New York that time with a sign around his neck saying "tell me off for two dollars".

Stuart realised Moe was waiting expectantly for the money. He counted out the coins and surveyed what was left. Pennies.

Things were not good. He'd better ring Professor Garrett today.

"There he goes again," said Moe.

Stuart looked up and out of the rain–streaked window; the astronaut was on the other side of the road, miming playing a golf shot for the amusement of two umbrella'd old ladies dragging tartan shopping trolleys. Whoever was in the suit seemed to feel Stuart's gaze and the helmet inclined slightly, as though returning his stare. Uncomfortably, Stuart gathered his purchases and mumbled a farewell to Moe.

By the time he got out of the shop, the astronaut was gone. The two old ladies scowled at Stuart from the other side of the road, as though his demeanour had spirited away their only entertainment for the day. A fat glob of rain hit him squarely on the nose and he looked up imploringly at the blackening sky. The dusk declined to meet his gaze, and spat on him again. Stuart hurried home.

He hadn't dared hope to catch Professor Garrett still at the university so late, but after three rings the familiar hesitant voice answered. Stuart shoved a finger into his ear to drown out the sound of drilling coming from somewhere unseen but nearby which shook the cracked, rain–streaked panes of the telephone box. Many of his acquaintances no longer had a land–line in their homes, but Stuart took an almost perverse pleasure in being the only person he knew who had never owned a mobile phone nor was ever likely to. It was a stupid affectation in a world where if you were not contactable you were almost beneath contempt, but he clung grimly to it, though he would have been hard–pressed to say why. The cost, he would have told himself. He could barely afford to eat these days, never mind keep a mobile phone in credit. He had a landline in the flat, which allowed him to connect to the internet, but the handset had broken some weeks ago and he'd not had the necessary to replace it. He was achingly aware that he was pumping the last of his change into the call box, that he was paying for the privilege of standing in a puddle of piss with his last few pence in the world. He'd better make this call count.

Professor Garrett seemed rather ambivalent to hear from him. "More money? This is highly irregular. Didn't we just issue a payment?"

"Two months ago," shouted Stuart. "I'm about to deliver chapters eight to eleven. Sixties crime–fighting shows through to Seventies youthsploitation fiction. I had to spend quite a bit of the money at Amazon on *Champions* DVDs and copies of *Suedehead*. You'd be surprised at how much... oh, hang on Professor–"

Stuart plunged the last of his change into the slot to see off the beeps. Professor Garrett started talking to someone else, his hand over the receiver to muffle his voice.

"Professor?" said Stuart, a little more shrilly and certainly much more desperately than he intended.

"Yes, yes," said Professor Garrett to Stuart. "We can bring the next advance forward, but we really must see up to and including chapter twenty before any future payment, Mr Balfour. And we'll need to see receipts for any research materials."

"Oh, thank you, Professor," said Stuart. "Thank you. Oh, before you go, Professor, have you any idea who Joey and Mikey—?"

But the connection was dead and he was listening to hissing static and the incessant scream of the drill. Still, mission accomplished. Stuart lit a celebratory Marlboro in the shelter of the telephone box and stepped out into the rain.

It would be too late for Professor Garrett to organise the payment tonight, reflected Stuart as he sat by the open window of his flat smoking the fourth of his packet of ten Marlboros. The earliest he could hope for the money to go into his account would be Friday, which would mean getting through tomorrow with no cash at all. Of course, if Garrett didn't sort out the transfer tomorrow he would be looking at spending all weekend penniless, which didn't bear thinking about. Of course, he could ask his mother for money when he went to visit her at the home on Saturday, but he always felt bad on the occasions he'd had to resort to that. And not a little pathetic, too; there she was, slobbering into her custard and imagining Zeppelins being constructed covertly by mean–faced dwarfs in the TV room after she had gone to bed and he was still tied to her apron strings, wheedling spare change out of her to buy cigarettes and sandwiches.

Stuart expertly flicked the cigarette out of the window. He didn't really like smoking in the bedsit, which was a hangover of his time with Jane. When they had their flat in Islington together she would never let him inside with his cigarettes, and he'd grown used to spending his evenings standing in the garden, puffing on a fag as he watched the planes and satellites wink overhead.

After the divorce he'd stuck to the outdoors habit, only recently allowing himself the luxury of smoking out of the open window of his third–floor flat rather than standing on the shared door–step. He'd been driven inside by a combination of the cold weather and the crack addicts with pin–prick lights in their black eyes who scuffed about on the pavement waiting for the dealer in the ground floor flat to open up.

Stuart watched the orange tip of the butt as it sailed downwards, bouncing off the slick sheen of rain on the street. It wasn't pouring anymore and the air felt a degree or two warmer. As the embers sizzled out in a puddle, something caught Stuart's eye, a white flash, a movement near the big, windowless red brick wall that dominated the other side of the street. It bordered a factory or a warehouse, Stuart supposed; he'd never really been moved to find out. A good twenty feet high, it was curled with rusty barbed wire on its top edge. Sometimes he stared at it for hours through his window; a quintessential bedsit view.

At ground level, just to his left on the edge of the penumbra bordering a pool of orange light from a street–lamp still working though its innards were hanging out, stood the astronaut. Stuart did a double take which doubtless would have been comical if there had been anyone in the room to see him.

The astronaut stood mutely by the wall, his arm raised slightly. Stuart's heart leapt into his mouth, but it wasn't a greeting; the astronaut was pointing at something. At the wall. Behind him was a mural, a fresh, brightly–coloured graffito which must have been done in the time since the rain stopped, because he certainly hadn't noticed it earlier. Stuart squinted to make it out in the darkness; two words, running into each other, the first in sloping, stylised italics, propped up against the solid blocks of capitals of the second.

*pop*CULT!

Apparently satisfied that whoever he was signalling to – me? thought Stuart crazily – had seen the artwork, the astronaut began to lope slowly off down the street, back towards the main road and the shops.   Stuart stared at the spray–painted words. *pop*CULT!   It had a ring to it. A band, perhaps, or a maybe nightclub, as Moe had suggested. Stuart shivered. It was getting colder so, shrugging, he fastened the window and sat down again at the bright, blank, accusing screen of his battered laptop. He stared at it for a while, then picked up the copy of *Suedehead* that had come through the post yesterday. He'd read it when he was a kid, though never owned it. A battered paperback had passed from desk to desk, devoured surreptitiously at break–times and during boring history lessons. Budding adults excited by the sex and violence and Seventies futurism. Most of his class–mates left it there and either grew up or moved on to real–life sex and violence, but the young Stuart used the books as a spring–board to *A Clockwork Orange* and later Stewart Home. He wasn't really built for sex or violence and instead became the bedroom anarchist, dreaming of chaos and outrage but scared to pass a group of more than three strange boys on the street.

The book gave him bad memories of a childhood of geekdom and he put it down with a shiver. The chapter on youthsploitation could wait. Despite what he'd said to Professor Garrett, chapters

9

eight through eleven weren't even started, let alone finished. Instead he decided to jump ahead a couple of chapters, and from the shelf in his room selected a handful of DVDs: The *Champions* one that came from Amazon with the *Suedehead* book, a couple of compilations of *Avengers* episodes and *Super Vixens*. Strictly speaking, Russ Meyer's pneumatic anti–heroines and his related canon of films didn't really fit the brief of British popular culture that Stuart was researching, but he did think a passing reference was in order for the chapter on the rise of strong female characters in movies and television which he had given the working title Leather and Lace. He watched the three episodes of The *Champions* on the disc, making dutiful notes on Alexandro Bastedo's screen presence. He broke off only to check his lottery numbers with a fatalistic glimmer of hope, screwing the ticket into a ball when he didn't get a single number. Then he watched two whole volumes of *The Avengers*, Emma Peel period, of course. Stuart had always wanted a life like John Steed. Sharp suits, polished shoes, a ready quip and good taste. And an immaculate flat in central London where a glamorous, intelligent, feisty woman would be guaranteed to call round at any moment. Ideally it would be Mrs Peel, demure and stylish but, at the drop of a carnation, a high–kicking minx. After that, he put on the Russ Meyer, and eventually crawled into bed at after one, where he masturbated furiously while thinking about his ex–wife Jane before collapsing into a sodden, sobbing heap and entering a fitful sleep haunted by women in tight leather catsuits laughing at him.

Two

Stuart spent Thursday working. He completed chapters eight and nine and did plenty of research for the later sections. Professor Garrett was true to his word and the money was waiting in Stuart's account when he checked in with the bank at nine on Friday morning. By way of celebration he washed his bedding, ordered a couple of books from Amazon and treated himself to a *Sun* and a sit–down brunch at the greasy spoon two doors up from Moe's. As he mopped up the remains of his fry–up with a slice of bread he was gratified to see a story in the newspaper about Joey and Mikey. One of them was an actor, the other a singer. Their relationship was back on, apparently. Stuart sighed. Things were moving too quickly for him. How could he hope to write the definitive, academic source–book on British popular culture when new celebrities sprung full–blown as though from the brow of Zeus every morning and then, to mix mythological metaphors, were torn like Prometheus' liver from the body of public perception by dusk? Culture was gathering pace, breeding with itself like a pair of rats, spawning sub–genres and movements which had the lifespan of butterflies. At this rate he'd be writing the book until the day he died.

But with money in the bank Stuart couldn't stay miserable for long. He drained the big mug of tea and folded the *Sun*. In the nanosecond it takes for an electrical impulse to spark in the brain, he'd assembled a complete and convincing argument tracing a direct lineage between *Adam Adamant* and Adam Ant, and he was anxious to get back to the bedsit and get writing.

On Saturday Stuart took a break from the book and after a morning spent watching cartoons he got himself ready to visit his mum. The home was a bus journey and two tube rides away; the best part of an hour. The bus was a nightmare. A drunk or a madman – or possibly a bit of both – stood in the aisle, ranting and raving.

"There's a thing under London," he roared. "There's pigs in the sewers. This thing's like nothing you've ever imagined. I've seen it. It's a fucking monster."

A woman with a brood of snot–nosed children tutted loudly. The drunk began to cry.

"It'll eat us all," he said pleadingly.

A square–headed man in a leather coat told him to shut up or he'd have him shot. Stuart stared out of the window at the grimy houses and boarded up shops until it was his stop.

In his darkest moments, Stuart would find himself wondering how much longer she would hold on. He had to remind himself that no matter what she said, what she did, she was still his mother. The senility had broken her down, made her old and frail before her time. But she was only in her sixties. The nurses said she was physically healthy, as strong as an ox. Theoretically, she could live out her life normally, if she continued getting round–the–clock care. It depressed him to think that he might still be making this dreadful journey every Saturday morning when he was as old as his mother was now. He wondered if the money from the sale of her house would still be paying for the home by then. Bang goes any hope of an inheritance, he thought gloomily as he filed through the white tiled tunnel connecting the tube stations, transferring him from the Northern Line to the Circle Line, then hated himself for thinking that anyway. He gave a pound to a silent, sullen beggar by way of penance as he emerged, gasping for air, from the Underground nearest to the home.

Elysian Fields, it was called, with no apparent intentional irony. There were CCTV cameras on the flat roof and they'd put razor–wire on the wall that circled the drab building since his last visit. Stuart tried not to think about what that meant.

He signed in and said hello to the nursing staff, idly wondering to himself how many visits it would take until he no longer noticed the smell of urine mingling with cheap disinfectant. Sam, the small, dark nurse who was privately graded "quite pretty" by

12

Stuart, asked him if he had a mobile phone, and if he had he'd have to leave it at reception.

"I don't," said Stuart. "What is it, do they interfere with machinery or something?"

"No," confided Sam. "Mrs Burton's son left his behind last weekend. We don't know who found it, but by the time he realised where he'd left it they'd passed it around and used it to cast votes for the talent show on the telly on Saturday night. They ran up more than a hundred and fifty pounds in two days."

"Christ," muttered Stuart. He wondered who his mum had voted for. The fat man with the bassoon, probably.

As they walked to the day room the wailing began. Stuart's heart sank to his boots. It didn't sound like his mum, but he couldn't really be sure.

"Don't worry," said Sam, offering him a wrinkle nosed smile. "It's not what you think."

No, thought Stuart to himself as he followed her into the day room. It's far, far worse. One of the old women was standing wrapped in nothing but a sheet, and she was doing the wailing. Then Stuart noticed they were all wearing sheets, his mum included. Several of them were abasing themselves at the foot of the wailing woman, which was no mean feat considering half of them could barely get to the toilet on their own.

"They're rehearsing a play," whispered Sam. "It's marvellous, really. *Medea*. I think they really wanted to do something nice like *My Fair Lady*, but Thom insisted they push themselves."

The thin man in black standing by the window with a clipboard under his arm must be Thom, Stuart decided. He wondered if he pronounced it with the 'th' sound, or whether that was Sam taking the piss slightly. Thom rubbed his chin then applauded loudly and shouted, "Wonderful. Wonderful. Let's take call it a day, team. I think visiting hour is upon us."

More than half of the residents glared with open hostility at Stuart standing awkwardly behind Sam in the doorway to the day room. Not a lot of them got visitors and he guessed they'd rather be hopping around in sheets rather than slumping in their easy chairs while the few progeny who did bother to come on a Saturday morning ate Rich Tea biscuits and talked about trivialities.

Stuart's mum was alarmingly out of breath when she came over to see him. "Are you sure you should be doing this, mum?" he said doubtfully.

"Och, stop fussing," she said airily. "Come and meet Thom."

She dragged him to where the thin man was making notes on the clipboard. He looked up expectantly. "You're Mrs Balfour's son? Your mother is very talented, young man."

Stuart bristled. He hated being called 'young man' by someone barely four or five years older than him. His mum, however, glowed with pride.

"I'm Thom Sinclair," said the man, pronouncing the 'h' and thrusting out his bony hand. Stuart took it and shook it limply, afraid the bones might snap. Thom continued, "I'm with Art Smash. We're funded by the Arts Council and the local government to do workshops in the senior community. I must say, the residents of Elysian Fields are among the keenest and most energetic I've worked with."

Stuart mumbled something, wanting to say, "That's because they're all half mad," but resisted the urge. He wondered if he'd be able to sue if this idiot pushed his mother into an early grave. Thom started packing up his things and Stuart steered his mother towards a battered leather chair. The spell of *Medea* broken and starting to fade, she began to revert to her normal self a little, her eyes grazing to the television screen in the corner. "I think it's time for my quiz," she said to herself.

Stuart squatted by the chair as his mum settled down, still in the white sheet. He suggested she might want to put something warmer on, but she ignored him. He tried to ignore her thin, stretched flesh and fragile frame as he ran through his usual questions about the food (probably poisoned), how she was sleeping (okay, apart from the noise made by the dwarves in the day room after dark) and how the staff were treating her (beating her daily. Stuart tutted at the non–existent handcuff marks on her wrists).

After a while of this Stuart started getting pins and needles in his haunches, and his mum said, "How's your Jane? Why does she never come with you to see me?"

Stuart sighed. "Mum, me and Jane got divorced more than a year ago. You know that."

"She's nice, Jane. You should bring her next time."

Now Stuart came to think of it, there wasn't really any reason Jane shouldn't visit his mum. They'd got on okay before she left him. Before his mum started to get a bit confused. In fact, it was a bit bloody shitty of her not to visit once in a while. Stuart felt himself starting to get angry at his ex–wife again. Not that there was much use. She'd be far too busy having dinner parties with that Quentin and his friends, and going to pilates and book group and Val d'Isere. All the kinds of stuff him and her used to take the piss out of when they lived in their little flat together, toasting their individuality and their unbearable hipness. Until she started screwing the accounts manager at her agency, obviously, and discovered that she had a choice between having all the things she professed to hate lavished upon her or living with Stuart with his rapidly diminishing prospects and rapidly growing mountain of tat.

It was funny how the things she used to find endearing about him were the reasons she said she had to leave in the end. "Look at this stuff," she'd said despairingly, casting her eyes around the spare room piled high with DVDs, comics, books, Lady Penelope dolls and *Confessions of a Window Cleaner* posters. "It's rubbish, Stuart. You value rubbish more than anything else. I can't live this way any longer."

"I'll change," he'd said dumbly.

She picked up his original vinyl *God Save The Queen* album. "Then throw this away. Throw it all away."

It was a good double bluff. She knew that he'd never do that, so it was a safe bet to imply she'd stay if he did. As a dramatic parting shot she ground the record under the heel of the smart new shoes Stuart had only just noticed she'd started wearing. Perhaps if he'd taken note of things like that earlier, she might not be walking out on him now.

"Christ!" he'd said, gathering up the shards of shattered black vinyl. "Do you know what this is worth?"

Jane had looked at him pityingly. "Do you?" she said, and left.

Stuart blinked. His mother was talking to him. "What?" he said.

"A mobile thingy, a phone," his mum said. "Can I have one?"

"No," said Stuart firmly. "I heard about what happened with Mrs Burton's son."

His mum giggled. It was like the *Evil Dead*, or *The Others*. Stuart shivered. Sam appeared and said visiting was over, and that the residents had to get out of their sheets and into their normal clothes. Stuart was intensely relieved and after giving his mother a chaste kiss on the cheek almost ran out of Elysian Fields. He leaned on the razor–wired wall and took deep lungfuls of air, suddenly hating everyone and everything. He hated his mum for going senile, hated the chemicals or electrical impulses in her brain or whatever it was that had brought on the Alzheimer's. He hated Jane for shagging Quentin and leaving him and setting up home with Quentin, in exactly that order. He hated Thom for making the pensioners put on stupid plays, for giving them hope where there was none. He hated the nurse, Sam, for never picking up on the sultry, sexy looks he directed her way. He hated himself for hating his mum and for wondering if Thom was gay when it didn't matter one bit and for not having the courage to ask Sam what time she knocked off and if she wanted to go for a drink.

And then he remembered it was Saturday and for a pound's worth of a punt on the lottery, life could change beyond all recognition. Cheering up considerably, he set off for the shop around the corner.

* * *

16

The shop was as different from Moe's as was possible. The booze was kept behind a locked metal grill that you had to ask for the padlock to be taken off. There were short aisles filled with dusty tins and packets, and a wall given over to magazines and newspapers. The beefy, tattooed bald bloke who always leaned on the counter invariably read either porn or motorbike magazines. He was always muttering under his breath about "bitches" or "Pakis". Stuart hated him, but felt it was his duty to experience life's rich tapestry, so he continued to make a habit of getting his Saturday lottery ticket there after visiting his mum.

He was reading porn today. He looked up at Stuart and a dull light of recognition glowed under his furrowed brow. He grunted a greeting and turned back to his study. Stuart headed over to the magazines and flicked through the celeb rags, and then some of the music magazines. He confessed he found them impenetrable these days. A sure sign of growing old.

The door to the shop opened and Stuart suddenly had the overpowering feeling that he really should turn around. Maybe it was the slightest hint of a scent in the musty air of the shop. Perhaps the barely audible intake of breath from the meathead who ran the place. Possibly – just possibly – the kiss of leather upon leather and the concentrated tapping of stiletto heels on the lino.

She was Stuart's dream of the previous night made flesh. The shopkeeper was appraising her unashamedly, rubbing his fat chin with the palm of his hand. She walked over to him, the leather of her black motorcycle outfit squeaking slightly as her thighs brushed together. On the crook of her elbow hung a sleek black helmet; down her back hung die–straight black hair. Stuart was staring and became aware that he wasn't breathing. He didn't feel like he could do both at the same time, and didn't want to tear his eyes away.

She was beautiful. Her leather all–in–one was shiny and fluid and she filled it as though airbrushed into it by a fantasy artist. Stuart's throat constricted as she glanced at him for a split second with almond eyes, her blood–red lips pursed and half–smiling. Then she turned her attention to the meathead.

"Eight hundred Marlboro," Stuart heard her say. Her voice was like treacle; dark, thick and sweet. "And can you put this in the window?"

He studied the printed card she handed him, making sure his fingers brushed hers as he took it. "Pound a week," he sniffed. "How long do you want it in?"

If she got the clumsy innuendo, she didn't react. Instead, she glanced again at Stuart, almost coyly. "Oh, not long," she said.

As the newsagent stuffed cartons of cigarettes into plastic carrier bags she unzipped a side pocket in the leather catsuit and pulled out a wad of notes. The shopkeeper rung up the cost on the till and took the money off her. She grabbed the carrier bags and walked straight out of the shop, not casting another look at Stuart despite his silent pleas.

The shopkeeper grinned at him as soon as the door shut. "Jesus Christ. Did .you fucking well see the state of that? Dripping for it, she was, dirty little fucking slag. Bet she likes it rough, all that leather. Blonde, too. Fucking bitch."

"Can I look at that card?" Stuart was all in a mess; he was too confused to pick up on the idiot calling her blonde when she was so incredibly dark, and too much in a whirl to do what he'd normally do at that language, which would be to tut and say nothing.

The meathead glanced down at the card as though for the first time. "What? Oh. Good idea. Bet it's got her phone number on it. Bet if I phoned her she'd say all sorts of filth while I pulled my knob. Dirty little slag."

Stuart took the card. He read it, then read it again. His head couldn't process the words, so he read it again. Then he didn't believe what he was seeing, so he had to read it through slowly one more time. It said:

Excellent DVD copy of ultra-rare "Carry On, You Old Devil".
Cost negotiable.
Interested? We'll contact you.

The shopkeeper snatched it back. "That's enough, sunshine," he said menacingly. "What's it say, anyway?"

Leaving him studying the card, Stuart finally processed the words and got to the door in two strides. There was the faint growl of a motorcycle engine on the breeze, but no movement on the street. He cursed silently to himself.

Then his eyes were drawn across the quiet road, to a wide, tall, blank brick wall. On it was a tag, a graffito in hastily applied white spray–paint that Stuart was pretty sure hadn't been there when he went in the shop.

A single word.

*pop*CULT!

Three

On the day that Stuart Balfour first saw the astronaut, when he was in the telephone box begging for an advance, Professor Garrett was somewhat distracted; as he was sitting at his desk in his office in the faculty of media and popular culture studies, the telephone in his hand, sitting opposite him was a woman who only minutes before had swept unannounced into the room and introduced herself as Miss Monroe. Dressed in a dirndl dress and orange leather boots, her strawberry blond hair in bunches and her lips and cheeks lightly rouged, she betrayed a rather shrewd insight into Professor Garrett's most secret, unspoken fantasies. As he spoke to Stuart on the telephone, Miss Monroe bent forward to fiddle with the chrome clasp on the heel of her boot, affording him an unhindered view down the front of her white blouse beneath the low apron of the dress. Absently Professor Garrett tugged at his collar and wondered if someone had cranked up the heating in his office.

Balfour was asking for an advance on the regular sums agreed he would be paid on delivery of chapters for the volume Professor Garrett had commissioned him to write, and was lately wishing he hadn't bothered to do so. The material he had sent in so far was good, true; Balfour certainly knew his stuff and could certainly write. But hitting deadlines wasn't really his forte, Professor Garrett was beginning to discover.

"More money?" he said into the telephone. Miss Monroe picked up an envelope from the desk and started to fan her face. "This is highly irregular. Didn't we just issue a payment?"

Balfour was talking again, but Professor Garrett wasn't really listening. Miss Monroe was unfastening another button on her crisp white blouse. Professor Garrett felt an erection forming uncomfortably in the folds of his trousers.

"Is it hot in here?" said Miss Monroe pleasantly. Professor Garrett could see the hint of white lace underneath the blouse. The phone was beeping at him now and Balfour was sounding rather hysterical. Professor Garrett wanted rid of him so he could find out just what this vision of loveliness wanted of him.

"Yes, yes," he said when Balfour was back on the line. "We can bring the next advance forward, but we really must see up to and including chapter twenty before any future payment, Mr Balfour. And we'll need to see receipts for any research materials."

Then he replaced the receiver and turned his attention to Miss Monroe. "I apologise for that. Urgent business, I'm afraid. Perhaps if you'd made an appointment I could have set aside more time to discuss..." he paused. "Ah, what exactly is it you wanted to talk about..?"

Miss Monroe wrinkled her lightly–freckled nose and Professor Garrett's stomach lurched. He surreptitiously tried to massage his groin into a more comfortable position.

"Professor Garrett," she said. "I represent certain... interests. We understand you have commissioned an academic treatise on popular culture... I take it that the Mr Balfour you were just speaking with is involved?"

"Stuart Balfour, yes. He's writing it. An excellent authority on the subject. He was a student of mine many years ago, he's worked in magazines and television since."

Miss Monroe crossed her legs. "What do you intend to do with this book?"

"Publish it under the university's own imprint, of course."

She fingered the next button on her blouse. "And what kind of print run are you anticipating? What market are you expecting to reach? Do you plan any publicity or author tours?"

"It is a fairly modest set–up, it's true, but we are a well–respected imprint and generally get good reviews in some of the broadsheets and specialist press. Um."

For the first time, it began to dawn on Professor Garrett that this woman had walked into his office uninvited and he was just handing over potentially sensitive information to her, purely because she happened to be his deepest kink made flesh.

"Professor Garrett," said Miss Monroe. "Do you work out?"

He blinked. "What? I'm sorry, what?"

She appraised him, a painted nail tapping her chin. "I apologise. I was thinking out loud. I was just wondering to myself though... you're what, forty–five?"

Despite himself, Professor Garrett flushed slightly. "Nearer fifty–five, Miss Monroe, actually."

She made a good show of looking surprised. Pleasantly surprised, noted Professor Garrett. She said, "I admire a man who looks after himself. Your wife must be very proud of you."

Professor Garrett grunted. He did exercise, true. He would love to say that Mrs Garrett did the same. If he did indeed look ten years younger than his age, then she looked a good five years older than she actually was. For a brief second he imagined his wife wearing the clothes Miss Monroe had on, and his erection wilted momentarily. Then Miss Monroe bent forward to brush an imaginary spot from her immaculate boot–toe and gave his kundalini a kick–start.

There was a pause. He said, "I'm sorry, you were saying..?"

Miss Monroe smiled. "I was saying that I represent certain interests who are keen to see this book published, Professor Garrett. We may be prepared to financially back this project to a substantial extent but we will be hoping to target as wide and as populist an audience as possible with the finished product."

"Well, naturally, that goes without saying. But... financial backing? To what degree? And for what purpose?"

"Considerable, I should say, Professor. However. There is a but. And it is rather a big but."

"I shall have to say now, Miss Monroe, that I am not prepared to allow any corporate hijacking of this publication, if that's what you and your interests have in mind."

She smiled again. "Not at all, Professor. It is just that there are other parties who may not be as enthusiastic about this book as we are. They may visit you. They can be very... persuasive. From what I've seen of you, you seem a very capable man who would certainly not be intimidated. But it is only right that I warn you."

Professor Garrett was at something of a loss now. "Other parties? Persuasive? Intimidated? Miss Monroe, what exactly are we talking about here? This book is to be an academic treatise. Are you sure..?"

She stood, smoothing her skirts. Another button on her blouse had slipped open, allowing him an unfettered view of the swell of her breasts. He feared he was gaping unashamedly, but couldn't stop himself. He pressed down on his lap again, trying to defuse his desire.

"We'll speak again, soon," said Miss Monroe. "In the meantime, could I have Mr Balfour's address?"

Before he had even thought about it Professor Garrett had flicked through the file on his desktop PC and printed out Balfour's details. He paused before releasing his grip on the piece of paper that whispered out of the printer as Miss Monroe accepted it from him. "And I shall see you again soon?" he said.

"Of course." She folded the paper and secreted it in the apron of her dress, fastening the stray buttons on her blouse as she did so. She walked to the door.

"Please, don't stand," said Miss Monroe, a smile playing on her lips. "I'm sure you have your hands full at the moment. I'll see myself out."

Professor Garrett watched her go, not fully understanding what had just occurred.

For a long time on the following Saturday, after his visit to Elysian Fields and his encounter with the mysterious woman in the shop around the corner, Stuart sat in the darkness of his flat, thinking hard.

He'd vaguely heard of *Carry On, You Old Devil*, but didn't believe it existed. No–one with half a brain thought it was actually real. It was just one of those silly internet rumours that bored nerds who liked to believe they were post–modern pranksters dreamed up and put around until they became urban myths. All he knew was that it had supposedly been filmed towards the end of the Carry On era but had never been released. In fact, the studio had apparently buried it, and no–one talked about it. Why this was meant to be the case, Stuart didn't know. There was talk of people dying, a curse or something. Not the type of thing Stuart generally took much notice of, but now he thought about it... if this thing really existed, and if this woman really had a copy on DVD, what a centrepiece it would make for his book. But he had no way of contacting her, just the memory of that flashing gaze cast over a leather shoulder as she disappeared from his life, only the cryptic card left behind: *Interested? We'll contact you.* It smelled of a hoax. But could he take the chance?

Stuart thought he'd better go and talk to Walter.

Stuart collected friends like he collected old movie posters, or comic annuals, or out–of–print books. He picked them up in dusty shops, tracked them down on websites, found them by accident and stumbled across them in the most unlikely places. At first, like so many things, it charmed Jane with its eccentricity. By the end, as she came home from working late or a gym session, she would barely try to hide her sighs and rolled eyes as Stuart littered the living room up with some loser and his particular fetish. Walter, though, she always tolerated. His affected Seventies gayness appealed to her sense of what was cool, and Stuart suspected she liked to boast about having him as a friend to her shallow acquaintances. But that was probably a little uncharitable on Stuart's part; Jane did seem genuinely fond of Walter, who always managed to mix fantastic cocktails from whatever bottles of booze they had lying around, and occasionally cooked marvellously dated meals for them featuring fondue dips and Black Forest gateau. He always noticed when she'd had her hair cut or bought a new dress, a social grace with which Stuart was distinctly unfamiliar. But at least he felt that Walter's attentiveness earned him some brownie points too, by association. Not that it did him much good at the end, though.

Walter answered the door wearing a safari suit and holding a glass of something vibrantly pink in his right hand.

"Dear boy," he said. "How nice to see you north of the river. I've just thrown together a jug of strawberry daiquiri. I trust you'll help me dispose of it?"

Stuart followed Walter up the steep stairs to his flat, which was dominated by a huge window affording views of the rooftops of Islington.

"I wish you'd telephone ahead, though. You're lucky you caught me in."

Stuart flopped on the sofa, accepting a cocktail from Walter. "The phone's still broke, Walter," he said. "And besides, you never go out. You're agoraphobic now, aren't you?"

Walter stood at the window, cutting a melancholy figure.

"True, dear heart. My world is now within these walls."

"Googie Withers," said Stuart, slurping the daiquiri through the straw.

"Chin chin," said Walter, returning the toast and sipping at his drink. "So how goes the writing of the definitive tome on popular culture?"

Stuart picked up a battered paperback from the coffee table. *The Lady Is Ready*, shouted the title garishly. Then smaller, "A Mark Caine mystery. By Jason King".

"Oh, not bad," said Stuart, flicking through the novel. "Hey, isn't this..?"

"Yes. A novel about action hero Mark Caine purportedly written by playboy, author and secret agent Jason King. Who was, of course, the character played by dear Peter Wyngarde in *Department S* and *Jason King*. And who, obviously didn't exist."

"This is a good mock–up, then. Looks almost genuine."

Walter took the book from him. "Odd, isn't it?" he mused. "Picked it up from a second hand stall on Camden Market. It actually looks like a real Seventies pulp novel – sniff those pages. It even smells old. But as far as I know – and that's pretty far as far as these things are concerned – no merchandise like this was ever released to support either *Department S* or the *Jason King* series. It's almost as though it's the real thing... dropped through a timewarp from another dimension, perhaps, where our magical television heroes are commonplace things..."

Walter had a faraway look in his eye and was in danger of getting maudlin, Stuart knew. He was a dramatic old queen stuck in the cul–de–sac of nostalgia, with his Barbarella dolls and Cathy Gale kinky boots, but there was no finer authority in London on trashy culture of the late Sixties and early Seventies, and Stuart had need of his expertise.

"Well," he said brightly. "Have I got a little mystery for you."

"A mystery? Very well, Stuart, I am piqued. Thrill me."

"What do you know about a 'lost' Carry On movie?"

Walter refilled his glass from the daiquiri jug and popped in a fresh umbrella. He smoothed his moustache with forefinger and thumb and sighed. "Which one? They're ten a penny. *Carry On Smoking*, from 1961, in which Sid James tries to train a group of bungling new firefighters? Or *Carry On Spaceman* and *Carry On Flying*, both 1962? Perhaps you mean *Carry On Again Nurse* in Seventy–nine – an X–rated disaster which was dropped at the planning stages after the poor reception of *Carry On Emmanuelle*."

"Oh," said Stuart, somewhat deflated. "I thought I'd stumbled on something. I suppose this *Carry On, You Old Devil*'s no big deal then, really?"

Walter paused as though freeze–framed at the end of a particularly dramatic episode of his favourite TV show. After a long moment, he whispered, "What did you just say?"

So Stuart told him as much as he thought was relevant. He didn't think to mention the astronaut, which was a shame because Walter had heard about him from one source or another, and later on Stuart might have found what he had to say useful. And although he would be very surprised at this later on, he seemed to have forgotten about seeing the *pop*CULT! graffiti twice. Instead, Stuart began with his visit to his mother and his confrontation with the woman in leather at the shop.

"How awfully *Matrix*," said Walter. "And the card definitely said *Carry On, You Old Devil?*"

"Mm," said Stuart, helping himself to the plate of nachos Walter had prepared while he told the tale. "But how is that more important than *Carry On Smoking* or whatever?"

Walter gazed for a moment into the lava lamp on the leatherette bar in the corner of his living room. "'Honest vulgarity is the central tradition of English humour'," he quoted. "Kenneth Williams. 'I think we will carry on 'til we drop, but it will have been a giggle – for everybody'. Sid James."

Walter finished mixing a fresh jug of daiquiri and joined Stuart on the sofa. "Sid carried on until he died, in 1976, that's for sure. But it wasn't always the giggle he would have hoped. If the rumours about *You Old Devil* are to be believed, it was anything but."

"I did a bit of research on the internet," said Stuart. "Something about a curse..?"

"By the mid–Seventies the Carry On franchise was coming to a natural end. *Carry On Girls*, in '74, was a foretaste of the descent into substandard porn rather than seaside postcard smut – and there is a huge difference – which was to characterise the last of the series. Sid's last film was *Carry On Dick* the year before he died. It was a return to the form that made the Carry Ons great – a historical context, surprisingly well realised; some great, punning gags; the sparking electricity between Sid and Barbara... magic.

"The minute it was over Pinewood Studios started work on what was to be the twenty–seventh movie – *Carry On, You Old Devil*. One of the most successful Carry On movies ever was *Screaming*, a pastiche on the old Hammer horror movies, and Pinewood wanted to recreate that. Inspired by the recent box office smash *The Exorcist*, and *Rosemary's Baby* and *The Devil Rides*

Out a couple of years before that, the producers decided that the subject of devil worship would make a cracking Carry On."

"I bet they would have been right," said Stuart. "I wouldn't have minded seeing that."

"It certainly had all the hallmarks of a classic," agreed Walter. "Sid as randy priest Father O'Toole, also known as 'the sexorcist'. Babs as Lucy Fare, the devil's daughter. Peter Butterworth as Sid's bungling assistant, Canon Fodder. Kenneth Williams as Bill Z. Bubb, High Priest of the Satanic cult, Hattie Jacques as his fearsome wife, Bella. And Charles Hawtrey in a cameo role as the devil himself."

"So how come it never got released?"

"It appears the movie was badly starred from the off," said Walter. "The writers had tried to research their subject matter as thoroughly as possible, even to the point of approaching the Catholic Church and asking them for advice on filming the exorcism scenes. Of course, the Church was incensed and refused to co–operate – and tried to get Pinewood to drop the film into the bargain. To the studio's credit, it soldiered on. But then came the accidents."

"Accidents?"

"On the set. A scenery hand was found dead, hanging from the rafters one morning. Suicide was assumed, but it didn't take tongues long to start wagging. Especially after the second death just a couple of weeks later, when a make–up girl was crushed by falling masonry on a location shoot in Scotland. And then there was Sid..."

"Sid James? What happened?"

"This is the conjecture bit, the rumour, the legend. The story is that Sid was the last one in the studio, having taken a nap after filming at the end of one day and had been accidentally locked in the sound stage. The security guard heard him hammering at the door, and when he let him out reported that he was as white as a sheet and babbling incoherently. The next day, Sid quit the film. He gave as his excuse his age – he was into his sixties, by this point – and previous commitments to appear on stage in *The Mating Game* during seventy–six, which he said he needed to prepare for."

"I suppose no Sid, no movie."

"Well, things were too far advanced for that. Windsor Davies was to brought in to replace him, but by then the rot had set in. Crew drifted away from the production, there were tales of strange things happening on set."

"Like what?"

"Well, the rumour is that the scriptwriters had been a little too thorough in their research, and some of the Satanic rituals filmed were actually based on genuine occult masses the researchers had found in some old books. The actors complained that the studio was freezing, things disappeared and turned up in unlikely places, the sound technicians were dogged by problems, hissing and roaring on the tapes. Eventually, Pinewood pulled the plug before they'd even started re–shooting Sid's scenes with Windsor Davies, and in a very quick turnaround they scrapped the movie and started work on *Carry On Behind*, which was released December 1975. And which pretty much signalled the end of the Carry On series as we knew it. Four months later, Sid died of a heart attack during a performance of *The Mating Game* in Sunderland. It truly was the end of an era."

They sat in silence for a while, contemplating their drinks. Eventually, Stuart said, "And what do you think? Is it true?"

"No–one I know's ever seen a copy, or knows anyone who has. Pinewood have never acknowledged the existence of it. If this all actually happened it was decades ago, remember, and practically everyone involved in the movie is now dead... giving rise, I suppose, to the curse theory."

"But what do you think?" pressed Stuart.

"What do I think?" said Walter. "I think, dear boy, that if you can somehow get hold of a copy of the footage that was shot for *Carry On, You Old Devil*, then you've got yourself one hell of a book."

* * *

Mr Grundy couldn't abide noise. If he had to nail down one particular thing that had helped to make his years on Earth utterly unbearable, it would have to be noise. Fortunately, as a man who could name a hundred hateful things before breakfast, he doubted he would ever have to narrow his list of intense dislikes down to just one. Still, he hated noise; particularly screaming. He turned up the volume on Mahler's Symphony Number Five until the screams faded and busied himself with his study of the third–quarter figures from one of his many business interests, the documents spread out on the mahogany desk which overlooked London from the upper floors of the tower block he owned in the heart of Canary Wharf. The screams were issuing from the room behind his expansive office where George and Escobar were busily employed doing what Mr Grundy paid them for; namely, torture.

Mr Grundy became engrossed in his figures and barely noticed that the CD had finished. Then the door opened and George emerged from the ante–room, his white apron covered in blood. Mr Grundy sensed that things had not gone well.

In the room George and Escobar had been torturing a man of advancing years whose name no–one had really used for some time. In fact, the last occasion he had even crossed anyone's radar was when Stuart Balfour had shared a bus–ride with him on Saturday afternoon. Then he had been shouting about a thing under London. Stuart had thought him either mad or drunk. In truth, he was at that time a little of one and substantially more of the other, but over the past hour he had recovered sufficiently to fervently wish that he'd kept his mouth shut.

George was broad and hairless and thought about what he said for some time before he opened his mouth. After a long pause while he considered the blood on his apron, he said, "Mr Grundy, I'm afraid things haven't gone quite as we would have wished."

"Escobar?" sighed Mr Grundy.

George nodded. Escobar was keen and always willing to help,

but had several times proved a tad over–zealous in the torturing stakes. George was a big man who many considered a little slow and unwieldy, but he prided himself in having a measure of finesse about these things.

"I'm afraid he died before we could ascertain whether he did, in fact, know anything."

Mr Grundy studied his reflection in the window, the brilliantined hair and the spotless Savile Row tailoring, the dark eyes and the flash of his watch peering from beneath his cuff.

"No matter, George. I'm sure he didn't really know much, anyway. Just another drunk shooting his mouth off on the streets."

Mr Grundy dug into his inside pocket and handed George a wad of notes. "For the overtime. Oh, and take Escobar for a drink and explain the finer points of the job to him again, would you, George?"

"Of course, Mr Grundy," said George. "And Mr Grundy? I'm sure we'll find them eventually."

"Yes, George," said Mr Grundy. "We'll find them. We'll find *pop*CULT!"

Four

There was a new apprentice in the workshop and the lads were having him on a sight. Thomas Grundy took no part in their fun, feeling a bit sorry for the new nipper. He'd come in with fancy designs, like so many of them do, of becoming the new Stephenson or Watt, which always gets the goats of those who've been there for a longer while. They did their usual tricks; sending him off to the foreman, Jackson, and telling him to call the boss by the name "Jacko", on account of he loved that, when all along they knew he hated it because the lads called him "Jacko of the Jungle" behind his back. It was Thomas who dreamt up that name, too; Jacko of the Jungle was one of the characters in the penny bloods he devoured and he thought Mr Jackson looked just like the illustration of the huge ape in the story.

Then the lads continued to take the nipper's measure, sending him off to the stores to ask for a half–round square and a long stand. The latter the storesman gave him by leaving him in the corridor for a good half an hour, until Jacko chanced upon him and clipped his ear.

But still, Thomas felt sorry for the nipper, a dark–haired, thin–faced fellow whose name was William. The lads had all done the same tricks to Thomas when he started, and more; he'd been called over on his first day to help get a chipping of iron out of one of the lad's eyes. The usual method for this, as Thomas had been taught, was to hold up the other fellow's eyelid and scrape it with your scriber – your pen–knife. Thomas was keen to do this as he thought it would help get him in with the lads, doing them a good turn and all that. The lads around the fellow with the chipping in his eye said they couldn't do it themselves because they had grease on their hands and didn't want to cause an infection, and as Thomas peered close the lad had let loose a stream of water he'd had in his cheeks for just the jape.

Thomas worked hard as Jacko wandered past his bench, whistling and giving the lads the once over. The foreman kept to a strict route around the workshop, watching out for slackers and shirkers and, all things being equal, he wouldn't pass by that quarter again for half an hour. Which meant a quick unofficial break for the lads, and the biggest test of the new lad William so far.

As soon as Jacko was out of sight the lads gathered around William. "You're to keep nix, see, and let us know if Jacko makes an unscheduled visit this way again in the next ten minutes," they told him. "But don't let him know what you're doing, mind, or we'll all catch it."

"I'd be partial to a small break myself," said William.

The lads laughed. "You're the new nipper, ain't you? When there's a new new nipper, then you can have a break."

Everyone silently and quickly filed behind the low wall which separated the workshop from the packing yard. Most of them lit up a smoke, a couple sneaked out small bottles of gin and took a tot. Thomas did what he always did at break times; took out the latest number of his magazine from his apron pocket and unfurled it, quickly turning to his marked spot.

Sometimes Thomas had a smoke as well, but this time he just wanted a quick read. He settled himself in a quiet corner, away from the rest of the lads, took out his periodical, *The Magazine of Curiosity and Wonder*, and stared at the illustration on the front page. A horrific figure loomed out of a window at the disgusted, fleeing crowd. "Extraordinary account of a woman with a pig's face", promised the caption underneath. Stuart began to read.

"There have been many reports at different periods, of a pig–faced lady, who was stated to have been born in London, and was to be seen publicly about the streets of the metropolis. For the truth of this account we cannot, however, undertake to vouch, though for our own parts, we should almost feel inclined to doubt it. We shall confine ourselves to the following remarkable account, which is extracted from a German book of the year 1704. It is embellished with a wood cut, from which our present engraving is a copy, and runs as follows—"

Thomas's lips moved slowly as he plunged into the awful narrative. He didn't know how long he had been reading when a shadow fell across him. He stuffed the magazine back into his apron pocket and scrambled to his feet, thinking Jacko had chanced upon him. But it was only William.

Thomas glanced over to where the lads were still smoking and playing cards. "You're supposed to be keeping nix," he said to William. "The lads'll have you if Jacko catches us."

"I saw you reading your magazine," said William. "Don't much care *for Curiosity and Wonder* myself."

"Don't you, now," said Thomas, clicking his tongue. The lads looked over and he signalled for them to get back to their posts.

"Have you seen the latest number of *The Ghost*?" asked William. "It's all about the dead devouring the living in Paris."

"I don't much care for *The Ghost*," sniffed Thomas, though he was warming to the new nipper. It wasn't often he found a fellow who took the penny bloods as often as he did. "I think *Tales of All Nations* has the edge on it. Are you reading *The Malefactor*?"

Their conversation was interrupted when Arthur Evans, the unofficial cock of the walk in the workshop, stormed over and cuffed William around the ear.

"Ow!" said William, rubbing the side of his head. "What was that for?"

"For leaving your post when you're supposed to be keeping nix," said Arthur Evans. "Blondie, tell him we won't tolerate it."

The lads called Thomas "Blondie" because of his hair, but he didn't mind. It was what the prostitutes called him back at the lodgings as well. In fact, it had been his nickname ever since he was a small boy. As Arthur Evans got back to work, William said sullenly, "I'd like to know where he thinks he gets off clipping me like that."

"There'll be a lot worse if you let Jacko catch us on a break," said Thomas. "Next time, if you're told to keep nix, keep nix. It ain't difficult. Now we'd best get back to it."

"Anyway, I was going to say," said William. "On account of you reading that number with the pig faced lady. There's a freak show on at Holborn and I fancied going tomorrow evening. Do you think you'd like to go as well?"

"Why, ain't you got a sweetheart?" asked Thomas, more viciously than he'd intended.

William shook his head. "I've to concentrate on getting my apprenticeship before I get mixed up in women, pa says. Besides, the pay's not enough to spend on a sweetheart. Have you got one?"

"I've got loads," said Thomas proudly, though in truth he didn't at all. Although apprenticed to the workshop, he was an orphan and lived in lodgings with the lower classes, and didn't have the means to romance a girl properly.

"Still," he mused. "It might be a lark to go to the freakshow. Holborn, you say? Shall I meet you there tomorrow? At seven, say?"

William smiled. "That would be smashing. I'll bring you the last number of *The Ghost*, if you like. I've read it now. Perhaps you could swap me that issue *of Curiosity and Wonder* when you've finished it up."

"I thought you didn't hold with *Curiosity and Wonder*," said Thomas.

"It's all right, I suppose," conceded William. "You'll see things a darn sight more surprising than that pig faced lady at this freakshow tomorrow, though, by all accounts."

Thomas lived in lodgings in Turk's Row in the parish of Chelsea, which as lodging houses went wasn't a bad one. Mrs Woods who was landlady kept a strict house and it wasn't as packed as some; Thomas had heard tell of lodgings where they slept three to a bed, eight beds to a room. He didn't exactly have his own room, it was true, but he did at least have a bed to himself and his room–mates were trustworthy, clean and friendly.

The reason Mrs Woods ran such a tight ship at Turk's Row

was that she was a madam, and the top floor of the lodgings was in fact a brothel. After escaping from the workhouse at thirteen Thomas had been taken in by Mrs Woods. He hadn't been a bad boy, but he had learned in the workhouse to be handy with his fists and he was big for his age. Mrs Woods gave him free lodgings and board in return for him keeping an eye on some of the girls. More than once he'd had to throw a customer out or box his ears. Thomas was wiry and stronger than he looked, but didn't like to show off. Which was why he let that Arthur Evans think he was cock of the walk at the workshop, though Thomas knew he could probably have him on his back with one punch.

The girls liked Thomas, too, probably because he didn't lech after them, and chatted to them as though they were proper people, not just whores. In return, they'd been free with their favours on occasion, which meant that although Thomas had no regular sweetheart as such, he was no new nipper in the ways of romance.

It was Mrs Woods who got him apprenticed to the workshop. Thomas suspected that some of the bosses were regular customers at Turk's Row, though he'd never seen any of them there, and Mrs Woods called in a few favours. However he'd got in, he'd excelled at everything he did and was one of the best apprentices there.

Although he was adept at machine–work, it wasn't really what he dreamed of. Thomas wanted to write for his beloved penny bloods, and when he finished work and climbed into his hard bed after a supper of chicken and potatoes provided by Mrs Woods, he lit his candle and took his paper and quill from the mahogany box he kept under his bed. Being the youngest, Thomas had the bed nearest the window, which was terribly draughty in winter and noisy in summer, when the shops in the street outside took their deliveries at first light. His candle flickered in the cold wind which rattled the pane, but stayed alight.

It was early still and the other three men who shared his room were out, carousing or begging or just walking the streets of

London. Thomas took out his copy of *Curiosity and Wonder*, laid it on the bed, and took up his quill and inkpot. He was writing a story about a murderer who preyed on lone women who were often to be found wandering dark corners of London at unlikely hours of the night. The killer strangled his victims with a silk scarf and Thomas was just at the climax of the story, where the dashing detective from Scotland Yard spots the self–same scarf around the neck of an hitherto unguessed at suspect (Thomas hoped), a Lord at a fancy social occasion.

He'd been writing an hour, squinting at the paper in the candlelight when the door to his room squeaked. Thinking it was one of his room–mates Thomas started to lay up his pen and ink; if they were drunk they'd want to read it (or have it read to them, depending on who it was and how drunk they were) and Thomas wasn't in the mood. But it wasn't a room–mate, it was Mrs Woods.

"Is there trouble upstairs?" asked Thomas, putting his paper back in the box.

"No, love," said Mrs Woods, bustling in. She had once been handsome, guessed Thomas, but the demands of her career weighed heavily upon her. "I forgot to tell you earlier; there's a letter for you."

Thomas felt his stomach somersault. There was only one person who could have written a letter to him. His mouth dry, he held out his hand and accepted the envelope from Mrs Woods, who waited expectantly.

He stared at his name and address written in sweeping script on the vellum. He'd never had a letter before in his life. "I'll go, shall I, Blondie?" said Mrs Woods eventually.

Thomas nodded wordlessly, not noticing Mrs Woods's disappointment as she gathered her skirts and sighed her way out of the room. He continued to stare at the letter.

It would be, of course, from Mr Edward Lloyd, the king of the penny bloods. He was the publisher of the greatest number of periodicals on the market, and Thomas had been bold enough to send a story for his consideration to his offices in Salisbury Square. He hoped beyond hope to one day see one of his pieces side–by–side with the thrilling words of his favourite writer, Thomas Prest.

With shaking hands Thomas carefully opened the envelope and extracted the thin paper inside. He closed his eyes tight as he unfolded the letter, then allowed himself to squint with one eye at the short message.

"...most amateurish story I have ever read..."

"...completely without any artistic merit..."

"...with all the thrills and tension of a dish of the worst jellied eels in London..."

Thomas had read enough. He crumpled Edward Lloyd's letter in a ball and flung it across the room. Then he took his sheaf of paper from his mahogany box and tore his latest story to shreds, before burying himself under his thin grey blanket and weeping until he fell asleep.

Thomas was in a foul mood all the following day, and almost cancelled his visit to the freakshow with William, but the lad coaxed him into it and after work they trudged through the streets towards Holborn.

"Where do your ma and pa live?" asked William, munching on an apple as they walked.

"They both died when I was a baby," said Thomas, who was starving and would have missed his supper at the lodgings by the time he got back from Holborn.

"Oh," said William, tossing the half–eaten apple into the gutter and pulling a lump of bread from his napsack. "My pa's the manager of a workshop in Limehouse. He wanted me to get apprenticed somewhere else, though, else the lads would think I'd been taken for favouritism, like. But after my apprenticeship he'll take me on. Probably as second–foreman. Then I'll find myself a sweetheart and probably get a house. Kensington, perhaps."

Thomas said nothing, still brooding about Edward Lloyd's

letter about his story. He wanted nothing more than to write for the penny bloods, and could no more imagine a life spent in the workshop than he could bear to admit he might never see for himself the far–flung places and fantastic countries described in such breathless detail in the stories in his periodicals, the jungles and plains of Africa, the temples of India, the dusty frontier towns of the Americas.

The freakshow had set up camp on a patch of cleared land in the middle of Holborn. They caught the scent of it first; the woodsmoke and sweet candy and damp sawdust. Then the sounds; the dull cranking of a wind–up organ, screams and laughter, music turned inside out on the breeze.

The sign said CORONATION PARADE OF THE GROTESQUE in big, red letters, and underneath in smaller script: In honour of our new monarch, the gracious Queen Victoria, though it had been seven months since the Queen's coronation. The freakshow was set out in avenues so that it resembled a small town or village within Holborn, bounded by a high fence. The gate was straddled by a mighty wooden giant, full thirty feet tall, and the visitors passed between his huge legs. At the giant's right foot a barker called out to the passing crowds.

"Many wonders inside, ladies and gentlemen. Vampires, we have, and wolfmen too, transported by moonlight from the far Carpathian mountains. See the cat with two heads and the dog with two tails. Have your palm read or your bumps felt and learn your future. See the man who has lived forever, and the woman who married a horse. Roll up, roll up, we have many wonders inside."

As Thomas and William approached the barker, who was dressed as a cannibal or pygmy or somesuch, with grass skirt and a bone through his nose, peered at them from beneath his feather head–dress. "A–ha! A couple of likely lads – apprentices, am I right?"

William nodded. "Do you really have wolfmen? And vampires?"

The barker leaned conspiratorially towards them, saying into the back of his hand, "And more, lads. A woman from the South Seas with three cunnies. New attraction. Only cost you tuppence to see, sixpence to touch."

William goggled at Thomas. "How much money do you have?"

"Enough, but I don't think I'll throw sixpence away on a touch," said Thomas, who doubted such a thing could exist.

"Well, I bloody will," whispered William, his face red and his voice oddly thick.

The barker ushered them in. "Pay at each attraction, my fine lads. Don't forget to visit the elastic–skinned man; he gets awful lonely over the far side."

The freakshow was a great disappointment to Thomas. The two–headed cat turned out to be the skeleton of a puss with a second cat's skull clumsily stuck on to the neck–bone. The vampire was a thin–man in a cage with sauce of some kind staining his teeth, who spoke in what Thomas was sure was cod–German. The wolfman was nothing more than a hairy half–naked drunk who gambolled around a straw–filled room on all fours, chained by the neck to a wooden stake in the floor.

"What rot," said William as they meandered past a juggler and a mime artist. "If the Queen ever came to see this sorry collection I'll eat my apron."

Thomas stopped him with a hand to the chest. "Didn't you want to see this?"

The were outside a black tent which had a sign over the entrance: UNUSUAL BEAUTY FROM THE SOUTH SEAS. ADMISSION IS AT THE MANAGEMENT'S DISCRETION.

A bull–necked man in a leather cap stood by the tent flaps, looking Thomas and William up and down. "Two is it?" he grunted.

Thomas shook his head. William dug in his pocket. "The man at the gate said it was, uh, sixpence, for..."

The man nodded him in, palming the outstretched coin.

Thomas turned to survey the rest of the sorry stalls. The sky was darkening and his belly ached. Across the mud track was a lonely tent, outside which sat an incredibly old man wearing faded velvet robes, puffing on a pipe. He caught Thomas staring at him and waggled his bushy white eyebrows. A toothless mouth opened within his grey beard.

"In case you were wondering, I'm the man who has lived forever," he said.

Thomas nodded. "Hello. I'm the man who has lived seventeen years."

The man grunted and shifted along the low bench, indicating for Thomas to join him. When he did, the old man ruminated for a moment then spat a stream of tobacco into the mud.

"So," said Thomas. "How old are you supposed to be then?"

The man glanced at him sidelong. "I am supposed to be able to remember the sinking of Atlantis, and the sacking of Rome, and the signing of the Magna Carta. You do know what the Magna Carta is, do you, boy?"

"'Course," said Thomas proudly. "I read about it."

"Hmm," said the man, spitting into the mud again. "That's what I'm supposed to remember, according to the management of the fair."

"Another fake," sighed Thomas.

The man nodded. "It would seem so. In truth, I can remember only as far back as the middle fifteen hundreds, or thereabouts."

Thomas laughed. The old man was good value, and he hadn't even had to give him ha'penny. "That would make you nearly three hundred years old, then."

"Hmm," said the old man again. "The first couple of hundred were fine, but I'm started to feel a bit weary. In fact, I'm thinking of giving it up, this living forever business."

"And how would you go about that?"

The man put his hand inside his robes and withdrew his clenched fist. "A good start would be giving this to someone. You."

Thomas glanced back at the tent where William had disappeared but there was no sign of him. Uncertainly, he held out his hand. The old man dropped a small golden–brown ball into his palm.

It was warm to the touch. Thomas plucked it with his thumb and forefinger and examined it. It was like a marble the youngsters played hundreds or conqueror with, except slightly spongy. It seemed to be lit from within, and the browns and yellows swirled around like oil in water.

"What is it?" he said.

"Haven't been able to find out in three hundred years," said the old man, relighting his pipe.

"Where did you get it?"

He pointed his pipe at Thomas. "You ever hear of a man called Doctor John Dee?"

Thomas shook his head. The old man carried on, "No matter. He was looking for miracles, for a way to turn lead into gold. He thought this might be the answer."

Thomas stared into its swirling depths. "Gold," he breathed. "Was it? The answer?"

The man chuckled. "Not in the way that old Dee thought it was. But he wasn't far off the mark, in some ways."

Thomas clenched his hand around the ball, felt its warmth. "But where did he get it?"

"Said it fell from the sky. But then, he said a lot of things. Claimed to be able to talk to angels."

"And you're giving it to me?"

The old man pointed with his pipe. "Looks like your friend is back. Take care of that, young man."

"What are you going to do?"

"Rest, I think. Yes, rest."

"What an absolute swizz," complained William loudly as the man in the leather cap bundled him away from the tent.

"Off with you," grunted the bull–necked man. "No refunds.

And stop causing bother."

William straightened his collar and stalked off, Thomas close behind him. "A bloody swizz," he said again.

"Did she not have three cunnies, then?" asked Thomas, struggling to keep up.

"Oh, yes," spat William.

"But?"

"But they were made out of stone. Like the rest of her. She was a statue. South Seas beauty indeed. Downright swizz."

They paused in the centre of the freakshow, Thomas looking around. "Do you want to see anything else?"

"No. I think I'll get home. See if my ma has any supper for me. See you tomorrow?"

"Yes," said Thomas, the ball throbbing in his tight warm fist. "See you tomorrow."

In his bed, Thomas cradled the golden sphere in his hands and watched the meandering colours. What it was he had no idea, but it was pretty. He put it in his mahogany box and covered it with his penny blood, and went to sleep.

He awoke drenched in sweat, the thin light filtering through the muslin window–hanging. His night had been assailed by dreams, none of which he could remember, but they clung to him like sand. Dressing quickly, he checked the box to make sure the ball was still there. It was. But a curious thing had occurred. His periodical had been replaced by a sheaf of blank papers. Angrily, he looked around, but the room was empty, the men having gone off to do whatever they did in the early morning. One of them had evidently stolen his magazine and replaced it for a jape. But when he inspected the blank papers, he saw that they were bound in the same manner as *Curiosity and Wonder*, and curled in the same way that he had rolled the magazine. There was even a folded corner on the fifth page, where he had been reading the previous afternoon. It was as though the pages had been literally drained of their ink. Puzzled, Thomas headed off to the workshop.

At work, he found he couldn't concentrate. His mind kept wandering and he felt a little dry in the mouth. Jacko commented on how pale he looked and, fearing he had some lurgy which would lay low the other lads, sent him home. Normally Thomas would have protested at the loss of half a day's pay, but he went without complaint. He wandered back to the lodgings in something of a daze, and it wasn't until Mrs Woods had ordered him to bed and he was frowning once again at the blank pages of his magazine, that the woolly, jumbling ideas in his head began to coalesce into something. At first he thought he was remembering his dreams from the night before, then he realised what it was. It was a story. He picked up his inkpot, his quill and his notepad, and began to write.

Thomas wrote until it went dark and he had to light his candle. Then he wrote until the other men came back to the room, grumbling and drunk. He put his paper and quill into his box and slept soundly until after eight the next morning.

He read what he had scribbled out the previous night. It was the best thing he had ever written. It might even have been the best thing he had ever read. It would be perfect for one of Edward Lloyd's magazines. Immediately, Thomas began to write a letter to Edward Lloyd, putting forward his story for possible publication. When he got to signing it, he paused. If Lloyd saw the name Thomas Grundy and remembered the story he'd rejected, he would likely as not throw this one straight on the fire. Thomas needed a nom de plume. He had already signed his Christian name, but that was common enough anyway. He looked out of the window, seeking inspiration, just as a meat wagon rolled up with stock for the butcher's shop across the road. Tyler & Sons, Epping, it said. As good a name as any. He signed the letter "Thomas Tyler", citing the workshop as his return address, then got dressed and delivered the manuscript by hand to Edward Lloyd's offices on Salisbury Square.

Three days later William was keeping nix as the lads had a smoke.

Thomas was reading the copy of *The Ghost* which William had brought in for him. Suddenly there was a low whistle; William's signal that Jacko was on his way. The lads rushed back to their posts and concentrated on their work as the foreman strode past the benches. He stopped in front of Thomas.

"There's a letter been delivered here for one Thomas Tyler. Do we have anyone here of that name who I don't know about?" he said, holding out the envelope.

Thomas reached out a shaking hand to take it but Jacko whipped it away. "Ah, Mr Grundy. I thought this might have something to do with you. This ain't some mailing address for you, you know, whatever name you decide to choose. It's a place of work, and I'll thank you to remember it."

Thomas nodded mutely and took the envelope. Jacko watched with narrowed eyes as he ripped it open.

"What's it say, anyway?"

Thomas read it through quickly once. William and the other lads had started to gravitate towards his bench, scenting something. "It's from Edward Lloyd."

"And who would he be, when he's at home?" said Jacko, one eyebrow raised.

Thomas folded the letter and put it in his inside pocket. Then he took off his apron and gave Jacko a beaming smile.

"He's my new boss," he said. "I reckon my apprenticeship's over."

Five

On Monday Stuart tried to get back into writing, but he couldn't focus. He kept going to the window of the bedsit and staring blankly at the *pop*CULT! graffito, which was being slowly eroded by the relentless rain. He kept imagining scenes from *Carry On, You Old Devil*, painstakingly constructing Sid James' priestly costume and inventing sequences of dialogue. It was as though the movie was seeping into his consciousness, until by lunch–time, as he leaned on the window frame smoking a cigarette and glaring at the blackening sky, he couldn't be wholly sure that he hadn't actually seen it at some point in his life.

When the weather cleared temporarily he went outside to inspect the graffito. He ran his fingers over the damp bricks. Chalk. He wondered about the astronaut. Had he done it? Stuart couldn't imagine his thick–gloved fingers manipulating the coloured chalks with enough dexterity. Then he noticed a signature, almost faded to nothing, just beneath the exclamation mark. He bent to inspect it.

Monty Cantsin, it said.

Stuart rolled the name around his tongue. "Monty Cantsin," he said. "Monty Cantsin." A teenager was walking past him, enclosed in a parka and strapped into a complicated shoulder bag. He snorted at Stuart and pointed his sculpted hair into the returning drizzle. Stuart said the name again. "Monty Cantsin." It had a rhythm, kind of like Charlie Don't Surf, or *Sally Can't Dance*, the Lou Reed song. And wasn't that the name of the transvestite from *Con Air*? That made Stuart think about Nicolas Cage, and *Wild At Heart*, and David Lynch. His mind pinballing off references, he began to whistle *Sweet Home Alabama* and by the time he'd crossed the road and escaped back into his bedsit, he'd arrived – by way of *Blue Velvet* and Kyle McLachlan – at an unconscious decision to watch his *Twin Peaks* DVDs.

Back in the bedsit, after abandoning *Twin Peaks* an hour in, he turned over the pieces of the puzzle. First there was the astronaut, who Stuart might have discounted as simply some urban attention seeker if he – or she, Stuart suddenly pointed out to himself – hadn't drawn his attention to the graffito on the wall outside his building. Then there was the scrawl itself. *pop*CULT!. And the woman in leather at the shop. There'd been graffiti there, as well, which he was pretty sure he hadn't seen on the way in. And finally the promise of the DVD. *Carry On, You Old Devil*.

Idly, he logged on to the internet and Googled the word popcult. Amid the morass of popular culture websites he managed to pick out a couple of mentions on obscure forums and messageboards, veiled references to some kind of group or organisation, but they were all to obtuse to hold his attention. Someone had posted a series of images on a photo–sharing site of similar graffiti tags to the one outside his flat, from all over London, which piqued his interest, but there was no further information, and the pictures were presented merely as an art project, without comment. One website did bring up a black page with simple, unadorned text that read *You found* pop*CULT!. Tough shit.* But there were no contact details, and no mention of *Carry On, You Old Devil.*

He wanted that DVD. Oh, how badly he wanted it. And the woman... the DVD meant seeing her again. Stuart stared at the blank TV screen, then at his laptop purring in the corner. Then he got his coat.

Sam, the nurse, looked pleasantly surprised to see him, Stuart liked to think, when he went to sign in at the Elysian Fields reception. Then a shadow passed over her face. "Oh, there's nothing wrong, is there? I mean, we don't normally see you in the week..."

"No, nothing wrong," said Stuart breezily. "I was in the area and just thought I'd pop in on mum."

"It's creative writing class," said Sam. "But they should be finished at four. You can wait in the office, if you like."

"Creative writing," marvelled Stuart as he followed Sam into the small office behind reception. And here he thought they just sat watching soaps and makeover shows all day, and reminiscing about the end of rationing.

"You're a writer, aren't you?" said Sam as she put the kettle on and Stuart perched on a plastic chair at the small table. "Your mum said you're writing a book about pop music, or something."

"Pop culture," corrected Stuart.

"Oh. Is there a difference, really? Do you take sugar and milk?"

"Milk and two sugars, that would be great, thanks. And yes, there is a difference."

Stuart scrunched his face up at how snotty that sounded. "I mean, pop music's pop culture, of course, but..."

Sam put the mug of tea on the table in front of him. "I used to be in a band. My boyfriend's. I was the singer. We were crap, though, so we packed it in."

"Oh, I'm sure you weren't," said Stuart, and winced. He sounded even worse when he simpered.

"No, I was, trust me," said Sam. "We cleared a pub in ten minutes, once. But the funny thing is, since I started working here, I've had some really fantastic ideas for songs. Arrangements, lyrics, everything. Really good, as well."

She blushed slightly at the self–praise as she sat down opposite him. "I mean, well, okay. I was thinking... well, that I might go on one of those TV talent shows. That's the only way to get a music career these days, isn't it?"

"Why not just start the band again?"

Sam scowled. "Oh, no. Not with Kev. Fired him off ages ago. He was a right cock."

Stuart perked up. This was the point, he knew, when he should offer to look at her lyrics, tell her he knew people in TV and the media and might be able to put her in touch with someone who could help, and perhaps she would like to meet him for a drink when she finished work to talk about it?

Instead, he made a grunting noise and said, "Shame."

Sam looked at him curiously. "Right. Well. They should be finishing up in the day room, I'll take you through."

Stuart drained his mug and followed Sam out of the office, silently punching his forehead with his balled fist.

His mum was, thankfully, not wearing a sheet this time. She blinked at him as he walked into the day room with Sam. "Stuart?" she said. "Is something wrong?"

The other residents gathered around expectantly, no doubt hoping for something at least as juicy as an accident, or a financial disaster, maybe even news of a death. Stuart backed off involuntarily, waving his hands. "No, no, nothing's wrong. I was just passing."

A small woman with a die–straight helmet haircut pushed through the small throng, brandishing a sheaf of papers. "Hello, love," she beamed at Sam. "All done here."

"Okay, Mrs P," said Sam. "Good session, was it?"

Mrs P studied the handwritten papers in her hand. "More than good, dear. Quite extraordinary, in fact. I've never known a group so... well, talented."

"Mr Balfour's a writer," said Sam.

Mrs P blinked at him. "Are you, then? And you'll be Mrs Balfour's son, I take it?"

Sam began ushering the residents away. "Let's get you all settled down with a nice cup of tea. I'll bring Stuart over in a minute, Mrs Balfour."

Mrs P leaned into Stuart conspiratorially. "Your mother's very gifted. Has she always had such a talent for prose?"

"Well, not as far as I know," said Stuart. "Can I have a look at what she's done?"

Mrs P leafed through the manuscripts and extracted one in Stuart's mother's familiar sloping handwriting. "Well, she must have been hiding her light under a bushel. Take a look."

If Stuart was expecting some stilted *what we did on our holidays* memoir he couldn't have been more wrong. The piece was untitled, but began: *Sometimes he was outside, sometimes he was inside, but he was always watching. Watching people on the street, watching the man in the shop brutally slicing joints of red flesh, watching the traffic warden slapping tickets on car windscreens with undisguised self-loathing, watching girls while imagining their fragrant cunts, watching boys and picturing their throbbing cocks. And all the while, as he watched, he dreamed of murder...*

"Oh," was all Stuart could think to say. "It's a bit..."

"Isn't it?" said Mrs P delightedly. "It's positively Carveresque. I tell you, I run classes all over the city and I've not seen writing like this in more than one per cent of them. And it isn't just your mother. They're all this good."

"Are they all like..." Stuart glanced at the paper again. Fragrant cunts. Throbbing cocks. "...ah, like this?"

"Not at all. There's an unimaginable variety. Memoir, poetry, genre fiction... this place has it all. I'm thinking of approaching the Arts Council for money to put an anthology together. I'm serious."

Stuart handed back the manuscript wonderingly. First *Medea*, now this. He shook his head as Sam returned. "You can see your mother now, Mr Balfour. Mrs P, I'll show you out."

Stuart's mother was settled in her chair, watching two men getting excited about a duvet on the TV. Stuart crouched at the side of her. She looked at him in surprise. "Stuart. Is it Saturday?"

"No, mum, it's Monday."

"Well, what are you doing here? Is something wrong?"

"No, mum, we've been through this. I was just passing."

"Oh." She returned, untroubled, to her programme. After a moment, she tutted. "They're stapling that pelmet. That'll never stay up."

"Mum," said Stuart. "I read your story. It was... where did you get the idea for that?"

"It's just a story," she said. "I made it up."

"I know, but..."

"I might write one about a pig next week."

Stuart paused. "A pig."

"Yes, you know." She made a startling snorting sound. "A pig."

An elderly woman in the next chair laughed and made the same noise. Then an old man moaned and told them to shut up. Three more of the residents made pig noises. Stuart looked around wildly as Sam came marching into the day room.

"That's quite enough!" she said sharply.

Stuart stood. "They're getting a bit giddy. Maybe I should go. See you Saturday, mum."

"Oink, oink," she said, and laughed. Then she turned to the woman in the next chair and shouted, "I told him, you can't staple a pelmet, can you, Marie? I told him, but they won't listen."

"We've got to start getting their medicine ready before tea–time," said Sam quietly.

"Yes, I've got to go anyway," said Stuart, intensely relieved.

Sam accompanied him to the front door. She bit her lip and then said, "Look, I was wondering. What with you writing a book about pop music, and all, if you wouldn't mind having a look at the songs I wrote."

Stuart was about to remind her of the difference between pop music and pop culture when he processed what she had just said.

"Um, yes. Do you want to bring them in on Saturday and I'll have a look at them when I come in?"

"Well... I thought maybe we could go for a drink. Are you busy tomorrow night?"

"Busy? Ha ha. No. Not busy. Well, busy, obviously, with the book. The pop culture... pop music. But not tomorrow night. Night off. Ha ha." Stuart had to stand on his own foot to make himself shut up. Sam named a bar in the West End and said she'd be there at eight. She closed the door and Stuart stood there for a moment, under the CCTV cameras and razor–wire, just staring. Then he remembered why he'd caught a bus and two tubes to this Godforsaken end of town in the first place.

* * *

Outside the shop, the card was still in the window. *Interested? We'll contact you.* Stuart pushed open the door and the meathead looked up from a magazine of naked, hairy women, grunting an acknowledgement. Stuart asked for twenty Marlboro Lights and said, "Uh, the card in the window..?"

"Which one?" said the meathead, punching the keypad on the till.

"I was in on Saturday. The woman on the motorbike. She asked for the card to go in the window..."

A light went on behind the newsagent's eyes. "Oh, yeah. That one. The blonde bit. Heh."

Stuart frowned. "Blonde? She was dark."

"She was fucking blonde, pal. Least, she was when I was thinking about her in the bath on Saturday night. What about her, anyway?"

"I just wondered if she'd been back in at all..?"

He laughed. "I'd fucking remember it if she had. Jesus."

Stuart pointed out of the window at the white *pop*CULT! graffito. "What about that? When did that go up?"

The meathead squinted through the grimy glass. "That? Fuck knows. They write all sorts of shit round here. What's with all the fucking questions, anyway?"

Stuart pocketed the cigarettes and left. He crossed the quiet street to look at the tag, this one spray–painted roughly, as though done in a hurry. He was sure the woman had done it in the moments between leaving the shop and roaring away on the motorbike. Stuart peered at the exclamation mark and there, scrawled clumsily in fading yellow chalk, was a signature.

Monroe.

Well, at least he had a name. Now all he had to do was find her. And the DVD.

Tuesday morning was overcast but so far without rain, and it found Mr Grundy on the roof of his tower block, where he liked to belt golf balls from a length of astroturf out into space and, eventually, on to the rush–hour commuters below. George was standing dutifully to one side with a flask of Lapsan Souchong, a supply of golf balls, and a clipboard, from which he was reading out loud.

"Shoreditch, Mr Grundy. King's Cross. Half a dozen places south of the river. And Islington, fresh last night."

Mr Grundy sliced a ball to the right and grunted. "Bloody juveniles. They're taunting me, George. That's what they're doing. All this graffiti. Vandalism, is what it is. Such a wasteful application of so much energy."

George pondered his list. "What should we do, Mr Grundy?"

"Have someone mark a map of London with all the places where this vandalism has been perpetrated. Then draw lines between them. Join the dots, George."

George made notes on his clipboard. As Mr Grundy hit another ball with a satisfying chock, he said, "For what purpose, Mr Grundy, if you don't mind me asking?"

Mr Grundy took the flask from the crook of George's arm and poured tea into a china cup by the astroturf. "Oh, it'll probably spell out some Assyrian obscenity or turn out to be in the shape of an obscure occult symbol of some kind. It's just the kind of thing they find amusing. But we'd better do it, just in case. Go through the motions, as it were."

"Tick all the boxes, sir," added George brightly.

"That's the ticket. Anything else from the morning report?"

George consulted his clipboard. "We believe we've had a sighting of the woman, Mr Grundy, the one they call Monroe. She was at one of the university faculties last Wednesday, and we believe she was visiting a Professor Garrett."

"They're up to something, George," said Mr Grundy, inspecting a golf ball closely before placing it carefully on the turf. "All this vandalism. Visiting professors. They're excited. I think perhaps you should pay this Professor... what did you say his name was?"

"Garrett."

"Professor Garrett. Let's pay him a visit." Mr Grundy sipped his tea. "Is that it, then, George?"

After a pause, George said, "Just one thing, sir. I said I'd ask. Escobar wants to know if he can have this Monroe woman for his wife when we destroy *pop*CULT!. I think he's quite taken with the idea of her."

Mr Grundy sighed. "Oh, George. Can you please tell him that he's in England now and he works for me and that's not how we do things? Oh, dear. That's quite put me off my swing."

"Sorry, sir. I said I'd ask."

"No matter, George. The traffic's thinning out down there anyway. Have someone bring my clubs back inside, would you? And if Escobar wants to let off a little steam, take him with you to see this Garrett fellow. But don't let him make a mess, George."

"Very good, Mr Grundy."

That morning, Professor Garrett was sitting at his desk with a cup of strong coffee, reading through the latest chapters Stuart Balfour had sent him in the post. It was, he had to admit, good stuff. But then, Balfour had been his brightest student. Professor Garrett felt a glow of almost paternal pride. This was going to be a good book. And it might even sell to a mainstream audience. Balfour knew his stuff and he had a nice common touch as well. Of course, with this extra backing the mysterious Miss Monroe had promised... well, anything could happen. Christmas bestseller, perhaps. Maybe they should come up with a snappy title, get it on the shelves at Waterstone's. *Balfour's Miscellaneous Pop Culture*, perhaps.

The phone on his desk buzzed. Professor Garrett frowned; it was only just after nine–thirty. He'd come in early to read Balfour's stuff and because his wife was getting on his nerves, but he wasn't officially at work until ten and wasn't expecting any calls.

He picked the phone up to Stuart Balfour.

"Professor Garrett, sorry to bother you so early but I'm on to something that might be really interesting, and wondered if you could shed any light on it."

"I'll try. The material you sent is looking good, by the way."

"Great. Listen, have you ever heard of *Carry On, You Old Devil*? It was made in the early Seventies but never released. I might be able to get hold of a copy."

"Not my field, I'm afraid," said Professor Garrett.

"Oh," said Stuart, pumping more money into the telephone. "Never mind. The thing is, the person who's got this DVD, I can't get hold of them. Don't suppose the word *pop*CULT! means anything to you?"

"I'm afraid not. Sorry."

"It doesn't matter. It's just I think this woman who has the DVD, this Monroe person, is involved in—"

"Wait, wait," said Professor Garrett. "Did you say Monroe? Miss Monroe?"

"I think that's her name. Do you—?"

"What does she look like?"

"Dark hair. Very attractive. Thin face. Do you know her?"

Professor Garrett sighed. "No, I don't think so. The Miss Monroe I know is... well, it doesn't sound like the same woman."

"Okay, Professor... oops, the beeps are going. I'll have some more stuff in the post next—"

The connection went dead and Professor Garrett replaced the receiver. How odd that Balfour was trying to find someone called Monroe just days after he'd been visited by the woman who still occupied most of his waking thoughts. He'd just begun to recreate her freckles and bunched hair in his mind when the phone buzzed again.

"Yes?" he said irritably.

It was the faculty reception desk. "Professor Garrett? There are two gentlemen here to see you. They say it's very urgent."

"Yes, we do represent Mr Windsor Davies. Is this a press inquiry?"

55

"Uh, not exactly. I'm a writer. I'm researching a book. My name's Stuart Balfour."

"And what can we do for you, Mr Balfour?"

"It's about a film. Which Windsor Davies was in."

"He's been in many films, Mr Balfour. Which particular one?"

"It was made but never actually released. It was called *Carry On, You Old Devil*. Back in Sev— hello? Hello?"

"Hello, is that the Pinewood Studios library?"

"Pinewood–Shepperton, sir. You're through to the archive department. What's the nature of your inquiry?"

"Well, it's about a film that was made there in the 1970s..."

"One of many, sir, ha ha. What was it called?"

"It was called... it was a Carry On film."

"Ah, that'll be Gerald you want. He's our Carry On expert. Infamy, infamy and all that. And you're writing a book, sir?"

"Yes, that's right. It's..."

"I'll just get Gerald for you. What was the movie again?"

"It was called *Carry On, You Old Devil*."

"*Carry On, You Old Devil*, sir? Hang on. Gerald? Gerald. Chap here on about *Carry On, You Old Devil*. Not one I've... Gerald? Good God, Gerald, what's... Sir, I'm sorry, can you call back later, please?"

"Hello, is that Jim Dale?"

"Er, yes, it is. Who is this, please? Do you know what time it is?"

"Mr Dale, my name's Stuart Balfour, I'm a writer. I wanted to—"

"Writer? How did you get this number if you don't mind me asking?"

"Mr Dale, I know you didn't work on it, but—"

"Who gave you this number? Are you calling from England? Do you know what time it is over here?"

"Mr Dale, it's about *Carry On, You Old Devil*..."

"Oh, for God's sake, when are you people going to leave this alone? You're right, I didn't work on that movie, because it didn't exist. Now I'm going back to bed and I'll thank you not to call again."

"Mr Dale, is it true the movie was cursed? That people died? Mr Dale? Mr Dale..?"

Stuart slammed the receiver back into its cradle. That last call to the United States had swallowed the last of his pound coins. Perhaps he should relent and get a new phone in the flat, he thought. His fingers were numb with cold and he had a headache coming on from the overpowering smell of disinfectant. Well, at least they'd tried to clean the call box up a bit. It was a marginally better odour than the piss. He decided to head off to Moe's and buy some paracetamol and a newspaper. The last thing he wanted was for a headache to ruin tonight. A date! His first in... well, since he split with Jane, really. He hoped he remembered what to do. It had been such a long time since he'd had to go into a West End bar and make small talk. Perhaps he could tell her about phoning Jim Dale. That might get a laugh. Then he thought that she might not even know who Jim Dale was. Sam was about twenty–seven, he estimated. Seven years his junior. Would she have even ever seen a Carry On movie? Still, it wasn't as if he was completely out of touch... he did, after all, know a thing or two about popular culture. He was sure they'd have plenty to talk about.

The main street was strangely quiet, apart from an old man folded into an overcoat and tottering along with a stick a hundred yards or so ahead of him. Stuart whistled tunelessly, looking up at the sky; it looked like rain again, surprise, surprise. When he glanced back at the street there were three youths crossing the road, just ahead of the old man. Stuart carried on walking, drawing closer as the kids stopped the pensioner in his tracks and began gesticulating at him. They were all uniformed in white tracksuits and baseball caps, their pale faces pinched and thin, one of them with his hood up over his headgear. Stuart's stomach flipped; he had a bad feeling about this.

One of the youths pushed the old man, who staggered slightly. Stuart was only twenty yards away now; he could hear their cod–hip hop patois as they demanded money.

He slowed to a crawl, putting one painstaking foot in front of the other. This was evidently a mugging in progress in broad daylight. He glanced nonchalantly around; there was no–one else on the street. Not a soul. The old man looked around and saw Stuart, his face instantly gratified. The three kids looked at him as one; their dark eyes warned him to back off. He was inclined to heed the threat.

Stuart stopped and inspected the non–existent watch on his left wrist. Then he bent and re–tied his shoe–lace. When he stood up again, the old boy had his back against the wall and was brandishing his walking stick at the laughing youths. Stuart looked around again. The street was still deserted.

"Help me!"

Stuart winced and pretended not to hear. He just stood there in the street while this mugging was going on ten yards away. What could he do? Surely there was someone else..? Desperately, he checked the change in his pockets. The old man shouted again.

"Please, they're after my pension!"

Stuart heard the pensioner moan and saw him hand over his wallet to the kids. He really should say something.

"Um. You lot," he offered, barely audibly.

Pocketing the wallet, the biggest of the youths gave the pensioner a shove and laughed as he staggered against the wall. Then he beckoned his mates and they started to walk towards Stuart.

Shit, he thought. Shit. A mugging was a certainty now, he realised with sinking heart. And he had about a hundred quid in his wallet as well. Stupid, stupid, stupid. All he could hope for now was that they didn't hurt him too much.

They were surrounding him now. Stuart backed against the wall. The leader pointed a finger in his chest.

"You know somethin'?"

"Um," said Stuart.

Suddenly, he broke into a huge grin. "You're on *Double Take TV*!"

Half a dozen people melted out of nowhere. Stuart's first thought was, thank God! until he processed the fact that half of them were holding TV cameras and sound booms. A tall black man he vaguely recognised, a former athlete or footballer, maybe, was standing right in front of him. He was holding a clipboard and wearing a matey grin wholly inappropriate for the situation, Stuart felt.

"Sir, you are on *Double Take TV*," said the man, gurning at the camera.

"What?" said Stuart. "What?"

"There's no mugging!" he said, laughing uproariously. "All the people you just witnessed were actors!"

The old man had joined them now. He took his cap off and nodded at Stuart. "Hello."

"Hello," said Stuart weakly.

The presenter now had his arm around Stuart's shoulder and was steering him towards a camera. He said, "What's your name, sir?"

"Stuart."

"Stuart, you're on *Double Take TV*! This whole situation was a set–up to see how normal people like you would react when confronted with street violence. How do you feel?"

Stuart looked at the camera, then at him. "You utter twat," he said levelly.

The presenter scowled and winked at the camera, and said, "What a sport! It's Stuart, ladies and gentlemen!" Then he drew his clipboard across his throat. The light on the camera blinked off.

"You utter twats!" said Stuart, more loudly. One of the youths sniggered. A young woman with blue hair and headphones presented a piece of paper on a clipboard to Stuart.

"Could you just sign this release sir, allowing us to use this footage in an upcoming episode of *Double Take TV*?"

Stuart looked at her, then at the cameras, then at the old man. "No, I most certainly will not."

The girl looked nonplussed. "What? But we can't use the footage if you don't sign... I know it's daft, but it's the rules."

"I don't want to sign because I don't want you to use the footage," said Stuart.

The presenter was looking back at him now. The girl said quietly, as though Stuart was stupid, "He won't sign."

"Sir," said the presenter. "Don't you want to be on TV?"

"Frankly, no," said Stuart.

The presenter and the girl looked at each other. The man glanced at him again. "Sorry, no?"

"No," said Stuart again.

"Oh."

The crew started to pack their stuff away, muttering to themselves and casting glances at Stuart. "He said no," he heard one of them say. They started to drift away down the street, in the direction of the greasy spoon cafe near Moe's. The presenter was the last one there.

"You're sure?" he said after an awkward silence.

"Positive," said Stuart. "I can't be the first one to not want to be on the TV, surely."

The presenter rubbed his chin. "Actually, I think you are. Ah well." He beamed at Stuart. "Always one, eh? Never mind. Take care, sir."

The man jogged up the street after the crew. Stuart shook his head and went to Moe's for his newspaper and paracetamol, which he needed more than ever.

It had started to pour as Stuart was on his way back from the shop, and he ran the last hundred yards, stamping his feet and shaking his hands as he closed the door behind him. Outside his bedsit was Mrs Zygmundewycz, the ancient Polish woman who lived in the flat next door. She stood there in her floral pinafore, wringing her bony hands, looking up at him through her thick glasses from her four–foot–nothing. She always looked to Stuart like she'd just finished a shift cleaning destroyers at some Gdansk shipyard. He hoped he hadn't been burgled.

"Mr Balfour, are you all right? You are as white as the sheet."

Stuart did feel a little shaken. He told her what had happened. She clasped her hands to her bosom. "Oh, it is terrible. They are mugging the people and taking the moving pictures of them?"

"No, it wasn't real, Mrs Zed," said Stuart. "It was... you remember *Candid Camera*? It was like that. It was for television."

"They are putting the muggings on the television?" she said incredulously. "Oh, if my Lech was here now, he would be turning in the grave."

Stuart fished out his keys as Mrs Zygmundewicz grabbed his arm. "Oh, speaking of the television, you know the Mrs Arlington? The lady who had the lump? The lady who does the washing for the people in the big houses?"

"No," said Stuart. He needed a cup of tea.

"The lady with the son, who wears the glasses?"

"No, Mrs Zed, I—"

"She won the twenty thousand pounds. On the breakfast telly. With the guessing the answers to the questions."

"Oh," said Stuart. "Well..."

"Oh, and there is the other thing. The telephone went and it was the call for you."

Stuart stopped fiddling with his keys. Mrs Zed had kindly agreed to take any important messages for him as he didn't have a phone. The only thing he could think of was that it was Elysian Fields and something had happened to his mother. He felt a little faint.

"Was it the home, Mrs Zed? My mother..?"

"Not the mother," she said. "It was the wife. She wants you to call her. She sounded very nice, Mr Balfour. Perhaps you are to get back together, eh?"

"The wife?" said Stuart dumbly.

"The ex–wife. The one who left you for the man."

"The wife," said Stuart again.

The woman called Monroe was not dark, nor blonde, nor wore red hair in bunches framing a freckled nose. Yet sometimes she was all these things. It was complicated, and she didn't fully understand it herself, so she tended not to think about it too much these days. She relaxed on a bench in Hyde Park, under the shelter of a weeping willow, its branches dripping with rain. Every man who had passed her, every jogger and cyclist and husband and boyfriend and father and pensioner and teenage boy, had stared openly at her, slowing their pace, provoking scowls and nudges from girlfriends and wives. Some of the girlfriends and wives had cast surreptitious glances at her as well, the same strange look in their eyes. They would all dream of her tonight, Monroe knew.

She flipped open her mobile phone and dialled with her thumb. It connected after one ring.

"Tyler. Monroe."

"Monroe, baby," came the fuzzy reply. "Let me get up a couple of levels, the signal's crap."

She waited, smiling at a man in an overcoat walking a dog, who turned for a second and third look at her as he passed, getting himself tangled in the lead of his yapping terrier. Then Tyler came back, clearer and laughing.

"Monroe. How's it going?"

"What are you laughing at?" she said suspiciously.

"Nothing, baby. I— ow!"

"Tyler," she sighed. "What's going on?"

He giggled. "We've got a new Karen Eliot. I'm just showing her the ropes."

"Well, tell her to get her hands off your rope and piss off out of it for five minutes. This is important."

There was mumbling and scuffling and then Tyler came back

on. "You have my undivided attention, Monroe. What's up?"

She scanned the park, but it was quiet. The rain redoubled its efforts and was starting to penetrate the shelter of the tree.

"I've been followed all day."

"Grundy?"

"Naturally. They can't keep up, though. I lost the last lot in Brixton. Put a new tag up, as well."

"Nice. Do they know about Balfour?"

"I don't think so. I've avoided his place though, just in case. Have you still got Luther on him?"

"Yeah, but I don't like him being away from the warehouse for too long. Grundy's up to something and I want as many of us as possible on–site in case we have to flit at short notice. Is Balfour ready for us, yet?"

Monroe pursed her lips. "Hard to say. But then again, when is anyone ready for us?"

"Good point. I think we should bring him in, then."

"Okay. When?"

"Tonight," said Tyler, and the phone went dead.

Six

While processing the information that Jane had telephoned him for the first time in the best part of a year, Stuart sat on the sofa and watched two–thirds of a BBC4 retrospective documentary on, quite bizarrely, *Bagpuss*. Bizarre because his abiding emotional memory of the time he and Jane finally, irrevocably split for good was a singing mouse.

Stuart had met Jane while she was working for the public relations firm which represented the small production company he was doing some freelance work for. She was in charge of promoting the series he was researching for, *I Know 'Cos I Was There*. In each hour–long programme a parade of talking heads would wax lyrical about the TV shows, the music, the ads, the movies, the books and any other disposable culture icons of a particular year. It was Stuart's job to find out just what was hot in each year and to organise the creation of a pack containing cuttings and DVD discs which was couriered round to each minor personality a couple of days before the show was filmed.

It was quite obvious in many cases that the featured C–list celebrities had either no memory of the shows they were supposed to be enthusing about, or that they were blatantly too young to have been anything more than a mewling babe–in–arms when they were meant to be glued to *The Tomorrow People*, playing Buckaroo or listening to *Tiger Feet*. Stuart would grimace as the cameras recorded each celeb getting excited about the same clip of *Black Beauty* or *Bonanza* he'd assembled for them, even down to the finest detail of clothing or incidental music which nobody in their right mind – much less a stand–up comedian famous for slopping pints of mild down his trousers or a ditzy children's TV presenter with bunches and a grating laugh – could possibly recall from a single tea–time viewing twenty–odd years ago.

For *I Know 'Cos I Was There – 1974*, Stuart had put together a series of clips on every child's favourite saggy old cloth cat, *Bagpuss*. He was watching some radio DJ gurning his way through a very bad impression of Professor Yaffle, the carved wooden woodpecker bookend. Then the DJ completely appropriated Stuart's briefing note that Yaffle was a gentle parody of the philosopher Bertrand Russell, which annoyed no end the magazine journalist who was next to be filmed and who had planned to use that little nugget herself. "Bastard," she hissed, flicking through the briefing notes to find something else to pass off as her own observation. "I never liked the moth–eaten fucking moggie anyhow."

It was at that point that Stuart first became aware of a slender young woman in combat pants and a vest who was standing nearby, staring daggers at the magazine journalist. Her hair was tied back and her face angular, make up–less, and quite, quite beautiful. Stuart recklessly edged closer to her in the darkened control booth facing the sound stage.

By the time the magazine journalist was up for filming, Stuart was standing behind the stranger. As the journo enthusiastically began gesticulating wildly and talking about the singing mice, her favourite one being "Harley", the woman, who looked maybe Stuart's age, maybe a little younger, snorted. "He was called Charlie, you silly cow," she muttered to herself.

"Correct," murmured Stuart, making the woman jump slightly. "I wish the talent would read the briefing notes as thoroughly as you, Miss...?"

She looked up at Stuart, embarrassed. "Gornall. Jane Gornall. And I haven't read your briefing notes, I'm afraid. I just remember Bagpuss as though it was yesterday."

Stuart was about to say something cringe–worthy about her not looking old enough, but she rescued him by continuing her introduction. "I'm from Buzz PR. We're handling the publicity on IKCIWT."

"Ickywit?" said Stuart, mystified.

"IKCIWT – *I Know 'Cos I Was There*. Sorry, you are..?"

"Sorry. Stuart Balfour. Researcher, briefing notes editor, general dogsbody. I..."

The director turned around and shushed them angrily, and Jane and Stuart grinned at each other in the semi–darkness. He pointed at the back of the director and made an up–and–down motion with his clenched fist.

Jane laughed silently and pointed at the magazine journo on the sound stage, who was saying, "Postgate? Are you sure these notes are right? Oliver fucking Postgate? I thought Bagpuss was invented by that French guy." She stuck her tongue into the space under her lower lip and mimed a pulling action from her forehead.

Stuart winked, thinking about his next gambit.

Tired of waiting, Jane mimed a drinking motion and raised a quizzical eyebrow.

Stuart shrugged and nodded.

She tapped her watch and held up five fingers.

Stuart nodded.

Jane winked, and slid silently into the darkness at the back of the booth, and out through the door, which let a shaft of yellow light in and then closed behind her.

Stuart nodded again, though there was no–one to see him, or his ridiculous smile.

Not long after *I Know 'Cos I Was There* completed filming a wrap party was held in a swish bar in Soho. Stuart and Jane had been on a couple of relaxed dates in between and though nothing more serious or promising had happened, Stuart feared he was falling for her. But when Stuart fell for someone, he generally ended up face down in all manner of shit, and besides, she was pretty and sassy and intelligent and way, way out of his league.

At the launch party everyone got very, very drunk. Jane unceremoniously presented Stuart with a small package – a goodbye gift, he reckoned. It turned out to be a toy, a small grey mouse with wide, white eyes, wearing a blue gingham shirt and trousers and a spotted tie. It was Charlie Mouse from *Bagpuss*. When you pressed his stomach, he sang a little song. "So you'll remember me," said Jane.

Stuart knew he should have taken her in his arms and planted a long, smouldering kiss on her lips. "So you'll remember me, too," he should have said.

Instead, he looked stupidly at the mouse and pressed its stomach. When the song had finished he gave Jane a crooked smile. "Thanks. I, er, didn't get you anything."

By the time the night was over, Stuart was utterly, soddenly, miserably pissed. Jane had left half an hour previously, giving him a chaste kiss on the cheek. He'd hammered bottle after bottle of something which tasted like Tizer but had a higher alcohol content than Stella Artois ever since she walked out of the door. Why could he never take the initiative? Why did he let beautiful women smile at him then walk out of his life forever? His work on *I Know 'Cos I Was There* was done now, and he'd never see Jane again. Of course, he knew where she worked and even had her mobile number following the couple of drinks they'd had at the bar round the corner from the production company's offices, but he knew he wouldn't phone her. He never did.

So when Jane swept back into the bar, pushing against the throng of people who were leaving, Stuart imagined her to be a product of the sugary, boozy drink he'd been downing with abandon. She marched straight up to him, smiling at him lopsidedly. Stuart asked her if she'd forgotten something.

"Yes," she said. "This."

Then she gave him the kiss he should have given her, long and deep and hot and wet. They kissed as he climbed into his coat, they kissed at the taxi rank, they kissed all the way back to her flat, up the stairs, through the door and into the bedroom. They kissed for two whole days and a whole night.

Two months later, they were engaged to be married. The proposal was hardly romantic, but then it wasn't Stuart who did the asking anyway. It was February 29, they were standing on the wobbling Millennium Bridge, an icy gale roaring off the Thames and threatening to have them in the black waters.

"If I fell in, would you dive in after me?" shouted Jane above the roar of the wind.

Stuart thought about it. "I suppose so. If there was no ambulance around, or anything."

Jane pondered his answer. "That'll do for me. Want to get married?"

And three years after that, it was over. In his imagination, Stuart tended to paint Jane as a horrible harridan who screamed and swore and grimaced at him as she told him how useless he was and that he had to get out of her sight forever. In fact, it wasn't like that at all. On the day that they both knew in their hearts that it had come to an end, Jane wept as much as Stuart did as she packed a bag and said she was moving out for two weeks, to give him time to find somewhere else to live. The flat he'd always thought of as theirs was, in fact, hers. He'd known that when he let her deal with all the mortgage applications and told her to put her name on all the documents because he was freelance and didn't have a regular monthly income, though he was never really out of work. They hugged and said they were sorry and told each other to take care, then Jane left.

Stuart paced around the flat for an hour, feeling strangely numb and partly excited, as though he was a teenage boy who'd been left on his own for a fortnight while his parents went on holiday without him for the first time and he could do exactly what he wanted. Then the enormity of it all crushed him and he sagged under its weight, sliding down the wall in the spare bedroom which had become, over three years, piled high with his records and books and comics and posters and DVDs and tat.

The tears came freely as his eyes lit upon Charlie Mouse, sitting on a pile of *TV Century 21* annuals. Stuart held the mouse tightly, causing it to burst into song.

"We will find it, we will bind it, we will stick it with glue, glue, glue. We will stickle it, every little bit of it, we will fix it like new, new, new."

He roared, then, allowing his sobs free egress into the still, quiet, abandoned air of the flat. Jane had gone. Left him. For good. He squeezed Charlie Mouse's stomach, listening to the song again. He was a piece of something that could never be fixed.

Stuart crouched there against the wall until he fell asleep, pressing Charlie Mouse's belly again and again and again until he, too, was as broken as Stuart, and the song came no more.

He felt a lump swelling in his throat and turned off the Bagpuss documentary. There was no way around it, he would have to phone Jane. It might be important. Something bad might have happened. Quentin might have been horribly killed in a freakish accident, perhaps by a safe or grand piano falling from a great height, and she might need the only person who really understood her, who really knew her. Unlikely, considered Stuart, but he'd better call all the same.

His last round of phone calls chasing his tail over the Carry On DVD had taken all his change, and he couldn't face going around to Moe's yet again to load up on pound coins. Wrapping himself up in his coat and scarf, he knocked on Mrs Zygmundewicz's door.

She blinked up at him from behind several security chains. "Mr Balfour. Have you telephoned the wife?"

"No, Mrs Zed," said Stuart as she unfettered the door. "I need money for the phone box. Don't suppose you can change a fiver, can you?"

"Neither the borrower nor the lender be, that's what my Lech always used to say," said Mrs Zygmundewicz, opening the door wide. "You can come in and use the phone to ring the wife."

"No," said Stuart. "I don't want to borrow money, I want to change a five pound note..."

Mrs Zygmundewicz shooed him into the flat, flapping a duster at him. "The telephone is in the living room. Ring the wife. It might be important."

Stuart did as he was told. The tiny living room was immaculate, antimacassars on the backs of the faded floral chairs, the smell of beeswax and cleanliness all around. What little light there was illuminated a black and white photograph of a smiling, kindly man in military uniform. The dear departed Mr Zygmundewicz, guessed Stuart. Mrs Zygmundewicz followed him into the room and perched on the edge of the sofa, watching him expectantly from behind her glasses, her hands clasped at the front of her yellow apron.

"Uh," said Stuart.

"Oh, it's okay. I am not the eavesdropper."

"Um. Fine."

Stuart dug in his pocket and pulled out his diary. In the back were the numbers of his few friends. In fact, most of them weren't even friends, by the time he'd discounted Elysian Fields, Professor Garrett and the Koi Temple takeaway on the main road. The number he wanted was listed as Jane (at Quentin's). Even after a year, he couldn't quite bring himself to accept that Jane and Quentin lived together permanently, rather than her just staying with him for a bit.

Glancing back at Mrs Zygmundewicz, who smiled broadly at him, he punched the numbers and waited, his stomach flipping in time with the steady buzz of the ringtone.

"Hello—", began Jane.

"Jane, it's—"

"—Jane and Quentin aren't in right now. Please leave a message after the beep!"

Stuart took the receiver away from his ear and stared at it. Jane and Quentin aren't in. Not *Quentin, whose house this is, isn't in, and neither is Jane, the woman who is living with him temporarily until she realises she loves her husband*, but *Jane and Quentin*. He heard the beep sound, and then suddenly a tinny voice shouting, "Hello? Hello?"

He put the phone back to his ear. It had been picked up.

"Jane?"

It was Quentin. "No, sorry, I'll just get her. Who shall I say is calling?"

In the comics, when someone spoke with venom or acidic nastiness, the letterer made the words quiver and drip. Stuart tried to make his voice do that. "Tell her it's her ex–husband."

There was a pause. "Ah. Stuart. Um, how are you?"

Stuart had met Quentin, of course. Before Jane announced that she was sleeping with Quentin, Stuart had run into him at various PR parties and shows and events that he often found himself dragged along to by Jane. Dragged along to less and less frequently towards the end, he noted. Actually, Stuart hadn't actually disliked him that much. He'd just considered him a typical, two–dimensional, shallow PR–type. Up until he found out that he was sleeping with his wife, he probably subconsciously thought he was gay, but then Stuart tended to think that of any man who was turned out better than he was which, he had to glumly admit, was most of the male population these days.

"Fine," said Stuart, trying to make his voice sound like he was anything but. "I'm returning Jane's call."

"Of course. Ha ha. She's here now. Well... good to speak to you again, ah, Stuart..."

Stuart said nothing and let Quentin hand over the telephone to Jane, who came on immediately. "Stu. How are you? Keeping well, I hope?"

"As well as can be expected. Um. You called me?"

"Yes. God, when are you going to get a new phone? Or a mobile, at least?"

What, like you're trying to get hold of me all the time? thought Stuart, then said, "Look, Jane, I've got loads on and—"

"Right," she said briskly. Was there a note of disappointment at his aloofness? Stuart suddenly felt his heart melt. And she'd called him Stu... no–one but Jane ever did that. But she was talking again: "Stuart, I thought it best you know, and that you hear it from me. From us."

Us?

"Know what?"

71

Jane took a deep breath. There was an electric pause. "Stu, I'm... we're having a baby. Quentin and me. We're pregnant."

A baby. When they'd got married, Stuart had tentatively raised the question of children. "God, no," she'd said. Babies didn't fit into the career path, the game plan, the lifestyle. "Besides," she'd said, rubbing his hair with her knuckles and gesturing at his various collections. "Who needs a kid when I've got you?"

"Stuart? Did you hear me?"

He coughed. "Uh, yeah. Yes. I'm..." He sought for the right words. "Happy. I'm happy for you."

"Oh, thank you, Stuart," said Jane with genuine warmth. "That means a lot to me. Really. So, come on, tell me. What's keeping you busy?"

"Well, there's the book..." began Stuart, but was suddenly aware of Mrs Zygmundewicz standing expectantly at his elbow.

"Oh, and the date. I've got a date tonight. Look, I've got to go, Jane, Mrs Zed..."

"A book and a date. I am impressed," said Jane. "Look, thanks for taking it so well and keep in touch, but before you dash off there's something else."

"Oh?"

"Just a little thing, really. Since I'm pregnant we thought, well, we thought we'd get married."

"Married?" said Stuart. Very often, he forgot that he and Jane were actually divorced. "Married," he said again.

"Yeah. February. And... look, I understand if you can't, but we... I'd like you to be there. Don't answer now, but think about it, okay?"

"Okay," said Stuart, then said goodbye and replaced the receiver.

"Bad news?" said Mrs Zygmundewicz hopefully.

Stuart slipped the fiver from his pocket and slid it under the telephone. "My wife's having a baby," he said flatly.

"Oh, the wife is having the baby!" said Mrs Zygmundewicz delightedly. "You must be so happy!"

Seven

Professor Garrett sat back in his chair, his head tilted as far back as it would, a bag of frozen peas clamped to his face. Evelyn, his secretary, had bought his story about tripping on the moth–eaten rug in front of his desk and banging his nose on the book–shelf, and had returned from the canteen with the peas with impressive haste.

The intercom buzzed. It was Evelyn. "Professor Garrett? I know you said no visitors, but there's a woman... I've sent her in."

Professor Garret groaned, bringing his head level just in time to see Miss Monroe walk into his office. He smiled as suavely as he possibly could, then remembered he had the peas on his face. He whipped them away and tried to smile again, but almost immediately he could feel blood trickling down his philtrum.

Miss Monroe stood with her hands on her hips. She was dressed, as far as Professor Garrett could tell, as Olivia Newton John in *Grease*, the coquettish Sandra Dee look with long skirt, tight blouse and bobby socks which Professor Garrett had fixed in his mind and masturbated over countless times, rather than the purportedly sexy leather and fuck–me heels look of the final frames.

"Oh, you poor dear," she said, her pony–tail swishing behind her. "What on Earth have you been up to?"

"I... fell," he said limply.

Miss Monroe took a seat facing him across the desk. She dipped into her handbag and withdrew a tissue. "You're bleeding. Allow me."

She leaned over the desk, her blouse gaping. Professor Garrett moaned slightly as she softly brushed the blood away from his nose, but it was more to do with the view and her nutty, woody scent than the pain.

Satisfied she had cleaned him up, Miss Monroe sat back down, a frown on her face. "Now, suppose you tell me what really happened. You've had a visit, haven't you? Like I said you might?"

* * *

73

The two men didn't introduce themselves. They walked into his office and closed the door quietly behind them. One was in his fifties, impossibly broad with a scarred, bald head and bright eyes shining from their cavernous orbits. His companion was small, wiry and Latino, with a tightly–cropped moustache. Both wore dark suits and black ties. Professor Garrett was suddenly very scared, and didn't know which of the men unsettled him most.

"You're Professor Garrett," said the big man.

"Yes," said Professor Garrett standing and holding out his hand, which was ignored. "And you are..?"

The smaller man wandered over to the bookshelves and feigned interest in the spines. The big man sat down, facing Professor Garrett across the desk. "Professor, you've been visited by a woman, who may be calling herself Monroe. Am I correct?"

His first thought was that they were private detectives his wife had hired. He smiled. "Yes, as it happens. On a business matter. A publishing matter. But I fail—"

The big man sat back. "A publishing matter."

"A publishing matter," echoed the other man. Professor Garrett looked up and was surprised to see he was taking notes in a spiral–bound notebook.

"Look, if my wife's sent you..."

The big man smiled and raised an eyebrow, causing the scars on his forehead to dance. "Your wife? Your wife hasn't sent us, Professor. We represent... an interested party."

Then Miss Monroe's words came back to him. *There are other parties who may not be as enthusiastic about this book as we are. They may visit you. They can be very... persuasive.*

"Oh, God," said Professor Garrett softly.

"Not quite," smiled the big man.

"George and Escobar," said Miss Monroe, almost to herself.

"You know them?"

"What? Oh, not really. Heard of them. They're Grundy's right hand men."

"Grundy?" said Professor Garrett.

"Never mind," said Miss Monroe. "Did they say what they wanted?"

"A publishing matter," mused George. "What's the nature of this 'publishing matter', please, Professor?"

Professor Garrett sat up as straight as he could. "I rather don't think that's any of your business," he said bravely.

George nodded sadly. "I was hoping you weren't going to be like this, Professor. In fact, I was so sure, I had a little wager with my colleague here on the way over." He turned to Escobar, who was watching Professor Garrett intently. "It looks like I owe you five pounds."

"Again," said Escobar.

"Again," agreed George. "I really should learn to trust his instincts more, Professor. He's right more often than I am. Do you believe in instinct, Professor?"

Professor Garrett said nothing.

George continued. "You see, your instinct should now be telling you to co-operate with us. You don't know who we are. You don't know where we're from. You're quite alone with us."

"Apart from my secretary," said Professor Garrett, immediately realising how foolish and frightened he sounded.

"Ah," said George. "Evelyn, am I correct? She is currently out in the car park, helping a young man who met with quite an unfortunate accident. We reported it to her on our arrival and she rushed to help."

"An accident?"

Escobar casually pulled what Professor Garrett believed to be called a kukri from inside his suit jacket. It was an evil–looking curved blade generally utilised by the Gurkhas.

"An accident," said George. "But back to instinct. What is your instinct telling you now, Professor?"

Miss Monroe leaned forward, hanging on his every word. "Oh,

my. What did you do?"

Professor Garrett pushed his shoulders back and his chest out slightly. "They didn't scare me, Miss Monroe. I told them to get out of my office, threats and kukri or not."

"Oh, God," said Professor Garrett.

"He knows how to use it, too," said George. "In many imaginative ways. Now, suppose you tell us all about this 'publishing matter'. A book, I suppose. What about?"

"You didn't tell them, obviously," said Miss Monroe, sitting back, a perturbed look clouding her face.

"Uh, obviously," said Professor Garrett. "The knife worried me, but I thought I could get the drop on the smaller one and take his weapon, and see off the other."

"My. How brave," smiled Miss Monroe.

Professor Garrett talked for ten minutes, never taking his eyes off Escobar who had the kukri clenched between his teeth while he took rapid notes. He gave them a full synopsis about Balfour's book and told them everything Miss Monroe had said on her visit. At the end, he said, "But why? Why is this so important?"

"Is that how you got injured?" said Miss Monroe. "When you... 'got the drop' on Escobar?"

"Pretty much," said Professor Garrett. "The big one – George? — was faster than he looked."

"I believe I'm asking the questions," said George, and without warning his right hand lashed out and slapped Professor Garrett smartly on the nose.

"Ow!" said Professor Garrett. "I'm bleeding!"

George looked at Escobar. "Do you want to cut off his ears? Like in that film you like to watch? What's it called?"

"*Reservoir Dogs*," said Escobar, showing his white teeth in a wide grin.

"Oh, God, please," begged Professor Garrett. "I've told you everything."

"Except one thing. Who's writing this book?"

"So you got the knife off Escobar and threatened George with it, but he managed to overpower you," said Miss Monroe. "You must have been terrified. And still you didn't give them what they wanted?"

"Of course not," said Professor Garrett, his face burning now. "I told you I wouldn't."

Holding his handkerchief to his nose, Professor Garrett called up the file on his PC and read out Stuart Balfour's address, which Escobar duly noted down.

George stood, motioning for Escobar to follow him. "You've been very helpful, Professor Garrett. Apologies for the violence but... well, you understand."

"Not really," said Professor Garrett from behind the handkerchief. "I don't understand any of this."

"Best to not worry about it," said George. "And I shouldn't think about going to the police or anything like that."

Escobar turned the blade of the kukri this way and that, as though disappointed he'd unsheathed it from his jacket and now wasn't going to use it.

"Unfortunately, the smaller fellow wasn't out for as long as I thought he would be. While I was struggling with this George, he pulled out a... another kukri and put it to my throat. It was a... a stalemate."

"A checkmate," agreed Miss Monroe. "And I suppose you had no choice but to tell them what they wanted?"

"No choice," agreed Professor Garrett weakly. "Then they left. Well, they punched me a couple of times in the stomach, then they left."

Miss Monroe stood and walked to the window. "Oh, dear," she said in a small voice.

"Look," said Professor Garrett. "Will you please tell me what's going on here? I mean, all this over a book on popular culture? I find it hard to believe."

"It's a very important book, Professor," said Miss Monroe, gazing out of the window. "Very important indeed. And now Grundy knows about it. Shit."

She turned and walked to the door. Professor Garrett stood hastily. "Wait! Where are you going?"

"To deal with this. If you're a very good boy, and you don't give any more secrets away, I might be back."

"Might be back?" said Professor Garrett. "But I thought..."

But Miss Monroe had gone.

Outside in the university car park, Monroe flipped open her mobile and dialled quickly.

"Tyler? Monroe. Listen, is Luther still on Balfour? Good. Tell him not to take his eyes off him. Garrett's only gone and spilled everything to George and Escobar. I know. I know. Shit, Tyler, I know! Don't worry, Grundy won't do anything yet. He'll be pondering what it all means. We'll bring Balfour in tonight and decide what to do long–term later. Okay. See you back at the warehouse."

Monroe climbed on to her Ducati, gunned the engine, flipped a finger at the three students who were staring unashamedly at her, and roared out of the car park and towards the river.

Mr Grundy, like his namesake Solomon, was born on a Monday. This made him, according to another old adage, fair of face, which despite his advancing years was still somewhat true. Many a man in his mid–fifties would have been more than happy to look like Mr Grundy. His nose was straight, his hair thick and only at the sides dusted with grey, his skin still taut, his eyes piercing. Fair of face yet somewhat puzzled. He gripped the cuff–

links holding his left shirt–sleeve together and wiggled them, which he tended to do when thinking.

"A book?"

George consulted the typed transcript of Escobar's notes. "Yes, sir. On popular culture. Written by one Stuart Balfour, who apparently is a former student of Professor Garrett's."

Mr Grundy stood from his desk and went to gaze out of the window at the sun being swallowed by the London smog somewhere beyond Ealing.

"Proceed, then, George."

George consulted his clipboard. "The book is to be published by the university's own imprint. It is to be an academic treatment of the subject matter. Professor Garrett received a visit from a woman who called herself Miss Monroe, and who promised substantial financial backing to get the book to a wider audience."

Mr Grundy wiggled his cuff–link again. He said, "But why is *pop*CULT! so interested in this book? What does it profit them to have it published to a wider audience? Why get involved?"

George looked at his clipboard again, but he knew the answers weren't there. Instead he said, "Do you want us to pay this Balfour a visit?"

Mr Grundy turned away from the window. With the setting sun the lights in his office were dimly rising. "No, I don't think so. We need to play this one a little sensitively, George."

"Softly, softly, catchee monkee, Mr Grundy?"

"That's the spirit, George. Have Escobar keep an eye on this Balfour fellow, but tell him to keep out of sight and not to approach him. I don't suppose you killed Professor Garrett, did you?"

"No, sir. You asked me not to let Escobar make a mess, if you remember."

"Pity. I should have let you boys have your head. He's probably already gone running to Monroe and *pop*CULT!. No matter; it would probably have caused more problems than it solved, to be honest. And it's good for them to know we're this close behind them."

Mr Grundy went to his cabinet and poured himself a Scotch. As he absently watched the chaotic swirls of the amber liquid, George asked, "Why do you think they're interested in this book, Mr Grundy?"

Mr Grundy took a sip. "I don't really know, George, and that's what bothers me. Usually you can second guess them easily. A bit of graffiti here, a prank there, a thumbprint of their's on a middle–of–the–night TV show or within the pages of a style magazine."

"All that flash–mobbing a while ago."

"Yes," agreed Mr Grundy. "That stank of *pop*CULT!. But it's all been pretty low–level stuff. A terrible waste of the gift they find themselves curating. They're up to something bigger this time, George. We're going to have to act very soon if all my plans are to come to fruition."

Stuart stood uneasily on the pavement outside the blacked–out windows of what he was sure was the place he was meant to be meeting Sam. A blank–faced bouncer kept tapping his ear–piece and ushering through the double doors groups of horribly well–dressed people with painstakingly–tended hair and curious facial topiary. Stuart felt wretchedly out of place. He'd raided his wardrobe and managed to come up with a pair of jeans, a shirt and a corduroy jacket, and had wrestled his hair into some kind of passable shape. He looked like a geography teacher, but was gratified to see that the geography teacher look seemed to be quite in vogue, if the groups of bright young things on the streets were anything to go by. He might just pull this off.

Above the windows was chrome lettering proclaiming the establishment to be BAR ESCHATON. Definitely the right place. Stuart gave his unruly hair a last smooth–down with the palm of his hand and strode as confidently as possible towards the doors.

The bouncer gave him the once–over and nodded him in. The bar was packed and seemed to be based along some kind of apocalyptic theme. There were TV–screens all showing different disaster B–movies, giant ants taking over the world, that kind of thing. The bar–staff were dressed in *Mad Max* gear, all leather straps and chains, and behind them a board offered the bar specialities, cocktails with names like Second Ice Age (Blue Bols, vodka, crushed ice and lemonade, apparently), The Day The Earth Caught Fire (Cointreau, Glayva and Dr Pepper) and Godzilla (creme de menthe, whisky and American cream soda). Stuart wondered if a beer might be too much to ask for. He also despaired of ever finding Sam in the throng. A group of people jostled him on their way to the bar; suddenly, Stuart felt threatened, though not in a sense that he was afraid of physical danger. It was more of a cultural threat, as though he was an interloper in this world of brand labels and haircuts, as if he was a cheat and an outsider. He shouldn't be there. It was enough for him to write about places like this, to acknowledge them in only the most abstract sense, as the breeding grounds and petri dishes of popular culture. That didn't mean he had to actually go to them. He began to back away towards the exit, and felt his heel crunch on a distressingly delicate in–step.

"Ow!"

Stuart turned to apologise and saw Sam hopping on one leg, rubbing her foot. A friendly face. He began to breathe again; the droplets of sweat forming on his brow cooled and started to evaporate. "Sorry," he said lamely.

Sam put her foot down and smiled at him. Her transformation from nursing home assistant to – well, *sex kitten* was the first guilty thought in Stuart's head – was amazing. She wore cargo pants hanging dangerously low off her hips, a snug spangly vest and a pair of electric blue heels, the left of which had Stuart's bootprint all over it. Her hair was a mass of dark curls piled high on her head and her face glistened with creams and glitter. Stuart suddenly felt like her dad, or, to be fair to himself, maybe her uncle.

"Don't worry about it," she said. "I just got in and saw you looking a bit lost. Haven't you been here before?"

"Erm, no. I usually go... um," said Stuart waving vaguely in the air. Truth was, he hadn't been to a bar like this since Jane left him.

"Let's get some drinks," said Sam. She skipped off towards the bar, weaving in and out of the knots of drinkers. Stuart lumbered through them, spilling drinks and earning glares as he hurried to keep up.

Sam had insinuated herself into the crowd at the bar and was already ordering. "I'll have an Illuminatus," she said. "Stuart?"

He was fumbling in his wallet for a ten. "Um, a beer, please. Lager. Anything."

Sam ordered him a bottle of something Japanese. He tried to hand the note to her over the heads of the customers who'd materialised between them but she shooed him away and paid for the drinks. Then she led him to a dark corner where, miraculously, there was a free table and two low, brushed–steel stools.

Stuart sipped his beer, which was cold and sharp and didn't really taste of anything. "So, what's in an Illuminatus, then?"

Sam looked at the swirling yellow drink in the tall glass. "God knows. But it's nice. Want a taste?"

Stuart shook his head and sucked at his beer bottle. Stop panicking, he told himself. You're having a drink with a pretty girl. Talk to her, you idiot. "So..." he said.

"I didn't bring the songs," said Sam. "I though it was a bit daft, really, bringing them to a date."

"I'd like to have seen them," said Stuart, wildly trying to assimilate the fact that she'd called their meeting a date.

"Maybe next time," she smiled at him. "So this book you're writing... is that what you do full time? You make a living from writing? You're, like, a writer?"

"A living?" Stuart thought about his bedsit. "I suppose so. It's the first book I've done. I've worked for magazines, though, and TV shows."

"Wow," said Sam. Stuart looked at her curiously to see if she was taking the piss, but she appeared to be genuinely impressed.

His confidence growing, he gave her a potted history of his career, starting with graduating with honours from Professor Garrett's popular culture degree course and, liberally peppering his story with some well–worn media anecdotes, finished up at the book.

"So this Professor who taught you at university just phoned out of the blue one day and asked you to write a book? He must really rate you."

"Yes," said Stuart, almost with surprise. "I suppose he does."

"In fact," said Sam, draining her glass, "he must think you're better than he is at this popular culture stuff, or he'd have written the book himself, wouldn't he?"

"I suppose."

Sam wiggled her empty glass. "Your round."

As Stuart joined the crush at the bar, he brightened considerably. This was going rather well. It had been a while since he'd impressed a beautiful woman simply by talking about himself. As he negotiated his way with the drinks back to the table he saw Sam glance towards him and smile dazzlingly. His stomach lurched. The expectation was unbearable. What might happen tonight? And what might happen next week, or the week after? Might he be about to embark on a relationship?

After four glasses of Illuminatus Sam was telling him what a lovely woman his mother was and what a good, thoughtful son he was. Stuart had been telling her how his mum had gone rapidly downhill after his dad died of a heart attack ten years ago. Sam's hand was brushing his knee. Suddenly her head snapped to one side.

"Oh," she said. "I love this tune."

Stuart became aware of the music, a church bell that juddered his insides, a fluting, electronic whistle underscored by a thudding bass heartbeat.

"*Millennium Fevre* by Desolation Angels," said Sam, starting to sway on her stool. "I'm not a big techno fan, but this is a classic. Takes me back. God, ten years. More."

The piece of music had somehow managed to pass Stuart by. He considered. She would have been a child when it first came out. He would have been in his twenties. The thought made him feel a bit funny. Sam suddenly grabbed his hand. "Want to dance?"

He looked around, panicky, at the tiny dancefloor in the corner, where people were frugging and shuffling with po–faced sincerity. "Erm," he said.

Sam's face loomed in close to his. "Or," she said slowly, "we could dance to it back at my place. What do you say?"

Stuart knew he should carry a book of one–liners to punt out in situations like this. Not that situations like this we're very common these days. He looked at Sam, his mind a blank, as she waited expectantly. Then he became aware that the music had stopped, and that the bar had fallen almost supernaturally silent. Sam had taken her eyes off his and was looking over his shoulder.

"Oh, wow," she breathed.

Stuart felt a prickling at the back of his neck, as though all eyes were on him. Had he tucked his shirt into his underpants again? He risked a glance behind him.

The patrons of Bar Eschaton were observing a respectful silence and the crowd had parted to create a passageway from the doors to Stuart and Sam's table. Striding along it was a tall woman with raven–black hair, dressed from neck to heels in shiny, fluid, jet–dark leather. Her green eyes were focused on his, a playful smile on her ruby lips.

It was her. It was Monroe.

Stuart looked back at Sam, whose puzzled gaze met his inexplicably guilty one. Then he looked up as Monroe addressed him directly.

"Stuart. Stuart Balfour. I said we'd be in touch."

"The DVD?" said Stuart.

Monroe nodded. "The DVD."

He looked at Sam, who was frowning. A small crowd was beginning to develop around them. "But how did you know where to find me..? How did you know I was interested?"

Monroe smiled tightly and raised an eyebrow.

"And what's *pop*CULT!?" asked Stuart.

Monroe's eyes were laughing now and she pursed her lips. "I think you'd better come with me."

Stuart half–stood then sat back on the stool. "What? I mean, now?"

Sam bristled. "Stuart, what's going on? Are you leaving with this woman?"

Stuart looked desperately between her and Monroe. "I... I have to, Sam. It's about the book... Should I ring you tomorrow?"

Sam snorted and looked away. Monroe was starting to turn back towards the door, the crowd parting for her once again.

"It's now or never, Stuart," she said, striding away from the table.

Stuart looked abjectly at Sam and made to follow. At the last minute he dug into his pocket and pulled out a ten pound note. "For your taxi," he said miserably.

"Piss off," said Sam.

Face burning, Stuart ran out of the bar.

Monroe was waiting for him by a sleek black motorcycle parked at the kerb. It was a Ducati, thought Stuart, although he wasn't well up on motorbikes. She had a black helmet on the crook of her arm, and was pulling a second one out of a pannier at the rear of the bike. When Stuart approached her she tossed the second helmet at him, which he caught clumsily.

"I still don't understand," he said. "How did you know I would be interested in that DVD?"

"Wait and see," said Monroe. "Sorry if I ruined your date in there."

"First one for a year," muttered Stuart to himself. "I think I was in with a chance as well."

"Don't worry," said Monroe, throwing herself on to the bike. She patted the leather seat behind her. "You're about to have the ride of your life."

Eight

Stuart awkwardly slid the helmet over his head and almost immediately Monroe's voice oozed around his ears. "Short–wave radio mic set–up," she said. There was a second's delay between her lips moving and the words bursting from the helmet's internal speakers. "Get on behind me."

Stuart did as he was told, glancing back at the bar. Several pairs of eyes were turned his way from the shadowy interior; none appeared to belong to Sam.

Monroe gunned the engine and the bike purred into life beneath Stuart. She dug into a zipped pocket on her arm and twisted around to tap Stuart's glass visor. "Open up," she said.

When Stuart did Monroe took his hand and dropped a small white pill into it. He brought it close to his face for inspection; it was round and flattish with a © symbol stamped on it. Stuart looked at it doubtfully. "What is it?" he said.

"Copyright," said Monroe. "Take it now."

"It's copyright? I don't want to steal it, I just want to know what's in it."

"It's called Copyright," said Monroe. It's a *pop*CULT! thing. Our own blend. A little DMT, bit of Ayahuasca, some LSD, and our secret special recipe."

"I don't really do drugs..." said Stuart, scrutinising the pill.

"You do now," said Monroe. "Or at least, you do if you want to come with me."

Do I want to come with you? thought Stuart furiously. *Is this DVD important enough for me to take unknown drugs and climb on the back of a motorbike with a woman I don't know?*

Monroe winked at him and popped two of the pills into her mouth, throwing her head back and exposing her delicate white neck, which undulated suggestively as she swallowed.

Yes, seemed to be the answer to Stuart's questions as he followed suit and gulped down the pill. Monroe laughed and gunned the engine again.

"Hang on," she said, and Stuart's stomach flipped as they roared away from the kerb.

"Where are we going?" shouted Stuart as they joined the main road and Monroe wove the bike tightly around the sluggish traffic.

"Ssh," said Monroe. "The mic's pretty sensitive; you don't need to shout. And hang on a bit tighter; when the Copyright kicks in you might feel a bit disorientated."

Stuart awkwardly put his arms around her waist. Monroe patted his hands and shifted up a gear, running a red light and hanging a sudden left.

"Where are we going?" asked Stuart again, more quietly.

"Wait and see."

In the absence of any further information, Stuart tried to concentrate on following the route. At first they seemed to be heading West, but then Stuart was sure they'd just crossed the river. He tried to get his bearings as they slowly picked their way through heavy traffic, but he couldn't make out any of the street signs and suddenly Battersea power station's unmistakable towers were looming up on his right.

"Are we going over the river again?" he asked.

"We're nowhere near the river," laughed Monroe, and when Stuart tried to look back at Battersea, he saw she was right. They were threading through parked cars in a tree–lined avenue which could have been Islington or maybe St John's Wood.

"Hold on tighter," said Monroe.

Stuart wrapped his arms around her, holding her tight and putting his head on her shoulder, drinking in the fruity smell of her hair trapped beneath the helmet, the cold scent of the leather. He felt incredibly horny and pushed himself into Monroe's back.

"...fuck you..." he heard someone say. He blinked. It had been him.

Monroe was laughing into his helmet. "Why, Stuart, we hardly know each other..."

He was suddenly mortified to realise his left hand was gripping her breast. He jerked backwards, but he seemed to be moving more slowly than his body, and it was a second or two before he felt married with it again.

"Monroe... I feel a bit strange," he said.

"That'll be the drugs," she said. "Hold on again, we're going off–road."

Stuart snuggled up against her back, careful to put his hands in relatively neutral positions along her ribcage. Off–road? Suddenly the lights disappeared and branches were whipping his face. He put down his visor, cutting out what little moonlight there was and plunging himself into insulated pitch–blackness.

They rode on for a few minutes in bumpy silence, then Monroe said in the blackness, "What did you think when you first saw me?"

"What? In the bar? Tonight?"

"No. At the shop the other day. I could see it in your eyes. I could see what you were thinking."

Hidden in the darkness of the helmet and emboldened by the drugs, Stuart said, "I thought you were beautiful. The most beautiful woman I'd ever seen in my life."

"More beautiful than that girl you were with at the bar?"

Stuart nodded against her back. As a reward, Monroe took his right hand and moved it up her torso until it cupped her breast. Then his face was filled with light again, and he flipped up his visor. The motorbike slowed and Monroe brought it to a halt. Stuart looked around. They appeared to be on the crest of a hill, London spread below them. But it looked all wrong. It looked too purple. They were in the middle of a dark common, pale streetlights like spider–eggs strung along the boundary on bristling twine. Stars danced above them in an angry indigo night.

"Son, he said, grab your things I'm going to take you home," sang Stuart softly to himself.

"It's a pretty humbling sight, isn't it?"

"Humbling," agreed Stuart. "I'm humble. I'm a humble Womble. The humble Womble from the rhombus hostel."

He paused. "Why are we up here? Are we there?"

"Not yet. We need a good run–up. We're going to ride as fast as we can back into London and then straight into a brick wall. Do you trust me?"

Stuart sighed. "Implicitly. In fact, I think I love you."

"Good," said Monroe. "Then let's go."

As she wheeled the bike into position, Monroe said, "Did you know that during the Iraq war, American soldiers psyched themselves up with Wagner's *The Ride of the Valkyries* in a direct homage to *Apocalypse Now* before they rammed into Saddam's strongholds?"

Music burst from the speakers inside Stuart's helmet. He heard himself moan weakly, struggling to keep a grip. He was having trouble keeping up with Monroe. "A brick wall?" he said.

Monroe revved the bike and suddenly they were falling, or at least it felt that way. Stuart tried to stabilise himself internally and realised they were riding downhill very, very rapidly. Streetlights flashed by and his stomach lurched as the bike left the earth for scant seconds as it mounted a speed bump. Monroe directed the bike between a line of cars crawling down a main road and above the Wagner Stuart heard a volley of angry horns.

With a series of rapid lurches Monroe kicked the bike into top gear. Stuart hung on to her tightly, his thighs gripping the seat. From somewhere, he heard a siren, then another one. Monroe whispered things he couldn't catch inside his helmet.

Gradually, Stuart's fear left him. He felt insulated in the slipstream, as though they were moving through time and space at different angles to everyone else, and no–one could catch them. They had left the built up area and were on a dark, deserted street. Monroe slowed the bike slightly, and swore quietly. Stuart looked over her shoulder and saw what she saw.

The astronaut.

He was standing by a dark alleyway, maybe a hundred yards ahead of them. The spacesuit had a yellow cast in the pool of a streetlight and above him Stuart noticed a street–sign bolted to the high brick wall.

"Him again," said Stuart.

"You've seen him before?" said Monroe, picking up speed.

"Yes, a couple of times. Who is he?"

"The Urban Spaceman," said Monroe. "I wonder what he wants?"

Monroe had reached top gear again and was directing the bike straight towards the dark alleyway, a sliver of blackness sandwiched between two high brick buildings. The spaceman stepped back as they approached, and as they flashed by Stuart registered a snapshot of the streetlight, the astronaut, and a blur of the street sign: Praxis Street.

Then they were in the alley, displacing air in the narrow space and whipping up vicious eddies of litter. Ahead of them, a high brick wall loomed.

"Monroe..." said Stuart, his voice rising.

Monroe laughed.

Stuart closed his eyes, and waited for the impact.

The bike slowed abruptly, but not as abruptly as Stuart was expecting. He opened his eyes and risked letting go of Monroe long enough to flip the visor. Monroe was bringing the bike to a halt in a narrow bare brick corridor, concrete underfoot and dull lightbulbs swinging in series above. Stuart looked back; the corridor disappeared into darkness behind them.

"How did that happen?" said Stuart as Monroe killed the engine at the bricked end of the corridor. "There was no way you could avoid that wall. We should be dead."

Monroe took off the helmet and shook her hair free. "If you hadn't taken the Copyright, you would be," she said. "It's complicated. How are you feeling, anyway?"

Stuart pulled off his helmet and climbed off the bike. "Not bad. Okay. Great. I think the drugs have worn off."

Monroe gave a tight smile and took the helmet off him. She gestured to a wooden door he'd only just noticed. A keypad was fixed to the wall beside the door. "Through there. Time to meet them."

"Meet them? Meet who?"

Monroe punched a series of numbers into the keypad and the door clicked. She pushed it open and gestured for Stuart to go in.

"*pop*CULT!," she said.

Taking a deep breath, Stuart stepped over the threshold. The door opened into a vast space, an old warehouse of some kind. Immediately his eyes were drawn to a huge number of television screens, all tuned into a different channel, piled haphazardly on top of each other in a precarious pyramid. Behind them was a vast graffito on the brick wall. *pop*CULT!, predictably enough. The other walls were hung with thick, dark drapes, and along one side of the room was a row of desks with half a dozen laptops all glowing gently ranged along them. There was music, bass–heavy electronica thudding against the drapes. There were people, as well, sitting at the computers or lounging on sofas and bean–bags in front of the TV screens, but Stuart couldn't assimilate them properly. He glanced at Monroe, a stricken look on his face, but she smiled and ushered him in.

Along the left wall was a series of bookshelves, and standing by them was a man. He looked up as they entered and snapped shut the book he was reading. The man focused Stuart's attention immediately. He was tall and slender, but had muscles like woven steel cables. He was shirtless and barefoot, his brown–and–blond hair falling over what was undoubtedly a handsome face. Even at a distance of fifty feet or so, his blue eyes pierced Stuart's discomfort, penetrating it and inflating it until Stuart wanted to turn on his heel and run.

"Aha!" shouted the man, and the other people around the space looked up and turned to him. "Ladies and gentlemen, fair Monroe is back among us, and if I'm not mistaken I believe she has brought with her Mr Stuart Balfour."

There was some scattered applause and a hoot. Stuart felt his face burning. The man strode towards them, holding out his hand. Stuart looked at it dumbly, then took it in his own. The handshake was firm and strong.

"This is Tyler," said Monroe.

Tyler bowed low and swept his arm around him. "Delighted, Stuart. And welcome to our humble home."

Stuart smiled wanly. He was beginning to get a headache. "Erm," he said. "I was... there was something about a DVD..?"

Tyler patted Stuart on the shoulder. "Plenty of time for that, my man. Monroe, what stage is he at?"

"He's been out of phase two for about ten minutes, I reckon."

"Woo–hoo," laughed Tyler, showing his white teeth. "Let the wild rumpus start."

"Phase two?" said Stuart doubtfully. "What do you..."

Then it happened.

[There's a sound of... what? Cellophane being urgently torn? Stuart... I, no, Stuart, no, I look back at Monroe. She's smiling calmly, but melting away from me. Tyler has already disappeared.

"What's happening?" I say. "Have you killed me?"

"It's phase three," she says kindly. "Don't worry; it doesn't last long. Maybe ten minutes."

The drapes in the warehouse have multiplied and grown like lush undergrowth. Did I say warehouse? I meant... what? Cave? Cellar? It feels like I'm deep underground, with the weight of the world above me, held aloft by huge vaulted ceilings and buttresses.

"Slow–release DMT... MacGuffin's done wonders... just sit back and enjoy it... can't kill you, unless it's death by astonishment..."

Monroe sounds like she's whispering through an immensely long tube. Stuart... I mean I... can't see her anymore. I'm lost and alone in a huge space of sensuous material. No. Not alone. There are people here, melting out of the drapes. But... not people. Peoplenotpeople. They're jewelled and built from crazy geometry and don't even look like people, more like footballs seen from every angle at once. They're like children, but impossibly old. And they're smiling, even though they don't have faces, they're smiling and they mean me no harm.

One of the peoplenotpeople reaches inside itself even though it has no arms and pulls out fractured syntax. It's speaking to me, giving me something of

92

itself, tearing part of itself away and it looks like diamonds or Faberge eggs and it holds it aloft and suddenly I think I know what's going on.

"Dad?" I say.

Another one pushes forward and presents me with a glowing pearl wrenched from its inner core. And I know exactly what it is, because it's speaking to me, it's talking to me and even though it isn't using words the things it's pulling from deep inside itself are words, in a language I've always understood.

"Dad," I say, and begin to cry.

And they're all around me, hugging me, filling me with warmth. And they're looking at me expectantly, like they want something. The eggs and pearls are being held towards me, and every time my heart beats the gifts change and become something else, something equally wondrous and bright and desirable. It's like a babble, a cacophony, a rising chorus and I don't know what they want of me. They're pushing the things towards me and I'm getting scared, now, I'm feeling threatened and I hold up my hands to ward them off but end up grabbing one of the things, one of the Faberge eggs, and suddenly there's quiet.

The egg is warm and soft and I hug it to my chest. And it sinks into my chest and I feel it inside of me, throbbing within my arteries and buzzing in my head, and at last I understand. They're not giving me gifts, they want to trade. I reach into myself the way they did, and I can do it so long as I don't think about my hands, because they don't have hands and they can do it. And I find it, the egg, deep inside me, and I can grab it and I pull it out but it's no longer an egg. It's different. It's mine.

And I give it back to the peoplenotpeople and they're smiling and singing because I've cracked it, I've got it. There has been an exchange, although of what I'm not sure. But I've got something of them in me and they've got something of me, and they seem happy with that. And because they're happy, they're melting away again, disappearing into the drapes and I've only just noticed the light they brought with them, because now it's fading and there's a darkening around the edge of my – Stuart's? – eyes and I can hear a voice, a proper voice, not one I could see like I did with the peoplenotpeople. It's someone I know. Monroe.

"Ten minutes, you said," I say and it feels wrong, the audible words coming out of my mouth. "It's been hours. Days."

93

And then I can see Monroe again, and Tyler, and the light's faded and Stuart... I mean... Stuart looks around and...]

Stuart pitched forward, throwing his hands out in front of him to break his fall. He lay there for a second and then his guts wrenched and he splashed warm vomit all over the stone floor. He became aware that Tyler and Monroe were crouching beside him, stroking his head and patting his shoulders.

"Sshh," said Monroe, and Stuart realised he was moaning. "It's okay. It's over. You're back with us."

He looked up at Tyler, vomit shining around his mouth, tears rolling down his face. "What happened? Where was I? Who were they?"

Tyler smiled at him. "Welcome to *pop*CULT!," he said.

Stuart huddled on the sofa in front of the bank of TV screens, surrounded by people. He felt wretched and just wanted to go home. Monroe sat by him and held his hand while Tyler stood in front, the screens casting a halo of blue light around him. Stuart had no idea who the other people were, and didn't much care. He wished he was back in Bar Eschaton with Sam. That felt like days ago. "What time is it?" he croaked.

Tyler laughed, throwing his head back and baring his teeth. Stuart had the crazy thought that he was being put in his place by the alpha male of the troupe.

"We don't do clocks here at *pop*CULT!, Stuart," he said.

Stuart closed his eyes and breathed deeply. He assessed the situation. No–one knew where he was. He didn't know where he was. He'd been given fuck knows what cocktail of hallucinogenic drugs and was currently in the company of mad people, or possibly worse. Criminals, without a doubt.

"I don't have any money," he said weakly.

"Sorry?" said Tyler.

Stuart opened one eye. "I don't have any money. Well, I've got about forty quid on me. You can have that. But there's no

94

point... kidnapping me or anything. I haven't got any money and neither has my family."

Stuart remembered how he felt when those... *peoplenotpeople* clamoured around him. "My Dad died ten years ago," he said in a tiny voice, then paused. "What were those things?"

Tyler sat beside him, and took his other hand. "Stuart, no–one's kidnapping you. You came here freely, and of your own will, right?"

"Right," said Stuart. He thought he might start crying.

"Those things..." said Monroe. "We call them Machine Elves. You can only see them when you're on Copyright."

"Were they real, then?"

Monroe looked at Tyler. "Real enough," he said. "When you can see them. What you've got to ask yourself, though, is what's real anyway?"

Stuart nodded, although he didn't understand. He looked around. "Who are you people?"

Tyler stood again. "Forgive me, Stuart. My manners are sometimes wanting. Allow me to introduce you to the gang."

Standing at the far side of the pile of TV screens was a tall Afro–Caribbean man dressed in an electric blue suit and a pink shirt. Tyler slapped him on the shoulder. "Luther Blissett. Merry prankster, master storyteller, and damned fly dude."

Stuart waved a hand. Luther nodded back. "Hi."

"Luther's been watching you," said Tyler.

"Watching me?"

"Keeping an eye on you, more like," put in Monroe. "For security reasons."

Before Stuart could ask more questions, Tyler walked over to a girl of no more than twenty who was perched on the end of the sofa. She wore pink and black striped tights, denim shorts, and a huge, shapeless knitted vest. Her face was pocked with metal shrapnel and lank pink hair fell over her face.

"This is Karen Eliot. Cultural terrorist, anti–artist, gender–rewirer. Say hello, Karen."

Karen pulled out her bolt–riven tongue at Stuart and looked away.

"Pay her no mind," said Monroe. "She's just jealous because she was the new baby until you turned up."

"You're new as well?" said Stuart to Karen, who was flipping her middle finger at Monroe.

"*She's* new, but Karen's been with us years," said Monroe, as though that was some kind of explanation.

"Oh," said Stuart. He felt a bit faint.

Tyler turned to a third man, a white guy with long, shaggy highlighted hair and dressed in sloppy surfer gear. "Monty Cantsin," he said. "Monty is our ace tagger, our cool–hunter, our adbuster."

"Dude," said Monty.

"I know you," said Stuart. "Well, I saw your name. On the *pop*CULT! graffiti outside my house."

Monty blinked. "I tagged your street?"

Tyler clapped him on the shoulder. "My man. This endeavour is well–starred indeed."

There was one final figure, a man in his late forties, maybe even his fifties. He was sitting on a swivel chair by the rank of computer screens, watching Stuart intently. He wore a strange contraption on the top of his head as though it were a pair of stylised spectacles, all lenses and magnifying glasses and battery–powered lights. He wore a brown coat, like the sort people who worked in hardware stores wore, and shapeless clothes underneath.

"And last but not in the least bit least," said Tyler, bounding over to the man. "MacGuffin. *pop*CULT!'s ideas man. Our weaver of dreams."

"Our Jim'll Fix It," said Monty, and everyone laughed.

"Our Cilla Black," said Luther.

"Enough, already," said MacGuffin, walking over to inspect Stuart through his glasses contraption. "Stuart Balfour. *Carry On, You Old Devil*, am I right?"

"The DVD," said Stuart gratefully. It was the one thing, bizarre though it was in itself, which anchored him to some kind of reality. He'd discussed the movie with Walter, with Professor Garrett. It gave him a reference point to his life.

"All in good time," said Tyler, steering him away from MacGuffin. "So. Now you've met the Pink Panther, the rinky-dink panther. First impressions, Stuart?"

Stuart slumped into his jacket. "I don't understand, really. I don't know what you're about. I don't know what *pop*CULT! is."

"*pop*CULT! is beyond 'is'," said Tyler. "You can't define *pop*CULT!, and to not define *pop*CULT! is to be a part of *pop*CULT!"

"That's nonsense," mumbled Stuart. He felt a little unwell. Cold sweat formed in glass beads on his forehead.

"If *pop*CULT! didn't exist, we would have to not invent it," said Tyler. "We are *pop*CULT!, do not listen to us."

Something was crawling up Stuart's spine, something deep inside, something like a scorpion or a tarantula. Tyler held his arms wide, welcoming Stuart to his naked torso.

"Join us," he whispered. "We want war with you."

Stuart felt his head spinning and couldn't really reconcile the angle the floor made with the walls. He staggered slightly.

"Phase four," he heard MacGuffin drawl.

"Here we go," said Monroe.

The lift was metal–lined and it required Tyler, Luther and Monty together to hold Stuart down as he clawed at the walls and began wailing about ovens as they descended so rapidly his ears popped.

"This is amazing," he kept saying over and over as he brushed the walls, the ground, the railway carriages all made of plush, red felty fabric. "This is amazing."

"This is the Velvet Underground," said Tyler.

"But how does it work? How do you keep it secret?" asked Stuart as the train hurtled into the blackness.

"The Machine Elves," shrugged MacGuffin. "We tell them what we want and they make it happen. Hold on; there's a bend coming up."

"Are you getting any ideas yet?" asked Tyler.

"Yes," said Stuart, who had been thinking about television as the velvet tube train trundled inexorably through the tunnels. "What about *Pet Swap*? The cameras follow a family of dog lovers and a family of cat lovers as they try to cope with each other's pet for two weeks. *It's Your Funeral...* the public get to vote on which terminally ill contestant gets to have the ultimate send–off with the funeral of their dreams. *Jailhouse Rocket*: Can celebrity chefs turn lifers in one of Britain's most notorious prisons on to nouvelle cuisine?"

"Are you going to fuck her? Monroe?" said Karen.

Stuart looked dumbly at her. "What?"

Monty laughed. "Everybody wants to fuck Monroe. She's the Venus in Furs..."

"The Morrigan," said Tyler.

"The Three–in–One," laughed Luther.

"The Lorelei," said MacGuffin.

Monroe just smiled.

The train was slowing and he was alone with Monroe. "I've been waiting for days," she said, slowly unzipping the leather catsuit.

"What for?" said Stuart, still dreaming up TV shows. *Snore Way Out!* A team of volunteers is sedated live on TV for a weekend. Viewers vote out contestants, who wake up alone in strange places. *Housebreak*. Unwitting victims go on holiday and come back to find their home has been broken into by a reformed burglar and completely redecorated by a team of celebrity designers.

Monroe took his hand and put it inside the cool leather. "For you to do this. To welcome you to *pop*CULT! properly, Stuart."

"Oh," he said, as she began to loosen his clothes.

"Oh my God, I think I love you," breathed Stuart.

At some point he realised he was naked and making low whimpering noises. He came, gasped and blacked out.

Stuart opened his eyes. Grey light was seeping through the window. His window. He was in his bedsit, flat on his back on the bed, his clothing in disarray and his throat dry and constricted. He raised his head and the hammers started behind his eyeballs. Stuart sank back on to the pillow, his neck stiff from where he had been sleeping awkwardly.

The clock beside the bed said it was a little after nine. He couldn't remember getting home. He couldn't even remember where he'd been. He remembered being in the bar with Sam, and then... and then...

He sat up suddenly. Too suddenly. His stomach lurched and his head swam threateningly. But he'd remembered; *pop*CULT!. *pop*CULT! and Monroe. Gingerly he lay down again, clutching his head. Good God, they'd drugged him. He patted his jacket pocket. His wallet still seemed to be there. And something else. Stuart reached inside and grasped the cold, hard plastic of a mobile phone.

Nine

Dawson City North West Mounted Police Incident Report
Filed by Sergeant M. Richard Eden, October 21st 1897

I wish to state as a matter of record that I am only filing this report on the strict orders of my commander, Charles Constantine, and although it is a true and accurate record of events as they happened I offer no comment on them nor offer no explanations for what I say happened.

It began with a complaint of claim–jumping laid on October first by George Bond of Seattle, regarding a patch of land some sixty miles north of Rabbit Creek. Bond is well known to this department and has faced several charges of brawling, assault and lewd behaviour. His complaint was against "English Tom", who has lived in a cabin nearby the disputed area for pretty much as long as anyone can remember. English Tom has been a peaceable resident of the region and comes into Dawson City maybe a couple times a year, with his dog, an amenable St Bernard–Collie mix called Buck, to pick up supplies. Arthur Koenig at the trading store knows English Tom best, and says that when the mood takes him he spins wild tales of life in London, England of sixty years ago or more. He also claims to have travelled to America from London on the SS Cuba with the writer Charles Dickens, but that would have been thirty years or more ago and Arthur says no way is English Tom that old. He says you shave off his beard and cut his hair, clean him up a bit, and he wouldn't be no more than twenty–five. He also says that he's been serving English Tom in his store since he, Arthur, was a boy of fifteen, which pretty much knocks that theory on the head as he's now forty if he's a day. That's Arthur again.

So George Bond comes into the office and says English Tom jumped his claim. Wants us to go up to the spot and arrest him. Now, Rabbit Creek is a fair hike from Dawson City and we tell Bond that we can't do that just on his say so, that we've got forty thousand people in Dawson City at the moment, and that if he can prove his stake to the land we'll do something about it but if not then he'll have to wait until we've either got men in the area to talk to English Tom or wait until English Tom comes into Dawson City for supplies.

Bond was not happy at this and only left after a forcible warning from myself that if he continued to use language as he was using then he would be locked up for the night. As far as I am aware, Bond then went to the saloon.

With no further evidence or complaint forthcoming from George Bond the matter was placed on file. Two weeks later, though, English Tom came to town. He was in the company of a San Franciscan named Jack London, who described his occupation as "writer". London had sailed to join the gold rush with his brother–in–law James Shepard in July and like many city dwellers who have made the trek to the Klondike, London seemed woefully unprepared for the territory and the weather and apparently soon fell into ill health out in the Yukon.

When English Tom brought London – who had left his brother–in–law guarding their claim – to Dawson, London was malnourished and suffering from scurvy. To be honest, he was half dead and I thought we would have another one for the morgue, but I directed them to Father William Judge, the Jesuit priest who runs the medical centre in the city. They also have English Tom's dog Buck with them. English Tom told Father Judge that he'd been hunting moose in the woods and had come across London, delirious and lost. He had supposedly been looking for the prospectors' camp to stock up on supplies from their tent, but had got confused in the woods. English Tom, unable to get any sense out of London as to where his brother–in–law was prospecting, brought him to Dawson.

While London was being cared for by Father Judge, the priest gave English Tom the use of his cabin in Dawson City, as English Tom said he would pick up some supplies in town and escort London back to his claim if that was what he wanted when he had been treated.

It was two days later, which would have been October seventeen, that George Bond spied English Tom in the street outside Arthur's stores. Bond harangued English Tom and repeated the allegations that he'd jumped his claim. Witnesses said that Bond appeared the worse for drink at this point and after a heated exchange Bond pulled a pistol on English Tom. Buck, English Tom's dog, went for Bond and savaged his gun arm, but Bond managed to get off a shot which hit English Tom in the stomach.

It was at that point that the police were called and I attended the scene, arresting George Bond and escorting English Tom to Father Judge.

In Father Judge's professional opinion, English Tom should have been dead from the shot. He said he was amazed that English Tom had managed to walk through the door, given that Bond's bullet had entered his stomach, passed through his gut and out his back, scraping his spine. Father Judge fixed up English Tom and gave him a bed for the night in the medical centre. English Tom asked that his dog Buck be allowed to stay by his bed and was quite insistent that a small wooden box he had brought with him and which was in Father Judge's cabin be brought to him. English Tom was indulged his wishes as Father Judge indicated to me in private that he was not expected to last the night.

The next morning I was all fit to be charging George Bond with murder when I got a message to go to the hospital. I figured that English Tom would be dead, but darned if he wasn't packing his stuff up preparing to head back into the hills. Father Judge was amazed and said that English Tom's injuries had all but healed overnight. He was calling it a miracle.

I volunteered to ride English Tom back as close to Rabbit Creek as I could, mainly because I was sorry he'd been shot in Dawson City on my watch, and wanted to make it up to him, but partly because I was curious about what kind of life he led up in the mountains. English Tom wasn't much for talking at first, but as we went on he opened up and told me he was from London, England, which was how he got his name, and had come on a visit to America to make his fortune. He said the writer Charles Dickens had told him to visit Canada and he'd been blown away when he come up here and seen all the countryside and such, as he'd not seen anything like it in London. He said he'd raised money for his passage by being a writer of stories for the magazines in London.

Then English Tom told me that he was nearly eighty years old and had left London because he lived in a whorehouse and people thought he had a pact with the devil because the whores kept on getting older and he just stayed the same, and when the madam of the house was on her deathbed she told him to get out and see some of the world, so that's what he done, but he liked the fresh air and open spaces of the Yukon so much that he stayed for thirty years.

Living alone up in them mountains can do things to a man's mind, and I told English Tom so, told him that what he was telling me was impossible, that maybe he should get down to Dawson City more often and mix with folks. English Tom just laughed and told me that he'd prove it to me when we got to his cabin.

To change the subject I asked English Tom why George Bond had accused him of claim–jumping. English Tom told me that although he'd taken no part in the gold rush he had watched the comings and goings of the prospectors with interest. He had met George Bond while English Tom was hunting moose and Bond had shown him a piece of gold he'd found somewhere near Rabbit Creek, although naturally he wouldn't divulge the full location. English Tom said he'd told Bond that he could tell him where to find much more gold, and perhaps they could go into partnership, and had asked to borrow the nugget for a moment. Bond had been suspicious but had agreed, so long as he didn't take it out of his sight. English Tom had agreed and placed the gold nugget in the box that he had asked for when at the medical facility. He then said that he'd had what he called an "insight" into Bond's plans, and so refused to share with him the information he claimed to have. He said he suspected Bond was going to kill him if and when they found any gold. Bond had got angry and left.

English Tom claims he had discovered the location of a huge seam of gold simply by placing Bond's nugget in a box. He says he got a picture in his mind of a spot and went there and started digging, and... well, he said he'd show me when we got to his cabin.

I didn't believe him but I delivered English Tom and Buck safely home after three days, and English Tom showed me into his cabin. I place it here as a matter of record that I have never seen so much gold in my life. It was piled up in the cabin, on every available surface.

I asked what English Tom's secret was, how he'd learned where the seam was. He showed me the wooden box – an Indian design, I think – which he always carried around with him. He said he didn't have a name for what was in it, but it had been given to him by a man who had lived forever and the thing had fallen from the stars. He said you showed it a thing, and it told you how to get more of it, or how to make a thing that was like it. By this point I was convinced English Tom was crazy, but I couldn't deny that he'd sure got a pile of gold.

Then English Tom showed me what was in his box. I don't know how to describe it here, except to say it was like water but thicker, but not as thick as gravy. It was about as big as a man's fist, and it was gold in colour itself, but maybe more brown on the inside. It moved like it was alive. I can't say I liked it much.

It was while we was talking that Buck, his dog, started barking like he was fit to kill something, and we saw a face that I would say was George Bond at the window. Bond, I later learned, had been released from the cells by my deputy who considered he had cooled off sufficiently. He had evidently tracked us back to English Tom's place. We got to the door but Bond had disappeared.

I said I was concerned that Bond had seen the gold and might try to attack English Tom again. English Tom said that if it wasn't Bond, it would be someone else, and besides, he was ready for city life again, and was planning to take his gold down to the bank and maybe get back to London, England. I took my leave of him and that was the last I ever saw of him.

Yesterday George Bond's body showed up in the Yukon River and I told my story to my commander, Charles Constantine. He has sent a patrol to call on English Tom, but in my opinion they won't find him there. And that's all I got to say.

Ten

For four days, Stuart worked. From the moment he had woken up, dishevelled, confused and with aching testicles, his mind had been teeming with ideas. Boiling with them. They roared inside his head, shouted each other down, cried and whined for attention, until Stuart had called a halt.

Drowning the weaker ones with seven glasses of water one after the other, he'd sat at his desk, flipped open his laptop, and let what was left flood forth. Only the strong survived, but that was enough. More than enough. He surfaced sometime around Sunday lunchtime, dimly aware that he'd snatched half–hours of sleep here and there throughout the last half of the week, that he'd been eating rotten bananas and cold beans straight from the tin, and that by the writhing, overflowing ashtray on his desk he'd broken his rule about smoking in the flat. But he also had a fresh twenty–five thousand words of the book backed up to his hard–drive; and they were good, too. When he'd wrung dry the last of his new–found inspiration he looked back at what he'd done, spending three hours reading it as though it was the first time he'd seen any of it. In a way, it was; between Wednesday morning and Sunday afternoon he hadn't quite been there; it was as though there wasn't room for him inside his own head, so his conscious self had been given a holiday while he got on with the job at hand. He felt more refreshed then he had any right to, as well.

The book was now a good four–fifths done, pending revisions and edits. Professor Garrett would be amazed at what he'd turned out this week. Stuart was amazed at what he'd turned out. It was only when he'd read everything through twice, printed himself out a copy of all the chapters completed so far, and backed everything up to disks did he relax, open the window to try to clear the fug in the bedsit, and allow himself to think about what had happened on Tuesday night.

The mobile phone squatted like a plastic, alien thing on the dusty mantelpiece. In his jacket pocket he had also found a charger, and had left the phone plugged in for the past four days. There had been no calls.

The phone was evidently a gift from *pop*CULT!, or maybe just Monroe. It at least gave him something real to focus on, to help convince himself that the whole episode hadn't, in the style of a Sixties American superhero comic cover blurb, been a hoax, a dream or an imaginary tale.

In the grey light of his bedsit, Stuart felt able to remove some of the veneer of mystery from his night at *pop*CULT!. A bunch of art–terrorists or Situationists, that's all they were, with a good source of high–grade hallucinogenic drugs. Pranksters. It was all probably an art installation, or a student project. They had been playing with him, the straight in the corduroy jacket. Did they even have a copy of *Carry On, You Old Devil* at all? Stuart had begun to doubt it. But he was intrigued now, not least by Monroe. They'd slept together, of that he was sure. He mentally slapped himself for his old–fashioned language. Slept together sounded so... sedate. Basically, they'd fucked like rats. He wondered if they'd used any protection.

Stuart had already decided that he had to visit *pop*CULT! again. The book, while good, still needed the Carry On DVD at its heart... and not just the DVD, but the whole attendant story of *pop*CULT! as well. By their very definition, they were an integral part of popular culture. They were the core of his book, if he got to know more about them, the difference between a simply academic text and... what? A piece of journalism? A bestseller? Stuart felt quite giddy at the thought.

With a start it dawned on him that it was Sunday. Which meant yesterday was Saturday. Which meant he'd missed a visit to his mother. His guts tied themselves in another knot at the thought of a visit to Elysian Fields, which would mean seeing Sam again. Perhaps he could take her out for another drink, explain about the book and the DVD, tell her that it wasn't what she thought with Monroe. Then he had a sudden, clear image of Monroe slowly unzipping her leather catsuit, and realised that it was exactly what Sam thought.

The clock on his laptop told him it was just after three. He could visit his mother and possibly head over to Islington to call on Walter. Tomorrow he would go to the university and hand over everything he had written so far to Professor Garret for safe–keeping; Stuart lived in constant fear that burglars would steal his laptop or one of the other residents in the house would burn the building down, and all his work would be lost forever. But first, he needed a shower.

George had Sundays off, but it was accepted that he would be available at a moment's notice should Mr Grundy require his services. To be fair to his employer, George rarely found his weekends interrupted, although he would not have complained if they were. His life was working for Mr Grundy; he had been his confidante, his aide and almost his friend for many years. And he was well remunerated for his loyalty, enough to own a decent property in a quiet street and to buy fresh fish every two days for his cats.

The only time Mr Grundy did prevail upon George on a Sunday was every four or five weeks when a visit to the cemetery was in order. Today was such a day.

George manoeuvred the black Bentley into a parking bay outside the graveyard. It was a drizzly day so George took an umbrella from the boot of the car and unfurled it so that Mr Grundy could step out from the back seat on to the cracked pavement in relative dryness. George reached into the passenger seat and took out the wrapped bundle of orchids. Mr Grundy accepted them with a sigh.

"George, does it always rain when we come to the cemetery, or am I just getting old?"

George considered telling the truth for a moment, that it was often not raining at all when they visited the cemetery, then decided against it. "It does seem that way, Mr Grundy," he said.

They walked slowly along the Tarmac paths, ignoring the knots of visitors huddled around marble headstones, whispering their news to long–gone family and friends. George dutifully held the umbrella over Mr Grundy, himself ignoring the fine rain that was soaking his collar and broad shoulders. They walked until they were in the bowels of the graveyard, where the plots were more tangled, where the paths more overgrown. They stopped.

Mr Grundy laid the flowers across the blue marble chippings of the grave and stood for a moment, holding his chin, frowning. George shifted, distributing the weight over either foot. He often felt awkward on these Sunday visits, uncomfortable with the occasional displays of emotion Mr Grundy could be given to. He found it hard to reconcile the frailty Mr Grundy sometimes exhibited at the graveside, which didn't square with the man he knew through the rest of the week. But it was only to be expected; it was his mother, after all.

"By mocking me, they sully her memory," said Mr Grundy suddenly. "*He* sullies her memory."

"Tyler, Mr Grundy?" said George, though he knew that was exactly who he was talking about.

Mr Grundy made a snorting noise. "Him and his little gang. His simpering, pathologically–disordered followers. He makes me sick, George."

The rain thickened and sluiced George's dome of a head. "Balfour eventually emerged from his flat today," said George. "Four days he's been in there. Escobar's on him now; hopefully he might lead us to them."

"I doubt it," sighed Mr Grundy. "They're too clever for that. Tyler's too clever for that. I loathe him, George."

"Yes, Mr Grundy," said George, grateful that his employer was now turning away from the grave and walking slowly back to the car.

"And him my own flesh and blood, as well."

Unsurprisingly, Sam was less than over the moon to see Stuart walk through the doors of Elysian Fields. She glanced at him and returned to the paperwork she was filling out at the reception desk.

Stuart smiled weakly. "Ah. Hi," he said.

"Mr Balfour, your mother's in the day room," said Sam without looking up. "Go through."

Stuart paused, started to speak, put his hand over his mouth, and smiled again. "Ah," he said. "Ehm."

Sam finally looked at him, her eyes cold. "Please do not say any of the following. Do not say 'I'm sorry'. Do not say 'it wasn't what you think'. Don't say 'I can explain', 'it was an emergency' or 'can we try again?'. In fact, don't say anything to me that isn't directly related to your mother's care. Is that understood?"

Stuart nodded quickly. "Erm. The day–room, you said?"

Sam returned to her paperwork. Stuart was about to say something else, but changed his mind and slunk away down the corridor.

His mother was having a bad day. She was sitting in her chair, staring at a football match on the TV. She looked up at Stuart glassy–eyed.

"Stuart? What day is it?"

For a second he considered lying, saying it was Saturday, but he said, "Sunday, Mum. Sorry I couldn't make it yesterday. Something came up."

"Stuart, when am I going home?" she said, her voice trembling.

He sighed. "You are home, Mum. This is where you live now."

"But I need to be getting back," she said, starting to rise from the chair. "Your Dad'll be wanting his tea."

"Dad's dead, Mum," said Stuart softly, laying a hand on hers. "Sit down."

She looked at him dumbly. "But he'll be wanting his tea. You know what he's like if he doesn't get his tea on time."

"What have you been doing today?" asked Stuart, his jollity sounding hollow as he gently helped his mother sit back in the chair. "Have you written any more stories?"

"I don't like it here, Stuart," she said, her eyes brimming with tears. "I get too much stuff in my head. I want to go home."

"Oh, Mum," said Stuart, his voice cracking. He hated it when she was like this. He suddenly felt exhausted and had to bite back a sob. "Come on, Mum."

"Will you go and get something in for your Dad's tea?" she said. "I haven't been able to get out to the shops. They won't let me go. They hate me here."

"Mum..."

"Get some pork. Shall we have pork?"

"Yes," sighed Stuart. "Let's have pork."

"Good boy," said his mother, resting her head back against the chair and closing her eyes. "You're a good boy, Stuart."

On his way out he was confronted by Sam who thrust an envelope into his hand without looking him in the eye. His first thought was that it was some kind of greetings card, an apology, until he realised she didn't actually have anything to apologise for.

"It's from Mrs Pecalanos, who runs the creative writing classes," said Sam flatly. "She's got funding to do that book she was going on about. She needs you to sign this if you want your mother's stories going in it."

"Right," said Stuart, pocketing the envelope. He had no intention of allowing his mum's stuff going in any book, at least not under her own name. He wasn't really sure getting people her age to write that sort of thing was strictly helpful. He did fleetingly wonder how old Henry Miller was when he wrote *Tropic of Cancer*, but pushed the thought away. There were more pressing matters.

"Look, Sam," he said.

Sam consulted her wristwatch. "I get off in ten minutes," she said.

"Oh?" said Stuart, brightening.

"Yes," said Sam. "And when I'm on my own time I can tell you that you're an absolute cunt, Mr Balfour. It's up to you if you want to wait."

* * *

111

Stuart decided not to. Instead he made his way laboriously across London to Islington to visit Walter, who he found in agreeable mood.

"You must tell me all the news," said Walter as he poured brandy for Stuart and himself.

"Well," said Stuart. "I had a date on Tuesday, which was gatecrashed by a woman in leather who gave me drugs and took me to meet a group of cultural terrorists called *pop*CULT! before shagging my brains out on a velvet tube train. Oh, and I think I might have seen some aliens or ghosts or something."

Walter handed the drink to Stuart. "And other than that..?"

It was dark outside by the time Stuart had finished putting together as much as he could about his visit to *pop*CULT!, and they had sunk half a bottle of brandy between them. Walter, who had been silent throughout the story, finally said, "And could you find it again? This warehouse?"

Stuart thought back to the nightmarish ride through London on the back of Monroe's bike. "I remember Battersea... trees on a hill... purple lights..."

"Oh dear," said Walter. "Set the controls for the heart of Pink Floyd, then."

"Wait a second... there was the astronaut..."

Walter sat up. "Astronaut?"

"Yeah. I've seen him a couple of times recently. He was wandering up and down the main road near where I live. Then I saw him pointing to some *pop*CULT! graffiti opposite my flat."

"The Urban Spaceman," said Walter quietly.

"That's it! That's what Monroe called him. You know him? What is he, some kind of performance artist or something?"

Walter pursed his lips. The CD he had put on had stopped so he went to change it. "*Big Brother and the Holding Company?*"

"Whatever. Walter, what do you know about this spaceman guy?"

"The Urban Spaceman," said Walter. "I've never seen him, but I've heard of him. There have been sightings since the

Sixties, I think. Pretty much around the time the space programme captured the public imagination."

"He's been going round in that outfit for half a century?" said Stuart, refilling both their glasses. "But why?"

Walter pinched the bridge of his nose. "They say the Urban Spaceman's a... a... Stuart, I'm not sure how to describe it. An omen. A portent. A harbinger."

"This is all a bit Tolkien, isn't it? A harbinger of what?"

Walter shrugged. "People who have seen the Urban Spaceman say he always appeared just before some important event in their lives, at some crossroads, before a crucial choice they had to make. It's all just an urban myth, Stuart, or at least I thought it was. They say he's kind of a signifier of things to come, an alarm bell. A sign."

"A sign..." said Stuart slowly. "He was standing by a sign. Walter, have you got a London A–Z?"

Eleven

They located Praxis Street on the edge of Walthamstow. "Wait here," said Walter, pouring the last of the brandy into Stuart's glass. "Study the map. Find us a route."

Walter emerged from his bedroom five minutes later wearing a beige safari suit. "I'm ready," he said.

As Walter fired the engine on his powder blue Triumph, which could have been described as "vintage" due to its age but was more likely to have been branded "illegal" because of its condition, Stuart said, "Ah, how much have you had to drink, Walter? And is this thing taxed?"

"We're going to Walthamstow, dear boy," he said as he pulled the car away from the kerb. "We're hardly likely to meet a policeman."

Stuart directed Walter by as many back roads as he could. "Anyway, I thought you were agoraphobic," he said.

Walter roughly dragged the Triumph over a roundabout. "I've given that particular affectation up," he said. "While it was a good excuse for keeping nice boys in my bed for three days at a time, it did rather preclude meeting them in the first place. I thought I might start smoking again, instead. That seems to be delightfully anti–social again these days. Do you have one?"

Stuart lit a Marlboro Light and handed it to Walter, who clasped it in his leather driving gloves. "So why has this Urban Spaceman started to follow me around?" said Stuart.

"As I said. An omen. A portent. A what–have–you."

"But why me?" pressed Stuart. "And what does he know? And who's in the suit anyway?"

"Questions, questions," said Walter through gritted teeth as he bumped the back wheel over a kerb. "I'm not an expert on the Urban Spaceman, but as to why you, possibly because you were about to get embroiled with a weird sex cult in a warehouse in Walthamstow. Unless anything else has happened to you that you haven't seen fit to mention?"

114

"But who is he?" said Stuart again. "And how did he know? Do you think he's involved with *pop*CULT!?"

"Well, here's where we find out," said Walter, stamping on the brake pedal and coasting the car to a halt in a pool of yellow light from a lamp–post. Stuart looked out of the window. They were on a long, dark road of tall, anonymous red–brick industrial buildings. It was deserted, without so much as a parked car. An unlit alleyway squatted like a leakage of midnight between two high walls. There was a sign on the wall, by the street–light.

"Praxis Street," said Stuart.

They sat silently in the car for a moment, then Walter said, "Stuart, tell me again why we're here?"

Stuart looked at Walter. "I have absolutely no idea," he said.

They both got out of the car. Stuart looked up and down the deserted street. "Think," he said. "I came to your flat, then we came here. What did we talk about?"

Walter pondered for a moment. Then he and Stuart said simultaneously, "*pop*CULT!"

Stuart joined Walter on the pavement. "But how could we forget? Both of us, just like that?"

Walter frowned. "I don't know. I don't know at all."

They stood on the pavement, under the streetlight. Stuart looked up and down the deserted street. Facing the dark alley was a side road that stretched up into darkness. Was this the road Monroe and he had rode down on her bike? Was this the alley they had spun into?

Walter nudged him and pointed down the street. A pair of headlights glowed distantly. Stuart grabbed Walter's elbow and, though he didn't really know why, he pulled him into the shadows of the alley entrance.

Some thirty thousand people disappeared in Argentina between the years 1976 and 1983. Joaquim Pablo Escobar was by no means responsible for all of them, but he did pride himself on the fact that his personal tally of the *desaparecidos* ran to treble figures.

115

Escobar had been a highly commended soldier in Peron's Dirty War. He had smashed down doors in the dead of night, taken subversives – journalists, teachers, doctors, activists, Marxists, Communists; by the end he didn't care who they were – away to secret compounds, bullied and beaten and raped and tortured them in grey windowless rooms, and eventually he'd killed them and buried them in unmarked graves.

In 1989 Escobar, disgusted that his former paymasters had accepted pardons from the new president Carlos Menem, made his way to the United States where he worked for a time with gangsters in first New York and then Los Angeles. But America failed to fire his imagination as much as he'd hoped it would, and after four years he took a passage to London where, trying to make a name for himself, he quickly got himself on the wrong side of Mr Grundy. Rather than having Escobar killed, though, Mr Grundy acknowledged his experience and tenacity and offered him a job.

A job he was now mortified to find himself failing in. He knew he was meant to be following someone, but as he coasted the black Audi along the quiet, industrial street on the outskirts of Walthamstow, he suddenly had no idea who.

Escobar purred along at barely fifteen miles an hour, trying to recall what he was doing here. He passed a parked car, a pale, decrepit Triumph under a streetlight. It rang vague, muffled bells, but not enough to make him stop. He gunned the engine and pushed on along the street, desperately trying to remember.

"Well, well, well. Lookee here." Tyler bent over MacGuffin's shoulder to see the monitor connected to the CCTV cameras in the alleyway outside the *pop*CULT! warehouse. "It seems that our Mr Balfour is more resourceful than we've perhaps given him credit for."

Luther joined Tyler. "Shouldn't the dampers be keeping them away?"

MacGuffin scratched his head. "Well, yes, in theory. But there's a bit of a glitch in the system; the dampers'll keep casual passers–by away from the alley, they'll kill off any curiosity that people have about what's down there, but if you already know about us, they don't work as well. You might forget what you're doing in that alley, but if you think hard enough you'll remember."

The three of them watched Stuart and Walter lurking in the shadows of the alley for a while.

"Who's the other guy?" asked Luther, lighting up a cigarette.

"I don't know," said Tyler thoughtfully. "I didn't expect Balfour to go blabbing about us so quickly; from Monroe's intelligence I'd been led to believe he was a loner."

"Do we really need him as much as Monroe thinks we do?" asked Luther.

Tyler smiled. "It took me a while to work out why. Tell him, Mac."

MacGuffin pushed back his chair away from the monitor. "He's writing a book, Luther. A book about popular culture. A book about us, really, and everything we stand for. It's going to be published by a university imprint. It'll be widely reviewed, probably be written about in the quality press, might make him a minor celebrity for a bit."

Luther shook his head. "I still don't get it."

"It's going to academicise popular culture," laughed Tyler. "We're going respectable, brother. We're going to be unstoppable."

Luther broke out into a broad, white grin as he slowly understood.

Monroe had a room at the back of the warehouse, which she'd made as comfortable as possible. There was a double bed and racks of clothes, a bureau with her cosmetics, shelves with books and CDs, a TV and DVD player, a smart Apple MacBook. Home. The only thing missing was a mirror. When everyone saw you differently, why have a mirror? Besides, Monroe hated her reflection. It was an unwanted portrait of a past she would rather forget.

Monroe lay on the bed, plugged into her MP3 player. She'd taken half of a Copyright and was still, almost lifeless, thinking. Thinking about The Waif.

The Waif was the only person in *pop*CULT! she'd ever been close to calling a friend. The Luthers and the Karens and the Montys came and went too frequently ever to get close to; MacGuffin was more like the uncle you were fond of but never too sure about. Tyler...

But The Waif was different. She was already part of *pop*CULT! when Tyler recruited Monroe. She was thin, fashionable and quite, quite beautiful. This was back when heroin chic and slightly off–kilter looks were the new black. Tyler called her his "little zeitgeist", the acceptable face of *pop*CULT!. The Waif had even been in magazines, fashion shoots, and was something of a face in London's after–hours party scene. She was almost a celebrity, which Tyler loved. And when she was gone... when she died... she was mourned for half an hour, which Tyler loved even more. That was the nature of celebrity, he'd said. That proved that The Waif was highly regarded, the fact that she'd been forgotten so quickly. Most of the time, it was hard to tell whether Tyler was being serious or not.

Like everyone else, The Waif had seen Monroe as she wanted to see her, she'd imprinted her own desires and passions on Monroe's blank slate.

"God," she'd said, staring at Monroe. "You look just like me. We could be sisters."

Sisters was almost what they became. They went shopping, listened to music and watched TV together in each others' rooms, went drinking and pulled men together. The Waif didn't even bear grudges when Monroe always got the good–looking one. "Guy," she'd say in her fake Valley Girl accent. "I wish I had what you've got."

No, you don't, Monroe would think.

And then she had to go and get herself killed.

It had been on one of Tyler's typically crazy missions. He'd wanted to tag Canary Wharf, a huge, vertical *pop*CULT! graffito to welcome and puzzle the Docklands at dawn. They'd got up there no problems, a combination of Monroe's charm and MacGuffin's fuzzy logic. But it was the abseiling that had caused problems when The Waif, stoked on coke and skunk, had wigged out in the harness and started screaming. She'd nearly had Karen over the edge, and her cries alerted security who busted the whole operation before it had begun. Tyler claimed he was hit by one of the security guards, and that was why he'd let go of the rope. They all watched, *pop*CULT! and security guards, as The Waif plummeted, screaming all the way down, to her death at the foot of Canary Wharf. *pop*CULT! had escaped in the confusion, the mission aborted, The Waif dead.

Tyler was insufferably insincere all the way back to the warehouse. And that was the moment, that was when Monroe started to think that maybe he wasn't all he made out to be. That was when she started to have her doubts.

The Machine Elves clustered around the periphery of her consciousness. Monroe started to shoo them away; she had no patience for their games at the moment. But they were offering something, and reluctantly, she capitulated. They wanted her memories of The Waif. And in return, they gave her a vision of Stuart, standing in the alleyway outside *pop*CULT! with another man. Monroe opened her eyes, startled. This was happening right now.

Settling back on the bed, she caught a wave off the Copyright, and began to sing softly to herself.

In the darkness, Walter felt a spot of rain on his forehead. "Marvellous," he said.

Stuart had ventured into the depths of the rubbish–strewn alley, remembering. This was definitely it. This was where Monroe had directed the bike at full tilt. He stopped before a brick wall, a dead end that stretched up into the shadows. This was how they had got into *pop*CULT!.

Stuart ran his fingers over the coarse, solid brickwork as

Walter joined him. "This can't be it," said Walter.

"It is," said Stuart. He paused. "Can you hear something?"

In her room, Monroe sang, "I don't want to lose you, this good thing that I got 'cause if I do I will surely, surely lose a lot."

Walter cocked his head. "No. Nothing. Look, you must be mistaken. Let's take the car around the block. There must be a door or a gate round the other side or something."

"No," insisted Stuart. "It was here. I remember the Urban Spaceman standing under that streetlight, pointing to the street sign, then we came down here, I closed my eyes... and we were inside."

Walter rapped his knuckles on the brickwork. "Ow," he said. "It's solid. Stuart, it's impossible."

Monroe sang, "'Cause your love is better than any love I know..."

It started to rain more heavily. Walter grimaced up at the sky far above them. "I think I'll go and wait in the car," he said.

Stuart nodded, trying to catch the faint sound he could hear on the breeze.

Monroe sang, "It's like thunder and lightning, the way you love me is frightening..."

He took a step back, his foot skidding on the garbage underfoot. His heel clipped the stone cobbles underneath. The sound wasn't right. Stuart crouched down and touched the cobbles. They felt real enough. He ran his hand over them. Was there the hint of a draught coming between them?

Monroe sang, "You'd better knock..."

Stuart clenched his fist.

Monroe sang, "Knock..."

He brought it down, hard, on the ground. It didn't sound like cobbles. His punch rang dully around him. It sounded like...

Monroe sang, "On wood, baby..."

There was a hissed shout from the top of the alley. Stuart looked up to see Walter's silhouette frantically waving at him in the yellow glow of the lamp–post. He took another look at the cobbles, then jogged towards Praxis Street.

Walter dragged him by the jacket towards the car. "Someone's coming," he said.

There was a car at the top of Praxis Street. Walter bundled Stuart into the passenger seat and then hopped around to his side. As they belted up the car, a black Audi drew level with them and slowed. A pair of piercing eyes in a dark face glowered at them.

Escobar had driven a mile out of Walthamstow before he remembered he was supposed to be following Balfour. He executed a U–turn and screamed back the way he had come, following landmarks such as pubs and shops although he couldn't, for some reason, recall where he had just been. He chanced upon Praxis Street by accident, but his reasons for being there drained away from him immediately. He saw some activity up ahead around a parked car and slowed, glancing at the occupants. It was only when he was a hundred yards past them that he realised it had been Balfour.

"He's stopped," said Walter, watching Escobar's progress in the rear–view mirror. He fired the ignition, crunched the Triumph into first, and put his foot down.

"But who is he? What's the big deal?" protested Stuart.

"I don't know," said Walter, through the mirror watching Escobar execute a three–point turn on Praxis Street. "I'm just a little tense. Shit, he's following us. Hang on."

Stuart had never had Walter down as a skilled driver before, but he was certainly impressed with the way he spun the Triumph out of Praxis Street, along a warren of residential avenues and back towards Islington, not giving the Audi the ghost of a chance to catch them.

They didn't speak until the Triumph was nosing along Walter's street. "Well," said Stuart.

"Indeed," said Walter, parking up.

"That was a bit... weird."

"Did you find anything in the alley?"

Stuart shrugged. "I don't know. I could sort of hear something. I felt I was being told to do something."

"What?"

Stuart sighed. "I don't really know. There was something a bit funny about the ground. Like it wasn't real. I don't know."

"I don't mind admitting, I was a bit freaked out," said Walter. "How could we both forget why we were there? And who was in that car? Was he following us?"

"I've no idea what's going on any more," said Stuart. "I just want that Carry On DVD."

"So you're going back?"

"Not tonight. Tomorrow, maybe."

"Do you want a lift home?"

Stuart shook his head. "I'll take the Tube. Maybe walk for a bit. I've got some thinking to do."

There was a knock at Monroe's door, then Tyler walked in. She took off her headphones. "Hi."

"Balfour was just here," said Tyler.

Monroe nodded. "Right."

He sat down on the bed, stroking her ankle. "You don't seem surprised."

Monroe stared at his hand as it crept up her shin towards her thigh. "No. Like I said, there's something about him."

Tyler leaned in towards her, his breath hot on her cheek. "He was a good find," he agreed.

Monroe turned her head and firmly lifted his hand off her thigh. "Thank you."

Tyler frowned, then stood up from the bed. "Okay. I think we should get him back in again. Tomorrow night, maybe. Tell him a bit more about us."

Monroe nodded. "Fine."

Tyler made to leave then paused at the door. "Monroe, you're up to something, aren't you?"

She smiled tightly. He shook his head and left.

Stuart walked for an hour, the rain soaking him through. He didn't want to catch the Tube, didn't want to be underground. He couldn't get Monroe out of his head, like she'd crept in there while he was in the alley and wouldn't get out. He wondered what was more important to him now, getting hold of the DVD or seeing Monroe again. After the last few days of intense writing, the book had receded in importance somewhat. He just wanted it done and out of the way. He wanted to see Monroe again.

As he walked, he felt a vibration near his heart. He stumbled mid–stride, clutching his chest. Good God, what was happening to him? Then a trilling broke out, the mobile phone he'd put into his jacket pocket bursting into life. He fumbled for it and glanced at the screen. Anonymous caller, it said. He spent another couple of seconds working out which button to press to receive the call, then put the phone to his ear.

"Hello?" he said uncertainly.

"So," said Monroe. "Are you ready for more, then?"

Twelve

Early in the morning, when it was as black as blindness but the city was breathing lightly and could awaken at any moment, Stuart stared at the ceiling and thought about those things, those presences, that had crowded him during his first night at *pop*CULT!, those... what did Monroe call them? Machine Elves?

He remembered what he thought he'd seen, but couldn't picture them in his mind any more. All he knew was that there had been some kind of exchange of something. He didn't know what he'd been given or what they'd taken from him, but he could remember the sudden, overwhelming memories he'd had of his dad. Of home.

Jimmy Balfour was a hard–working man who loved his family but tended not to show it too much. The Balfours had lived in Glasgow up until Jimmy had been made redundant from the Govan shipyard and had transferred the family south to London where a new job and a new life awaited them. Stuart had been five or six; he couldn't remember much of his life in the north, except the long weeks his father was at home between losing his job and moving the family to England. His father would sit in the front room of the tiny terraced house, reading the paper by the dull light that filtered through the heavy curtains, while his mother smoked at the table. Stuart remembered one summer day, sitting at the table with his mother, drawing dinosaurs on rough, yellowish paper.

"Do you no want to play fitba with the other lads, Stuey?" his dad had said from behind his paper.

Stuart had listened for a moment to the shouts and echoing rebound of the leather ball off the brick walls of the narrow street.

"I'm drawing."

His mother had regarded him through the blue smoke of her cigarette. "Do you no like the boys, Stuart?"

"They're all right."

His dad had grunted.

"What?" said his mum.

Jimmy Balfour folded his newspaper. His hair was thick and black and his short body was an even mixture of fat and muscle. "I'm just sayin', is all, the lad'll have tae buck up a bit if he's goan tae get on at school."

"He doesn't like fitba," said his mum. "He likes drawing and comics and stuff."

Stuart could sense an argument brewing. He sunk into the chair, his shoulders drooping, concentrating on pencilling the teeth of the dinosaur. As big as kitchen knives, said his book. Row upon row of them, hard and sharp. He imagined them tearing into the hide of a Triceratops. The Triceratops roars in pain and anger, bringing around its horned head, trying to butt the Tyrannosaur in its delicate belly. But the Tyrannosaur is too fast, and sinks its mouthful of deadly incisors deep into the Triceratops' back.

The argument has indeed started and moved to the kitchen. Stuart can hear them shouting through the thin wall, even though the door is shut.

"Well, perhaps if you did'nae sit around all day doing nothing and acted like a father once in a while..."

"Now, Pat, that's no fair. I'm trying tae find work. It's no like you're goan tae keep the family afloat, is it..?"

"You're a bastard, Jimmy Balfour. You know I'd get work if I could. You know I'm bad with my nerves."

The shouting became crying and his mother stamped off up the narrow stairs to the bedroom. His dad slumped back in his chair and stared at the newspaper.

Stuart slipped off the dining chair and presented his picture to his dad. It was three dinosaurs, a family of Tyrannosaurs, hunkered down over the steaming corpse of a killed herbivore.

"That's you, that's mum and that's me," explained Stuart.

Jimmy Balfour looked uncomprehendingly at the drawing. "Jesus Christ," he said softly.

"Dad?" said Stuart. Jimmy Balfour had started to cry. Stuart had never seen it before.

Jimmy scooped up Stuart in his strong arms and held him close. "It'll be all right, son," he said, choking back his tears. "Dad'll get work. It'll be all right."

And against the odds, it was. There were jobs going down in London at the docks on Canary Wharf. Pat didn't want to leave her parents and friends, but Jimmy was adamant. He wouldn't let his family live on the dole. Not when there was work going. He was going to get on his bike and go to London, and the family was going with him.

By degrees, Stuart forgot his early years in Glasgow and became a London boy. Traces of his accent were slowly eroded through each successive school term, until by the time he was a teenager he spoke like a native, and in truth could only ever remember living in London. And then Jimmy Balfour lost his job as the Canary Wharf docks closed around him, and this time there was nowhere else to go.

At eighteen Stuart left the broken, soulless Balfour home for university and Professor Garrett's popular culture studies degree class. He returned home infrequently, discomfited by his surrendered, abandoned father and his hopelessly jolly mother.

"What exactly is this course you're doing?" his dad had grumbled once.

"It's like media, isn't it?" his mum answered for him. "We're awful proud, Stuart. He'll be reading the news on the telly one day, Jimmy, mark my words."

"Reading the fucking newspaper in the dole queue," Jimmy Balfour had muttered, staring at the TV.

Later, in the kitchen, as Stuart and his mum had coffee and Jimmy had gone to the pub, she said, "He doesn't mean it, Stuart. He just doesn't understand, really."

"He hates me," said Stuart. "He thinks I'm wasting my time. Thinks I won't get a man's job, like he had. He thinks I'm gay."

"Aw, don't be silly," said his mum, putting a hand on his arm. "He does'nae think any of those things." She paused, looking at her coffee. "Ah, you're not, are you? Gay?"

Stuart's first job after university was with a small independent production company which made TV ads and music videos, and which later made its name with a docusoap set on a landfill dump. It didn't pay much and his job title of "research assistant" covered a multitude of manual work, but it was his first step on what he was sure would be a glittering media career.

"You're a fucking tea–boy," grunted Jimmy Balfour when Stuart outlined his new job. "A gopher. Jesus Christ, is that what all those years at university were for?"

"At least I've got a job," said Stuart.

Jimmy Balfour nearly hit his son, then. He didn't, though. In fact, he barely moved. But Stuart saw it in his eyes, and they both knew how close he had come. They didn't speak again for a year, by which time Stuart had left the production company and was working on a London listings and arts magazine as a writer. At an old warehouse on Canary Wharf there was an exhibition of photographs charting the last days of the docks, and Stuart used his free tickets as an olive branch to repair relations with his parents. Jimmy Balfour, his face scrubbed and shaved, his hair combed, his collar itching, had tears in his eyes at the huge monochrome images recounting in minute, unflinching detail the death of the industry he had given his life to. He drank too much red wine and had to be led away early by Pat, but not before he clapped an embarrassed Stuart on the shoulder and said loudly, "You're a good lad, Stuey. Make a go of this, you hear? Make me proud."

Stuart inched inexorably up the media ladder for the next two years, while Jimmy Balfour sunk further into a sewer of drink, TV and horse–racing. There were arguments when Pat started to forget little things; she'd put his tea in the oven but not turn it on, she wouldn't remember to tape a film while he was at the pub for the afternoon, she'd go to the Post Office and stand in the queue, wondering why she was there even as she had the books for electricity and gas stamps in her hand.

Stuart was back in television when he got the call. He'd got a position as a senior researcher with a company making documentaries for Channel 4. He was juggling three calls to three different people when the receptionist put Pat Balfour through to him.

"Stuart, it's your mother. It sounds urgent."

"Christ," muttered Stuart. "Mum? Look, I'm really snowed under at the moment. Can I... what did you say?"

Jimmy Balfour had always been a big man, but on the hospital bed, invaded by tubes and wires, he seemed so thin, so pale, so small. Stuart stood by what surely must be a badly–fashioned waxwork of his father, his hand on his mum's shoulder, listening but not comprehending the doctor's words. *Massive heart attack* was all he made out. That and *we're terribly sorry*, which he knew from *Casualty* meant there was no hope.

After the machines had been switched off, Stuart stood with his mum in the hospital foyer, waiting for the taxi. When it arrived she gave the driver the address of their old house in Glasgow.

"Mum," reproached Stuart gently, giving the driver the proper address.

"Oh, yes," she said. "I forgot. I forget so much, these days."

Stuart abandoned his bed and his memories and showered for a long time, flaying his skin red raw under the needles of hot water. Dwelling on the past wasn't going to give him answers to his present conundrum. He dressed and gathered up his manuscript, sliding it into a large padded envelope, then went out to get some breakfast before his visit to Professor Garrett. And after that...

"Are you ready for more, then?"

Mr Grundy liked the Thames in the rain. A small leisure boat enveloped in glass was at the ready at all times and he'd had George order it out at eight. He took breakfast as the boat nosed slowly up–

river, listening intently to the patter of the rain on the glass roof as George waited patiently to begin the morning briefing.

George was a little perturbed. Late the previous night Escobar had turned up at his house in something of a state. When the door–bell rang George had been studying a letter which had been waiting for him on the doormat upon his return from work that evening. Perhaps "letter" was too strong a word for the missive; a simple form communication from a large London literary agency. His name was hastily pencilled at the top of the letter, under the masthead, and then it said:

Thank you for allowing us to see samples of your work. As I'm sure you're aware, the publishing industry is extremely competitive and literary agents can only afford to take on work they feel passionate about, and I'm afraid I didn't have that feeling about your writing.

Please do not feel down–hearted, as another literary agent may well feel differently.

Apologies for the form nature of this letter, but with between 50–100 unsolicited submissions a week we are unable to reply to each personally.

George carefully added the name on the bottom of the letter to a list in a small notebook, a list which in idle moments he dreamed of working through with various implements of torture, then he filed the letter away with the others in a box–file. There were many others. In fact, George had worked through most of the big literary agents in London. Three chapters, a synopsis, a covering letter and the all–important stamped, addressed envelope. He had grown used to seeing his own handwriting on buff A4 envelopes staring up at him from the doormat, silent testimonials to yet another failure. At first he had ripped open the envelopes almost with excitement, before he realised that if anyone was interested in his work they wouldn't be posting it back to him in his own envelope. Now he opened them with clinical detachment, copying the names out and filing the letters and throwing the returned pages in the bin.

George had written a novel. It was an old–fashioned sort of novel, where people fall in love and wars happen and there are deaths, misunderstandings, passions and jealousy. He thought it was rather a good novel, the kind he would have liked to read himself. Unfortunately, no–one shared George's view. In more than a year he had singularly failed to get a literary agent to ask to see more than the requisite three sample chapters. Occasionally there would be scrawled messages on the letters, things like: *Well–written, but not for us* or *An interesting idea... perhaps not quite commercial enough, though.* Keen to find out just what was commercial, George had visited WH Smith and browsed the paperback shelves. They were packed with books about young women with tangled love–lives working in the media, or men bringing up babies, or confessional memoirs of abused children, or drugs and violence. Not the kind of thing George liked to write about. Especially the drugs and violence; he got enough of that at work. It seemed that not only was George uncommercial, he was also desperately unfashionable.

As he was filing the letter the doorbell rang. It was Escobar, drenched and confused. George frowned; he did not encourage Escobar to visit him at home on his own time. He lived in a respectable neighbourhood. But Escobar looked unusual; frightened, almost. As soon as he was inside and George had the kettle on, he spilled forth about his failure to keep tabs on Balfour.

"I never forget to do a job before in my life," exclaimed Escobar, rather startlingly breaking out into huge sobs. "Mr Grundy, he is going to have me killed."

George assured Escobar that Mr Grundy was not going to kill him, and made him repeat the story from the beginning. It was this story George was going through in his head, preparing a suitable version of it for consumption by Mr Grundy as soon as he had finished breakfast.

Mr Grundy chased the last forkful of kipper around his plate before tiring of the sport, spearing it and popping it into his mouth. He wiped his hands on his napkin and parachuted it on to his empty plate. Draining his tea–cup, he pushed the breakfast tray away from him.

"George," he said, strangling a polite belch in his fist. "The morning report, please."

George went through the business minutes first. Mr Grundy had considerable business interests, and this morning there seemed to be a lot of news. George admitted to being baffled by the deep financial information, but he soldiered on and tried to sound as if he knew what he was talking about. Mr Grundy didn't complain or ask him to clarify anything.

"Any other business, George? What's the latest on Tyler and his infernal band?"

Carefully, George outlined a mild version of Escobar's adventures following Balfour the previous night.

"Perhaps, Mr Grundy, it's time to pick him up," said George. "Give him the treatment."

"The treatment, George?" asked Mr Grundy, looking slightly aghast. "Torture him, you mean?"

George said nothing, a little nonplussed. Mr Grundy continued, "No, I think that would be a terrible decision at the moment. Besides, I've been having a think, George. About Mr Balfour and his book. Why do you think *pop*CULT! are so interested in this book, George?"

It was a question George had already failed to provide an answer for on numerous occasions. Mr Grundy went on, "Think about it, George. A book on popular culture. An academic book on popular culture. Given what they've got hidden away in London somewhere, I'm surprised this didn't occur to them long ago. It could increase their power quite significantly. They must be very, very pleased with themselves at having stumbled across Mr Balfour."

"So we shouldn't pick him up, then?" said George. "Even though he's so useful to them? Even though he could tell us where they are?"

"No," said Mr Grundy. "We need to... have you ever fished, George? For salmon?"

"Yes, Mr Grundy. When I was younger."

"Give them line, George. Give them some line."

"Play them, Mr Grundy?"

"Exactly, George."

"Very good, Mr Grundy."

"That's not to say we shouldn't do our best to find out where they are, though. What did you say this chap's name was who accompanied Balfour last night?"

George checked his notes. "Vaughan. Walter Vaughan. Lives in Islington." He lowered his voice. "A sodomite, Mr Grundy, according to Escobar."

Mr Grundy peered through the glass walls of the boat at the rain plucking holes in the surface of the Thames. The river was getting rather choppy now.

"I suggest we go and see Mr Vaughan," decided Mr Grundy.

George frowned. "We, Mr Grundy? You wish to go along too..?"

Mr Grundy stretched his arms out in front of him. "It might do me good to get out. Flex the old muscles." He paused for a moment, watching the rain. "George, I'd rather like you to go and find me a tart, now. A rather common, dirty one, I think. I have something of a hunger on me."

"Will there be a body to dispose of afterwards, Mr Grundy?"

"Quite likely, George."

"Very good. I'll make the necessary arrangements."

Thirteen

Thomas Grundy was ninety–six years old when he enlisted for the 1st Battalion, the Queen's Own Royal West Kents, but he didn't look a day over twenty six. He was vaguely disappointed not to see Lord Kitchener himself in the recruiting office, but once he had been handed a commission and informed that he would be joining the British Expeditionary Force as a Sergeant, in charge of a platoon section of ten men as part of 13 Brigade heading for Belgium in August 1914, he didn't mind too much.

"Ever been abroad?" asked the gruff recruiting officer in the small, dusty room where Thomas signed his papers with the name Tyler Grundy. He thought it best not to mention his three decades in the Land of Opportunity.

"A little with my family when I was younger," said Tyler, carefully. "Italy and France."

"You'll be seeing France with different eyes than when you were on your jollies with mater and pater," sniffed the officer. Since a little before turn of the century, when "English Tom" had cut his hair, bought a suit and banked his gold in both the Americas and London, Thomas had been cultivating the persona of a member of the gentry. And he'd rather enjoyed it. He had three clubs in Soho and it was while drinking there that he had been inflamed by tales of the Boer War.

"Will I be allowed a personal baggage allowance?" asked Tyler Grundy.

"You keep your nose clean and your moustache clipped and you might be allowed your own batman, with your pedigree," said the officer. "Sign here. Yes, you can have a personal allowance. Two small trunks. We shall see you a week Thursday, Mr Grundy. Or, should I say, Sergeant."

Tyler Grundy liked the sound of that. He went for a drink at one of his clubs, not even the presence of huge numbers of anti–war protesters in Trafalgar Square souring his mood. Haigh, a florid blusterer who was cultivating gout and who had marched with Smith–Dorrien's Brigade on Bloemfontein, bought him a congratulatory brandy when he told the old boys the news. "Sticking it to the Hun!" he said dreamily. "Give the Boche one for me, Grundy. I envy you, boy. It'll be a bloody good adventure."

Some weeks later, on the hot, dusty road from the banks of the Marne to the Belgian border, shouldering his pack and keeping a nervous eye on the truck ahead which carried his two trunks, it did not feel like the bloody good adventure Haigh had promised. He had been cursorily introduced to the ten men in his section, all muscular, tanned farmhands from the Home Counties or pitmen and factory workers from the North, no less well–built but with a less healthy pallor. They had treated him with the respect his position demanded yet had not seemed overly friendly. Apart from Cole, a private from Bradford in Yorkshire, who had fallen into step with Grundy as they marched between dying, untended fields and through picturesque villages already abandoned and ghostly as rumours of the advancing German forces swept the countryside.

"Do you know where we're headed, Sir?" asked Cole cheerily, his forehead already reddening in the heat.

"It's classified, apparently," muttered Grundy, squirming as he walked to redistribute the weight of his pack. "They did tell me some weeks ago that we'd be heading for Paris, but we appear to be going in the wrong direction."

"'All warfare is based on deception'," said Cole. "I read that in Sun Tzu's *Art of War*."

"Sun who?"

"Chinaman," said Cole. "Knew a lot about scrapping. Used to read an awful lot on my breaks. Worked in the wool–comber's up Thornton Road in Bradford."

He pronounced it *Bratfert*. Grundy had no desire to go there if men earned their living combing wool. He was warming to Cole, though. He saw a lot of himself as a young nipper in the affable Northerner.

"Anyroad," continued Cole, squinting into the dusty distance. "Safe money's on Mons."

Tyler glanced at him. "You know that?"

"Don't you?"

"Well..."

"I know," laughed Cole. "It's classified. Don't worry, sir. Everybody knows which road we're headed. Question is, where they'll stick us. Reserve trenches or front–line, would you say?"

Grundy was becoming more miserable with every step in the hot August afternoon. The interminable march in the dry heat, the uncertainty of their destination, the fact that he seemed so out of sorts, the veiled, hostile stares of the other men. "You seem eminently more suited to commanding the section than I do," he said.

Cole laughed. "Me, sir? Who'd take orders from a wool–comber? See that Corporal up front? Knew him back in Bradford. His father owned a mill. Think he'd be told what to do by the likes of me?"

Corps HQ was located in a grand chateau, the grounds a sea of tents hosting tens of thousands of men. It stank like a latrine already. Grundy had never been so relieved to kick off his boots and gorge himself on the meagre rations. They all had to stand to attention as the Corps commander, a frowning Lieutenant General with a silvery handlebar moustache, did his rounds.

"He'll be dining on steak tonight, no doubt," whispered Cole. "Or pork. Bet that big house has a fine larder."

As darkness fell, they sat and listened to the distant thump of artillery fire. The horses of the cavalry units whinnied. "Hear that?" said Cole. "The Germans. We'll be at the front tomorrow, I reckon."

Grundy sipped at his tin mug of milky tea in silence, staring at their campfire. Then he said, "Why did you enlist, Cole?"

The other man shrugged. "They're already calling this The Last War. We're going to destroy the Hun, take Germany for the

King. It'll be written about in history books. England will rule Europe. I suppose I just wanted to be part of that. They reckon our losses will be pretty minimal. I just hope I'm not one of the unlucky ones. What about you, sir? Any regimental links with your family?"

"My family..? No, Cole. No. Like you, I suppose, I just wanted to be part of it. Part of something big. An adventure, someone told me it would be. I just thought..."

"Sir?"

Grundy shrugged. He looked around. "I don't know. There are so many men here. It just seems a little... impersonal, I suppose."

Cole rose and stretched. "Plenty of opportunity to be the conquering hero tomorrow, I should dare say, sir. I think I'll turn in, now."

At dawn the section packed up and joined four other sections to make up a platoon under the command of a Lieutenant who was even younger than Grundy appeared to be. He had a hairless top lip and was white as a sheet. He looked terrified. Grundy began to have a very bad feeling.

They marched through the artillery gun lines, over the churned up fields, and passed through the brigade reserve trenches to great cheers from the reserve battalion men. The sky was cloudy and flat, the air dry and still as they marched towards where 13 Brigade had dug into trenches alongside a railway bridge. The shaking young Lieutenant told Grundy to get his section ready for action and to prepare their rifles.

Cole popped his head above the lip of the trench, dirt shored up by reclaimed wood. "Just think," he said. "The Boche are just over there. Think they've got any idea what's about to hit them?"

"Get down, Cole," said Grundy irritably as he arranged his trunk in the small personal space he'd been allocated. The rest of the section were checking their rifles. Grundy felt sick. He summoned Cole quietly.

"That book, by the Chinaman. You don't have it, do you?"

"The *Art of War*? 'Course. Want a quick look before the bother starts?"

Grundy ordered his men to take a quick break and took the leather bound book to his quarters. He had two chests, one filled with clothing, books and his wash–bag. The other... Although he could hear the shouts of men just yards away, he was alone. He unlocked the trunk with shaking fingers and opened the lid. A golden–brown glow suffused the tiny timber–lined room. The thing waited, expectantly. Grundy placed the book inside the trunk and it was swallowed up. "Please," he whispered. "Give me guidance. I don't think I can do this. These men don't realise what's happening."

There was a shout and Grundy snapped the trunk lid down as Cole popped his head around the corner. "Sir! The Lieutenant wants us up front. The Germans are massing in the fields!"

Grundy nodded and curtly dismissed Cole. He opened the trunk again. There wasn't time for the thing to work its magic. It shuddered as it felt his distress. He despaired. What could he do? Then, something happened that he'd never seen before. The writhing, glowing mass within the trunk extended an almost–tentacle, curving upwards and over. A droplet appeared at the end of the pseudopod, dangling tentatively. Uncertainly, Grundy placed his hand palm upwards under the droplet, and flinched as the tiny ball separated from the rest of the thing and dropped warmly into his hand.

"What?" he said. "What am I supposed to do?"

"Sir!" It was Cole again. "You really need to come now!"

Grundy locked the trunk again and stood, the tiny pellet still clutched in his fist. Without knowing why, he took one more look at it, then popped it in his mouth and swallowed it down.

"Sergeant Grundy!" called the Lieutenant. "So glad you could join us. If you'd care to take a look above the trench wall, you might see the Fusilier battalion of the Brandenburg Grenadiers debouching in our general direction."

Grundy did as he was told. Through the scattered rolls of barbed wire he could indeed make out lines of distant men coming closer. "Good Lord," he said under his breath.

"Gentlemen of the Royal West Kents!" roared a voice from out of sight along the trench. "We are about to engage the enemy. Section commanders, have your men fire when ready."

There was a scuffling and clambering up the trench wall and suddenly the still morning exploded with fire and flash.

"Sir?" said Cole. Grundy realised he was swaying and staring into nothingness. "Oh, yes," he said absently. "Fire at will, men."

Grundy's mind was ablaze. It began at the very core of his being and spread out like oil on water, separate from him yet covering him totally, skewing his sight–lines, making him feel divorced from his body. The book that Cole had lent him was suddenly in his head, its lines writ across his brain, the words in bruised relief on his flesh. But it was mixed and diluted with the thoughts and fears of the thousands of men around him. The thing had absorbed too much, was unable to shut out the emotional firestorm raging around it. Grundy suddenly felt connected to every single one of the men, felt his finger tighten on every rifle trigger. Foreign voices screamed in his mind as they were cut down on the Mons fields, the disciplined firepower of the Brigade mowing down the advancing enemy. He managed to crawl to the lip of the trench and through the fog of rifle fire he saw the bodies piled in mounds and the Germans grimly forging ahead.

Grundy became aware that his face was pressed into the dirt wall of the trench, drool dribbling down his chin. He was unable to speak, unable to operate in the normal world. It felt as though there was something in him, something desperate to get out. He touched his top lip; blood slicked his moustache. His ears needed to pop and the sounds of battle seemed so very far away.

Then he felt them, sliding out of him, squeezing out of his eyes, his nostrils, his ears, his arsehole. There were seven of them, and they were unlike anything he had ever expected to see in his life. Dizzyingly wrong in their perspective, hopelessly trying to tack to the summer winds of a world not set up for their presence, writhing and turning in on themselves like infinitely layered Mobius strips, inside out and upside down and filling spaces that simply weren't there.

And, Grundy knew, they were somehow alive.

There was a pause, a silence. Cole was looking up. He breathed a word. Grundy couldn't hear it but he could lip–read. Cole had said, "Angels."

Other men were looking up as well, then a shout went up.

"They're backing off!" someone called and a cheer sounded.

"Keep firing!" shouted the Lieutenant. Grundy felt the presences above him fade, felt his body returned to him somewhat, felt the dirt and noise become more real around him.

Beside Grundy, Cole kept firing until his rifle clicked emptily. He threw it away from him and joined several other men clambering out of the trench and jumping and flicking the Agincourt salute at the retreated Boche. It's over, Grundy thought. We've done it. We've won.

Then the shelling began.

The first 5.9 inch shell exploded just in front of the trench. Grundy saw Cole surrounded by a yellow halo and then his head was no longer there. The West Kents dissolved into chaos and when the noise finally began it was the screaming of the damned in hell, as far as Grundy was concerned. As the soldiers began to fall back under an onslaught to which they had no defence, Grundy pushed towards his quarters.

It was night when he finally felt unable to go on any further. He had been dragging his trunk behind him for miles, in which direction he had no idea. His Brigade had been fractured and dissipated by the vicious shelling and, as far as he knew, were probably regrouping at Corps HQ. He stopped at a deserted farmhouse and after finding some stale bread and having an unquiet sleep on a hard bed, awoke to dim sunlight and the realisation that he had deserted his unit. If he was caught now he would be shot. Taking off and burning his uniform in the grate,

Grundy found an ill–fitting dirty white shirt and a pair of shapeless black trousers, and pulling a cap tight down on his head he squeezed his feet into a pair of muck encrusted boots two sizes too small and set off walking with his trunk, eventually sighting a stream of lost, frightened and hungry men, women and children streaming along a dusty road. He stopped a weeping woman and asked in halting French where they were going.

She pointed to the horizon. "Le Pyrenees," she said. "Et liberte."

After a moment's hesitation, Grundy joined them.

Fourteen

Monroe returned to Praxis Street after two hours nosing her bike around the Congestion Charge zone in a failed bid to shift a headache. She should have acted on her first whim and gunned the machine down to Brighton and back, but didn't want to drift too far from *pop*CULT!. Something was brewing and she felt itchy and uncomfortable. The feeling intensified as she walked into the warehouse and slung her helmet on to a bean bag.

"What's up?" she asked brightly. Karen turned and shushed her with a finger to her purple lips.

"Tyler's televining," she mouthed.

Monroe curled her lip at the girl and feigned indifference. She fiddled needlessly with a clasp on her boot and cast a sly glance to where Tyler's silhouette perched Buddha–like and fuzzy in the halo of the bank of glowing TV screens.

Each one wore the same image; the endlessly–looped collapse of the World Trade Center, soundtracked only by the whistling wind and the tinny, unbelieving, androgynous voice of the holder of the camcorder, breathing out *oh. my. God.* as the second plane exploded in bone dust and aviation fuel against the standing tower just as the first was falling in on itself like a dry sandcastle. There were flies around the zenith of the tower, or maybe lovers leaping to one kind of death to escape another, and then the camera lurched and showed careening blue sky as the owner retched and swore. Then there was the tiniest of blips, like the feeling of falling off a kerb you get when jerked out of shallow sleep on a comfortable couch, and the whole process began again.

The images made Monroe feel queasy and she looked away. Surrounding Tyler was the rest of *pop*CULT!, assembled languidly around him. Karen was perched on the back of one of the plump sofas, her knees drawn under her chin. It was the new Karen she'd taken an instant dislike to. Monroe knew that Tyler must have fucked her already, and if he hadn't it would only be a matter of time. She would be pathetically grateful, and would try to be nonchalant and act like a good soldier when she inevitably found Tyler boning someone else, when all the time she was crushed inside. Monroe hoped that was soon, so the new girl could stop following him around like a lost puppy.

Monroe gave a little wave to Monty, who sat smoking a Marlboro a little way from the group. He was Monroe's favourite Monty, he'd been with *pop*CULT! a couple of years and was pretty relaxed by the whole thing. Standing a few feet in front of him was Luther Blissett, the one who liked the Armani suits and had that strange, tribal scarification on his face. And finally, MacGuffin was at the desks that lined the walls, his chair spun around so he could observe the performance.

Monroe toyed with just going to her room and plugging into her MP3s, but curiosity got the better of her. It had been a while since she'd seen a televination, and Tyler always gave good value for money. Before 9/11 he'd used tapes of Princess Diana's funeral and before that the newsreel footage of the starving masses in Ethiopia which had kick–started the Band Aid appeal. Anything with a violent emotional kick which had been seen by millions of people around the world and was imprinted into the global consciousness would do to get him into the necessary state for televining, but the Twin Towers footage seemed to work especially well.

She watched quietly with the rest of them for a while, until Tyler abruptly bowed his head, the only movement he had made since Monroe walked in.

"I'm ready," he said in a small, laboured voice.

Karen Eliot was immediately at his side, clicking off the DVD loop and replacing it with snowy static, and handing Tyler a thick, black remote control. Connected to the bubbling sub–strata of popular culture via the public execution of thousands of innocents, he was ready to accept the messages of the ether and the guidance of the ghosts in the machine.

Tyler weighed the remote control in his hand and then looked up from his lotus position on the rugs before the bank of crackling TV screens. "What should we do?" he whispered, and then began to thumb the buttons.

The control was one specially designed by MacGuffin to operate all of the TV screens simultaneously, sending a random channel–change command to the individual digital switch–boxes which controlled each monitor. Immediately they leapt into life, each one showing a different picture with a Babylonian cacophony rising from the pyramid. Tyler's eyes flickered over the screens, like those of a quiz show contestant seeking the right answer on a high–tech game–board. There were news programmes, commercials, soap operas, movies, gardening programmes, makeover shows, shopping channels, porn, dramas, cartoons, discussions, celebrity game shows, music videos, comedy sketches. Monroe often thought that it was only when you saw television in its entirety that you realised just how little of it there actually was. When you were limited to one channel at a time, the medium stacked up behind it seemed immense and full of promise. But viewed as a whole, it was rather limited. And largely crap, thought Monroe, although it would have been blasphemy to say as such here within the walls of *pop*CULT!, devoted as it was to the worship of the goggle–box god and the wider church it presided over.

Suddenly, Tyler flung out his arm and shouted, "There!"

He pressed a button on the remote and the picture on one of the screens to the far right of the bank froze, a sit–com family caught in amber around their kitchen table.

"And there!" A newsreader paused, his eyes half–open, his mouth yawning.

"And there!" Homer Simpson was captured in mid–pratfall.

This continued for a minute or more, until at least half of the TV screens were in freeze–frame, then Tyler flung the remote from him and fell forward, hugging his chest. Karen materialised at his side, a hand on his heaving shoulders, and Luther took a step forward.

Tyler stood shakily, leaning on Karen for support. He turned to the group and gave them a wide smile. "Th–th–that's all, folks!"

Monroe realised she was holding her breath, and slowly let it out.

"I'll edit that stuff together on to a DVD," called MacGuffin from his work station. "Half an hour okay?"

"Perfect," called Tyler. He glanced at Monroe. "I could do with a shag."

Karen leaned into him, looking up at him with her kohl'd eyes, waggling the stud in her tongue in the gap in her front teeth. Tyler gave her a grin.

To be honest, it was the last thing that Monroe fancied. Her head was pounding and she thought she might be about to come on. But it was time the newest Karen Eliot learned the harsh lessons of life in *pop*CULT!. It would do her good in the long run, especially with a mission coming up. Monroe waited until Tyler glanced at her again, then ran her tongue over her top lip. "Your place or mine?" she said.

As Tyler bucked and thrusted on top of her, whooped and hollered and punched the headboard of Monroe's bed, she made all the appropriate noises and gripped his tight buttocks with her diamond–hard nails, just as he liked, but in truth her heart wasn't in it. Another paradox; Monroe had never really liked sex. Not actively disliked it, but never enjoyed it as much as people thought she did. Which was probably hardly surprising, given that in her pre–*pop*CULT! life she had sold her body to the ministrations of sweating, stinking, overweight men just to survive.

Monroe – or rather, the woman she was before she was Monroe – didn't consider herself a very good prostitute. Not that it was really possible to be a bad one; so long as you were willing to hitch up your skirt and allow hard–faced men to fuck you against a brick wall for fifteen quid in well–used notes pushed into your cold hands, it was steady work. But, like the fat girl always picked last for school sports, Monroe often found herself overlooked and ignored on the streets, forcing her to take the punters that none of the other girls would, the weirdos who wanted to quote Scripture at you while you sucked their reedy cocks, the fat businessmen who punched you as they came, the carloads of young men who wanted to pass you round their mates for only an extra tenner. The lonely, middle–aged bachelors in cardigans who wanted you to tell them you loved them as they sucked your nipples. That sort.

It wasn't so much that she was ugly, more that she was invisible. Plain, mousy, nondescript. Always in the shadows, afraid to speak, unheeded except by those with a nose for pathetic vulnerability.

Until Tyler found her, of course. When he'd walked up to her that rainy night, she thought he merely wanted directions or was looking for someone else. And fifteen minutes later, as he pressed a fifty pound note into her hand then rogered her rigid with a tenderness that surprised her, she still couldn't understand why someone as good–looking and lithe as him had picked her from the rain–swept gutter. And when he told her that he was going to take her away and cast a spell on her that would make her beautiful and give her the life that the rest of the girls on the street could only dream about, she almost believed him.

And then he brought her to *pop*CULT!, and she realised that he was telling the truth.

Feeling a surge of fondness towards Tyler at the memory, Monroe allowed Tyler's thrusts to bring her to orgasm, and she arched her back and began to gasp as his howling hit fever pitch and he came noisily inside her.

Stuart was stopped at the university gates by a uniformed security guard who asked him what his business was.

"I've an appointment with Professor Garrett in the popular culture studies department," he said, nonplussed.

The guard repeated Stuart's name into a walkie–talkie and after a hiss of static to the affirmative he waved Stuart inside. "Can't take too many precautions these days, sir. We've had a bit of trouble on the campus recently."

Stuart found Professor Garrett in distracted mood. He had at least been hoping that the sheaf of paper he presented would have elicited a mildly enthusiastic response.

"Have you been in a fight?" asked Stuart.

Professor Garrett fingered the bruise on his lip and instead of answering studied the chapters that Stuart had brought with him. "Well. You're certainly... well. Keep it coming, I say."

Undeterred, Stuart pointed out some of the passages he was particularly proud of, and when Professor Garrett struggled to maintain interest Stuart began to panic inside and worried he was going cold on the project.

"There's something else, as well," he said.

Professor Garrett nodded for him to go on.

"I've stumbled across something... a DVD. Of a movie that was never released. *Carry On, You Old Devil.*"

Professor Garrett did a double take. "*Carry On, You Old Devil?* You've seen a copy?"

"Not yet," said Stuart. "But I'm close. There's this group, this *pop*CULT!, and they've got it. I just need a bit of time to get in with them."

Professor Garrett sighed. "I'm worried time is something we don't have too much of."

"Professor..? Has something happened?"

Garrett looked pityingly at Stuart. How could he tell him that he'd handed over his name and address to two thugs who evidently had some interest in Balfour's book that he couldn't fathom? Dangerous thugs who carried around Gurkha knives and split people's lips?

"Stuart... Look, just be careful, okay? And if... if you see anyone hanging around your flat, call the police."

Stuart was startled now. "Hanging around my flat? Like who? Look, is this something I should be worried about?"

Professor Garrett put his head into his hand and waved Stuart away. "No. I don't know. Just be careful. Go away for a few days, if you can. Finish the book somewhere else. Take a holiday."

Stuart wanted more, but it was evidently not forthcoming, so he left. The security guard nodded at him as he walked thoughtfully out of the gate. "Take care, sir."

Stuart stopped. "What do you mean?"

The man shrugged. "Just a figure of speech."

Stuart was jumpy now. He cast around the streets as he walked, trying to spot people who might be watching or following him. He looked at his watch. He had two hours until he was supposed to meet Monroe again in Hyde Park. He didn't want to go back the flat, not after what Garrett had said, nor did he want to be standing alone in the park while he waited for Monroe to show. All things considered, Stuart decided that he deserved a drink.

Karen Eliot was in a sulk and Monroe couldn't resist giving her a grin as she emerged from her room with Tyler in tow. MacGuffin swiveled round at one of the computer terminals and plucked a DVD from the tray of the rewriter.

"All done, Tyler," he called, flipping the disc over to Monty Cantsin, who caught it deftly and popped his forefinger through the hole.

"Well, let the show begin," said Tyler, flopping on to a sofa. He lifted an arm expectantly, but Monroe went to the fridge against the far wall and popped the tab on a can of lager. Karen Eliot snuggled against Tyler's legs on the rugs as Monty loaded up the DVD and Luther sparked up another Marlboro.

All the screens in the TV pyramid glowed blue as Tyler manipulated the remote control. "TV's like the Holy Spirit, man," he said, almost to himself. It's all around us. It's a comfort. It gives guidance."

"What did you ask it?" asked Monty.

Tyler looked thoughtful. "We need a mission," he said. "*pop*CULT! needs direction. And verily, here it comes..."

Tyler hit PLAY. A group of brightly–dressed, beaming presenters on a children's channel sang in close harmony, "The time has come..."

Homer Simpson looked frustrated and said, "Marge, when I join an underground cult I expect a little support from my family..."

"You're makin' a big fuckin' spectacle of yourself," shouted Nicky Santoro in *Casino*...

"Here I am, invisible to the eye," riposted Giles in *Buffy*...

"Of course, the real trick to survival lies not in running and hiding, but in removing your enemy's capacity to hunt you down," answered Liam Cunningham in *Dog Soldiers*...

Doc Emmett Brown, *Back to the Future*: "This is it! This is the answer! It says here... that a bolt of lightning is going to strike the clock tower at precisely 10.05pm next Saturday night... If we can somehow harness this lightning... channel it... into the flux capacitator, it just might work..."

"You know, they say the truth is revealed under pressure. Veritas Inextremas. Like when you're stuck in a lift?" suggested Karl in an episode of *Neighbours* at least twenty years old...

From *Sex and the City*: "There's no such thing as bad publicity..."

A monochrome ferris wheel turned slowly, and Orson Welles spat, "Would you really feel any pity of one of those dots stopped moving forever? If I offered you twenty thousand pounds for every dot that stopped, would you really, old man, tell me to keep my money, or would you calculate how many dots you could afford to spare.."

"Panic attack! Panic attack! Panic attack!" shrieked Eddie in *Absolutely Fabulous*...

Amid the heat and dust of *Zulu*: "The way of the Lord has been shown to us..."

And Richard Hannay hung from the monstrous hands of Big Ben, legs kicking until the frame stalled and was frozen, and the image melted away.

"So what does the Holy Ghost tell us?" said Monroe before taking a swig of her beer.

Tyler grinned. "It tells us that it's about time we went public."

Stuart sheltered under a weeping willow as the rain battered Hyde Park, chain–smoking Marlboros and convincing himself that Monroe wasn't going to show. For reasons he couldn't really understand he felt wretched, as though he was embarking on something which should have been exciting but which he had deep, undefined misgivings about. He thought about ringing Jane, but what would he tell her? That he had "met someone"? What exactly did he feel for Monroe... lust, sure. Like every other man who met her. Was he in love with her? He stamped on his cigarette butt in disgust. He hardly knew her. He wasn't even sure if they'd actually slept together, or whether his cotton–wool memory of it was simply the result of the narcotics they'd fed him. He was behaving like a teenager. He pulled the unfamiliar weight of the mobile phone from his jacket pocket and scrutinised it for missed calls, but there was nothing. He opened it up and his thumb hovered above the first digit of Jane's number, then he changed his mind and punched in Walter's landline.

"Stuart," said Walter. "I take it you're going back?"

"Yes," said Stuart wretchedly. "I don't know why, though."

Walter paused, chewing thoughtfully on an olive. "For the DVD, surely."

"Yes, I suppose so."

"And..?"

Stuart was sure Walter had a raised eyebrow and a glint in his eye. He sighed. "And the woman. Monroe. If she ever shows up."

"If she does, be sure and ask her how they do that trick on Praxis Street. There are, dear boy, quite a few people I would like to forget where I live. And find out who that brute was who followed us, while you're at it."

"Will do," agreed Stuart. Then he added, "I don't suppose you want to come with me, do you?"

"I think this is your adventure, Stuart. I am but a bit–player, a walk–on part, another anonymous face in the crowd. Besides, I have company tonight. A new agency has advertised in the local rag and they are sending a young chap around this evening who will hopefully give me a right good seeing to."

"Well, be careful," said Stuart.

"You too, dear boy," said Walter, just as Stuart became aware of the scent of rain–sluiced Alpine slopes creeping through the dripping branches. He was barely cognisant of Walter hanging up when Monroe sidled into his view, a sheen of water on her biking leathers, her fragrant hair mussed and static–y from the motorcycle helmet she held in her gloved hands.

"Round two," she grinned.

Later, after an indulgent soak and a little primping, Walter idly glanced at the advertisement placed in the previous day's newspaper while he smoked a Gitane and sipped a Manhattan, comfortable and cool in his silk robe. It could almost have been designed to appeal personally to him, and to no–one else.

Are you out of step with the world, or is the world out of step with you? Do you crave for an age of romance that you suspect might never have really existed? Are you holding out for a hero? Then call us. Discretion is assured. Your expectations are not.

Walter smoothed his moustache for the umpteenth time and paced about the flat, flicking imaginary crumbs from the sofa and running his finger along the bar–top for non–existent dust. It was almost eight. He wondered what Stuart was doing now, what mysteries had been revealed to him. Walter lit another Gitane and freshened up his glass, pondering whether the Mantovani was too twee, just as his doorbell sang. With one last look in the mirror, he strode to answer it.

"Mister Vaughan?"

Walter tried not to look nonplussed. He had been expecting

someone younger, he had to admit, someone a little less... weathered. And someone a little taller. At least he was clean, and smartly dressed. Walter inclined his head slightly.

"I am he. And you..?"

"Escobar."

They considered each other for a moment in the doorway, then Walter remembered his manners. "Escobar, please, do come in and make yourself comfortable."

As he led his way to the lounge he asked, "I can fix you a drink?"

Escobar sloughed off his overcoat. Walter was mildly thrilled to see evidence of solid muscle beneath the black suit he wore. He came closer until Walter could almost see his reflection in Escobar's brilliantined hair.

"I prefer to get down to business," said Escobar, and Walter let loose a little animal squeak as the other man's hand darted inside Walter's robe, seeking out his business end and settling quick–bitten nails around the package, as though he was weighing apples.

"Well..." said Walter, forcing a smile. Escobar grinned back and squeezed.

"Steady on, old chap, you're not doing the FA Cup draw down there, you know," gasped Walter as Escobar's grin grew wider and he began to really, really hurt.

There was a sound of splintering wood, which Walter dimly recognised as his front door being kicked in, and then he was aware of two other figures, a hulking, bald brute with the face like the proverbial bulldog chewing on a wasp, and a slighter yet strangely more imposing man in his fifties, adjusting his cufflinks and glancing around the living room with a slight curl of his top lip.

"Escobar, you can release Mr Vaughan's genitals now," said the man, smoothing back his salt–and–pepper hair and taking a pair of leather gloves from his coat pocket. Escobar relaxed his grip and Walter groaned, stepping back and steadying himself on the bar–top.

"George, please secure the door."

"What's going on?" said Walter. "I must say, there shall be a strongly–worded letter to the introduction agency..."

The man smiled, his eyes dancing. "There is no introduction agency, Mr Vaughan. Merely a confection of my own devising, to encourage you to invite us over your threshold, that is all."

"Who are you?" said Walter, his anger dissipating as he at last began to appreciate his situation.

"Please allow me to introduce myself," said the man, pulling on the leather gloves as the one he called George reappeared behind him and Escobar withdrew a frankly terrifying curved, shining blade from within the dark recesses of his jacket. "I am a man of wealth, and taste."

Fifteen

"**W**hat are you doing here?" asked Tyler. He was dressed in a thick, cabled sweater, khaki cargo pants shoved carelessly into leather boots, a furry Russian hat on his head, the flaps dangling.

Stuart looked uncertainly at Monroe. "Erm," he said. "Monroe brought me... I thought..."

Tyler grinned. "No. What are you doing here? Why are you here? What brings you back to us?"

Stuart closed his eyes and drew a deep, ragged breath. Monroe had made him take another dose of Copyright before climbing on to the back of her bike. "Like I said before," she'd told him. "You don't take it, you don't come."

He hadn't wanted to. He wasn't sure that most of what he experienced last time wasn't just one long hallucinogenic trip.

"It's okay," she said. "It's not as intense after the first time. Once you've got it in your blood, you're just kind of topping up the levels. You won't feel as whacked out."

It was true. He'd buzzed and shivered as the drug did whatever it did to the muscles and nerves at the base of his skull, but he'd felt in control, on top of things. He even saw how they managed to pass through the brick wall at the end of the alley off Praxis Street; as they flew along the deserted roads Monroe had flicked a switch on the handgrip of the Ducati and ahead of them in the shadows the ground – the cobbles that Stuart had felt were somehow wrong when he'd tried to find the place again with Walter – had seamlessly slid back, revealing a shallow ramp which led into the concrete–lined corridor at the end of which lay the massive warehouse that was home to *pop*CULT!. Stuart had been very impressed.

"It's the Machine Elves," Monroe had said carelessly as she coasted the bike to a halt. "We want something doing, MacGuffin asks them to do it, it gets done."

Now he was inside again, insulated from the world in that cavernous space crammed with technology and mystery. Monroe smiled at him and said, "Stop teasing, Tyler."

"I'm not," said Tyler, throwing himself down on a huge pile of beanbags in front of the pyramid of TV screens, all tuned in to a different channel. MacGuffin was working at one of the computer terminals, scratching his wild grey hair. There were three other people, only one of whom Stuart recognised; the girl – Karen something? "I just want to know what Stuart thinks he's getting himself into, and why."

Monroe took the bike helmet that was hanging limply in Stuart's hands and tossed it, together with hers, on to a table beside the TV screens. "I'm going to freshen up," she said.

Stuart cast her a stricken glance. *Don't leave me here alone.* Monroe wrinkled her nose at him and Tyler patted the beanbags. "Stuey, baby. Chill out. Sit down. Monty!"

One of the other people, perched on the back of one of the several sofas arranged around the TVs, raised his hand. "Dude?"

"Some refreshment for Mr Balfour,"

Monty eased himself from the sofa, pushing his long hair out of his face and tying it deftly at the back with a rubber band. He wore a T–shirt that said APE SEX. "Beer, dude?" he asked Stuart.

Stuart nodded, sitting awkwardly at the side of Tyler, who clapped him on the shoulder. "Stuart, man, cool your jets! You're among friends here, you know. You want me to remind you? The guy getting your drinks is Monty Cantsin. He's the guy who tagged your street with the *pop*CULT! graffito, remember?"

"No it's not," said Stuart pointedly. "The guy who tagged my street was a good six inches shorter than him, and he had dark hair. And one of those little surfer beards."

Monty laughed from the big American–style fridge behind the TVs. Tyler laughed with him. In fact, they all laughed – the girl with multicoloured streaked hair called Karen Eliot and the black guy with the bushy afro and the John Lennon glasses whose name was Luther Blissett. Even MacGuffin turned from his monitor and grinned.

"Stuart," said Tyler, accepting two cold bottles from Monty and passing one over to him. "We're going to have to give you the tour.

But first, you haven't answered my question. Why are you here?"

Stuart took a sip of the beer, suddenly realising he was parched. "For the film," he said.

"Ah," said Tyler. "The film. *Carry On, You Old Devil*, am I right?"

"If it even exists," said Stuart. He was beginning to doubt it, beginning to wonder why he had even believed it in the first place.

"Oh, it exists," said Tyler. "That right, Mac?"

MacGuffin touched his forehead in a small salute. "Of course."

"Everything exists," said Tyler. "Everything you can imagine, and quite a lot you can't. And that's why you're here, Stuart. Because you've been given a glimpse into a world you never even knew existed, and it's right here beside you, underneath you, all around you. We're everything you ever dreamed of, Stuart, every little flight of fancy you ever took, every adolescent power trip and wank fantasy, every single I wish I wish I wish..."

"Bollocks," said Stuart, rising awkwardly from the bean bags, the drained bottle in his hand. He felt a little light–headed, unsure whether it was the alcohol or the drugs. "You're just a bunch of... I don't know what you are."

Tyler grinned. "Want me to show you why else you're here?"

He rose, took Stuart's elbow, and guided him away from the central living area. Stuart followed and then pulled his arm away. "Where are you taking me?"

Tyler put his finger to his lips, and beckoned for Stuart to follow him towards a shadowy doorway near the back of the warehouse. The sounds from the TV and the rest of the group receded as they were absorbed into the spongy blackness of a warm, airless corridor. Tyler took off his hat and stuffed it into the side pocket of his pants.

Stuart allowed himself to be propelled along the darkness, his eyes becoming accustomed to the gloom, until Tyler halted and indicated an open square hatch at chest level. "In there," he said.

Stuart complied without knowing why, pulling himself up and

scraping his knees as he hauled himself ungraciously into a tight passageway that sloped gently upwards. When he was inside Tyler deftly vaulted in behind him, patted him on the arse and indicated he should crawl forward to where a vague, indistinct light glowed diffusely.

After a minute or so they came to a grill, the light bright behind it and the sounds of running water all around. Stuart crept up to the grill and peered inside, drawing back involuntarily as he saw Monroe, naked under the shower a few feet below them.

"She's beautiful, isn't she?" whispered Tyler under the hiss of water. "What do you see?"

"Raven–black hair," said Stuart, mesmerised. "Cheek–bones. Soap running off perfect breasts. Legs. Perfection."

"You know what I see?" said Tyler distantly. "Mousy blonde hair. A little weight around the arse. Breasts too small for her torso. Round shoulders."

Stuart wasn't listening. He was nursing an awkward erection in his crouched position, entranced by the deliciously clandestine view of Monroe as she languidly soaped her tummy.

"You should have seen her before I found her," murmured Tyler. "You wouldn't recognise her. You wouldn't look twice at her. *pop*CULT! made her the woman she is."

Stuart blinked as Tyler came up close to him in the cloying, claustrophobia of the ventilation shaft. "Is that what you're here for?" he whispered. Then he placed a hand on Stuart's groin and gripped him tightly.

Stuart tried to shuffle away but the space was too tight. "What are you doing?" he hissed, slapping Tyler's hand off his cock.

"Free your ass and your mind will follow," said Tyler into his ear. "It's the only way."

Stuart pushed him away again, banging his head on the grill. Below them, Monroe stopped, cocked her head, and looked up.

"Tyler?" she said, turning off the shower taps. "Tyler, is that you up there? Jesus, just fuck off out of it, will you?"

Tyler laughed, no longer attempting to hide. "Monroe, baby.

Whoever said cleanliness is next to godliness never witnessed you in the shower. You're a bad, bad girl."

Monroe threw a sponge at the grill, the water splashing Stuart's face, shocking him into embarrassment, then she stalked out of the white tiled shower room back into her quarters. Tyler laughed again and began to reverse out of the shaft. "Come on, Stuey. Let's get on with the tour."

They emerged from the corridor and back into the light and conversation of the central area, Tyler bouncing along happily and Stuart hanging back, frowning. Tyler led him to the sofas where Karen Eliot was watching cartoons and Monty and Luther were playing some kind of car–racing computer game on two of the TV screens at the bottom left–hand corner of the pyramid.

"*pop*CULT! is seven," said Tyler, disappearing behind the bank of screens and returning with a fistful of beers, which he distributed. "It's our lucky number. It's Gilgamesh's gate of seven bolts and felling the seven cedars, it's the creation of the world, it's the ears of corn and years of drought in Joseph's dreams, Snow White's dwarves, it's the seventh sons of seventh sons and the ancient wonders of the world, the ages of man, the pillars of wisdom, the heavens and the hells."

"I can get as much from Old Moore's Almanac," said Stuart dryly.

"*pop*CULT! is seven," repeated Tyler. "And at the heart of the seven is the infinite; the triumvirate of Luther Blissett, Karen Eliot and Monty Cantsin."

Luther and Monty abandoned their game and turned their heads to Tyler, as might acolytes to a high priest. Karen stood and insinuated herself under his arm, a hand lightly placed on his stomach.

"Luther, Karen and Monty are multiple–name projects," said Tyler. "Anyone can be them, with a couple of loose rules. Luther's usually black, Monty's usually male, Karen Eliot's usually bonkers."

The others laughed and Karen pouted and slapped Tyler softly across the face. His hand snaked to hers and gripped her wrist, turning it ever so slightly until the pressure made her wince and she skulked back to the sofa and her beer."

"That's why I see different people every time I come," said Stuart, interested despite himself. "So how many Luthers are there?"

"One," said Tyler. "Only one Luther, only one Karen, only one Monty. But the people who *are* them are countless."

"So it's role–play," said Stuart.

"No," said Tyler. "Everyone you see in this room is who they claim to be. But sometimes the faces are different. You see?"

Stuart balled his fist and rubbed it into the bridge of his nose. "No, not really."

Luther was standing now, and patted Stuart on the shoulder. "Don't fret about it. Just accept that whatever we look like, we're the same people with the same memories of you. Have you ever seen me before?"

Stuart looked into the wide brown eyes behind the round glasses. "No."

"Even so," said Luther. "I remember the last time you came. We rode on the Velvet Underground. And you got jiggy with Monroe."

Stuart's face burned, both with the memory of it and of his spying on Monroe in the shower just moments before. And right then she emerged from one of the darkened passages ranked at the rear of the warehouse, wearing a pale blue Lycra catsuit, her black hair tied at the back of her head, lips glowing blood–red.

"Luther, Monty and Karen are the ever–revolving heart of *pop*CULT!," continued Tyler, "but its brain, its lungs, its circulatory system, that's us. Me, Monroe and MacGuffin. Ever–present, never changing, always moving."

MacGuffin had moved away from his work on the computers to get a beer and was standing by Monroe, who regarded Stuart with a lively, dancing stare. Tyler stood front and centre, his foot–soldiers displayed around him. "We are *pop*CULT!," he said, opening his arms expansively.

"But *pop*CULT! is seven, you said," pointed out Stuart. "Where's the seventh member?"

Monroe glanced at Tyler. She said, "There was The Waif. She died."

"We need to close the circle, Stuart," said Tyler, his arms still outstretched. "Join us."

Stuart laughed. "Join you? And do what? Sit around in a squat all day, watching TV and talking rubbish? I don't even know what it is you claim to be doing, here. Just what is *pop*CULT! all about?"

The TV screens lit up Tyler in a sickly glow, casting grotesque, dancing shadows on the bare brick walls. "Revolution," he whispered.

Sixteen

"**R**evolution?" asked Stuart as Tyler hauled closed the concertina'd lift door and jabbed at the buttons. The dim light set into the ceiling of the metal box flickered as the lift juddered into life and began its jerky descent.

Tyler paused for a moment, as if considering his words. Then he said, "The world is at war, Stuart. And the prize isn't land or oil or creed or expansion, it's our minds. It's our time. It's what we look at with our waking eyes, what we dream about with our sleeping souls, what we talk about over the water cooler and argue about in the pub. There's a cultural assault taking place and you have to decide which side you're on, or you're just going to be collateral damage."

Stuart sighed, memories of his student days staying up all night smoking and drinking and quoting latter–day French philosophers. "Common–room Situationism, then," he said, a trifle disappointed.

Tyler grinned. "We're the Situationist Comedy International, and our bible is the Society of the Funny Spectacles... our eyes goggle out on springs at the wonder of the world."

"So you're not declaring war on the media, then?" said Stuart. "Not condemning the herding of the masses like sheep, not trashing the dumbing down of culture?"

"Trashing it?" laughed Tyler heartily. "We're embracing it! Western civilisation is constantly pushed into grasping for what it doesn't need. And I'm not talking about washing machines and designer clothes and games consoles... we *need* this shit! It feeds our souls! It's the product of the world we've created... it would be rude not to! It's the art snobs and the culture vultures who are strangling the general populace, making them feel guilty for watching a trashy movie or reading a chick–lit novel."

"'All art is quite useless'," said Stuart.

"Exactly!" enthused Tyler, punching his shoulder. "Art is timeless, and as such, out of time. Popular culture is here and now and who cares if it's gone tomorrow, because we enjoyed it today. And you know what the best thing about it all is?"

Stuart shrugged. Tyler brought his face close. "The people are doing it for themselves. They're no longer in thrall to the faceless TV executives with their Oxbridge welts on their true blue arses, they're getting up and storming the studios and making their own entertainment. Reality TV, Stuart. Ordinary people watching ordinary people. Bloggers telling the news and giving the opinions that the corporate media can't or won't. Self–published writers throwing off the shackles of editors and marketing departments. Bedroom rock stars releasing their music straight on to the internet.

"It's like a modern–day peasant's revolt, Stuart. You're an educated man; you know your Marx. What happens when you give the working class the means of production?"

"They become the ruling class," said Stuart slowly.

Tyler leaned back against the shuddering wall of the lift, the glow of a self–satisfied smile on his face. "Exactly."

The lift slowed and cruised to a jerking halt. Tyler pulled open the cage door.

"But what's this got to do with you? With *pop*CULT!? It's just happening anyway. It's nothing to do with you."

"That's where you're wrong, Stuey baby," said Tyler, leading him out of the lift. "And if you really want to – I mean, really, really want to, I'll show you why."

They stepped out into the warm glow of a dimly–lit platform, where the two carriages of a Tube train waited in fuzzy repose, nose and tail facing off into the blackness of a tunnel.

"Then I didn't dream it," breathed Stuart. "The Velvet Underground..."

He squatted and brushed his fingers over the tightly–cropped fur of the ground, stood and trailed them along the walls with their swirling patterns in slight relief. The curved roof was the same; even the rails and the ground they ran on, disappearing into the maw of the tunnel. Even the carriages...

"Welcome to Flock," said Tyler, striding towards the front carriage. The doors slid open noiselessly as he approached. "This is our base station at the moment; the Velvet Underground snakes across pretty much all of Central London; we have five other stations, all close to *pop*CULT! safe houses: Makhmal, Broccade, Hemp–Weft, Corduroy and Void, the end of the line. Come on, climb aboard."

Stuart touched the velvet–covered doors of the carriage. "But how?"

Tyler reclined on one of the seats and indicated for Stuart to do the same. He shrugged. "The Machine Elves did it for us. They can do anything. Within reason."

The doors whispered closed and the carriage moved smoothly off, the redness of Flock receding behind them until the tunnel swallowed the carriage. "The Machine Elves. You mean those things I saw when I was on the Copyright trip... Are you telling me they were real?"

Tyler nodded. "In a sense. You can't touch them or hear them, but you can sense them when you're on Copyright. There are seven of them. We ask them to do things, they do them. From us they take things; memories, emotions, feelings, sensations. They seem to think it's a fair swap."

Home.

Stuart recalled them clustering around him, the feeling he'd had that some kind of exchange had taken place. "Are you telling me they're alive?"

"They exist," said Tyler. A scarlet light approached from over his shoulder. "I told you before; everything exists, certainly in some form or other."

The train slowed but did not stop at a station, picked out in lush, Eastern–flavoured velvet. "Makhmal," said Tyler. "Pretty close to Bermondsey."

Stuart pondered what Tyler had said, eventually saying, "But they can't have just carved out fresh tunnels under London. Are these those abandoned Tube stations I've heard about?"

Tyler shook his head. "There are seven deep level lines on the Underground: Bakerloo, Central, Jubilee, Piccadilly, City, Victoria and Waterloo, Northern. There are abandoned stations on those lines, it's true; Aldwych, Hidden Holborn, Brompton Road. We've used a couple ourselves when we've had to. The Velvet Underground goes much deeper than that. It's only the one line; we suspect it was bored before the rest of the Underground was made as a trial line or maybe for some military purpose. Whatever the reason, it was abandoned; probably too deep. No–one really remembers it, and the Machine Elves make sure no–one stumbled across the stations."

"Like on Praxis Street, when we kept forgetting why we were there," said Stuart.

"We got them to put in dampening around all the stations. Unless you're really focused, you'll start thinking of something else and wander straight past us. It's saved our arses more than once."

The train rattled around a bend. Stuart shook his head, standing unsteadily and grasping for one of the suede straps looped overhead. "No," he said. "No. I can't believe we're having this conversation. Machine Elves and secret tunnels. It's just too insane. What am I doing down here with you? You're mad. You're all mad."

Tyler smiled. "The only people for me are the mad ones, the ones who are mad to live, mad to talk, mad to be saved, desirous of everything at the same time, the ones who never yawn or say a commonplace thing but burn, burn, burn..."

Stuart sighed and sat down again. "Jack Kerouac. You're just quotations and slogans. You're all style and no substance. Why would I join you, for fuck's sakes?"

"Because you worship us, Stuart. Because your life's work is popular culture. Because you're the key to our success."

"Me? Why?"

"Your book, Stuart." The train slowed to pass through a green velvet station, shapes and words picked out in ornate stitching on the walls. "Brocade. Look, Stuart, the book you're writing, it might well turn out to be the most important work in modern times. No, I'm serious. It will give us the means to go global, to take the message of *pop*CULT! to an ever wider audience."

"But how do you know?" said Stuart.

"The Machine Elves told me," said Tyler. "They're very excited about you, Stuart. Monroe has an eye for these things, she brought you in to us, but it was the Machine Elves that convinced me. I've never known them so animated, so excitable. You're very important to us, Stuart. And therefore, to the enemy as well. That's why we need you to join us. Because if you don't, you might fall into their hands. And then..."

"And then..?"

Tyler shrugged, glancing out of the window as they rattled through Hemp–Weft, its thick, cable–like sculptures looming grotesquely in the dim yellow light. They sat in silence for some minutes, Stuart processing everything he had been told, Tyler drumming his fingers on his knees and whistling tunelessly. Corduroy was as Stuart had expected, brown and linear and inviting. Questions tumbled around Stuart's head, but he didn't know how to phrase them, suddenly didn't feel he had the mental toolbox to put them into words. He hunched over in the seat, his spine curving into the living question mark that he felt he had become. He opened his mouth to say something, then shut it again.

Tyler looked at him kindly. "I know, I know. It's a lot to take on board. Best thing is to just go with the flow. It's episode one of season one for you, Stuart. You're just getting to know the characters, just gleaning the plot. It'll begin to make sense soon."

The train slowed and eased to a halt. Stuart thought they had broken down and panicked a little, until he realised they had stopped at a station that was fashioned entirely from jet–black velvet. The doors slid open and Tyler beckoned him to stand.

"Void," he said, stepping out into the vague darkness. "The end of the line."

Stuart followed Tyler uncertainly into the gloom. Tyler had already moved swiftly ahead to a velvet ladder, almost invisible against the softly curving walls. "Up here," said Tyler, beginning to climb.

Stuart fell in behind him, feeling his way until his head bumped against Tyler's feet. Tyler was grunting as he pushed open a hatch in the ceiling, and the bitter stench of raw sewage made Stuart pause and exhale. Retrieving a flashlight from one of his trouser pockets, Tyler illuminated the space above and deftly pulled himself through, turning to pull Stuart up behind him.

"Jesus," said Stuart, pulling the sleeve of his jumper over his hand and covering his nose and mouth.

Tyler nodded and flashed the torch around; they had emerged on to a narrow ledge in what was evidently a major sewer tunnel. A foul soup of organic matter flowed sluggishly by, the light bouncing off visceral lumps bobbing along the sludge. There was a tinny echo of squealing and Stuart jumped as a rat scurried away from the light some feet along the ledge. Tyler motioned for him to follow and then stopped, digging into his pockets and pulling out the furry Russian hat he had been wearing earlier.

"Put this on. MacGuffin's seeded damping tech into the flaps, so pull them tight around your ears. You'll start to get some pretty wild ideas in a minute; if it feels like it's getting too much give me a shout and we'll get out."

"Tyler," said Stuart, inching cautiously along behind him. "What's this all about? Why do you keep talking about an enemy, and safe houses, and a war?"

Tyler said nothing until they had been walking for five minutes or more. Then he stopped, holding his hand up for Stuart to be silent. Stuart tried to listen but the flaps of the hat muffled pretty much everything. He thought he heard some kind of low grunting bouncing off the slime–drenched walls of the sewer, but couldn't be sure.

"We haven't much time," muttered Tyler. Stuart realised they had stopped in front of a muck–encrusted metal door set into the brick wall. "Tell me a story."

"What?"

"Give me a plot, one sentence. A novel you'd write if you had the time."

And funnily enough, Stuart had been thinking about books... stories tumbled in his head, snatches of dialogue, whole chapters. "Uh," he said. "Okay. It's about this guy who meets a girl in a bar but the next morning he doesn't want anything to do with her. Then she... she gets a job at his company, which is in quite a bit of trouble financially. This woman turns out to be a bit of a business genius and she saves the company so everyone thinks she's great. She turns into a bit of a stalker and pursues the guy, and he feels he can't knock her back straight off because she has so much influence in the company, so he applies for a transfer to another town. She follows him and tricks him into sleeping with her, disguised as someone else, and she gets pregnant... and that's about as far as I got."

Tyler reached into one of his many sidepockets and pulled out a paperback book. He shone the torch on it; it was a slim Penguin edition of *All's Well That Ends Well*. "Close enough," he said, flipping the pages. They were all blank. He tossed it into the sewage.

Stuart frowned but Tyler had already pulled a key on a leather thong from around his neck and started unlock a large padlock on the metal door. As he slid the huge bolt back, he turned to Stuart. "It is a war. A war for hearts and minds. A war for everything you, Stuart Balfour, hold dear. And this is our weapon of mass destruction. Hold on to your hat."

Tyler pulled on the door handle with both hands and it squealed protestingly, eventually giving with a shower of brick dust. As the crack widened a faint golden glow painted Tyler's face, his eyes wide and shining with something that Stuart had never seen there before, but which unnerved him to the point of wanting to tear screaming back to the hatch and the relative familiarity and safety of the Velvet Underground. Tyler suddenly looked much more than the sum of his parts; older than his thirty–odd years, more imposing than his wiry frame suggested, forged of an alloy with more depth and facets than his almost adolescent posturing belied. Stuart looked at him with a newfound respect, but for reasons he couldn't fathom.

"Look," said Tyler softly, opening the door wide.

Stuart looked.

[Stuart looked. Stuart looks. I look. The space it occupies is vast, a yawning red–brick cavern which shows evidence of having been expanded over years, of walls having been removed, floors sunk, ceilings shored up, walkways and gantries added haphazardly around the perimeter. And in the huge recess between, it sits... it glows gold and brown, like an electrical storm boiling behind a veil of dried blood, sloshing between the walls like a raging sea, a haze of phosphorescence hovering above its liquid, mutating surface like an infinite cadre of angels whipped into a crazy St Vitus dance on the heads of a million pins. Urgent pseudopodal periscopes break the surface, ebbing and flowing randomly... although not randomly, no. They sniff the air like cobra tongues, tasting the crackling space dust that roams invisible in the dank air, the raw eddies of abstract data being flushed from the city above. As the river of human shit and refuse flows contained by the brick channel behind me, so the flotsam and jetsam of all we see and hear and read and dream is sucked down, down, down to where the massive sweating bulk of the thing rolls and turns like a crippled whale trapped in the shallows. And suddenly Tyler has receded from my eyeline and they are here... seven of them, announcing their arrival with the ripping rent of celophane, unfolding their impossible geometry from within itself, downloading into my state of being and clustering around me, communicating without speaking, extracting from within me the marrow of long–dormant memories, of the subdued sensations of love and loss, of the joy and horror of life from the wail of new–birth to the cold fear of midnight.

Home.

Of dad and mum and death and the things that have been taken away, and the magma of happiness which lies beneath the memories. Of Christmas presents and Easter eggs and dinner money and Saturday morning cartoons and of dad letting go of the seat of my bike for the very first time and me wobbling along, pumping my legs and terrified and exhilarated all at once.

And in return they give something to me.

Home.

Of rioting angles and a storm of perspective, of solid emotion that you can touch, of a vast, world–sized library of feeling and thought, and of its custodians, who are like the seven who cluster around me and yet who number in their millions.

And the thing beneath us sings an anguished song of overfeeding and obesity and growth beyond nature, and its dirge hurts my eyes and it rolls again feebly and shows its soft underbelly and then I think I know what they're trying to tell me but the thought stays hidden at the core of me, unable to find the concepts to latch on to, to relate itself to and then I awake. I awoke. Stuart awoke.]

Stuart awoke. He had time to take in the fact that he was lying in an unfamiliar bed in a room he didn't know, before his stomach flipped and he leaned over the bed and noisily threw up into a plastic bowl on the floorboards. He puked and puked until the vomit slopped over the edge of the bowl and splashed over a bright rug. Stuart sank back on to the bed and focused on the smiling face of Monroe, perched on the edge of the mattress, a bottle of water in her hand.

"Hi," she said.

Stuart accepted the water from her and drunk deeply. When he had drained the plastic bottle he said, "How long have I been out? What time is it? What the hell happened?"

"You've been asleep about three hours. It's a little after one," said Monroe. "And as to what happened... you've seen *pop*CULT!."

Stuart closed his eyes. "That thing. It was real? You've seen it?"

Monroe nodded. "Twice. Tyler's pretty protective about it. I didn't expect him to show you so soon."

"But what is it?"

Monroe shrugged. "Tyler told me to take you to him when you were feeling okay. Are you?"

Stuart swung himself off the bed. "Pretty much." He looked down at his shoes. They were soaked and stinking. There was what appeared to be blood on his jeans.

Monroe led him out of her room and along the corridor to the central area, where Tyler and MacGuffin where talking in low voices, silhouetted by the glowing TVs. Tyler's left arm had been bandaged and he carried it in a sling.

"What happened to your arm?" said Stuart.

Tyler grinned. "We had a bit of hog trouble," he said. "Nothing too bad – I just picked up a flesh wound. But we had to run for it. Sorry I had to pull you out so quickly."

"I can't remember anything after seeing that... that..." Stuart stopped and rubbed his forehead. "Tyler, what was it? And what do you mean, 'hog trouble'?"

"All will be revealed, Stuart. But only if you join us."

Stuart sat heavily on the sofa. "I'm just writing a book," he said softly. "I just wanted to watch the film. Why's everything gone so weird?"

"Join us and you'll get everything," said Tyler. "The movie, the answers about *pop*CULT!... everything." His eyes flicked towards Monroe.

"What does joining you involve, exactly."

Tyler rubbed his hands together. "At last, we're getting somewhere. Well, first off you have to move in here with us."

"Move in!" said Stuart. "But I've got a flat... work to do..."

"You can do your work here," said Tyler. "And you can keep up the lease on your flat; we'll pay your rent. But if you join us, you've got to live here."

"I don't know..." said Stuart doubtfully. "What else?"

"A mission," said Tyler. "Tomorrow night. To prove yourself."

"What kind of mission?" said Stuart.

"Say yes and I'll tell you."

Stuart paused. Was it all worth it? Just for the movie? He could well write his book without it. But that thing he'd seen...

"No," he said firmly. "No, I'm not joining you. It's ridiculous. I don't know what you've done to me, what drugs you've fed me, but it's not going to work. I'll leave, if that's okay."

"Sure," said Tyler, turning away from him. "But there's no

movie, no answers, nothing. You never get to see any of us again. And don't bother trying to find us, it won't work. Given time, Stuart, you'll forget all about us. Still want to walk away?"

Stuart bit his lip. He wanted the movie and he wanted to know what he'd seen in the sewers and the thought of never seeing Monroe again was like a knot in his gut. But he also wanted his life back, the life he had before seeing that damned notice in the shop window, the visits to his mother and chats with Walter and the eternal hope that Jane would take him back.

"Yes," he said. "I want to walk away."

Tyler shrugged. "Monroe, take him home."

They cruised in silence through the quiet streets, Stuart holding on to Monroe, soaking in the feel of her body against his and the scent of her hair and the leather. He wanted her to say she was disappointed, to beg him to join them, but she said nothing until she nosed the bike into his street and stopped outside his building. In the doorway of the crack house, pin–prick lights from suspicious eyes regarded them coolly.

Monroe killed the bike and took off her helmet. Stuart shed his and handed it over to her, watching her slide it into the pannier and click it shut. "So..." he said.

Monroe smiled at him. "Don't worry about it. Our life isn't for everyone."

"I don't suppose..?" He stopped, not know what he wanted to say. *I don't suppose we could meet for a drink?*, perhaps. As though a glass of wine in a bar with him could in any way be as exciting as the life she lived.

"Stuart," she began, but he had been distracted and looked up. Had he left the lights on in his flat? It seemed unlikely. She stopped and said, "What's the matter?"

He set off for his front door, scrabbling for his keys and stamping up the stairs. The door to his flat was ajar, the lock splintered. "Oh, shit," he said.

Monroe was behind him and put a hand on his shoulder.

"Don't go in," she whispered, crouching with her hands held out in front of her. She kicked open the door and took a cat–like step over the threshold.

The flat was empty, but it had been wrecked. His books and DVDs were scattered all over the floor, the TV was off its stand, the furniture upturned. He followed Monroe in and buried his face in his hands. "Oh, bollocks," he moaned.

Monroe bent down and picked up a DVD from the carpet. Stuart distractedly noticed that it was an *Avengers* compilation, Emma Peel ready for action on the sleeve. "Is this how you see me?" she said quietly.

He fumbled in his pocket for the mobile phone. "I'd better call the police," he said.

"Wait." Monroe skipped across the room to where his PC hummed quietly, the monitor glowing. "Did you leave this on when you left home?"

Stuart joined her and tapped at the keyboard. It was gone. The book, his notes, everything. The hard drive had been wiped.

"What the fuck?" he said.

"This isn't a burglary," said Monroe. "It's Grundy."

"Grundy?"

Monroe said, "You have a copy of your work somewhere?"

"Who is this Grundy?" said Stuart, picking through the debris until he found a copy of the *Beano* annual from 1976. Inside the cover was Blu–Tacked a memory stick with his book and research backed up on it. There was also the copy of the book he'd left with Professor Garrett. It was then he remembered Garrett's vague warnings, his suggestion to get away from his flat.

"Monroe, am I in danger?" he said, hating himself for sounding so pathetic.

She nodded tightly. "Have you anywhere you can go?"

Stuart shook his head. "Is it too late to... you know?"

"Come back with me, you mean?"

Stuart nodded wretchedly. "Do you think that would be all right?"

Monroe smiled. "Come on. Let's get out of here."

171

Seventeen

The Deposition of Howard Phillips Lovecraft.

I am, by my own admission, a man of nervous disposition and as a child I was prone to frequent illness. Until a little over a year ago I lived in self–imposed hermitry that had lasted five years following certain academic failures and a freely–admitted nervous breakdown, during which time I pursued my passions of astronomy and poetry.

Indeed, it was poetry which initiated my return to the living world. A voracious reader, I often took *Argosy* magazine, but found myself increasingly angered by the continued publishing of unimaginative romances from the pen of one Mr F___ J_____. Moved one day to write, in verse, a criticism of this editorial policy, I embarked upon a lively discussion with supporters of Mr J_____ in the pages of *Argosy*. Following the printed exchanges, I came to the attention of Mr Edward F Daas who invited me to join the United Amateur Press Association, which I did in 1914, and I am in the process of producing my own journal, The Conservative, which I plan to publish on a regular periodical basis this year.

You may, of course, verify this with Mr Daas, although what I am about to relate will demand that you require no evidence further than the written testimony of my own experiences which I now humbly place before you.

You may – in fact, you will – dismiss my story as the ramblings of one who should be admitted to a sanatorium. But I assure you, every word is true. How I wish it weren't! How I wish that my eyes had never been opened to the cosmic horror that I have been forced to witness! How I wish that I had never taken a walk on the beach that fateful Fall morning towards the end of last year.

Yet walk I did. I lived then, as I do now, with my mother in Angell Street, a rather cramped house compared to our former abode, which we had to leave due to financial difficulties arising from the mismanagement of my late grandfather's finances and business affairs. Mother is ailing, and beset by many maladies, and I have considered it a not inconsiderable part of my duty to take care of her since my father died in 1898, when I was but eight years old. After ensuring she was as fit as she could expect to be for the day, I embarked upon my morning constitutional towards Narragansett Bay, where sometimes I might see seals at sport in the distant surf.

It was cold, that October morning, yet fresh and clear. I remember that I had hoped the outlook would remain fine into the evening, so that I could partake in a little stargazing after mother had retired. The beach where I preferred to walk was deserted, the cold, choppy waters pushed through Watchemoket Cove by the Atlantic tides. I found it tolerable for thinking and often composed poetry, inspired by the wild and rugged coastline I had loved since childhood. Paradoxically, I was also wary of the sea, feared the batrachian shapes I imagined swum in its inky depths, pondered the tales of civilisations long lost and their once–proud cities gone to crumbling on the briny ocean floor. From those fears grew anxiety at the wider universe beyond our own world, at the far–flung, cold reaches of space, at the sheer insignificance of our planet in the boundless wastes of lifeless galactic blackness. And if a place so huge and still incompletely charted as our own world is but a speck of dust in the universal scheme of things, what then mankind? What then one man, walking alone on an empty beach on an October morning? He is, surely, as naught. But, by and large, I managed to keep my fears and anxieties bottled up and locked away in favour of more pedestrian and workaday pursuits.

Until, that is, I met him.

At first I thought he was a seal. Out in the bay I could see a small black shape bobbing between the waves. I watched it for some moments until it sunk quietly, and I fancied it had dived in pursuit of some fish or other meal. Then it broke the surface again, and I could see it was no seal. I made out a waving arm and the wind carried a cold, distant shout. I panicked, being alone on the beach and far from any authorities I could alert as to his predicament. But he had evidently seen me and the prospect of rescue seemed to give strength to his limbs. He began to flail about in the water and, as chance would have it, the tides were on his side. As he drew closer I saw that he was using a large trunk as a flotation aid.

Within minutes he was in the shallows and managed to stagger to where the foam–flecked waves crashed on the shingle, collapsing breathless at my feet and dragging the huge oak chest behind him.

"Thank God," he whispered through cracked, black lips. "Thank God. Where am I?"

He spoke with an English accent, and appeared to be a man in his mid twenties. His hair was fair and had once been neatly cut, although it showed evidence of some weeks' growth and a lack of attention. He had a full moustache and the beginnings of a beard. His dress was merely a white shirt and shapeless mariner's trousers, and his feet were bare.

"Just outside the city of Providence, in the state of Rhode Island," I said, crouching beside him and taking his pulse, which though faint was steady. His shirt was open and the ribs poking through his chest betrayed a lack of nutrition in recent days. "In the United States region of New England."

He closed his eyes and lay his head back in the wet pebbles, and laughed. "Better than the Old England, eh?"

Then he coughed violently and expelled a quantity of sea water from his stomach. "You should receive some medical attention, sir," I said.

"No," he whispered. "No. Just a place to stay for a few days, to recuperate. Some food and water. Could I impose on you, Mister..."

"Lovecraft," I replied. "Howard Lovecraft. I live with my mother a short walk from here. Do you think you can make it?"

He rolled himself over and rose, not without effort, to a crouching position. "We need to bring this," he said, patting the trunk.

I looked doubtfully at it. "You are in no position to carry such an object, sir, and I am afraid I am not in the best of health myself. Perhaps we could send for it later."

"No," he said firmly. "It does not contain anything too heavy; in fact it is no heavier than the chest itself. It must come with me."

He stood uncertainly and took a handle at one end of the trunk. Seeing that he would not be talked out of his course of action, I took the other handle. He had been correct; the trunk barely weighed anything at all.

"Might I inquire as to your name and how you came to arrive here in such an outré manner?" I asked him as we moved off up the shingle beach.

"My name is Grundy, lately a captain in the British Expeditionary Force serving against the Boche in France," he said. "And as to how I came to be here..."

After Mr Grundy had taken a bath and been dressed in some of my clothing, I introduced him to mother and ensured she was comfortable before taking him into the kitchen and fixing him a sandwich and a pot of coffee, which he consumed greedily and without pause. The wooden trunk, on which he kept a possessive eye at all times, was stowed under the table between us. Did I imagine warmth emanating from within? Was there the faintest suggestion of movement?

"I will not impose on your hospitality longer than a few days, if that is all right," said Mr Grundy. "I have business interests in the States and will need but a short time to put them in order and obtain funds. I shall re–imburse you for your efforts."

I waved away his offer, hungry for his story. He had all but admitted that he was a deserter, fleeing his military unit following some disaster at a battle between the British and the Germans in Mons, which I believed was in France. I must confess that I had not been following closely the reports of the conflict in Europe.

"I am indebted to you for taking me in, but I have a favour to ask," he said. "No–one must know of my shame on the battlefield. I will no longer be known as Grundy on these shores. Please refer to me in future as Mr T_____ T_____.

Mr T_____ told me that after fleeing his unit he had made his way, laboriously and not without danger and adventures, towards Spain, along with other refugees from the war. From there he made his way to the coast and took passage on a ship bound for the States, albeit as a stowaway. The ship, a merchantman, was bound for Boston, and he had been discovered by the crew as it neared land. Rather than allow himself to be handed over to the authorities, Mr T_____ took the drastic step of throwing himself, and his baggage, over the side and into the cold Atlantic.

"I was half dead when you saw me," he said. "Had I not seen your figure on the beach, I might well have given up and sunk into the sea there and then."

Mr T_____ turned out to be a companionable sort. Once his strength had returned he ventured into Providence to make inquiries regarding his mysterious "business interests" at the one of the city's branches of the First National Bank. He returned from the first outing angry at the fact that the bank officials had apparently not wanted to take his word that he was who he said he was, and that they would have to wait for confirmation from their offices in Boston and Alaska before they would release the funds he believed he was entitled to. He prevailed upon me to stay a further few days, and given that he seemed an intelligent sort with an easy manner – of which I was somewhat envious – I, with mother's permission, agreed. I admit to a burning curiosity, however, regarding his mysterious chest and even – to my shame – tried the lock one afternoon when Mr T_____ was out on business. It was firmly shut and could not have been breached without leaving a trace, so I tried, rather unsuccessfully, to put it out of my mind.

One evening, when mother had retired and Mr T_____ and myself took a little brandy, I accompanied him to the yard where he liked to smoke a cheroot. It was a clear, cold night and we gazed together in silence at the stars far above us. "You have an interest in astronomy," he said, puffing on his cigar.

I nodded. I pointed out the Great Bear, and Orion, and Venus low and bright in the sky.

"Tell me, Howard," said T_____. "Do you believe that life could exist on such stars?"

I looked at him curiously. It was indeed something I thought about often, but a military man such as himself I would have thought had no time for such fancies.

"Perhaps," I said carefully. I did not know T____'s attitude to matters of faith and did not want to anger him by talking of things beyond the ken of Christian teachings. "Our sun is simply a star like those we see in the night sky; other stars may well have planets like our own Earth circling them. Some of those planets could also support life. But I would imagine it is life very different from what we know."

We contemplated the sky for a moment, then T____ said, "And could things travel the distances between stars? Could things fall to Earth?"

"Rocks very often do," I told him. "Shooting stars and meteors and the like—"

"No," he said, grinding his cheroot underfoot. "Things with... abilities. Things that can..." He sighed, shaking his head at his own inability to express his thoughts. "I think I shall retire, Howard. Good evening."

That night, the dreams began.

No sooner had I laid my head on the pillow than did sleep seem to claim me at a preternatural rate. I found myself torn from my body and danced through the night sky at speed, leaving the Earth far behind and raging ahead into the cold blackness of infinity. But I seemed to be outside of space, looking at it in its limitless entirety from some impossible vantage point. Stars swirled in a mad, chaotic dance and at the centre of it all was a boundless, blasphemous *something,* a formless, eldritch obscenity which danced blindly to the beating of some infernal, colossal drummer and the painful whining of an unseen demonic flautist. My skin prickled with loathing at the very sight of it, and when the spaces between the stars seemed to whisper its name, I retched in my dream–body and was flung back to my solid form, awaking with a half–shout and drenched in sweat. My wristwatch on the bedside table gave the time as just moments since I had turned off the lamp, and on the cool air the name *Azathoth* lingered, as though breathed by bees.

Despite my confusion, sleep was not long in coming again. This time I found myself in the deep, green abyss of the sea, fronds of alien plant–life waving in the sub–oceanic currents, a dark mass rearing up ahead of me, avoided by all submarine fauna, large and small. Drawing closer I saw it a muck–encrusted citadel, though one that could have been built by no human hand. And crowning the citadel, as though *of* it yet *separate* from it, was an abomination that was surely against anything mankind could have summoned from his darkest, deepest nightmares. It was octopoidal, yet had more in common with the dragons of myth than the real creatures of the sea bottom. Rudimentary wings sprouted from its monstrous, scaly body, and it clung to the slime–coated stone of the citadel with malign claws. I thought it dead, or sleeping, but as I drew near it opened its loathsome, pulpy eyes and regarded me with a glassy stare of such terrifying malevolence that I immediately awoke, gratified to find myself once more in bed.

The third dream took me once again far from earth, to a plain at the foot of gigantic mountains, into which was set a stupendous gate carved by huge hands. Before it swayed a column of iridescent globes that glowed with malign suggestiveness and which commanded hordes of crustaceans which scuttled towards my dream body with murderous intent.

And so on, throughout the night, until dawn came and gave my ragged mind some relief from the horrors.

Over morning coffee, T_____ regarded me most curiously as I recounted my nightmares. He questioned me most closely about whether I had suffered such dreams before he had arrived at the house, and whether I was prone to fancies and imagination. After breakfast, a telegram was delivered to the house for T_____, and he informed me that the First National was now satisfied with the financial transactions he wished to carry out, and that he would be able to remove himself from Angell Street forthwith and continue with his business, after making one or two calls in Providence that afternoon.

I was somewhat saddened at the prospect of T_____'s departure, having grown used to having a confidante in the house. Mother had recuperated enough to join us for dinner that night, and we spoke of many things, including T_____'s plans. He was intending to travel to Boston and then on to New York, then possibly to the West Coast.

We enjoyed brandy and a cheroot in the yard, until T_____ announced his intention to retire for the evening. I took myself to bed but anxiety at being claimed by further night–terrors meant sleep did not come easily. I heard the clock in the sitting room chime one, then two, and sighing I decided to return to the kitchen and make a cup of cocoa.

Passing the guest–room I noticed the door was ajar, and through the thin opening I could see T_____, resting in a deep sleep. At the foot of the bed was his mysterious trunk, which he had either kept with him at all times or locked up in the guest–room when he had to leave the house.

What impulse drew me, what spontaneous madness overcame me, I cannot tell. But slowly I opened the door further, allowing the hall light to cast a sickly yellow glow over the crate. Two steps and I was inside the guest–room, my hand hovering over the chest's catch. T_____ remained steadfastly asleep, and taking a deep breath I sprung the latch and lifted open the lid.

O, what horror! As if wrenched from one of my sweat–drenched nightmares, the *thing* within the chest was an abomination against God. It glowed from within, golden and brown, formless shapes swirling within its malevolent depths. It was neither liquid nor solid, yet some formless in–between state, writhing and turning within its wooden prison, pseudopodal structures rising and investigating its expanded surroundings. I felt sickened by the very sight of it, and my mind was crowded with the intense feeling that the room was suddenly filled with presences – presences not of this Earth! The demons and monsters from my dreams came rushing back into my head, the swirling idiot–god at the centre of the universe, the batrachian shapes swimming towards me from the murky depths, huge, bat–winged creatures able to transverse the freezing, lifeless spaces between the stars. The thing in the crate took my deepest fears and made them as flesh. And the most terrible realisation was that the thing in the crate was – impossibly, incredibly – *alive*!

I let out an involuntary cry, and within a heartbeat T_____ was awake and leaping towards me.

"You fool!" he cried, slamming shut the chest lid. The glow faded and the creature was locked away once more. But the nightmares it had summoned remained branded upon my mind.

I returned to bed as one in a daze, and slept soundly and dreamlessly. When I awoke in the morning, T_____ had gone, the chest of horrors with him, and a quantity of bank–notes left in an envelope on the dresser, an amount far in excess of what was necessary to pay his way. Despite my investigations, I could find no trace of T_____ nor did I ever see him again.

The visions summoned during his short stay, however, I do not think will ever leave me.

Attached to the manuscript is the following note from the then editor of *Argosy* **magazine:** *Dear Mr Lovecraft, While I have enjoyed your correspondence in the past and am in no doubt of your abilities, I am a little perturbed that you are presenting this story to us for use as a factual piece. While I find your ideas interesting, I am in no way inclined to risk the magazine's and my reputation by publishing it as a "true story". If I may* *be allowed to offer advice, might I suggest that you take some of the themes you have touched upon here and build upon them for future works of fiction, which could well find a home in the likes of magazines such as* Weird Tales. *Best wishes for the future.*

Eighteen

Stuart awoke from a deep sleep to find himself in a dimly–lit, bare brick room with a disorientating lack of windows. He lay in a double–bed and groped on the bedside table, from which a dull lamp cast fuzzy shadows, for his watch. Squinting at it he made out that it was almost eleven. He had returned with Monroe to *pop*CULT! at around two and had almost immediately collapsed into the bed he was shown to, which meant he had slept soundly and dreamlessly for a good nine hours. It was the best night's sleep he could remember for a long time.

Turning up the light, he surveyed his surroundings. A bathroom lay beyond a half–open door beside him, on a mezzanine floor along with his bed. Muslin drapes hid the sleeping area from the loft–style open plan kitchen–diner and living area below. Christ, it was bigger than his flat. There was a TV and DVD recorder, and an iPod docked in a Bose speaker system. In a corner by itself was a PC set–up. Only the lack of a window stopped it from being the kind of place he'd always dreamed of living in when he was clawing his way inch by broken–nail inch up the media ladder.

On the bedside table was a note: *Hope you had a good night. When you're up, come and see us – out of your door, turn right, straight along the corridor. See you then. XX M.*

Stuart pondered the significance of the two kisses and realised he was nursing a thick erection under the fabric of his boxer shorts. He stumbled into the bathroom, the note crumpled in his hand, and efficiently wanked himself off into the toilet bowl before standing under the shower until he'd washed himself something approaching clean.

Before they'd left his flat, Stuart had gathered together two small cardboard boxes of books, DVDs and a few other research materials, as well as a carrier bag containing some clothes and toiletries. As he tried his best to patch up the damage to the lock and at least make it look as though the door wasn't broken, Mrs

Zygmundewicz had opened up her door a crack, and when she had seen Stuart and Monroe she'd closed it again, slid back several bolts and unhooked two or three security chains, and emerged in hair–curlers with a large quilted dressing gown pulled around her.

"Oh, Mr Balfour!" she exclaimed. "I thought you would be never coming back. Have you had the trouble with the door?"

"Burglars, I'm afraid, Mrs Zed," said Stuart.

She clapped her hands to her mouth. "Oh! The burglars! We will all be killed in the beds. Did you get the police?"

Stuart shrugged, and said, "I'll call them tomorrow. Don't worry, I don't think they'll be back."

As he gathered his bags, a thought struck him and he scrabbled in his pocket for the mobile phone. "Look, I'm going away for a bit. Not long. Just to write the book."

"Oh, like the writer's retreats I was reading about in *The People's Friend*?"

"Yes, something like that. I've got a phone, so if my mother or Jane or someone calls, I can give you the number..."

As Stuart wrote down his number on a scrap of paper, Mrs Zygmundewicz regarded Monroe. She leaned in to him and whispered loudly, "Is this the new lady friend?"

Monroe smiled and looked away as Stuart blushed. "Ah, this is Monroe, Mrs Zed."

"A good, stout girl," said his neighbour. "Not like the stick thin ones you see in the street with the bare bellies and no backsides."

As Stuart pressed the paper into her hands, Mrs Zygmundewicz retreated into the comfort zone of her distant past. "She has the look of the girl I knew when I was the youngster, the one who's father ran the farm. The one who took me into the barn on the summer night and gave me the vodka. The one who taught me so much, before I met the husband..."

Coughing to halt Mrs Zygmundewicz's reverie in its tracks, Stuart ushered her back into her flat and told her that he would be back in no time at all. When she had shut the door, he turned to Monroe and said curiously, "Why do people seem to see different things in you?"

She smiled, her tongue dancing over her teeth. "It's my thing. It's what *pop*CULT! does for me."

"Tyler said that *pop*CULT! made you what you are. He didn't mean the group, did he? He meant that... that thing in the sewers. Monroe, what exactly is it?"

"Come on," Monroe had said. "Let's get back. I'm sure you'll get everything you want in time."

Someone had taken the liberty of laying out fresh, clean clothes across the sofa in his new quarters. Stuart held them up – utilitarian cargo pants, boots, thick socks, white T–shirts and shirts and pale knitted jumpers, all in his size. He shrugged and pulled on the trousers, a T–shirt and a dark blue fleece, locating a wardrobe back in the sleeping area and hanging the rest of the stuff up. His books and notes were still in their boxes, dumped on the floor near the PC. On a whim he turned it on, flicking through a spiral–bound notebook stuffed with newspaper cuttings and printouts from the internet while it booted up. The computer hummed to itself as a *pop*CULT! screensaver, the same typeface as the graffiti he'd seen around town, bounced slowly around the monitor.

He retrieved the disc and loaded up the work he'd already done on to his book on to the computer's hard–drive. So now he was part of *pop*CULT!, and he was expected to live here and finish his book... and then what? Then he remembered Tyler's talk of a mission, and he switched off the computer and let himself out of his room, into a stark concrete corridor. He followed Monroe's instructions and followed the corridor until it opened into the central area dominated by the pyramid of glowing TV screens, in front of which an argument appeared to be in full flow.

"Mac, I know you can do it. What I don't understand is why you're so fidgety about it."

MacGuffin rubbed his hand over his lined face. "Tyler, how many times have I got to tell you? It's not natural. The Machine Elves are anxious... can't you feel them? They know it's not right."

"Of course it's natural, Mac. I only want a bit of fog. You telling me a bit of fog on a winter's night in London isn't natural?"

MacGuffin closed his eyes and breathed deeply. "No, I'm not telling you that. The fog is natural, of course. But the fog at a time and place that you demand isn't natural at all."

Tyler sighed. Monroe was ignoring them both, watching a day–time soap on the TVs. An Asian girl in a bright pink shalwar–kameez, her nose studded with gold rings, sat cross–legged near Tyler's feet. Stuart guessed this was the latest incarnation of Karen Eliot. The Monty was the same as the one he'd seen yesterday; Luther Blissett was a statuesque black woman wearing a yellow tracksuit, her hair in tight cornrakes against her head, purple lips pursed as she watched the back–and–forth between Tyler and MacGuffin from behind opaque wrap–around sunglasses.

"So, are you telling me they're not going to do it? That *you're* not going to do it?"

Mac threw up his arms in defeat. "They'll do it. I'll do it. I just wanted you to know that they're not happy about it."

"And what about you, Mac?"

"Okay, I'm not so fired up about it either, Tyler. There are rules, you know. Parameters. Boundaries. And we're starting to cross them, to push them. And neither of us know what might happen if we push them too far."

Tyler noticed Stuart, hovering at the shadowy corridor. "We'll worry about that when it happens, Mac," he said quietly, then called, "Stuart! I trust your first night with us was a good one?"

Stuart self–consciously stepped forward. "Uh, yeah. Great. Thanks for the room... I mean, if it's my room..."

Tyler laughed. "Of course it is. Pretty cool, yeah?"

Stuart nodded. "Pretty cool. So, uh... what now?"

Tyler leaned back against the sofa. "We've got step one out of the way, Stuart. You're here. Next you've got to prove yourself to us."

"The mission?"

Tyler nodded. "The mission. Listen, Stuart, you ever done any rock climbing..?"

"You're absolutely insane," said Stuart when Tyler had outlined his plan. "I'm not climbing that."

The bean–bags and rugs in front of the TV screens had been pushed back to accommodate a huge technical drawing of the Palace of Westminster clock tower. Stuart looked at it again, and shook his head. "No. I'm not climbing Big Ben. I can't."

"You said you'd done some rock–climbing," said Tyler.

"When I was at university. A bit of bouldering in Wales. Not Big Ben."

Tyler laughed. "It'll be a breeze, Stuart. Trust me."

In the space on the other side of the sofas, a huge amount of climbing equipment was being laid out by Monty and Luther. Ropes, harnesses, helmets, ascenders, pitons, and plenty of other stuff that Stuart had no words for. Luther gave him a big, white–toothed grin and said, "Don't worry, babe, you're in safe hands."

Stuart pinched his nose between his thumb and his forefinger and counted quietly to ten with his eyes tight shut. When he opened them again, the madness hadn't gone away. "Okay," he said. "Supposing I said yes. Supposing I actually could climb Big Ben. Supposing we managed to do it without getting shot by armed police. Why would I want to?"

"It's the mission," said Tyler. "I told you that you had to come on a mission with us to prove yourself to *pop*CULT!. This is it. Do this one little thing for us, and you get everything we promised you."

Stuart looked to Monroe for help. "Are you in on this too?"

She nodded. "It really will be okay, Stuart. Once you've prepared."

"Prepared!" shouted Stuart. "But you want to do this tonight. It would take me a month of preparation. No, a year of preparation. I can't just go out and climb Big Ben in... in..."

"In three hours," said Tyler.

"Oh, God," said Stuart, sitting down heavily. "I'm in the company of mad people."

"Right," said Tyler, crouching over the drawing. "Are we all aware of our positions? Me, Monroe, Luther and Stuart will be doing the climb. We'll be free–climbing for the first thirty feet or so; the whole tower is about three–hundred and sixteen feet tall, but we'll only be climbing as far as the clock–faces, which are about two hundred feet off the ground. Once we get as far as we can by free–climbing we'll be ramming some pitons into the architecture and using the ropes for the rest of it."

"The clock–tower's limestone," said Monty. "Just like the rock–faces you climbed in Wales, Stuart. And that Victorian gothic architecture means there are plenty of hand–holds and crevices. It'll be a walk in the park."

Tyler pulled out a blown–up photocopy of the A–Z. "We'll be going over this security fence here, near the junction of Parliament Square and Whitehall. Karen and Monty will be on this rooftop over here, where the newsagents and souvenir shop is on the ground floor. They'll be organising our escape route."

"Wait a minute," said Stuart. "If we're here..." – he jabbed the map – "... and they're here, how the hell is that going to help us escape? If we're going up Big Ben, the only way we can escape is to come down it, right?"

Tyler grinned. "Wrong. This is going to be spectacular, Stuart. This is going to be audacious. People will be talking about this for days."

Tyler stood and stretched his bare arms in front of him. "MacGuffin will remain here to co–ordinate the operation. How's my little diversion coming along, Mac?"

MacGuffin stood from the computer screen he had been working on, his eyes puffy and his complexion sallow. "As you

187

wished, Tyler. But like I said, they're not happy."

Tyler shrugged. "And the other stuff?"

MacGuffin tossed over a small bottle which Tyler caught deftly and unscrewed. He emptied into his palm four large capsules in green and white. "Excellent. We might as well take this now."

Stuart suspiciously scrutinised the pill that Tyler handed him. "What is it?"

"This is what's going to get you up Big Ben," said Tyler, accepting a bottle of water from Karen and gulping down his capsule. "Take it now."

"What's in it?" asked Stuart as Tyler handed the water over to him.

"Just a little something MacGuffin cooked up. Look, it's not going to fuck your head. It's not Copyright. You'll feel better about the mission once you've had it."

Stuart closed his fingers around the tablet. "I need a few minutes to think about this. Can I make a phone–call?"

Tyler glanced at Monroe. "Who to? We've got a bit of a policy here, Stuart. Nothing is allowed that would bring people to *pop*CULT!. I'd need to know who you're phoning, and why."

Stuart frowned. "Am I some kind of prisoner here?"

Tyler laughed again. "Not at all. But we need to protect our interests. It's a fair question."

"Okay. I just want to talk to Walter. See if he's okay."

"The guy who you came with when you were looking for us?" asked Tyler.

"Uh, yeah," said Stuart. "How did you know we were there?"

"*pop*CULT! has eyes everywhere," said MacGuffin.

Tyler said, "You've still got your mobile. Give him a call. Just don't tell him where you are."

Stuart retreated into a quiet corner and fumbled with the phone until it brought up Walter's number. He let it ring for some time before sighing and killing the connection. Walter had obviously got over his agoraphobia. He was about to return to the group when, on a whim, he jabbed Jane's number in. She answered after three rings.

"Jane."

"Stuart," she said guardedly. "Hi. Are you all right?"

"Of course," he said. "Why wouldn't I be?"

"No reason," said Jane, and he registered the puzzlement in her voice. "Just a turn of phrase. What can I do for you?"

"Jane, where did it all go wrong for us?"

She sighed. "Stuart, have you been drinking?"

"No. No, I just wondered. What was it about me that made you want to leave?"

"Stuart... we've been through all this a thousand times. Are you sure you aren't drunk?"

"Please, Jane. It's important."

"Look," she said sternly. "I'm only having this conversation because Quentin's out at his dad–to–be class." Stuart snorted and she ignored him. "You've got to accept that it's over, Stuart, and it's over for any number of reasons. But probably the chief one among them is the fact that you never do anything."

"I'm sorry? What do you mean?"

"You've always been happy to let life lead you by the nose, Stuart. You've never done anything you didn't fall into by accident. Christ, we'd never have got together if I hadn't asked you to go for a drink. You've lived your whole life being pushed into one thing and pulled into another. You've surrounded yourself with tat and trivia. Everything you hold dear is just rubbish, Stuart, unimportant crap. You're only happy if you've got your nose in a book or watching some old TV show. You're a voyeur, Stuart. A spectator. An audience looking for a drama. I just wanted a leading man for a change, that's all."

There was a silence as Jane got her breath back. Stuart was stunned. He took the phone away from his red–raw ear and looked at it before gingerly placing it back there. "Jesus," he said.

"Well, you asked," said Jane flatly. "And please don't tell me you can change, Stuart, because it's too late for that and I don't think you can anyway. Look, I'd rather you didn't call me again."

"Jane..." he said, not knowing whether he was trying to hide the anguished desperation in his voice or whether he was laying it on even thicker.

"Stuart," she said, more kindly. "Look, I just want to get on with my life. Why don't you do the same?"

He listened for some seconds to the harsh, empty air of the dead connection, then pocketed the phone. He looked back to where Tyler, Monroe and the others were looking expectantly at him.

"Well?" said Tyler as Stuart returned.

He opened his hand and inspected the pill one last time before popping it into his mouth and forcing it down with three gulps of water.

For a long moment, nothing happened. Then Stuart was slapped with a vertiginous upending of his senses. He stumbled and steadied himself on the back of the sofa, his skull buzzing like a hive of angry bees. "What the fuck..?" he began and then realised he was conjuring up memories of things he was pretty sure he'd never done, such as hauling himself up the outside of buildings in the middle of London and vaulting over chimney stacks on rain–slicked rooftops. He felt something expand within him, as though a store of knowledge was being filled up. His fingers itched to stroke rough, bare stone, his toes curled and longed to be gripping the merest of crevices.

"Woah," he said slowly as information downloaded into his mind. "I know crampons..."

Tyler watched him with his arms folded, his chin resting on one hand. "Show me."

Clenching his fingers, Stuart walked to the bare brick wall. He ran the tips over the brick–work, sensing the places where mortar had long–since fallen away, working out the reach between potential hand–holds, looking for a starting place. Tucking his toes into a broken brick four rows up from the floor, he hauled himself up, his fingers rammed into a line of rotted pointing. His left foot sought for a slight bump on another brick and he propelled himself up to where a jagged lump of plaster afforded another grip. Within minutes he was fifteen feet up. He looked down to where Monty was applauding and Tyler smiling smugly.

"Awesome," said Luther.

Monroe smiled.

"Game on," said Tyler, laughing. "Game on."

Nineteen

The light was failing when twenty–seven officers from the Metropolitan Police converged singly, and in twos and threes, at an office block which, from its uppermost floors, afforded views of the Thames and Canary Wharf. Although in civilian clothing, most of them had already worked a full shift; some of them were on annual leave, others not on duty that day. One or two were on long–term sick. They exchanged brief nods as they filed towards the reception desk in the neutral lobby of the building. The receptionist was blonde, young and pretty, and attracted a private, business–like appraisal of her shaggability from the every single man of the twenty–seven. Each of them was handed a blank name–badge with "delegate" inscribed upon it, and directed towards the lifts which would take them to the fifteenth floor.

They dutifully waited at the lifts, filling the carriages up six at a time and travelling in silence to the appointed floor, where another receptionist indicated they should enter a bright, airy waiting room decorated in cream and brown. There were leather seats lined around the windows and a table was adorned with small snacks, a water cooler, bottles of whisky, vodka and gin and cans of lager.

Some of the men knew each other well. Some were sleeping with the wives of others. Some were superiors and some were subordinates. But in accordance with the instructions they received, they engaged in no small talk other than the slightest nods and greetings, merely gathering drinks and food and standing by the windows, watching the lights come on across London.

After fifteen minutes or so, the receptionist entered and asked the men to follow her through the double doors on the other side, which opened into a smaller room in which chairs were ranked before a screen set up for a presentation. A smaller door at the far side of the room was closed. The twenty–seven off–duty police officers settled themselves in the chairs and waited.

192

As darkness proper fell over the capital, the smaller door whispered open and a large, hairless man stepped softly across the brown carpet to the screen and regarded the faces of the men assembled before him.

"Gentlemen. My name is George, and I represent Mr Grundy, who shall be with us in a moment. I would like to thank you all for coming here this afternoon."

"And thank you for the overtime," called out one of the younger men.

George nodded and smiled slightly, breaking the atmosphere that was strained over the room like a film. He knew that Mr Grundy liked the men to be efficient and of a businesslike manner at all times, but he also knew that men of the type which he was dealing with very often needed to be allowed to let off steam occasionally, and he was happy for them to do that before Mr Grundy arrived.

"So, what have you got for us, George?" said a man whose face was composed of angles and regimented, cropped hair. "Whose arses need kicking?"

"Whose heads, more like," said the man who had spoken first, and there was an exhalation of air, a release of pressure, one or two laughs.

George held up his hands in a mock appeal for calm. "Mr Grundy will explain fully. Needless to say, you have been hand–picked for this assignment because it is of the utmost importance. Mr Grundy is keen for this endeavour to go without any hitch whatsoever. Which is why he shall be sanctioning the use of firearms."

There was a growling whisper around the room, one or two surprised faces, more eager smiles.

"Is this about those fucking hippies?" asked a man as large as George, with thin eyes hidden under a frowning brow.

George nodded. "I don't think it would be stealing too much of Mr Grundy's thunder to say, yes, it does indeed involve the group of criminals who like to be known as *pop*CULT!."

George turned as Escobar popped his head around the door and stuck up his thumb. George cleared his throat and said, "Now, gentlemen, Mr Grundy will address you."

There was hard, no–nonsense applause as Mr Grundy, immaculate in a grey suit, walked with purpose across the room and took his place at the screen. George seated himself at a small table to one side, on which a laptop hummed quietly, poised for the presentation.

Mr Grundy closed his eyes and shook his head at the applause, smiling quietly to himself. "Please, gentlemen, please," he said. "Such a welcome should be reserved for yourselves. After all, it is heartening to know that you can still find a policeman in London should you need one."

When the laughter had died down, Mr Grundy clasped his hands behind his back and surveyed the officers, as though gathering his thoughts. Eventually he said, "Many of you will be familiar with my ongoing battle against a group of anarchist terrorists operating in London – indeed, many of you will have been imposed upon by me in the past with regards to hitherto unsuccessful attempts to curtail their noxious activities."

There was a general consensus of agreement in the room. Mr Grundy continued, "Largely, they carry out childish pranks and student japes. However, it is my belief that these activities are merely a smokescreen to disguise their true purpose, to wit the planning of an atrocity that threatens our very way of life in this country.

"Perhaps some of you might be wondering why I do not simply turn over my files to the appropriate authorities and let justice take its course."

Mr Grundy paused, knowing full well that the amounts of money currently landing in each man's bank account ensured that no such questioning of his motives would ever take place. Still, he went on, "The reason is simply this, gentlemen: I know full well that at the heart of this group is a dangerous individual who would use every resource at his disposal to evade the might of the

British establishment and, sadly, he is quite capable of doing so. Is there a man here who has not been frustrated at the vagaries of the British judicial system which has allowed nothing better than scum to walk free from the courts thanks to a mere technicality or the weasel words of a liberal viper?"

There was not. Mr Grundy, however, had a confession to make. "And I must admit to a desire for my own advantage in this venture, I am afraid. *pop*CULT! has something that I want to make use of for myself. Should this item fall into the hands of the authorities, I am very much concerned that it should not be used to its full capacity for the good of the British people. If any man finds my motives lacking, then I quite understand, and he is free to remove himself from this room and take no further part in the evening's activities. The monies already paid shall, of course, stand."

Mr Grundy surveyed the room. No–one moved. Mr Grundy smiled. "Now," he said. "Before George briefs you as to the fine points of the mission, does anyone have any general questions I can help them with?"

A detective inspector with a scar across the bridge of his nose raised his hand. He grinned viciously and said, "Did someone mention guns?"

"This is the man you need to watch out for," said George, stepping back to allow the officers to scrutinise the photograph on the screen.

"Pretty boy," said one of the men.

George looked at the photograph, a grainy, night–time shot taken at a vertiginous angle, but nevertheless allowing a decent view of the wild, blond hair and the angular, tanned face.

"Tyler," said George. "Other aliases used on occasion, but that should suffice for you. He's the head of *pop*CULT!, the driving force. The rest will look to him for direction and guidance."

"So we take him out and the whole group collapses?" said a thin man with a cracked voice.

Mr Grundy, who had been sitting on one side, coughed. "Theoretically, yes, Robert. But in practice, no. I apologise for any inconvenience caused to you gentlemen, but I'm very much afraid that I must insist that Tyler is taken alive."

The man grunted and George continued, bringing up a new photograph on the screen. "MacGuffin. Older, in appearance at least, than the rest. Should not put up much of a fight. Is dangerous in other ways, however, and should not be allowed to get too close to any computer equipment or anything resembling pills and medicines."

The next picture was a blurred photograph of a woman in dark glasses and a long coat, striding through a busy shopping street in central London. Someone let out a low whistle.

"Monroe. Good hand–to–hand combat abilities, has knowledge of sidearms and other weapon use. May initially be confusing because of her appearance; it isn't solid or fixed. Disable early to avoid any threat of disorientation."

George clicked off the picture and on to a shot of the *pop*CULT! graffiti on an inner–city wall. He said, "There will be at least three others present: Luther Blissett, Karen Eliot and Monty Cantsin. It is pointless showing you the images we do possess for these three because the people who inhabit the roles shift on a regular basis."

The photo changed again, this time to a clear shot of Stuart at the university. "Stuart Balfour is an associate of *pop*CULT!, and our intelligence leads us to believe he may be spending time with them, and possibly on–site when we go in. He is to be treated as the other members of the group, aside from Tyler."

"Which is?" asked one of the officers.

George glanced at Mr Grundy and inspected his notes. "Collateral damage. We would prefer it if they were not in a position to cause us any further trouble after this evening."

"What about the woman? Monroe?" said someone else.

George shrugged. "The same."

"Shame."

George smiled thinly. "What you do with her before you silence her is your business, gentlemen, so long as it does not jeopardise Mr Grundy's plans."

As the murmuring peaked and faded, George brought up a road map showing Praxis Street. "This is the target. It is slightly unusual; you will all be given printouts of this map with the entrance to the premises clearly marked. You might find yourself forgetting why you are there; please remain focused and refer to your briefing notes if this happens. If you stay in groups of four or more at all times the technology they are using should not cause problems; it is designed to put off casual passers–by, not an organised force such as this."

George glanced at his watch. "Now, gentlemen, if you would like to accompany Escobar into the next room, he will outfit you all with the necessary clothing, weapons and equipment for tonight's mission."

As the men filed through at Escobar's behest, Mr Grundy brought up the photograph of Tyler on the screen again. "Do you think I am being overly sentimental, George, in requesting that they spare his life?" he said quietly.

George paused, considering his response. "He is family, after all, Mr Grundy."

The other man nodded sadly. "And, as we are all aware, we cannot choose our family, George. Although we can, of course, choose our friends. You are a good friend, George."

George fidgeted awkwardly as he switched off the laptop and began to clear away the presentation equipment. *That's because you pay me well* seemed a rather inappropriate response, because although it was true, George did in fact care a great deal for Mr Grundy. He struggled to find something to say; although he felt himself very eloquent on the written page, sometimes the right words failed him when a verbal response was called for. Thankfully, Mr Grundy saved him by merely patting him on his thick bicep and saying, "Perhaps you should supervise Escobar with the equipment, George. I want all those firearms logged out and accounted for at the end of the night. Boys and their toys, and all that."

"Very good, Mr Grundy," said George as his boss wandered towards the lift.

197

It was close to seven when George and Escobar were satisfied that they had briefed and kitted out the twenty–seven off–duty officers of the Metropolitan Police to what they believed would be Mr Grundy's satisfaction. George felt a slight tremor of anticipation run through his body; was this actually going to be the night that Mr Grundy's plans came to fruition, and they succeeded in smashing *pop*CULT! and claiming the entity for themselves? It had felt like they had been fighting a war of attrition for so long that any kind of progress no longer seemed viable. And yet, everything could change by tomorrow morning. London might awake to truly a new dawn, one with Mr Grundy at the controls rather than Tyler and his rag–tag mob.

The men were getting tense and impatient to be off. George understood that they were a necessary part of Mr Grundy's plans, but he could not help but find them brutish and distasteful. In George's hands violence was a beautiful thing; with a knife for a bow and a fresh human body for a violin, he could create beautiful music which would not be forgotten in a hurry. But these policemen with their boots and fists and grunting, animal lust could not be described in the same breath as George. They were poles apart. They were a stampeding herd of fools, while he was an artist.

Mr Grundy would want to inspect the men before they departed. George and Escobar were to accompany them as far as Praxis Street and then wait in Escobar's car, watching the proceedings through a video link via a camera carried by one of the officers, just so that George could intervene should the officers look like they were about to disobey Mr Grundy's orders. George had suggested to Mr Grundy that he allow one of the other members of the group to be taken alive; it was unlikely that Tyler would give up the location to the entity willingly and given he was of the same blood as Mr Grundy this was a potential weakness in the plan should Mr Grundy balk at allowing George to extract the information via torture. Mr Grundy had at last relented and ordered that the woman, Monroe, be captured as well. There was some disgruntlement from those among the police officers who had intended to visit indignities upon her. Mr Grundy had assuaged them by saying the men could still have her so long as she was left alive. George, frankly, found the whole thing distasteful, and secretly hoped the woman would perhaps die of a bullet well before she could be captured alive by the police officers.

The officers were now clothed pretty much as a Met armed response team would be, minus the insignia. The body armour and black trousers and close–fitting jumpers would ensure that any members of the public who saw them would assume it was a regular operation. Each man was equipped with a Glock 17 self–loading pistol, while one in four carried a Heckler and Koch MP5 carbine rifle – all standard S019 issue. Now they lounged around drinking coffee and getting quietly psyched. One or two watched a TV in the corner, some late–afternoon show fronted by a loud, vulgar celebrity accompanied by clashing colours and discordant music. Precisely the sort of thing that would die a long–overdue death when Mr Grundy took control of the entity in the sewers. George was looking forward to the new world order. It promised to be a lot quieter.

The programme was interrupted by a "breaking news" banner. As the pictures unfolded on the screen, there was a sharp intake of breath in the room; George decided it was time to alert Mr Grundy.

When George had arrived on Mr Grundy's private floor and the lift doors whispered open, his boss was already watching the newsflash on a plasma screen television on the wood–panelled wall. He turned, his face breaking into a broad smile.

"Oh, this is excellent, George. It couldn't have been planned any better. Tyler has practically handed us his own head on a plate."

"Should I mobilise the men, Mr Grundy?"

"Oh, I think so, George, don't you? Tyler will be strutting like a peacock after this. No doubt they'll be indulging in a celebration when they return to their headquarters. Their defences shall be down. Let's gate–crash their little party, shall we?"

Twenty

The bus driver regarded them coolly. "Fancy dress party, is it?"

Tyler dropped a handful of pound coins on the tray. "Children in Need, innit? Four for Parliament Square, please."

As the tickets printed out, the driver frowned. "That's not until next week."

"Early start," said Tyler, leading them along the aisle to the back of the bus, where he dumped his rucksack on an empty seat and sat down beside it. Stuart did the same, his face burning at the glances from the other passengers for once abandoning the London practice of totally ignoring anyone else breathing the same public transport air as themselves. He glanced at his reflection in the night–blackened bus window. Thankfully, the mask hid his blushes. And besides, most people were staring openly at Monroe.

She sat herself across the aisle from him, squeezing her long, bare legs in besides her own back–pack. She wore the smallest of red briefs, an impossibly–tight white T–shirt with that famous "S" symbol stretched across her breasts, red leather boots and a small cape.

Behind Supergirl was Luther, who attracted not a few admiring glances herself, poured into a purple leather catsuit. "Hope you're going to change those stilettos for something a bit more practical, Catwoman," said Tyler.

Luther patted her bag. "Got my climbing shoes in here."

Stuart looked down at himself. He didn't fill the green and grey one–piece costume half as well as Tyler did his Batman outfit. It came with the over–sized domino mask, but the way his gut pushed out and the logo lay almost concave on his chest didn't fill him with much self–pride. Still, it could have been worse; at least the Green Lantern costume covered the whole of his body. At least he wasn't dressed as Robin to Tyler's Dark Knight.

"Tell me again why we're dressed as comic book characters," he hissed.

Tyler sighed. "We're about to break into the Mother of Parliaments and climb one of the most famous landmarks in the world. There are going to be armed police on our arses before we're out of the range of a pea–shooter. We're going to have rucksacks on our backs. What would you rather we dress as, Brazilian electricians?"

Stuart had to admit he had a point, although he still wasn't convinced they had to dress as anything. However, he secretly thought the costumes were pretty neat.

"It also why Karen's on rescue duty rather than in the first team," said Tyler. "Cops see an Asian face among us, they're not going to give us second chances. Besides, there aren't too many Asian super–heroes."

"Was Catwoman black, by the way?" asked Luther.

"You could count Eartha Kitt in the Sixties TV series," mumbled Stuart. "And Halle Berry in that movie a few years ago. But in the comics, not as far as I know." His heart was beating to fuck. He was certain he had to do this, but wasn't particularly sure why. All he knew was that it was time to stop watching and time to start doing. At the same time, he was running through the climbing moves that had suddenly, madly, implanted themselves in the core of his being. It was as though climbing was as familiar and ingrained to him as riding a bike, or writing his own name. After studying Tyler's close–up photographs of the clock–tower, he somehow instinctively knew how to get started, where to put his hands and feet, how to haul himself up and use his momentum to keep moving. In a strange way he was actually looking forward to all of this.

Earlier, Stuart had asked what was in the pill, why he now had these abilities. Tyler had simply said, "*pop*CULT!."

"No," said Stuart. "I don't mean what's in the pill in a philosophical or metaphysical sense, I mean what's actually in the pill?"

"*pop*CULT!," said Tyler again.

"You don't actually mean... bits of that thing?" Stuart felt a bit sick.

"Same as Copyright," said Tyler. "There's a little bit of *pop*CULT! in all of us, you know."

"But it... isn't it alive?"

"Possibly," said Tyler. "But not in any sense that we know."

Stuart's mind was whirling. "You can download abilities from it, presumably by... what? Chucking a couple of copies of *Rock Climbing Monthly* in to it?"

Tyler smiled as might a special needs teacher over a particularly backward child who had just mastered some basic concept. "Pretty much."

"But the possibilities are endless," said Stuart. "The potential applications... we could all be brain surgeons or airline pilots or... or..."

"Or soldiers," Monroe had said. "Or assassins. Or spies."

"Ah," said Stuart. Suddenly he saw.

"Or," said Tyler, smiling, "super–heroes." Then he'd unveiled their costumes.

Tyler pushed the bell. "Here we are. Please remember to collect all your belongings before exiting the vehicle."

They filed down the aisle, the packs over their shoulders. Luther and Monroe earned a couple of wolf whistles. As the bus slowed and the doors sighed open, Tyler turned to the passengers, raised his fist and yelled, "RIGHTS-4-PARENTS!"

"What the hell was that about?" hissed Stuart.

"Cover story," said Tyler. "Look in your bag."

Stuffed in the top of Stuart's pack were dozens of leaflets, each headed RIGHTS–4–PARENTS. They read: *We are all parents who, through no fault of our own, are not allowed to see our sons and daughters. We are carrying out this high–visibility protest to raise awareness of our plight and that of thousands of British parents like us who, up to now, have not had a voice. Please support our cause by taking this leaflet home and signing our online petition, details below.*

It all clicked into place. "Like the guys who climbed up Buckingham Palace and Tower Bridge," said Stuart slowly.

"And did they get shot by armed police?" asked Tyler sweetly. "Now, start handing 'em out."

The bus stop was busy, and a few passers–by had slowed to take in the spectacle. A couple of cars honked and Monroe waved at them. Stuart took his eyes off her backside and started giving the leaflets to the people waiting at the bus stop.

"I think what you're doing is brill," said a Welsh man with a black beard, folding up the leaflet. "I ain't seen my little girl in two years."

"We should be on CCTV by now," said Tyler. "They'll be coming round to check us out. I reckon we've got about thirty seconds. Go!"

Big Ben was separated from the road by a black, wrought–iron fence, which rose to encompass a stone gate–house right where they were standing. Tyler and Stuart pushed their backs against the gates and knotted their fingers, creating stirrups for Luther and Monroe to step into. The fluidity of the move surprised Stuart; it was though they had rehearsed it a hundred times. Grunting, he pushed upwards with all his strength, propelling Monroe upwards. For a moment she hung in the air, Supergirl to Luther's Catwoman, then they both grabbed the railings and deftly vaulted to the flat top of the stone gate–house.

A fraction of a second behind Tyler, Stuart turned and began to scale the gates. He certainly wasn't any fitter than he had been yesterday, but he seemed to know how to use his body better, how to knit gravity and kinetic energy to create a seamless movement that brought him, scrabbling and suddenly ungainly, to the top of the gates. Monroe hauled him up and he chanced a look backwards; the passengers waiting at the bus–stop were staring and pointing and cars were slowing to get a better look.

"Come on," hissed Tyler, leaping down to the other side, where the clock–tower reared up above them, illuminated in cold yellow light. Stuart, Luther and Monroe followed suit, dropping cat–like to the ground and racing towards the limestone tower. Stuart heard the slap of shoe–leather on wet stone.

"They're on their way," said Tyler. "Stuart, climb!"

Tyler's plan was to have Stuart and himself go first with Luther and Monroe following, on the basis that any trigger–happy cops would probably be distracted by the site of Catwoman's leather–clad arse and Supergirl's tiny briefs for just long enough to make them think twice about shooting. On the one hand, Stuart was suspicious of Tyler's motives and didn't feel very gallant in having Luther and Monroe acting as a human shield; on the other, he was acutely aware that within seconds there were going to be guns trained on his back and anything that was between him and them was quite welcome.

"Thirty feet then we switch to the ropes," grunted Tyler, taking a grip on the stonework and hauling himself up. Stuart brushed his fingers across the limestone. It felt welcoming to him, like his natural environment. He could sense the very whorls of his finger–tips slotting in with the faintest ridges of the stone, creating friction and a strange, preternatural attraction. Taking a firm hold of the ridged masonry he placed the rubber sole of his boot against the tower and launched himself into the climb.

Stuart had become almost weightless, but he barely noticed. The wind, the dampness, the road traffic, even the shouts from the police and security guards, who must have been just around the corner now, were lost to him. His world had condensed to the expanse of stone cladding that dominated his sight–line, the fine grain of the limestone magnified to infinity, his senses super–clarified so that his fingers were reaching for the next hand–hold even as his eyes identified it and his feet pushed him outwards and up, the laws of physics seemingly sidelined and forgotten as his body arced at impossible angles while he made vertiginous leaps of faith.

"This is the police. Stop climbing, I repeat, stop climbing. Stay where you are."

The voice was tinny and seemed very far away. For a moment

Stuart's exhilaration lurched and he almost faltered, almost felt the inevitable thud of the bullets into his back. "Keep going," said Tyler. "Don't look at them."

Stuart couldn't help himself. Casting a glance downwards, he saw Luther and Monroe right on his heels, almost waiting for his feet to move so they could claim the holds. Beyond them, maybe ten feet down, were the heads of five police officers, their firearms matt black shapes against their uniforms. One was holding a megaphone. "Shit," he breathed, and snapped back to the clock–tower.

They kept climbing until Tyler, who had pulled ahead by a good body length, called, "Belay!"

Stuart reached him and hung on, suddenly feeling drained. Luther and Monroe were behind them almost instantly, Monroe cheekily flapping her cape with one hand and wiggling her backside at the officers.

"We are armed and demand that you desist immediately and return to the ground," sounded the loud–hailer.

"We're going to be fucking shot!" whispered Stuart harshly.

Tyler, who had swung his pack off one shoulder and was rooting in it with one hand, said, "Just throw them some leaflets down. It'll be fine."

As Tyler deftly pulled on a harness belt hanging with pitons and caribiners then began to clip a rope from his pack to one of the hooks, Stuart awkwardly reached into his own rucksack and tossed a handful of leaflets outwards. They fluttered down to where the police stood. Sirens wailed close by, and quite a crowd had gathered on the pavement beyond the fence. There was a beeping noise and Luther freed one hand and tapped a Bluetooth earpiece inside her mask.

"That was Mac," she said. "He's spoken to the TV and press; they're on their way."

"Excellent," said Tyler. "I'm going to go up; Stuart, get your harness on and run this rope through it. If I fall before I've hammered a couple of pitons into the cracks, then fucking brace yourself."

The police had been poring over the leaflets, and the megaphone crackled into life again. "RIGHTS-4-PARENTS, please cease now. This is not the way to make your protest. There are proper channels you can go through."

Stuart relaxed a little. Tyler was right; no–one ever shot a disgruntled dad who couldn't see his kids. He looked out across Parliament Square as two police vans hoved into view. Behind them was an outside broadcast unit from *London Tonight*.

He felt a tug on the rope. "Climb on," shouted Tyler. Agile as a lizard, he'd made his way another twenty or so feet up and was resting, loosely hanging from the edge of the clock tower. Stuart began to zone in on the stone again, as Monroe began her own climb just behind him.

"You okay?" she said as she drew level. Stuart nodded, trying not to take his eyes off the stonework. Just because climbing came naturally to him now, it didn't mean he wasn't scared shitless, nearing fifty feet from the ground.

As he reached where Tyler was resting, the wind whipped around the edges of Parliament, threatening to unbalance him. The climb was getting tougher now, Stuart's fingers feeling the cold. He dipped into the bag of chalk hanging from his harness and rubbed his fingers together.

"Don't worry," said Tyler, preparing to move off again. "Now we're roped together we shouldn't be able to fall very far. It won't be long now."

Stuart hung himself out as far as he dared and looked up to where the face of Big Ben glowed impossibly large, like a huge harvest moon. Something so intrinsically obvious suddenly occurred to him that he felt a little dizzy with stupidity. "Tyler," he called at the retreating red trunks above him. "What exactly do we do when we get to the top?"

Tyler tossed a grin down at him and said, "Wait and see."

While Stuart belayed he glanced up at Monroe, who had overtaken him and was rapidly catching up to Tyler. Even now, he thought, even hanging off the side of Big Ben with guns trained on my head, I'm still stealing sly glances at her arse and nursing an inappropriate erection. Jesus Christ.

Luther drew level and paused, catching her breath. "Smile," she said. "We're on Candid Camera."

Stuart looked down. There were at least three camera crews filming from Parliament Square, and the flash–bulbs of press photographers popped like fireworks around them. Making sure his mask was in place, he nodded at Tyler's "climb on!" and began to drag himself up, feeling for the pitons that Tyler had driven into the stone cladding. There was going to be hell to pay for this, one way or another. If they didn't get shot they'd at least be charged with trespass and criminal damage. Stuart thanked God no–one knew it was him up there.

Half–way up the next section, after another belay and a round of threats from the police megaphones, Stuart got the fear. The weight of London abruptly pressed down on his back as he realised just how much of it there was out there, all behind him. His legs buckled and his left foot slipped from its housing. He pulled backwards, the rope spitting tight, and for one dizzying moment the cityscape swirled around his eyeline until Monroe grabbed his forearm and brought him back to equilibrium.

"Oh Jesus oh Christ oh fuck," he gabbled. "I can't do this I can't do this get me down."

"It's okay," soothed Monroe into his ear. "You can do this. I know you can."

Stuart steadied himself, trying to ignore the world roaring and flashing around him, and focused his mind on strengthening his fingers and stopping his legs shaking. He took a ragged breath and managed, "I'm fine. I'm fine."

By the time he got moving again, they were a matter of ten feet from the clock–face. The minute hand was about to hit twelve; the hour hand on five. "Stay where you are," shouted Tyler. "This is going to be fucking crazy."

Twenty One

SS Arcadia
Somewhere near Gibraltar
February 16 1957

Dear Ellen,

I'm writing this on the boat, which is silly – I won't be able to post it until we dock at Tangier, by which time I'm sure I'll have much more to tell you. But I wanted to write a letter at sea – it's so romantic!

I can't believe Andre Deutsch has sent Carl all the way to Africa to hand over a cheque – and that they've paid for me to go with him as well! Carl says they're a super company and that I should try to get a job with them – they're always looking for secretaries and girls for the typing pool. I told him that it wouldn't be a good idea – how would he be able to keep his eyes off me and do important work like editing manuscripts and commissioning cover art if I was sitting in the typing pool? He just said "hmmm". Sometimes he's such a cold fish, Ellen.

The plan is to visit this Jack character at his hotel, stay in Tangier for a couple of days, then come back via Gibraltar. It's so nice to have a bit of sun in February, Ellen – I'm sure it's just beastly for you in London at the moment. Gibraltar was quite pleasant – Carl took me for a Valentine's Day meal, just as you predicted. However, he didn't propose, so that's half a crown you owe me! Maybe next year..?!

Anyway, better go. Carl's being violently sick again – he certainly hasn't found his sea legs yet!

Lots of Love,

Joy

Muniria Hotel
Tangiers
February 18 1957

Dear Ellen,

Forget what I said about the sun in February – I wish I was back in London, sleet and wind or not. It's just too hot here in Tangiers. And dusty. I feel parched all the time, and wish I could just come down to the Traveller's Rest with you and the girls for a shandy. You honestly can't walk down the street on your own here – well, I suppose the boys can, but not girls. The Arabs make this clicking noise with their tongues, like they're calling a dog or something. The cheek of it! I wore my shorts on the first day but I've been covering up in public since then – won't make the same mistake twice! It would have been quite frightening if Carl hadn't been with me.

The Muniria Hotel is where this writer, Jack, is staying, so we've got a room there too. It's a little basic, but what you'd expect for a place that seems to have become some kind of artists' and writers' retreat. The smell of what Carl reliably informs me is hashish (how would he know!?) hangs in the air, and the rooms are dreadfully hot in the day, and bitterly cold at night.

The writer was terribly pleased with his cheque from Andre Deutsch – £150, which he says could buy him half a year in Tangiers. He's an odd sort – quite handsome, with strong features and dark hair, a little stocky. He's 35 but acts younger – very enthusiastic. His book's called *On The Road*, so you'll have to watch for it. There are others here, a slightly creepy old man called Bill who lives a couple of floors down from Jack, and they're waiting for the poet Allen Ginsberg – they were quite impressed when I said I'd heard of him! There's another writer as well, who lives on the same floor as Jack. His name's Tom and he seems very sweet. He's British but has spent a lot of time in the States. He has this intense look in his eye and seems to drift off into other worlds at times. He's already cornered Carl and asked him to take a copy of his manuscript back to London. Carl seems quite impressed with it, as far as Carl can show enthusiasm for anything.

We're planning to stay here for about four or five days, I think. I'm sure I'll get used to the heat, and Jack and Bill have promised to take us to a deserted beach where there are no Arabs and it's okay for a girl to bathe. There's another English girl living here, she used to be a teacher, seems very nice. She's promised to take me to a souk tomorrow, which is apparently a big market. I'll see if I can pick up a present for you – if I don't get whisked away by a handsome sheikh for his harem! Not that Carl would notice...

Lots of love,

Joy

Muniria Hotel
Tangiers
February 20 1957

Dear Ellen,

Had a wonderful day shopping in the souk. Esther, the teacher, taught me how to haggle for silk wraps and leather sandals – the Arabs come up with an outrageously inflated price, you offer them about half of what you think the thing's worth, and you tend to meet somewhere in the middle. It's great fun.

The beach was beautiful, as well – practically deserted. Would have had a wonderful time but for Carl going into one of his sulks. You know Carl doesn't like swimming, so I went out a little way into the sea with Tom, who's a strong swimmer. Carl had a terrible temper tantrum when I got back and stormed off. You know, Ellen, I'm sometimes not really sure if I want him to ask me to marry him at all.

Also – and you must keep this secret – I tried proper hashish for the first time. They smoke it all the time here, and it's not like the stuff they pass round in the pub in London. It's really strong and makes you feel all... well. I don't know what the word is. Needless to say, Carl didn't approve.

Will write again soon,

Joy

Muniria Hotel
Tangiers
February 22 1957

Dear Ellen,

Oh, God, you would not believe what goes on here. Everyone tends to walk in and out of each other's rooms here at the Muniria, and yesterday I walked in on the writer, Jack and the guy Tom (the one who I went swimming with) in bed. Together! I was really embarrassed and ran out, and later Tom found me in the courtyard and told me not to worry – it wasn't anything to get flustered about. He was telling me about how we should all be free to love each other, man or woman. Then he touched my cheek. It was a good job Carl wasn't watching. In fact, I don't know what Carl is doing with his time – he never seems to want to be around me. And we're supposed to be leaving in a couple of days.

Anyway, see you back in London!

Joy

Muniria Hotel
Tangiers
February 27 1957

Dear Ellen,

No doubt you've seen Carl by now. No doubt he's filled your head with nonsense and lies. Well, if you're still reading this, then all I can do is beg you to believe me: it wasn't my fault. Carl's an utter pig and he should hardly be surprised that he drove me into the arms of another man.

It happened the day Jack left for Marseilles, which coincided with the arrival of Allen Ginsberg and a friend of his, Peter Orlovsky. Carl was muttering about how many more men were going to be showing up, and disappeared on one of his long walks into the city centre. He didn't even ask me to go with him – yet again. I was quite upset and was having a little cry in the hotel lobby when I heard Ginsberg and Orlovsky talking to Tom. They didn't see me and Ginsberg was asking Tom if he'd had any "action". I think they were talking about boys, Ellen. I know, I know. Anyway, Orlovsky said something along the lines of "Naw, he's balling the fat-assed English chick with the mousy hair". Well, you can imagine how upset I was. I ran out of the hotel and didn't stop running until I was totally lost. Tangiers is not a good place for a white woman to be lost on her own. There were men on street corners making horrible noises at me. I was really scared and then suddenly he was there, Tom. He'd seen I was upset and followed me out of the hotel. He apologised for what the others had been saying and insisted he'd never claimed to have had sex with me. I'm afraid I was so relieved to see him I just fell into his arms. I don't know what happened next but either he kissed me or I kissed him.

You probably know the rest. Two hours later Carl walked straight into Tom's room and caught us in bed. He just sneered at me and left.

If you do see him, Ellen, you can tell him from me that he's a rat and I never want to see him again. I know what I did was wrong but it was his fault, and he didn't have to abandon me in Tangiers like that.

Anyway, I need to sort out getting home so I'll see you soon.

Love,

Joy

Muniria Hotel
Tangiers
March 19 1957

Dearest Ellen,

Sorry for taking so long to write. You haven't been worried about me, have you? Listen. I've decided to stay on for a little while in Tangiers, at least until the gang decides to go back to America. I've never felt so free in all my life, Ellen. Never felt so good. Or loved; me and Tom are an item, now. You'd love him, Ellen, you really would. He's incredibly handsome and knows everything about everything. Don't believe anything you hear about them, or anything Carl tells you. It's not all drugs and free sex. They actually treat women really well, treat us as equals, not as possessions or little girls who can only do the unimportant stuff. I've been writing poetry; Allan Ginsberg reckons I've got a talent for it.

Anyway, later.

Love and peace,

Joy

Muniria Hotel
Tangiers
May 25 1957

Ellen!

I'm so excited! We're coming home! I'm not going to write too much now, because I want to tell you everything in person. But get this: I'm having a baby! Yes, I know. Don't tell my mum and dad – I want to tell them myself. Tom's coming with me and we're going to get married. If it's a boy – which Tom is sure it is, men! – then we're going to call him Thomas.

See you soon, darling. Can't wait!

Joy

Twenty Two

As the hand ticked on, Stuart felt a gut–wrenching thud. At first he thought he was falling, then realised it was the clock–tower itself that was shuddering. He looked wildly around and then pulled himself close to the tower, his face scraping the stone and his eyes tight shut as Big Ben creaked into life and began to chime the hour.

"Fuck... me..." he shouted, although no–one heard him. He stayed that way until the last bong reverberated into a dull ache in his head, replaced by a roaring sound. It was Tyler, laughing like a maniac.

"Hey, Stuart," he shouted. "What did Big Ben say to the Tower of Pisa? I've got the time if you've got the inclination."

"Just climb," said Stuart through gritted teeth.

Tyler laughed again. "Me and Stuart are going up to the left of the clock face. Luther and Monroe, you take the right. Stop when you get to three o'clock, ladies."

They diverged and began the last section of the climb. Stuart could hear shouts above them; the police had evidently climbed the stone steps inside the tower and were cutting off the only possible exit. They were trapped.

The clock face actually made the climb easier, allowing Stuart to grip the metalwork and speed up his ascent. Soon he reached Tyler, who patted him on the shoulder. "Tremendous, Stuart. Take a breather."

Stuart glanced over to where Luther and Monroe were belaying on the right hand side of the clock–face. Luther was digging in her pack and pulled out a tightly–rolled tarpaulin or canvas, which she passed to Monroe. There was a thin cord attached to it, with a weight on the end, which she started to swing like a gaucho spinning a bolas, twirling it into a widening arc until she shouted, "Now, Tyler!" and let it fly.

It spun towards them and Tyler deftly plucked it from the air, fastening it to a caribiner he'd attached to the clock face frame and giving Luther the thumbs up.

"Supergirl, Catwoman and Green Lantern," laughed Tyler. "Thank you for an excellent climb. We're nearly done, now, Stuart. The mission's almost over."

"What the hell are you doing?" he shouted.

Luther had attached the other end of the tarpaulin on to her side of the clock face and Tyler began to pull the cord. As it jerked towards him the tarpaulin began to unfold and Stuart saw that it was very fine and rolled up extremely tight. It was very big, a huge, vertical, brightly–decorated banner pretty much the width of the clock–face, and as Tyler secured it at the framework it fluttered down a good thirty feet. The flashbulbs far below sputtered into a crackling display.

"Luther, get Mac on the blower and tell him to send in the cavalry in three minutes, when the TV has got plenty of footage," shouted Tyler. "Stuart, you might want to take a look at this before the lights go out."

Leaning back as far as he dared, Stuart looked awkwardly under his arm–pit at the banner. It took a moment before the shapes coalesced into words, and then a stunned second more for the enormity of it to dawn upon him.

*pop*CULT!, it said. *The definitive guide to modern popular culture. A new book by Stuart Balfour, out in Spring.* There was even the name of the university and what appeared to Stuart to be Professor Garrett's direct telephone number.

"Oh, shit," breathed Stuart. "Oh, fucking shit, Tyler, what have you done?"

Tyler brayed. "Isn't it just the living end? Everyone in the fucking country will be getting this on the tea–time news."

"But... that's my name," said Stuart weakly.

"Yeah, hope you don't mind the liberty of us giving your book a title, Stuart, but you have to admit *pop*CULT!'s got a nice ring to it."

"But why, Tyler?" Stuart felt sick. Proper, heart–felt, throwing–up sick.

216

"Because everyone needs to read your book, Stuart. Because words are power and *pop*CULT! is magic and when you put power and magic together it's like a fucking nuclear explosion and we'll be unstoppable, Stuart, we'll be absolutely, unbelievably unstoppable. And I didn't realise it at first, not when Monroe brought you to us, but you're the missing piece of the puzzle, it's like *pop*CULT!'s been waiting for you all this time. As soon as I realised how important you and your book was, the Machine Elves went bananas. They love you, Stuart. Because they know. They know that you hold the key to making this work."

Stuart sagged, no longer having the strength to grip the stonework. Tears rolled down his face. He was going to be in so much trouble for this. He'd never been in trouble before, never even asked a policeman the time. He might be going to jail. He wouldn't survive in prison. They'd eat him alive.

"Heads up," said Monroe. "Looks like MacGuffin's delivered."

The fog had begun as a slight river mist on the surface of an unseasonally warm Thames somewhere near Vauxhall. The breeze had pushed it up–river, and as it rolled it gathered moisture and density, touching both banks by the time it reached the Tate. Traffic on Lambeth Bridge had to slow and eventually stop as the mist became thick fog which could be pierced only a few feet by headlights even on full beam. Lambeth Palace and Millbank were completely engulfed as the fog slopped up the Thames, spiralling up to entwine with the low–lying cloud.

"A good old London pea–souper. Lovely," smiled Tyler as the fog turned inland and seeped over Westminster, approaching like a wall of greyness infused with the dull orange glow of swallowed streetlights. Within a minute it crashed silently over Big Ben and Stuart gasped with the thickening of the air in his throat. Luther and Monroe were lost to him, then Tyler faded to an indistinct shape. Only the clock–face offered any kind of illumination. Stuart hung on grimly.

"Are you still there?" he called tremulously.

"Not going anywhere without you, Stuey," said Tyler. He reached into his bag and pulled out the last item, shucking off the pack and letting it fall empty into the fog. Hanging on to the dampening masonry, Tyler tucked the device under his arm and braced himself against the wall.

"ResQMax Tactical Line–Launcher," said Tyler, bringing up his knees to balance the gun on. "Delivers three thousand pounds per square inch detonation pressure, non–pyrotechnic. Goes off like a fucking rocket."

"Goes off to where like a fucking rocket? I'm sure it hasn't escaped your notice that we're hanging off Big Ben," shouted Stuart.

Tyler peered into the fog and then adjusted his position slightly to the north–west. He closed his eyes and released the trigger. With a thud that knocked the wind out of him, the launcher propelled the grappling hook into the mist.

"Now what?" asked Stuart as Tyler quickly secured one end of a thin cord to the clock–face frame just as it went taught with a whip crack.

"Now," said Tyler, pulling four leather straps from his belt, "Monty and Karen are hopefully securing that grappling hook to something extremely stable on the roof–tops across Westminster Bridge."

As Tyler looped the straps over the cord and fastened them underneath, Stuart was appalled to realise what he was planning. "We're not going to slide down that," he said in horror.

"Stuart," said Tyler, as Luther and Monroe appeared out of the fog beneath Stuart. "This is seven mil Nylon over Spectra. It's going to be fine. Just get hold of this."

Stuart wrapped one hand around the leather loop. "Tyler..." he said.

"Just do it," snarled Tyler. Stuart's stomach lurched as he reached for the strap with his other hand and for a moment dangled in space, before Tyler put his boot on his arse and pushed him out into the fog.

"Oh, fu–" began Stuart, then gasped as the cold air hit him as he started to slide, gathering speed, his legs kicking spastically.

The wind and moisture plastered his hair to his face and mask and he set his mouth in a determined grimace as he abruptly emerged from the fog and into the night sky above London. He couldn't see the end of the rope, just the darkness of the rooftops facing Westminster, coming closer as he slid lower and lower. He risked a glance down; no–one was looking at him and he suddenly felt free and exhilarated, gliding noiselessly above the traffic. It's just like flying, he thought. Big Ben was still encased in fog and behind him he could make out the shapes of Monroe and Luther emerging from the smog. As he sped towards the darkness, he hoped that Monty and Karen were going to be there to catch him.

Tea–time at Elysian Fields had not gone well. Mrs Scattergood had let out an anguished cry and soiled herself before the pudding came. She had been led away to be cleaned up but the incident had upset the other residents. They'd been taken into the TV room and given their sponge cake and custard on their laps, but a good portion of it had ended up on the rugs.

Sam was on her knees, scrubbing custard off the carpet. Two hours into a ten hour shift. She wondered why she hadn't spent her morning doing something more constructive than watching day–time TV and painting her toe–nails.

"That's my Stuart," said Mrs Balfour.

Sam looked up, turning towards the door. "Where, Mrs B?"

"On the telly."

Sam sighed. Looked like Mrs Balfour was going downhill again. She wondered where Stuart had been? She hadn't seen him since he had walked out of the bar with that woman. "Now, Mrs B," she chided gently, "what would Stuart be doing on the television?"

The Six O'Clock News was on. Sam glanced at the pictures on the screen; something to do with Big Ben, and looked back to Mrs

Balfour. Then she slowly turned back to the TV. The announcer was saying, "And these were the pictures at Big Ben just minutes before the entire Palace of Westminster was shrouded in a sudden fog. The two men and two women wearing comic book super–hero costumes had initially posed as a group called RIGHTS–4–PARENTS in order to dramatically scale the clock tower, but when they reached the clock–face they released this banner."

And there was Stuart's name, so much larger than life.

"Jesus," said Sam. Mr Roberts tutted.

The picture changed to Whitehall surrounded by dense fog, the clock–face of Big Ben glowing weakly. "This is the scene now," said the newsreader. "The four climbers have not yet descended and armed police are waiting for them. Although this has turned out to be a publicity stunt for a book, questions are already being asked as to how four people managed to carry out such a flagrant act of trespass at the heart of Parliament."

"Jesus," said Sam again.

Jane was looking witheringly at the pak choi. Quentin loved it but she thought – like so many of the fashionable foodstuffs he seized upon – that it was pretty tasteless. She was just thinking that Stuart was probably sitting down to a Chinese takeaway right about now when her eyes grazed to the fold–down plasma TV screen fitted to the cupboard underside.

"...flagrant act of trespass at the heart of Parliament," said the voice–over. "And here, in pictures taken just before the fog closed in, we can see close–up shots of the four."

There was a long–haired Superman, a pneumatic Supergirl, a lissom Catwoman and then the camera lingered on a rather familiar–looking man in a green and grey costume that Jane vaguely remembered from Stuart's comics. Then she started at the unruly hair and the set of the mouth below the domino mask. Just then the camera panned back to take in the wording of the banner. popCULT! *The definitive guide to modern popular culture. A new book by Stuart Balfour.*

220

"Fucking hell, Stuart," breathed Jane, the pak choi rolling out of her hands to the laminate floor. "When I said you should get off your arse and do something, I meant clean the flat and put a few shelves up…"

Professor Garrett felt sure that his wife did it simply to annoy him. Just seconds after nagging him to pick the phone up, there she was hollering for him to come and look at something on the TV. And as usual, he couldn't find the bloody handset. Cordless phones were all well and good if you didn't have a wife who conspired to hide them in cupboard or leave them on shelves. At last he located it behind the bread crock and jabbed at the button to still its insistent ringing.

"Peter, come quickly!" shouted his wife.

Professor Garrett made a face at her through the kitchen wall and barked, "Hello? Yes?"

As he walked slowly to the lounge he said, "Yes… no… no, I've no idea… well, yes… The press..? I mean, of course… publicity budget..? Not that I… yes, I think you're right… right away, yes…"

Margery was kneeling in front of the TV watching the news as he walked in. "Peter!" she shouted again without looking around.

He put his hand over the mouthpiece. "Margery, for God's sake, I'm on to the Dean. Something about Balf–"

As he took in the pictures on the news, his mouth slowly opened and then closed again.

And in his insulated space looking out on Canary Wharf, Mr Grundy settled back in his leather armchair to watch the early evening news with interest.

The excitable journalist was stalking along Westminster Bridge, gesticulating towards the sky. "…and once the fog had cleared – as quickly and mysteriously as it arrived – it became apparent that the four trespassers had, in a daring escape worthy of a Hollywood blockbuster – fired a grappling hook all the way from the face of Big Ben to these rooftops over here…"

The camera panned over to the buildings on the other side of the river, on which police officers in Day–glo yellow tabards could be picked out. Overhead a police helicopter hovered, casting a tight beam of light on the buildings. The reporter stopped dead in the middle of the road and faced the camera, "...then they fearlessly slid along the rope, across the river, over busy Westminster Bridge, and made their escape even as the police were still plotting how to get them down from the fog–bound clock–tower."

Mr Grundy leaned over his desk and jabbed at the intercom. George answered directly, "Mr Grundy?"

"George, have the men gone out yet?"

"Just left, Mr Grundy. Just left."

Mr Grundy smiled, switched off the intercom, and leaned back to watch the re–runs of the banner being unfurled over the face of Big Ben. "Very good, George," he said quietly. "Very good."

Twenty-Three

After abandoning their super–hero costumes and changing into the dark clothing which Monty and Karen had waiting for them, the six shinned down a thick drainpipe to the rain–slick cobbles of an alley and followed Tyler into the darkness, vaulting over railings and swinging themselves up fire escapes, dashing in half–crouched, single–file across low rooftops, somersaulting across gaps between buildings.

"Fucking hell," grinned Stuart, as Tyler paused to let them catch their breath, well away from Westminster. Over the dark roofs they could see the fog clearing around distant Big Ben.

"I had MacGuffin factor a little *parkour* into those pills we had," laughed Tyler. "Thought you might be up for a bit of free–running, Stuart."

At a bus–stop near Trafalgar Square they watched themselves on a bank of televisions in a Curry's shop window. Stuart giggled uncontrollably. "That's me," he said. "Up Big Ben."

"Sshh," said Monroe kindly, putting a hand on his shoulder.

"Yeah, button it, Stuart," said Luther. "We're not out of the woods yet."

Stuart nodded, but couldn't take his eyes off the TV screens. He was goofily high, grinning like the first time he'd tried Ecstasy. Only he felt better than that, better than he could ever remember feeling.

"You're still getting an adrenaline rush," said Tyler quietly as the bus pulled up.

"Does that mean I'm going to crash soon?" frowned Stuart.

Tyler broke into a beaming smile. "No–one ever crashes at *pop*CULT!, Stuart."

When they arrived back at the warehouse, Monty hopped over to the fridge and broke out an armful of beers.

"Not yet," said Tyler. "First we need to give thanks."

He solemnly handed out Copyright to each of them and

watched while they swilled it down, then led them all, including MacGuffin, who had been tinkering at his computer, down the lift to Flock. The velvet carriage was waiting for them, humming patiently in the dim light.

"*pop*CULT! makes things like that happen for us, Stuart," said Tyler as the Velvet Underground whispered through the quiet tunnels. "Facilitated by the Machine Elves. They have given freely and selflessly, but it is only right that we give them something in return."

"How do you feel after your first mission?" asked Luther.

"Drained," said Stuart. "High as a kite. Empty. Hilarious."

"You're one of us, now, Stuey," said Monty.

"What are we doing when we get to *pop*CULT!?" said Stuart, nervous about another encounter with the organism.

"Communion," said Tyler. "*pop*CULT! feeds off emotions, memories, ideas. We have eaten of it, now it must eat of us."

Stuart remembered that exchange of images, of how *pop*CULT! always made him think of home and his parents. He remembered the dizzying, alien landscape it showed to him.

"It's the only way to make the connection," said MacGuffin. "Taking *pop*CULT! into yourself makes you more... pliable to the Machine Elves. It helps them work their magic on you."

"It makes you one of us," said Tyler. "We're here. Stick close and if you hear anything, shout out."

"The hogs," remembered Stuart as they filed off the carriage and into the darkness of Void. "We were attacked the last time I came here..."

"The Hampstead Hogs," said Tyler. "MacGuffin, do you want to field this one?"

As they climbed the ladder, MacGuffin said, "First thing you've got to appreciate is a little about how *pop*CULT! works. It feeds on what you might call psychic emanations."

"Only if I was insane," muttered Stuart.

MacGuffin laughed and went on, "Say you're up there, in a cafe in Hoxton, reading a magazine and listening to your MP3 player. There's a movie poster on a billboard across the road, maybe there's a soap opera showing on the TV in the corner. You're taking all these things in, some of them more intently than others. And while you're thinking about the magazine article or the song you're listening to, or maybe about the plot of the movie that's being advertised, *pop*CULT!'s listening to your thoughts, drinking it all in."

"It reads minds?" puffed Stuart as he climbed through the hatch into the darkness of the sewer.

"Not like you think," said MacGuffin, helping him to his feet. "It just takes the imagery and sense of what you've been thinking about. Then comes the clever bit.

"*pop*CULT! doesn't only eat psychic emanations as well, it excretes them. It sucks in our thoughts and feelings, takes the essence of them, and expels the trimmings. So far as we've been able to work out, anyway."

"So..." said Stuart, trying to understand. "So, say I'm reading this magazine and thinking about, I don't know, the new *Gavrilo Princip* single..."

"Then *pop*CULT! might suck in what you're thinking about the band, file the memory and the experience and your thoughts, expel it out in a watered–down form and someone walking past the cafe you're sitting in might suddenly get a hankering to listen to the new *Gavrilo Princip* record."

"Or, even better," said Tyler quietly once they were all standing beside the sluggish channel of the sewer, "they might go home and decide to form their own band, to become the new *Gavrilo Princip*."

Stuart nodded briskly. As ridiculous as this sounded, it also made a kind of sense. "So when there's a TV show on, some reality show, a bunch of celebrities locked in a castle or something..."

"*pop*CULT! will eat and digest what people are thinking about it, then it'll send out its own psychic emanations, which other people will pick up. Someone will have a bright idea... maybe a show about a bunch of slebs locked on an oil rig. And the whole process starts again."

"But..." said Stuart. "The entire basis of modern popular culture, the repetitive cycle of recent years, the recycling of trends and fashions... you're saying it's all so much... so much..."

"Shit," said Tyler, gesturing towards the sewage. "*pop*CULT! shit."

Stuart frowned in the dull light from the low flashlights that Monty and Luther carried . "But that's so depressing."

"Balls," said Tyler. "It's empowering. Anyone can have a bright idea, thanks to *pop*CULT!. We've made it okay to believe that 'celebrity' is an achievable career option. We've made it okay to write a sit–com or novel or movie and think you have the right to get it published. We've made it okay to believe in yourself. What's so depressing about that?"

"It's just..." said Stuart as they moved off slowly along the ledge. "What about human creativity?"

"*pop*CULT! enables human creativity," insisted Tyler. "It puts the arts in reach of the masses – not just by consumption, which *pop*CULT! enables anyway by making art more accessible, but by putting production and creativity in reach of everyone."

Stuart pondered this for a moment, half of him marvelling that he was even having this conversation in all seriousness at all. "But what about these hogs? How do they fit in?"

Tyler stopped outside the metal, slime–encrusted door set in the brick wall. "MacGuffin?"

"Sometimes," said MacGuffin, "*pop*CULT! does more than just excrete psychic emanations. It creates real, solid forms. We don't know why – possibly when there's an overwhelming public perception of something. Back in the Nineteenth Century, there was an urban myth that a pregnant sow had got into the sewers and given birth to a brood of piglets, which fed from offal and garbage and grew to huge proportions. They bred and became vicious and wild with each successive generation, and the story has it that they haunt the sewers. You get sightings every decade

226

or so. We think *pop*CULT! took this image and made it flesh."

"And they're real? The Hampstead Hogs?"

Tyler showed Stuart the bandage on his arm. "They attacked while you were communing with *pop*CULT!. I barely got you out in one piece."

"Jesus," said Stuart, glancing around.

"Don't worry," said Tyler, hauling open the door. "We'll be safe inside."

It was just as Stuart remembered it. The glowing, swirling golden brown light, the fuzz of fairy–dust ebbing and flowing above its plastic surface, the inquisitive tentacles prodding the air, knitting together the millions of half–formed thoughts raining down upon it.

"I don't have a hat," realised Stuart, suddenly panicking.

Karen snickered to herself. "Guy," she said, shaking her head.

"Communion," whispered Tyler, securing the metal door behind them. Stuart felt abruptly claustrophobic, wanted to get out. "We give freely."

Tyler and Monroe squatted then sat cross–legged on the damp stone floor, the others following suit. Stuart did the same, closing his eyes with the rest of them then opening one with a squint a second later, to check everyone was still there. They were.

"*pop*CULT!, we thank you for the music, the song you're singing," said Tyler reverently. Stuart glanced at him again to see if he was taking the piss, but he was straight–faced. "Thanks for all the joy you're bringing. In return, we open our minds and share with you our thoughts, memories and secrets."

Stuart barely had time to breathe. The seconds suddenly stretched and yawned, golden–coloured gaps dropping into infinity between them. He tried to speak but couldn't formulate the correct words. Something was sucking hard on his ear.

It felt like someone was carving his brains out with a butter–knife. Stuart looked in anguish at the others, but they were all silent and serene of face, their communion with *pop*CULT! an apparently pleasurable experience. Stuart felt like it was ripping the memories out of him and they blurred past like a home movie speeded up to critical mass, images blurring into each other, emotions passing through his breast like speeding trains. And then the direction of the traffic changed, and *pop*CULT! was hammering stuff back into him, filling his mind, swamping his most basic motor functions until he felt himself let loose his bladder and he gasped, crumpling to the floor as the Machine Elves crowded around him, screaming without words:

[HOMEHOMEHOMEHOME/KILLKILLKILLKILLKILL.]

"I told you, Tyler. I fucking told you."

In the depths, surrounded by diffuse light, Stuart held his breath and kicked through the oil for a distant surface.

"Chill, MacGuffin."

"No, I fucking told you." Anger. Shouting. "They're not happy, and this is what happens. Why won't you listen to me?"

"He's fine. Look, he's coming round."

"But he might not be, Tyler. Who knows what effect it has on people who aren't used to it?"

"Mac..."

"Why Stuart, though, I wonder?" Monroe. "Why him, and not any of the rest of us. Apart from Tyler, we're not exactly used to seeing *pop*CULT! at close quarters."

Stuart chanced opening one eye. He was lying on one of the sofas, in front of the wall of TV screens, the others looming over him. He breathed. It seemed okay.

"We're asking too much of them, Tyler, and this is how they show it. We're stretching it too far."

Tyler noticed that Stuart was stirring and squatted behind him, placing a hand on his shoulder. "Hey," he said softly. "You back with us?"

"What happened?"

Tyler glanced at MacGuffin. "You blacked out. We carried you back. This is becoming a habit, Stuey."

Stuart struggled to a sitting position. "It was like... Christ, it was like being overloaded." He placed a hand over his crotch. "Ew. I pissed myself."

"Like, really?" said Karen, rolling her eyes.

Tyler straightened up. "Go clean up, Stuart. That goes for all of you. We've done good tonight, we all deserve a bit of r'n'r. I'm going to sit here and watch us on the news; the rest of you guys do what you like."

Stuart shaved and scrubbed his teeth then stood under the shower for half an hour. Sitting in the easy chair in his quarters, a towelling robe loosely gathered around him, he smoked a cigarette and wondered what he should do now. His limbs were beginning to ache and his tendons were sore, but he didn't feel in the least bit tired. Pangs of doubt and unaccountable feelings of loss alternated with euphoric recollections of the assault on Big Ben that had him giggling out loud.

Energised, he was considering firing up the computer and doing some work on the book when there was a knock at his door. "Uh, come in," he called, still unsure of the etiquette around the warehouse.

It was Monroe. She stood in the doorway wearing a long, beige coat with military styling. Her black hair tumbled silkily over the epaulettes and she considered him with her green eyes, glowing almost luminous in the dim lighting.

Stuart stood awkwardly, pulling the robe tight around him. "Erm. Hi."

Monroe stepped inside and closed the door behind her. "Feel better after a shower?"

"Yes, great. Better. You?"

She laughed. "You are funny, Stuart."

"Am I?"

They were facing each other now, in the space between the sofas and the work area. Monroe stood with her hands on her hips, her head cocked to one side, as though considering him. "You did good today. I was proud of you."

Stuart beamed. "Really?"

"Yes," she said. Then she slowly pulled at the knotted belt at her waist and allowed the coat to fall open. Monroe had come to Stuart's room naked beneath the coat, but as it fell away she felt his desire clothing her, his anticipation painting her with the whisper of silk and the rasp of Nylon, his fantasies raising her on vertiginous stilettos and clamping her waist with whalebone. She looked down at the basque, the stockings, the garter belt. Her hair had woven itself into a tight bun, small, square–framed spectacles balanced on her nose. "Why, Stuart," she chided, a smile playing on her lips. "How rather obvious of you."

Stuart could only moan softly as Monroe shucked off the coat and covered the distance between them in two strides. "You're the most beautiful woman I've ever seen in my life," he whispered.

"I know," she said. Monroe reached for him, sliding her hand – suddenly covered in a leather, elbow–length glove – inside his robe. She moved down until she gripped his erection, then Stuart whimpered and came violently all over the inside of her forearm.

"Oh, God," he said in a tiny, appalled voice. "I'm so... I don't usually... I mean, that's never happened to me before..."

"Don't worry," she smiled. "It happens to me all the time. I'm sure there's plenty more where that came from."

Monroe steered Stuart backwards and he clumsily climbed the steps to the mezzanine floor in reverse. By the time she pushed him on to his bed he was indeed, to his pleasant surprise, back in the saddle, as Walter might have put it. Monroe took off her glasses and tugged at the bun at the back of her head until her hair tumbled over her bare shoulders. "Help me out of this corset, it's killing me," she said. "And then fuck me like there's no tomorrow."

Later, they lay on the trashed, twisted sheets of Stuart's bed, him with his head resting lightly on her breasts. "Jesus Christ," Stuart said for about the seventeenth time.

"Was that good?" she whispered, kissing the top of his head.

He looked up at her. "You're joking, right?"

She smiled at him, tousling his hair. "We've done it before, you know. Don't you remember?"

"On the Velvet Underground, that first night I came to *pop*CULT!," said Stuart. "No, I don't really remember. I wish I did. I was too strung out on Copyright."

"Was tonight better?"

Stuart inched up the bed until he was facing her on the pillow. He could already feel himself stiffening against her thigh, and she languidly stroked the underside of his balls. "What about you? Did you enjoy it?"

She looked into his eyes for a long moment, then nodded. "I did. But I wished I didn't."

Stuart frowned. "What do you mean?"

Monroe sighed. "I am what *pop*CULT! makes me, Stuart. It puts a... a glamour on me. People see me as the fulfilment of their heart's desire. And every time someone casts a lustful glance my way, every time a teenage boy goes home and masturbates with my image fixed in his head, every time I have sex... it's like I've been recharged, like I've got an electric current running through me, like I'm unstoppable. And I love it. I love the feeling. But I know it isn't real, Stuart. I know it's only *pop*CULT! making me feel this way. But whether I want to or not, I can't stop myself. I can't stop myself doing this..."

She kissed him, long and deep, then pulled away, sowing kisses along his neck and his chest, down his stomach to his cock, which she engulfed in her warm, hot mouth. After an agonising moment she stopped and released him. He moaned. "I need to ask you something, Stuart. I need you to help me. Will you help me?"

He nodded, closing his eyes and willing her to carry on. Stuart had questions of his own, too many questions, but they were all swept away as he abandoned himself to Monroe and felt himself bucking and shuddering as he surged towards another climax, fireworks exploding behind his eyes, the bed – no, the room – shaking, shrill alarms ringing and ringing and ringing and –

"Fuck," said Monroe, lifting her head and wiping the back of her hand across her mouth. The alarm was still ringing. It wasn't in Stuart's head. He blinked and hunched himself up on his elbows.

"What's that?" he said.

"Fuck," said Monroe again, rolling off the bed. "We've been breached."

Twenty Four

Mr Grundy's police officers had split into three teams of seven and one back–up team of six. Of the seven in each main squad, three officers were armed with the carbine rifles and the other four had Glock pistols. Two teams were at the entrance to the alley on Praxis Street and the third had made its way via a circuitous route to the roof of the building. The back–up team was waiting within a black Transit van with tinted windows, which also contained George and Escobar, who were maintaining radio contact with the leaders of each squad and Mr Grundy.

The headsets George and Escobar wore crackled with sound from the roof–top team. "The building's completely sealed off from above but we might be able to break through some damaged roof–tiles. Do you want us to proceed?"

"Hold steady for the moment," said George, switching the frequency to the street teams. "Gold Leader and Red Leader; advance into the alley."

The Gold squad went first, weapons drawn, their black uniforms merging with the darkness. The Red squad followed twenty yards behind them.

George and Escobar waited.

"Dead end," reported Gold Leader. "Brick wall. This can't be the way in."

"We have done a complete circuit of the block," insisted Escobar. "There are no doors from the outside. Either they get in and out via one of the adjoining buildings or..."

"Or a tunnel?" mused George. "Gold Leader, check the ground near the wall."

There was a little scuffling about and some light banging. Gold Leader hissed, "It feels odd. Looks like cobbles but feels a little hollow."

"Pull back and assume a covering role," said George. "Red Leader, see if your team can break through the ground. We need to move quickly, now. I'm sure they'll be aware that we're here."

***

Stuart pulled on his trousers and a shirt while Monroe fastened up the long coat. "Fucking hell, Stuart," she said. "How am I expected to fight in stilettos and a basque?"

"Fight?" said Stuart, alarmed. "Fight who?"

"Whoever's trying to get in the warehouse," said Monroe impatiently. "Come on."

She opened the door to see Monty outside, breathless and about to knock. "The filth," he gasped. "Two dozen of them, at least. They're about to bust in. Tyler's organising an evacuation."

"The police?" said Stuart.

Monty nodded. "Looks like Grundy's bent copper army. He's tried to use them before, but it's the first time they've found us."

"If we're evacuating, better bring anything of value," said Monroe. "Get any personal stuff or documents with your name on and meet me up front."

Stuart frantically cast around for his wallet, the shrieking of the alarm making it difficult to concentrate. Finding it under a book, he stuffed it in his pocket and was just about to leave when he remembered his manuscript. Ejecting the CD tray on the computer, he pocketed the disc and headed at a run after Monroe and Monty.

Tyler, Luther and Karen were already in the main area, standing in front of the pile of TV screens which were all tuned to the CCTV cameras in the alley off Praxis Street. To one side, MacGuffin was frantically bashing in concert at several keyboards on the computer bank. Stuart stopped short and stared at the images on the screen. "Fucking shit," he breathed. "Are they carrying *guns*?"

Tyler ignored him, instead calling out to MacGuffin, "Mac, what the fuck are you doing?"

"Wiping the hard–drives," said MacGuffin through clenched teeth.

"Don't bother," said Tyler, turning back to the screens. "Just prime the place for Closedown."

234

"I said, are they carrying guns..?" repeated Stuart.

Monty nodded. "It's the filth."

"Is this because of the Big Ben thing?" said Stuart.

"No," said Tyler. "Because of the Grundy thing. We'd better get out of here."

On the screens, a team of the black uniformed, helmeted officers were attacking the fake ground in the alley with pick axes and jack–hammers.

"They're in," pointed out Karen. "Shouldn't we go?"

Tyler strode to a one of the wall–mounted cabinets and shuffled through a set of keys before unlocking it and taking out four pistols.

"Oh, Christ, now *we've* got guns," moaned Stuart.

Tyler ejected the ammo clip on one of the guns then slammed it back in, and tossed three of the guns to Luther, Monty and Karen. The fourth he slipped down the waistband at the back of his trousers. "Monroe, Mac, Stu," he said. "Take the lift to the Velvet Underground and wait there. If we're not down in ten minutes, or these guys make it down before us, go to Hemp–Weft."

Tyler reached back in the cabinet and pulled out a mobile phone. He threw it to MacGuffin and said, "You remember how to do a Closedown, don't you?"

"I programmed the system, Tyler," sighed MacGuffin. "But—"

"No buts," said Tyler as the last of the policemen disappeared off the CCTV link and down the hole that had been smashed into the wooden ramp outside. "Just go. I'll see you downstairs."

George tapped the headset and switched the connection to Mr Grundy. Behind him, in the van, the third squad was tooling up. "Gold and Red teams have entered the tunnel, sir," he said. "I'm about to send in Blue team."

"Get Red Leader to switch on the video camera, George," sighed Mr Grundy. "I want to see pictures of this."

George nodded to Escobar, who switched his connection to Red Leader. "Mr Grundy, he says make sure you get the camera pictures," he ordered, then turned to the Blue team. "Go now. Secure the alley."

George glanced upwards through the windscreen. A torchlight flashed three times; Green team on the roof reporting there was nothing to interfere with the mission.

The police officer known for the evening as Gold Leader, but who was usually referred to as Chief Inspector Westwood on a day to day basis and as "Frank" by his whining bitch of a wife, held his Glock at arm's length as he led the way through the dark, concrete tunnel, flanked on either side by a rifle–wielding colleague with flashlights fitted to their carbines.

"The corridor's sloping upwards," he murmured into the mouthpiece fitted to his helmet. "Only a few degrees. Lift that light up! Looks like we're coming to a dead end... wait. There's a door – metal, by the looks of it – in the wall to our left."

Gold Leader motioned for one of the snipers to check the door. It was locked, with a key–code pad on the wall beside it. The officer chanced a touch of the door with his gloved palm; it was solid and immovable.

Gold Leader whispered, "Red Leader, we'll need the explosives."

Monroe led Stuart to the shadowy corridor that led to the lift–shaft, MacGuffin following close behind, connecting the mobile phone Tyler had given him to a battered netbook.

"I don't know..." Stuart was saying. "If it's the police, can't we just talk to them? Explain the situation?"

Monroe laughed humourlessly. "What *is* the situation, Stuart? And presumably you didn't fail to see that they were armed to the teeth. Like Monty said, they're not normal coppers... they're on Grundy's payroll."

"Then maybe we should go to the proper police, tell them what's happening..."

Monroe laughed again.

As they entered the corridor, Monroe stopped and held up her hand. There were noises coming from behind the door that led to the tunnel to Praxis Street. She glanced back at the CCTV shots; a further half–dozen or so of uniformed men had taken up position around the smashed–up camouflaged ramp.

"Why aren't Tyler and the others coming with us?" hissed Stuart.

"They need to buy us time," said Monroe, setting off at a run for the lift shaft. "Mac needs to prime the Closedown and it takes a while. How are you doing, Mac?"

MacGuffin swore under his breath as he jogged alongside Monroe, his fingers dancing over the netbook's tiny keyboard. "I never thought we'd actually have to do this, you know."

"What exactly are you doing?" asked Stuart.

Monroe and MacGuffin shared a glance, then she said, "Never mind. Just hurry up."

Tyler watched them disappear into the blackness of the corridor. Beside him, Karen Eliot was trying to strangle a terrified sob.

"We're going to die, aren't we?" she said in a small voice.

Tyler checked his clip again. "I won't. You might."

Monty was tying a bandana bearing a Japanese insignia around his forehead. "Blaze of glory and all that, eh, Karen? It was all there in the contract."

"It's just..." began Karen, looking up at Luther. "I never thought..."

Luther remained impassive behind her shades. "I'm just glad I'm female today," she said. "Black guys are always the first to buy it in these situations."

There was a noise that sounded like "crump" and the metal door buckled and collapsed on itself. Through the smoking portal two men in full–face helmets, black clothing, bullet–proof vests and holding Heckler and Koch carbines dropped to their knees.

"Don't fucking move an inch!" someone with an authoritative voice called.

"Stay behind me," whispered Tyler, taking the gun out of his waistband. "We only need to distract them long enough for Mac to prime the Closedown. We'll run at them then veer off down the corridor. But *stay behind me* and you might be okay."

"Since when was Grundy so soft on you?" said Monty, one eyebrow raised.

"He's a sentimental old fool," said Tyler, tensing as more police officers poured through the door and took up position. "He always has been."

"I repeat, don't fucking move," called out Gold Leader, stepping through the remains of the door, his pistol held straight. He could see four of them, Tyler and three others who were edging behind him in single file. A hippy, a tall black woman and an Asian girl. All armed.

"Where's that Monroe bitch?" muttered a young officer peering down the barrel of his Heckler and Koch. "I'm going to do her first."

"Get in the fucking queue, kid," said Gold Leader. "You're a fucking constable, it'll be like waving a conductor's baton in the Albert Hall by the time you get your go. If you really have to, you can have the Paki or the nigger while you're waiting. What's left of them, anyway."

Gold Leader, when he was known as Frank, had two daughters, one nineteen and one seventeen. If he ever heard a boy using language around his girls like he himself had just used, Frank'd kick his fucking bollocks to Stepney and back.

Gold and Red teams were assembled in the warehouse now, their guns trained on Tyler and his mob. There was a big pyramid of TV screens, all showing jerky footage of another seven officers in the alley. At least Blue Team were awake, thought Gold Leader. Pity there'd be no shooting for them tonight. Or shagging. Unless they were happy to have a go after the likes of this kid constable had finished up. "Right," said Gold Leader loudly. "Let's take this nice and easy. You put your guns on the floor and your hands up, and no—one's going to get hurt."

Tyler said, "Now."

Red Leader, whose name was Barry, was the most educated of the twenty–seven officers, and probably the least at ease with what was happening. He was only doing it to pay off the loan and credit card debts he'd run up without his wife knowing over the past seven years. Well, she would insist on holidays in the Maldives and two cars. He was only a sergeant. To Barry, the thing that ran towards them looked like one of those Hindu gods, a single entity with four pairs of arms all waving madly, an unearthly scream issuing from four mouths, three of them hidden.

"Hold your fucking fire," hissed Gold Leader. "Tyler is not to take any damage…"

Running at full pelt, Tyler held up his gun and fired. Gold Leader's chin exploded in a mess of blood and bone. Someone screamed "fuck". From behind Tyler, Luther popped off a shot and Red Leader crumpled to the floor.

"Hit a left," shouted Tyler, and broke for the dark corridor leading to the lift shaft. For a moment, the police paused. Tyler turned and banged off half a dozen random shots.

"Fuck!" roared one of the officers, breaking the spell, and their guns barked.

Stuart stopped, glancing over his shoulder as Monroe hauled open the lift gate and pushed MacGuffin, still tapping at the keyboard, inside. Stuart had never heard real, live gunfire before, and it took him a moment to realise what it was. "Jesus," he said. He felt weak, as though his muscles were atrophying under him. His head spun. People were *shooting* at each other.

"Get in the lift!" hissed Monroe, grabbing his T–shirt.

"But Tyler…" said Stuart.

"He'll be fine," said Monroe, jabbing at the buttons. The lift started to descend.

Six bullets hit Luther Blissett, the first one to her ribcage just about where her heart was. She kept running, but the next one tore her right knee off. As she fell, two more thudded into her right arm, one into her thigh, and the sixth to her head.

Monty Cantsin was hit once; but it was enough. The bullet caught him square in the nose as he risked a glance at the cops, the flaring barrels of their guns blinding him momentarily. He never recovered his sight as the bullet tore through his brain. The last thing he had seen was a bright light.

Karen Eliot almost made it. As Tyler was swallowed by the shadows she stumbled and fell forward, and as she did so a bullet ripped into her pelvis and flipped her over like an omelette. She was still conscious as the first officer got to her, and she could hear the sound of Tyler's footsteps fading along the corridor. The faceless helmet regarded her for a moment, then put a bullet into her forehead and stepped over her body in pursuit of Tyler.

The lift ground to a halt and Monroe, MacGuffin and Stuart tumbled out. Monroe sent the lift straight back up but Stuart barely noticed; his head was both a whirling mass of unformed terror and, paradoxically, a large, empty space. He leaned into the velvety wall and vomited.

"On to the train," urged Monroe. "Mac, you nearly there?"

"Just about," said MacGuffin. "Where the hell's Tyler?"

They sat in the softly–humming carriage for what seemed like an age.

"It must be ten minutes," gasped Stuart. "Let's go."

"Wait," said Monroe. The lift was cranking and rattling down the shaft.

"Has anyone," moaned Stuart, "worked out what we're going to do if that *isn't* Tyler in the lift?"

"The train'll have us out of here before they've set one foot on

240

Flock," said Monroe. "It's... look."

The lift cage was dragged back and Tyler half–walked, half–stumbled out. He wiped snot from his nose with the back of his hand then tossed the gun away from him, limping to the carriage and falling inside.

"Jesus," said Stuart, horrified. "You're bleeding."

"Flesh wound," said Tyler through gritted teeth, rolling up his trouser leg to expose the gash where a bullet had grazed his calf. "They weren't shooting to kill. Let's get the fuck out of here."

"The others?" said Monroe quietly.

"Unfortunately, they *were* shooting to kill *them*. Let's go," said Tyler.

As the carriage moved off smoothly and began to gather speed, Tyler dragged himself up to a seat and said, "Mac, did you get the Closedown primed."

Mac said nothing but unclipped the mobile phone from the netbook and handed it to Tyler.

Tyler dialled quickly with his thumb and put the phone to his ear.

In the warehouse, Tyler had left the three officers who pursued him to the lift dead, two bullets each. Four more were pounding on the lift doors, waiting for it to return. Three others were searching for another way to get to the floors below. Gold Leader II had taken charge of the operation, as Gold Leader was dead and Red Leader critically injured.

George relayed this information to Mr Grundy via his radio headset. Mr Grundy was not pleased.

"He got away, George, is that what you're telling me?"

"We managed to get three of them, sir," said George carefully.

"The three most unimportant," sighed Mr Grundy. "George, I–"

Mr Grundy was interrupted by a broadcast cutting across the signal. George heard it too, as did Escobar, as did every surviving officer, both on their headsets and from loudspeakers within the warehouse.

"Big Brother house, this is Davina," sounded Tyler's voice. "You are live on Channel 4, please do not swear."

Gold Leader II looked doubtfully around. He changed frequency to speak to George. "Are you getting this..?"

"Yes, shut up," said George, concentrating.

"You have all been evicted," said Tyler. "You have exactly fifteen seconds to get out of the warehouse. Closedown is commencing."

For two of the fifteen seconds, George thought about this. Then be barked into his mic, "Gold Leader II, get them out of there! Get everyone out!"

Tyler took the telephone away from his ear and looked at it. Monroe put a hand on his arm. "Are you sure..?"

Tyler nodded and pressed the hash key with his thumb, then tossed the phone to MacGuffin.

"What now–?" Stuart started to say, then stopped as he felt a low rumble under the carriage. A wave of pressure buffeted the train and a sigh of air shunted them along, a cloud of brick–dust enveloping them and billowing ahead, shards of stone tapping on the windows.

"What just happened?" said Stuart.

"The warehouse is gone," said MacGuffin quietly. "Flock's gone."

Tyler held out his hand and asked Stuart for his mobile. "All telephone privileges hereby revoked, for everyone, until I know we're safe," he said. He was about to shove it in his pocket then thought again and tapped in a number.

In his darkened quarters, Mr Grundy let his desk telephone ring for a moment, then picked it up.

"Thomas," said the voice. *His* voice.

"I was expecting your call," said Mr Grundy.

"Don't think I'll let you get away with this," snarled Tyler. "Don't think this has finished, just because your private army of bent coppers is lying under a ton of rubble. Don't think I won't be coming to get you."

The connection went dead. Mr Grundy replaced the handset. Tyler was getting rattled. He sounded angry, anxious, losing control. Mr Grundy smiled.

On the train, Tyler jammed the phone back in his pocket and stared straight ahead. They continued their journey in silence.

Twenty Five

Now start a revolution.
By Steve MacGuffin
SOUND AND FURY magazine
Edition: June 1979
Pages: 12–17

You want to know about Sid, don't you? You want to know what he was like, whether he was really so crazy all the time, whether he could actually play bass or not, what underwear he wore and what books he read and what bread he ate. You want to know what his last words were and whether he shat himself when he died and what his corpse looked like, after a life lived fast and a death died young.

Well, fuck you.

You can get all that shit from the other magazines, from the Sunday newspapers, from every slumming rich kid wearing a safety pin and a plastic bin–liner and swearing that they were right there through it all, through the whole punk thing.

You want Sid? Then go to Heathrow airport. Stand in the arrivals lounge. Breathe deep. When she came back to Britain after Sid's funeral, his mother dropped his ashes and they scattered across the floor at Heathrow, got sucked up into the vents, and are circulating through the air conditioning *right now*. That's where Sid's ghost is. Not at the 100 Club. Not at Hackney Technical College. Not at Virgin Records or SEX or the Hotel Chelsea.

Let me tell you something: It's not all about Sid.

There. I've said it. It's not all about Sid. It never was. It's not about Johnny or Jah or Malcolm fucking McLaren. It's not all about me, though there were times when I was convinced it was. Like when I was strung out on heroin, vomit on my T-shirt, my hand up the tartan skirt of some doe-eyed student with green hair. Maybe that was you. Maybe, for that moment, you thought it was all about *you*.

What it's all about, is all of us. All of you. That's all it was ever about. All it's ever going to be about. And it took Tommy Tyler to show me that.

Tyler was, like me, one of the Bromley Contingent. It's funny how many people I meet these days who claim to have been a part of it, like it was some mythical army of underground freedom fighters. People I've never met before who reckon they were there when Johnny Rotten auditioned for the band wearing his home-made "I hate Pink Floyd" T-shirt. People who swear blind that you can just see them in the photos of the gig at the Screen on the Green, there on the far right, looking straight at Souxsie's bare nipples.

But I was there, and so was Tyler. His hair was spiked with glue and he wore skin-tight black jeans. He was the first person to wear a safety pin, put it straight through his nose in SEX and got blood all over the Westwoods. Vivienne went bananas at him and he told her to fuck off. He's a great bass player, Tyler, and Malcolm McLaren wanted him in the band, but he just laughed. "Why should I?" he snorted.

"I'll make you famous," McLaren had answered.

Tyler had laughed. "Darling, we're *all* going to be famous. I don't need to make money for *you* while I'm at it."

McLaren never really liked Tyler. Everyone was into the "no future" thing at the time, but Tyler hated it. He said there wasn't just going to be a future, but that we were going to *be* the future. Punk was the first stages of liberating the masses. You didn't have to be able to play bass to be famous, he said. You just had to want it hard enough.

Tyler talked a lot of sense. If the Sex Pistols made you want to bang your head against the wall, Tommy Tyler gave you a reason for wanting to do so. It was him who came up with the *God Save The Queen* idea, whatever the fuck Rotten or McLaren might tell you. When the Pistols signed to A&M it was Tyler who suggested they do the publicity stunt outside Buckingham Palace.

"Fuck off," Rotten had said. "Why?"

"Because that raddled old bitch has been on the throne for a quarter of a century," Tyler replied. "That's a fucking life–time, for some. It's time we showed her what the next generation looks like."

When they brought Sid in to replace Glen Matlock, he couldn't play bass to save his life. He asked Tyler for lessons, but he refused with the words, "You'll give more hope to more disaffected kids on the dole if they see you thrashing around with your amp turned down than if they see you playing properly."

Not that Sid and Tyler were ever big mates. Tyler didn't like the Nazi stuff, the Swastika patches. Never explained why. I remember Tyler punching Sid out once at the 100 Club when he revealed he'd got on heroin after meeting Nancy. Tyler didn't approve. Called them "John and Yoko" under his breath. Said Sid was going to kill the band.

Then, Nancy died. We all know what happened. Dead on the bathroom floor in Apartment 100 of the Hotel Chelsea in New York. Stabbed in the gut. Tyler was there, you know, visiting the Big Apple and staying over at the Chelsea for a couple of nights. Said that Sid was so strung out, anything could have happened.

After that, Tyler said he'd had a bellyful of punk. Said we needed to look to the future. Said a revolution was coming and we were going to be part of it.

I don't know about you, but I believe him. Sid's gone, but what he stood for lives on in Tommy Tyler.

Remember Sniffin' Glue, the fanzine? It printed three pictures of chords with the caption: "This is a chord, this is another, this is a third. Now form a band."

That's what punk gave us, says Tyler. That "fuck it, I can do that" attitude. A couple of weeks after Sid's death Tyler took me up on to the roof of an old warehouse in Walthamstow. Reckoned he'd just bought it.

"Why?" I asked.

"Something's needed to take the place of punk," he said. "I've got three words for you: *pop*CULT! is coming. Now start a revolution."

Ends – approx 1,000 words

Memo
From: The Editor
To: The Features Editor

Jay, what the fuck is this? When I ask for an obit of Sid Vicious, I expect an obit of Sid fucking Vicious. Has MacGuffin totally lost it? I know it's late in the day, but this has got to go on the spike. Tell MacGuffin not to bother submitting anything else until he's got his shit together, and in the meantime get in touch with that Tony Parsons who's always on the phone and ask him if he can do a quick thousand words on Sid.

Cheers,
Rog.

Twenty Six

By the time they reached Hemp–Weft, Stuart was barely keeping it together. He had to be helped from the carriage and into a lift set back in the shadowed recesses of the platform, and when the doors hissed open and they walked out into an almost exact replica of the warehouse space they had left behind, complete with a jumble of TV screens and a wall of computer equipment, Stuart moaned softly. But it was when he noticed Luther Blisset, Karen Eliot and Monty Cantsin lounging on the bean bags and sofas in front of the televisions that he lost the use in his legs, sat down heavily on the floor, and began dry–retching until his eyes clouded with tears.

"You didn't think I'd blow up our Fortress of Solitude and not have a spare, do you?" said Tyler.

Stuart dragged himself over to the sofas. It was Luther, Karen and Monty, but not the ones who had died in the warehouse. They were different people.

"Hey, Stuart," said Luther, passing him a beer. "Had some tinnies on ice for you, mate."

Stuart pulled himself up and popped the tab on the can. He took a long swig and wiped his hand across the back of his mouth, then pointed his finger at Tyler. "All those policemen. You killed them?"

Tyler took a beer and flopped down. "Hopefully, though I'm sure a few got out."

"Jesus Christ," whimpered Stuart. "How could you?"

Tyler shrugged. "They killed Monty, Luther and Karen. They would have killed Monroe and MacGuffin. They'd probably have raped Monroe first. They were going to kill you, Stuart."

"But they were the police..."

Monroe put a hand on his head and ruffled his hair. "He's right, Stuart. They weren't... *proper* police. Well, they were, but they were on Grundy's payroll. They really were going to kill us, Stuart."

248

"But..." said Stuart, waving his hands around. "All this..."

"It's late," said Tyler kindly. "Go get some sleep, Stuart."

Stuart did feel tired. Tyler said, "Mac, give him something to cool his jets."

MacGuffin dug into his pocket and handed Stuart a small pill.

"Copyright?" said Stuart.

"It'll help you sleep," said Tyler. Stuart put the pill on his tongue and washed it down with beer.

"Where's my room?" he said.

Tyler pointed his thumb towards a corridor leading off the main area. "Same place, Stuart. See you in the morning."

It was a little before seven when Stuart surfaced from a deep, inky abyss of dreamless sleep. He felt rested but anxious, and when the night's events came rushing back to him he sank back on his pillow, knowing he should weep but for some reason feeling he was about to laugh.

His room was laid out as before, a mezzanine floor with bed and bathroom, living area below with kitchenette, storage, PC set–up and wide–screen TV. How the hell had Tyler enough money to outfit two identical places like this? And were there any more like it around London?

Stuart showered and dressed, finding the disc he'd hurriedly brought with him from the last base. He left it on the keyboard. The book was the last thing on his mind at the moment. Instead he turned on the TV.

Seconds later he was running down the corridor, yelling. He emerged into the central area, where Mac and Luther were watching the TV screens while Tyler, off to the left, was pushing bacon and eggs round large sizzling skillets. Cooking smells filled the still air and Stuart realised he was famished. The TV screens were showing what he'd seen on his room set – the pictures of them climbing Big Ben, endlessly looped footage of the banner being unfurled, Stuart's name writ so much larger than life. He had a stupid grin on his face as Monroe joined him.

"Christ, was that only yesterday?" said Stuart as Tyler walked over, balancing plates of food on his forearms.

"Get it while it's hot," said Tyler.

Monroe shook her head. "Think I'll just get some fruit," she said, then looked at Tyler. "You went out late last night."

"Couple of errands to run," said Tyler, smiling. "Anyway, there's fresh fruit over there, as well as coffee."

"You're chipper," observed MacGuffin.

Tyler balanced his plate on his lap and dug in. "It's a new dawn," he said through a mouthful of sausage. "We have burned in the fire and have risen from the flames afresh. We have a new headquarters, a successful mission all over the TV and *pop*CULT! is seven once again, despite Grundy's best efforts. We're moving faster than we ever have before."

"What now, then?" said Monroe.

"Now," said Tyler, "Mr Balfour must finish his book, and we must give him space and encouragement to do so. The rest of us, we must prepare, for a time of change is upon us. But nothing that won't wait until after breakfast, eh? In the meantime, let's see what they're saying about us."

Tyler turned up the volume on the TV, zoning in on one of the breakfast news programmes.

"...police say they have a number of leads and are making extensive inquiries at the university which is publishing the book '*pop*CULT!'. Its author, Stuart Balfour, is believed to be a former student of the university and although it has not yet been confirmed that he was one of the four people involved in yesterday's audacious publicity gimmick at Big Ben."

The TV cut back to the studio, where the newsreader said, "Back to our top story now. Nine police officers are dead and six are in a critical condition in hospital following the collapse of a warehouse in East London late last night.

"Scotland Yard said the men were on a training exercise in the area when the derelict building began to fall in upon itself. The officers rushed to the scene to see if there were casualties but several of them were caught up in the collapse. Public health officials are on site and an operation to recover the bodies is continuing this morning."

Tyler barked a laugh. "Training exercise. Love it."

"Oh, God," said Stuart. "We killed them."

Tyler shrugged. "You heard the man. A derelict building collapsed. The officers were on a training exercise. It was on the TV news; it must be true."

"But we killed them," said Stuart again. "We're murderers. What was it, a bomb, then?"

"MacGuffin laced the walls with explosives, just like he's laced the walls of this place with explosives. We can't risk our work getting into the hands of Grundy, Stuart." Tyler tossed him a pill. "Take some Copyright. Calm down."

"I don't want to take some Copyright," said Stuart angrily.

"Go on," said MacGuffin. "You need to write. Copyright'll put you in the right frame of mind."

Stuart sighed and swallowed the little white pill. Immediately he felt warmth spread through his bones, felt his jangled nerves untangled and smoothed. He barely noticed when Tyler handed him another pill and he took it without comment, not catching Monroe's reproving glance towards Tyler. Stuart finished his breakfast and was about to wash his plate when a familiar face was flashed up on the TV screen. It took him a moment to realise the still photograph was of Walter.

"And this just in," said the newsreader. "Police have launched a murder inquiry after the body of a man was found in his flat in Islington. Walter Vaughan, forty–eight, had been bludgeoned to death. There was evidence that his flat had been broken into. Police say it appears the motive was robbery, although Mr Vaughan was apparently well–known in the city's gay community and officers will be concentrating their inquiries there."

"Oh, shit," said Stuart. "Oh, shit."

"Grundy," Stuart heard Tyler say as though through a very long funnel, and then the second Copyright kicked in and he checked out.

Stuart was browsing through the musty paperbacks in the dark recesses of Uncle Einar's, his favourite second–hand bookshop in the whole of London. He had a pile of potential purchases under the crook of one arm, the *Necronomicon*, the *Celestial Homecare Omnibus*, *The Secret Mirror*, and other imaginary texts. He removed another book from the Borges section and was surprised to see Walter's eyes twinkling at him from the other side of the shelf.

"I thought you were dead," said Stuart.

"I am," said Walter, swinging around the shelf to his side.

"Is this some *pop*CULT! thing? Are you trying to speak to me from beyond the grave? To issue a warning or something?"

Walter stroked his moustache. "Afraid not, dear boy. I'm merely a construct of your poor, overloaded brain. You really should watch it with all those pills, you know. You don't really know what's in them, after all."

Stuart sat down heavily on one of the stools Uncle Einar dotted about the labyrinthine shop for customers to reach the racier texts he placed on upper shelves and to sit down and peruse them when they finally got their hands on them. "This is where we first met, isn't it?"

Walter nodded. "Sadly, the books on offer that day were slightly more pedestrian than the fictional books you appear to be buying. Although I did find a first edition of Colin McInnes's *City of Spades*, if I recall correctly. Or rather, if you recall correctly."

"I was looking for old *TV Century 21* comics. I think I found a stack right at the back, but they'd got dried cat sick on them."

"Hmm, I recall the smell," said Walter, wrinkling his nose. "You thought I was trying to pick you up but, dear heart, I'm afraid I never sleep with a boy who smells of regurgitated Whiskas."

"Not on the first date, anyway."

Walter laughed lightly. "And it was that humour which made me like you, Stuart. Although you were very quick to introduce me to your wife. Just to avoid any confusion, I expect."

"Ex–wife," said Stuart morosely. "As I have to keep reminding myself."

"Anyway," said Walter briskly. "I suppose we'd better get on with this."

"With what, exactly?"

"You know, message from the id, subconscious red alert, all that kind of thing. It's your sensible side of the brain talking now, just to let you know that all this wild sex and casual murder and strange entities with psychic powers, it could just push you over the edge. So be careful."

"What do you think that thing is, in the sewers? And those Machine Elves?"

"Isn't it obvious? They've told you, in their own way. Or at least tried to."

"All that stuff about home. And their home. A vast library of feelings and experiences... but it's like nowhere on Earth."

"Exactly."

"Aliens?"

"Well, what do you think?"

"But... aliens? And what about the thing, *pop*CULT!? Is that an alien, too? What's the relationship between *pop*CULT! and the Machine Elves?"

Walter looked at him chidingly. "Stuart, isn't it blindingly obvious?"

Stuart pouted. "No."

Walter sighed. "Stuart, they're its–"

Stuart came to lying on his bed. His watch told him it was four hours since he'd wigged out; almost lunch–time. He was hungry. He rolled his legs off the bed and stood up, noticing as he stretched that the computer was humming in the corner. He flicked the mouse to kill the screen–saver and frowned, scrolling back through the document on the screen. Someone had added at least ten thousand words to the manuscript since the last time he'd written anything. And it was damned good stuff, too. As he read it back, gradual recognition that he had actually written it filtered through to him. So he hadn't been out cold, as he'd assumed; he'd been sitting here, working. That Copyright was, as Luther might say, the shit. He ventured out into the corridor to see if he could find some lunch, and maybe one or two more pills. It was only when he emerged into the central area that a huge, racking sob escaped from him and he stumbled, the full enormity of the fact that *Walter had been murdered* hitting him a glancing blow against the head. Monroe and MacGuffin were at his side immediately, helping him towards the sofas.

"But why? Why Walter?" he managed.

"Because he knew where we were," said MacGuffin. "Grundy couldn't get at you, so he got Walter. That's how he found us."

Stuart doubled over as though with stomach cramps. "God," he moaned. "I've killed him."

"Take this," said MacGuffin.

Stuart gratefully swallowed the pill

"Can I have some more?" he said.

Stuart took Copyright pretty much constantly over the next three days, breaking off from his frenzied writing only to eat or use the bathroom, or to snatch troubled sleep in half–hour sessions here and there. He avoided the others, concentrating on the book, on driving it along, on formulating his theories and drawing his conclusions, and when he finally emerged from the fog he pretty much had it finished. Some of it was so good that he almost cried, but he didn't know whether that was at the beauty of his prose or the fact that it was a book built on the foundations of Walter's grave. It was almost finished, but not quite. One thing remained to do.

"Stuart," said Tyler. "Man, I thought you were hibernating."

"He looks as though he has," snickered Karen, eating an apple. "Your hair's wild, Stuart."

They were still talking about the Big Ben escapade on the news, Stuart noticed distractedly. It looked like the lunch–time bulletin; he had absolutely no other idea what time of day or night it was in the windowless coffin that was the warehouse. The murder of Walter and the deaths of the police officers in the "accident" had long fallen off the news agenda. On the TV, Professor Garrett was saying, "...no idea of Mr Balfour's whereabouts, and I can only re–iterate that this publicity gimmick was in no way sanctioned by the university. We have no real evidence that Mr Balfour was actually involved or even behind the incident. Yes, we will be releasing the book as normal. Yes, it should be in the shops soon."

"They want to interview you on Richard and Judy," laughed Tyler. "Stuart, you're going to be huge when this book comes out. How's it going, anyway?"

"Nearly finished," muttered Stuart, sitting down and accepting a pill from Luther. "Just need one thing."

Tyler opened his arms. "Here to serve, Stuey. Name it."

"The reason I'm here," he said. "The DVD. It's about time you showed me *Carry On, You Old Devil.*"

When Tyler explained it to him, Stuart had to laugh in the way that you have to laugh or otherwise you'll roll into a ball of seething, frayed nerves and weep into your chest. The movie didn't exist. Not didn't exist as in *pop*CULT! didn't have a copy of it, but didn't exist. Had never existed. Was a lie, an insubstantial rumour, a ghost.

"But people have heard about it," said Stuart. "Walter heard about it. They talk about it on the internet."

"You remember I told you MacGuffin was a weaver of dreams, when you first came here? Well, that's one of his talents, one of his *pop*CULT! super–powers. He can create new myths, insert lies into the public consciousness and make them truth. He can weave whispers and create facts that you are absolutely certain you know, yet which have never, ever been true. When

MacGuffin puts the word on the street, the word becomes real. Or as real as anything. And when enough people believe something, well, it has to be true, doesn't it Stuart?"

You know how people used to say *never believe anything you read in the papers?* was how Tyler tried to explain it to Stuart. Well, now they don't believe anything unless they read it in the papers or the magazines or see it on the TV or catch it on an internet bulletin board.

"Experience is all," said Tyler as Stuart nodded and threw back more Copyright. "But it doesn't have to be your own experience. So long as someone says they've done something, that's good enough for most people."

"So *Carry On, You Old Devil*, it's just a rumour. A lie. It doesn't exist."

Tyler shook his head. "It is a rumour, it is a lie, but it also exists. It exists because people think it does."

"No, it doesn't," said Stuart. "It doesn't exist in a physical form, I can't actually hold it in my hands."

Tyler gave Stuart a crooked grin. "You could if you wanted to."

Stuart sighed. "But how?"

"This is *pop*CULT!," laughed Tyler. "We can do *anything*!"

While MacGuffin wove his magic, Tyler took Stuart to the lift.

"The Velvet Underground?" said Stuart. "Are we going to see *it?*"

Tyler shook his head and pushed the buttons. The lift jerked and began to move, but upwards. "Let's get a breath of air," said Tyler.

When the lift stopped, he pulled back the cage and let them out into a bare, musty room, edged with dirty windows letting in the dull afternoon light. Tyler unlocked a door and ushered Stuart out on to the flat roof of the warehouse above Hemp–Weft. The river was close, almost running past the warehouse. Stuart could see the usual landmarks wreathed in mist on the horizon, but couldn't place just where they were. "Near Putney," said Tyler vaguely.

"Putney?" said Stuart. "You're telling me there's a big warehouse in Putney that hasn't been transformed into loft apartments? And no—one knows we're here?"

"Hide in plain sight, and all that," shrugged Tyler. "Plus a bit of MacGuffin's tech. People just don't seem to notice us."

Stuart walked as near to the edge of the asphalt roof as he dared and looked out over the rooftops. London was teeming and out there, somewhere among them, beneath them, was *pop*CULT! itself, sucking their thoughts, their emotions, their experiences, and expelling them out again, to be picked up and thought about all over again.

"What's the point of it all?" he asked.

"Are you talking to me, or to God?" asked Tyler.

Stuart didn't take his eyes off the skyline. "Why, Tyler? Why devote your life to this... this crusade? Why do you care?"

For a long time, Tyler didn't answer. Stuart half turned and then jumped as Tyler whispered in his ear, "Because someone has to."

Stuart pulled himself back from the edge and Tyler went on, "I've seen men die, Stuart, and I'm not talking abstract concepts like bent coppers buying it in a booby—trapped warehouse. I mean that I've seen men die, close—up and personal. And they didn't even know why they were dying. They were just following orders. And they were following the orders of people who thought they were better, thought they led more worthwhile lives, thought they were more cultured, thought they had a right to send other men to their deaths.

"Ever since that moment I've embraced the power of low art, Stuart. Celebrity. The cult of personality. And slowly, over the years, the gap's been closing, Stuart, between them and us. To the point where it's barely distinguishable. Rock stars get invited to Downing Street. Reality TV shows dominate the front pages for weeks on end. The rich ape the lowest strata of society and call it fashion. Anyone, anywhere, can become a millionaire just by choosing six numbers. We can all be famous, Stuart, if only we want it enough. That's why. That's why *pop*CULT! exists."

Stuart pondered them in their millions, every man, woman and child with a story to tell, everyone with a book in them, everyone packed and ready for their curtain call, their alarms set for their fifteen minutes of fame.

"But it's just London," said Stuart. "The world's bigger than London."

"That's why your book must succeed, Stuart. That's why you must plant the seed of the irrevocably vital role of popular culture in every mind. This is just the first phase. Every city in Britain – every city in the world – needs its own *pop*CULT!."

"But there's only one," said Stuart. Then, after a pause, "There is only one, isn't there?"

The sky was darkening and Stuart felt a spot of rain on his forehead. Tyler had squatted down and then sat, swinging his legs over the parapet. Below, traffic honked and crawled and the Thames sluggishly rolled by.

"You know if you cut an earthworm in two you get two earthworms?" said Tyler. "*pop*CULT!'s a bit like that. Take a piece of *pop*CULT! and it'll eventually become a separate entity, absorbing its own emanations and growing at its own rate. You take a half a glass of *pop*CULT! and put it in a busy city and pretty soon you're going to have another *pop*CULT!."

"And have you done this?" said Stuart cautiously.

"No. Not yet. But imagine... Manchester, Birmingham, Leeds, Liverpool, Bristol, Glasgow, Edinburgh... Imagine, Stuart, New Fucking York. Hollywood. Mumbai. Paris. Tokyo. Bangkok. Half a glass, Stuart."

The rain came thicker. A wind grew up around them, swirling leaves and brittle litter up from the street. Stuart pulled his jacket around him. "Yes, but is the glass half full or half empty?"

Tyler laughed. "Depends entirely on your point of view, Stuart. Come on, I think MacGuffin should have cooked up a nice little surprise for you by now."

By the time they got back down to the warehouse, Monroe had

appeared and was watching TV, picking at a plate of nachos that Luther had prepared.

MacGuffin handed Stuart a shiny disc and a thick pink–and–yellow capsule.

"What's this?"

Tyler smiled. "*Carry On, You Old Devil*, like you wanted."

"But it doesn't exist."

"Everything exists. Especially if you take that pill."

Stuart looked at Monroe, but she refused to meet his eyes. He shrugged and took the disc and the pill back to his quarters. When he'd loaded up the DVD player he forced the capsule down, hit play, and settled down to watch.

Twenty Seven

It begins with moonlight, and the dark outlines of trees, rushing towards Stuart. Or rather, Stuart is rushing towards the trees, one with the camera. A flock of dark birds rise and caw as the camera dips dizzyingly and scoots low through the midnight fields of middle England. As a fence and stile flash beneath the music rises, ominous drumming and the underlaid voices of a choir, chanting in sinister Latin voices and rising to a crescendo which bursts as the camera leaps up, up, up and pans back to reveal a panorama of a typical English country village, at which point trumpets and keyboards intrude into the music, tempering the tune into a jolly music hall number.

PINEWOOD STUDIOS PRESENTS, says a caption.

A PETER ROGERS FILM.

Blood starts to drip unconvincingly from the top of the picture.

SID JAMES

PETER BUTTERWORTH

KENNETH WILLIAMS

BARBARA WINDSOR in...

The screen is now all bubbling blood.

CARRY ON, YOU OLD DEVIL!

The scene fades to a shot of a dusty room lined with books. At a desk sits Kenneth Connor, wearing bejewelled finery and a lopsided mitre. Before him stand Bernard Bresslaw and Terry Scott, dressed in black cassocks.

THE VATICAN, says the caption.

"Excellency, we bring grave news," twitters Terry Scott.

"The child of the Beast has been located!" says Bresslaw. "It is about to reach maturity! We must act now!"

Connor puts a hearing trumpet to his ear and squints. "What? Wildebeest? Where?"

"No, Excellency," booms Bresslaw. "The child of the Beast! The devil's daughter!"

Connor mugs and gurns in astounded surprise. "The devil's daughter! We must act now! We must contact the local priest! Where is this abomination living?"

The picture begins to fade as Terry Scott says, "England, Excellency." The Vatican is replaced by a pastoral village scene. "A small village called Elsteeth..."

It is a perfect English village, a chocolate box scene of glorious Home Counties sunshine, thatched roofs, a village green with duckpond, an olde pubbe with the sign "The Fiddler's Elbow" swinging in the slightest summer breeze. Down the street prances Babs Windsor in hotpants and tightly–stretched T–shirt, a shopping basket over her arm. She giggles at a barrage of wolf whistles from a group of thatchers working on a house roof, among their number Robin Askwith.

Askwith curls up his Jagger lips and grins. "Phwoar. Wouldn't mind a bit of that on my tea break."

His mate nudges him. "Not 'alf. That's Lucy Fare, that is."

Beneath their ladders, a stern–faced woman with her coat buttoned up stops and tuts. "She's a bad lot, that one, mark my words. She's no better than she ought to be."

Askwith brays like a donkey. "She's a damned sight better than you, love. I don't think I'd be crawling over her to get at you in bed."

The scene shifts to the inside of a village shop, where Lucy appears through the door, the bell above announcing her arrival. The shopkeeper, whose face Stuart knows from a hundred saucy old movies but whose name he can't recall, leers at Lucy over the counter. "'Ello, Lucy," he grins. "What can I do for you today?"

Lucy giggles and places her basket on the counter. "Ooh, you are naughty, Arthur. What would Mrs Trumpington say?"

Right on cue, Mrs Trumpington emerges from the back room of the shop, her face the archetypal bulldog chewing the wasp. She grimaces and snaps, "She'd say that girls like you ought to be a bit more respectful to your elders, Miss Fare. Now what are you in here for?"

"Crumpets, sauce," says Lucy, looking at her shopping list. "A

261

bit of the other...”

The shopkeeper snickers and his wife clouts him around the head. “I beg your pardon?”

“A bit of the other beef I had last week, not the one I’ve been getting,” says Lucy, a picture of innocence. “Father O’Toole reckons it plays havoc with his guts.”

Sid James is Father O’Toole, and his craggy face peers around the kitchen door in the presbytery of Elsteeth Parish Church, “Phwoaar,” he mutters, in the way only Sid can.

Lucy is bending over the cupboards and putting away the shopping. She giggles and says, “Is that you, Father O’Toole? Only I couldn’t get everything you wanted.”

Father O’Toole, wearing a long black cassock, comes into the kitchen. “It looks okay from here...”

Lucy, still bending over, says, “They didn’t have any of that rump you like.”

The camera lingers on Lucy’s behind and Father O’Toole grunts, “Oh, I think I’ll be all right...”

Later they are having a cup of tea in the garden. Lucy is upset. “I do wish they wouldn’t say all those nasty things about me.”

Father O’Toole pours a tot of whisky into his tea. “Let him without sin cast the first stone, and all that.”

“I’m not that bad, am I, Father?” says Lucy, dabbing at her eyes with a tissue.

Father O’Toole twitches and goes around the garden table to comfort her. “No, Lucy. In fact, you’re very, very good.”

She smiles. “Am I the best you’ve ever had?”

O’Toole gives a Sid double take. “Pardon?”

Lucy giggles through her tears. “The best housekeeper. Oh, you are naughty!”

Father O’Toole is in his study with the Vatican’s emissaries, Scott and Bresslaw. Sid can’t believe his ears.

“What? The Devil’s daughter? Here in Elsteeth? Don’t be ridiculous.”

262

"It's true," intones Bresslaw. "And our Holy Father has despatched us here to... you know."

"No I don't know," snaps O'Toole. "What?"

"Get rid of her," hisses Scott.

"Get rid of her?" says Sid incredulously. "You mean, *kill* her?"

Bresslaw says, "She *is* the off–spring of the Beast."

"But who is she?" says O'Toole in exasperation.

As the scene changes to the village high street again, Scott says in voice–over, "That we don't know. But she is someone who will already be leading men into temptation – that much is for sure..."

Lucy is up a ladder leaning on a thatched roof. Robin Askwith and the thatchers are at the bottom of the ladder, looking up at her hotpants–clad behind.

Lucy says thoughtfully, "Well, like I told you, I don't know much about roofs, but it looks okay to me."

Askwith winks at his colleagues and says, "We just wanted a second opinion, Lucy. What do you think of the pointing under the guttering?"

"Yes, I certainly think you boys have filled all the cracks."

The thatchers guffaw and Askwith gurns again. "Not quite all of them, love. Not yet, anyway..."

Later, having established that Lucy is the Devil's daughter, the two Vatican emissaries embark upon a number of comically–doomed schemes to kill her off. Lucy is exercising in the garden of the presbytery, touching her toes while wearing a revealing swimsuit. In the bushes, Scott and Bresslaw are lurking, Bernie peering along the sights of a crossbow.

"Have you got a clear shot?" whispers Terry.

"Oh yes," says Bernie, tugging at his dog collar.

"Are you going to let her have it, then?"

Bernie is sweating. "Do you really think I should..? Oh, yes. I see what you mean."

"I can see her," hisses Terry. "She's bending over now. I can see right up her–"

There's a comedy TWANG sound and Bernie's eyes roll into the back of his head.

"You made me shoot my bolt," he sighs.

Towards the finale, Lucy has been kidnapped by Bill Z Bubb, the local Satanist played with aplomb by Kenneth Williams. His acid-tongued wife is Hattie Jacques as Bella Z Bubb. They are in the woods near the village, Lucy tied to a tree. Both Bill and Bella wear loose purple robes.

"Hand me the chicken," announces Kenneth imperiously.

"They didn't have any," says Hattie apologetically.

"What? No chickens? How am I supposed to do a ritualistic summoning without a chicken?"

"I got this," says Bella, taking out of a carrier bag a rubber chicken.

Bill holds the chicken and regards it in disgust. "A rubber chicken? You want me to perform with a bendy cock?"

"It'll be an improvement on your usual efforts," says Hattie lightly.

In the trees, Sid and his faithful verger Canon Fodder, played by Peter Butterworth, are about to rescue Lucy. Fodder is watching proceedings with a pair of binoculars while Sid refers to an ancient book on Satanism.

"What are they doing now?" whispers Sid.

"Oh, lumme," says Butterworth. "They're taking their clothes off."

"Skyclad, they call it," says Sid, reading from the book.

"Now that Bella's got her robes off and she's dancing around the tree – in the buff!"

"Widdershins?" asks Sid, still reading.

"Widdershins," says Butterworth, taking the binoculars away from his face. "Widder knees, widder belly, widder..." he holds his hands at his chest, balancing two invisible hefty weights.

When Bill and Bella finally summon Satan, he steps from a none–too–convincing billow of red–tinged dry ice in the form of

Charles Hawtrey, wearing a tank–top and thick glasses. A rubber tail hangs from his behind and he has little horns poking through his neat hair.

Bill and Bella prostrate themselves at his feet. He smirks slightly and says, "Oh, I say! Do get up."

"Dark master!" proclaims Williams. "Welcome to Earth!"

Hawtrey glances at Williams' off–screen nether regions. "Bit cold for the time of year, isn't it?"

Bell gives her husband a reproachful glance. "I told him it was too chilly to do naked rituals, but he is a stickler."

"Yes, that's what I'd call it as well," muses the Devil.

Turning to Babs, still strapped to the tree, Bill says, "Lord Satan, we present to you... your daughter, Lucy Fare!"

Lucy writhes and struggles in her bonds. "Get me out of here! He's not me dad."

Hawtrey chuckles. "Now don't be a naughty girl, or I'll have to put you over my knee."

Bill says hopefully, "I could do that for you, Master..."

Then it's the white hats to save the day as O'Toole and Fodder swoop on the Satan worshippers and their master.

Bill Z Bubb runs at O'Toole with a stick, shouting, "Away from here, holy man! You are in the presence of a greater god!"

Sid swats him away with a punch and mutters, "You know, you're getting right on my Wicca."

Sid is uncertainly stalking towards an unperturbed Hawtrey, his crucifix held aloft. He hisses, "Get behind me, Satan!"

The Devil smirks. "Ooh, if you insist."

Then O'Toole and Fodder are wrestling with Hawtrey.

"I've got the tail!" announces Butterworth.

"I've got the horn!" shouts Sid.

"Ooh, you are naughty!" giggles Hawtrey.

When the Devil has been despatched back to hell, Sid rescues Lucy from the tree, and she swoons into his arms. "Where did he go?" she sighs.

Sid, his face grimly set, says, "Back to where he came from. A place where there is no light or goodness and the damned cry out in torment."

"Balham?" muses Canon Fodder in the background.

Sid picks Lucy up in his arms and stalks away from the woods. "What are we going to do now?" she says.

Sid grins. "How's about you and me go back to the presbytery, run a nice hot bath, and break open a couple of bottles of communion wine?"

Lucy looks mock–horrified and giggles, "Father O'Toole! I thought you'd taken a vow of celibacy!"

Sid cackles. "Yeah, I think I've got some celery in the kitchen. Whatever tickles your fancy! I won't tell the Pope if you don't!"

In the closing scenes, Bernard Bresslaw and Terry Scott are peering in through the presbytery window while, off–screen, Sid cackles and Barbara giggles.

"Do you think we should report back to the Vatican now?" whispers Bernie.

Terry is up against the window as far as he can possibly go. "In a minute. Let's just... erm, check on things for a little while longer..."

They then jump like scalded cats, and behind we see Peter Butterworth training a hose–pipe on them. The two emissaries flee.

Butterworth turns off the hosepipe and shakes his head. "Good Lord above," he mutters. "What a carry on!"

Twenty Eight

As the credits rolled, Stuart didn't know whether to laugh or cry. This was what it had all been for, the whole reason he had allowed himself to be drawn into this madness. The whole reason Walter was dead.

Was it worth it? He wanted to say no, of course. He wanted to take the disc out of the DVD player and snap it in two. But for ninety minutes he had been enthralled, dutifully dipping into the bowl of Copyright pills on the sofa every quarter of an hour as instructed. He felt exhilarated and empty all at the same time. Now he'd seen *Carry On, You Old Devil*, he could finish his book. But... what then? Would it all be over?

Unsteady on his feet, Stuart sought out MacGuffin. He was sitting alone in the central area, tinkering on one of his PCs. The others were all in their quarters, or out doing whatever they did.

Stuart tossed the disc on to the computer desk, startling MacGuffin out of his concentration. He looked at the disc then up at Stuart. "So," he said measuredly. "What did you think?"

Stuart considered the question. "It had all the ingredients of a classic," he began. "But with the flavour of the later Carry Ons – a little jaded, a bit tired. In short, it was perfect. It was as I would have expected. But..."

"But?"

"But it wasn't real, was it? It was never made. Tyler told me the whole thing was just a rumour, a hoax put out by *pop*CULT!."

MacGuffin nodded, inviting Stuart to sit beside him. "It never existed. It was just a rumour. But a rumour made real, at least temporarily, at least for you."

"But why?" said Stuart. "Why go to all that trouble?"

MacGuffin shrugged. "Just following orders. It was designed to bring you to us."

Stuart thought about this, about the card he'd seen Monroe put in the newsagents' window what seemed a lifetime ago. It was bait, purely to entice him into *pop*CULT!'s web, purely to get him on–side so he could write his book in the rarefied atmosphere of Tyler's sphere of influence, purely to further *pop*CULT!'s ends.

"But if you can do that..." said Stuart, gesturing at the disc.

MacGuffin shook his head. "I didn't do it. *pop*CULT! did it. I just facilitated it, teased it in the right direction, told it what we wanted."

"But it's a miracle," breathed Stuart.

"It's like the Hampstead Hogs," said MacGuffin. "And the Urban Spaceman."

Stuart remembered the Urban Spaceman. "You mean he's a *pop*CULT! construct too?"

MacGuffin nodded. "He appeared at the tail end of the Sixties. He's mankind's wonder at the mysteries of outer space made flesh. *pop*CULT! picked up on that and created him, and now he wanders the streets of London. Mostly invisible or unnoticed, but sometimes he appears at important moments. We don't know what draws him. Making the film was just like that, but we harnessed the creative spark, kneaded it, directed it into what we wanted. Well, the Machine Elves did, anyway."

There was a book on MacGuffin's desk and Stuart picked it up. A paperback with a lurid cover illustration. *The Lady Is Ready*, by Jason King. Where had Stuart seen that before?

"That's another one, like the Carry On film," said MacGuffin, pointing at the book. "Made it years ago; can't even remember what for, now."

"Are the Machine Elves constructs of *pop*CULT! as well?" asked Stuart. Since they'd moved to the Hemp–Weft warehouse, he had been ever more acutely aware of their presence. He presumed it was something to do with all the Copyright he'd been taking.

"I think so," said MacGuffin. "I'm not really sure. They seem to exist in a... a different space to us. I can't really explain it. But I'm pretty sure *pop*CULT! made them as well."

"No," said Stuart absently flicking through the book. "I've just worked out what Walter was trying to tell me. The Machine Elves aren't *pop*CULT! constructs..."

He stopped, looking up into the middle distance. A fanfare was sounding in his head, an explosion of colour and light behind his eyes. The Machine Elves were rejoicing and clamouring around the periphery of his vision.

"They're its *crew*," he whispered.

Stuart had left MacGuffin at a run, heading back to his room where he collapsed on the bed, momentarily blinded by the storm in his head. He still clutched the book in his hand. The Machine Elves were jostling and pushing, throwing images and emotions at him, hammering home the fact that he'd finally got it, what they had been trying to tell him all this time. Now he had finally picked his way across the gulf between their consciousness he was being dazzled by data, gasping for breath as the info–dump swamped him, as the presences – no longer Machine Elves, such a pedestrian, human description would never do now that Stuart had a handle on how to communicate with them – embraced him.

Now he knew why they had constantly plucked memories and images of childhood and home from him, and clumsily tried to reciprocate with visions of their own far–off origins. The thing in the sewers was some kind of craft and they had travelled vast interstellar distances within it. Stuart opened his eyes.

[Stuart opens his eyes. I open my eyes. They speak to me without words, without pictures, but in bursts of pure emotion. Through their unhuman eyes I see what they see, their world, occupying a space between the atoms of our own. An ordered, peaceful world with a massive understanding of the greater universe, of the life–forms that teem within it, and with a desire to document, to catalogue, to preserve for eternity every imprint made upon the canvas of infinity by every single living thing. I see their ship, their craft; of them but not them, sentient but not intelligent, seven–fold berths and a riot of colour and joy as they leave, one among hundreds, thousands, spreading like dandelion–clocks on the currents of the universe, logging and recording everything they

269

see. They try to offer me feelings to convey how it works.

"Ontology?" I suggest, but they shimmer with non–understanding.

"Ideas," I say, and they oscillate through several frequencies.

"An ideas drive?"

They rejoice. A ship powered by ideas, propelled by the jetsam–stream of waste thoughts and concepts. Even as they collect, they move. On and on through all infinity.

Through their eyes I see a land of giants, a morass of humanity, life and death, filth and finery. It is Earth, five centuries ago or more. They are moving from the space within space into the proper space, but something is wrong. The ship is malfunctioning. It is crippled. It shifts from the space within to the space without, to our space, but they, its crew, do not. They are trapped between spaces and their craft is listing and groaning, collecting and collecting but unable to move forward or back, just to grow bloated and fat on the burgeoning thoughts of a world embracing its most rapidly expanding period. I understand. Stuart understands.]

Stuart understood. Or at least, he thought he did. They had come to Earth to document humanity, and had ended up stranded here. And now they wanted to go home. The concepts were too big for him to get his head around. Not knowing what else to do, Stuart fired up the PC, switched off his mind, and got to work on the closing stages of the book.

Stuart worked for most of the day and into the night, then collapsed exhausted into bed. As he was surfacing from a deep, dreamless sleep twelve hours later, Tyler and Monroe took a light brunch on the roof of the warehouse.

"He's probably just about finished, now," said Monroe, taking a bite from a muffin.

Tyler swallowed a mouthful of coffee. "Mmm. Time for the next phase of the plan, then."

"Which is?"

"We need to take the manuscript to the university. I want you to go with it today, get this Garrett chappie to nail down a publication date. Make sure he's got his marketing and PR strategies in order."

"And then?" asked Monroe.

Tyler reached around to the waistband at the back of his jeans and withdrew a handgun. He checked the ammunition cartridge and slammed it back into its cradle. He handed the gun over to Monroe.

"And then, you know what to do."

For a long time after he woke, Stuart ignored the rumblings of hunger in his stomach and the pressure on his bladder, and just gingerly descended the steps from the mezzanine floor to sit at his still–humming computer monitor. Gingerly because for the past few days his world had been this windowless room, his personal hygiene lacking and his diet mainly consisting of Copyright. And even as the thought occurred to him, he absent–mindedly dipped into the dwindling bowl of pills for his first one of the day.

The book was, as far as he could tell, finished. True, he could keep putting it away and coming back to it, and tinker with it to destruction. But really, it was finished. Completed. Done. His plan to place *Carry On, You Old Devil* at the heart of the book had obviously come to nothing, but instead he had consoled himself with a peregrination on the memetic nature of popular culture, how ideas could spread like viruses until they became, for all intents and purposes, real.

Stuart felt... nothing. Empty. As though he'd wrung every drop of himself out and poured it into the book. He was a monochrome reflection, devoid of thought, deed and word. It was all there in front of him, the history of popular culture, its place in modern society, and the very essence of Stuart Balfour, encompassed in one hundred and twenty thousand words which marshalled themselves quite nicely under the banner of "*pop*CULT!".

He ran the words around his tongue. "*pop*CULT!, by Stuart

Balfour. Stuart Balfour's *pop*CULT!. Hi, I'm Stuart Balfour, author of *pop*CULT!."

Stuart saved the work to a CD and ejected the disc, placing writing the title and name on the back in marker pen and placing it carefully in a jewel case. It was time to tell them he'd finished.

Professor Garrett was rather surprised to see his secretary usher Miss Monroe into his office. It had been some time since he had seen her, and he had begun to think she would never walk through his door again. This time she had inexpertly bleached blonde hair with a spider of black roots at the crown, and was wearing a black mini–skirt, long faux leather boots and a slightly soiled garish pink vest, which, by co–incidence was the outfit he had seen on a prostitute on the streets as he took the bus home yesterday evening, and who had invaded his sleep in the small hours of the morning.

"Miss Monroe," said Professor Garrett, pulling out a chair for her. "I was concerned that your people had severed links with the project after all that unpleasantness on the news this week."

"Unpleasantness?" smiled Miss Monroe sweetly.

"Yes," said Professor Garrett. "All that Big Ben nonsense. I can categorically assure you that the university was in no way involved with the stunt and, as far as I'm aware, it is not something that Stuart Balfour would get involved in, although I've been unable to reach him since it happened and his flat seems to have been visited by the police, according to his neighbour, a very sweet Polish woman—"

Miss Monroe cut off Professor Garrett with a hand in the air. "My... *people*, as you put it, are still very much interested in this project, Professor Garrett. I have been sent here to find out what your plans are regarding the marketing of the book and when you plan to release it."

"I believe Balfour has now decided that it's to be called *pop*CULT! or something," said Professor Garrett. "Which is not a title I would have chosen—"

"The title is not up for negotiation," said Miss Monroe sharply.

Professor Garrett shrugged. "Anyhow, we have printers and book–binders ready and plan to get the book into circulation by early Spring."

Miss Monroe delved into a shabby handbag she was carrying. First she removed a piece of folded paper. She handed it to Professor Garrett and he opened it. It was a cheque.

"Good Lord," said Professor Garrett, goggling at the figures.

"That is a contribution from my *people* towards production, marketing and distribution costs of *pop*CULT!. Please spend it wisely and spend it all, Professor. We want to see this book reviewed in every newspaper and magazine, read in every coffee shop, on display at every train station and airport. If you have to employ a team of marketing specialists, then do so."

"B–but I haven't even seen the manuscript, yet," said Professor Garrett, still staring at the cheque.

Miss Monroe dipped into the handbag again and withdrew a shiny CD. She pushed it across the desk towards Garrett. "I think you will find all this in order."

"This is the manuscript?" said Professor Garrett, picking it up. "Then you have seen Balfour?"

"Mr Balfour is... safe," said Miss Monroe shortly. "He is in a place conducive to creativity and industry. No doubt you shall be hearing from him soon."

She stood to take her leave and Professor Garrett felt a surge in his trousers. "Miss Monroe?" he said in a small voice.

She smiled. "Oh, yes," she said, leaning forward and allowing him to look down her vest. Then she inched up her skirt. She wasn't wearing any underwear. Professor Garrett came politely in his underpants and Miss Monroe nodded then left.

After eating with a surprisingly subdued Luther and Monty in the living space, Stuart went back to his room for a long bath, during which he pondered what would happen next. Presumably he would have to do some publicity for the book, author tours and such–like. There might even be newspaper interviews, radio features, TV appearances. He began to get quite excited at the prospect. He held his breath and sunk under the water. He was going to be a proper author, he realised. He might even become famous.

Stuart had just dressed and was towelling his hair, thinking he might be due for a hair–cut, when there was a curt knock at the door. It was Monroe.

"Hi," she said, coming into his room and closing the door behind her. She was wearing a loose, long cardigan, jeans and a T–shirt, her hair in a pony–tail. She glanced down at herself. "You must be tired, Stuart. I'm not in suspenders and a basque today."

He nodded, helping himself to a Copyright. "Pretty tired. But good. Glad to have the book finished. Speaking of books, I found this on MacGuffin's desk and..."

Stuart's voice tailed off as he picked up the paperback. He'd remembered where he'd seen it before. *The Lady Is Ready*. It was Walter. Walter had it. And if *pop*CULT! had it now...

Stuart sat down heavily on the sofa. "It wasn't Grundy," he breathed. "It was... Tyler?"

Monroe joined him on the sofa. She looked into his eyes for a long time. "He figured out it was Walter who had told Grundy about the warehouse. He went to see him the night we were raided. It turned out Grundy's men had visited your friend, roughed him up a little, got the Praxis Street location from him. Tyler got a little... angry."

Still smiling sadly Monroe reached into her cardigan and removed the gun, placing it between them on the sofa. Stuart looked down at it. "What now? More missions? More killing?"

"This is what happens next," said Monroe, her hand still on the gun. "This is the next phase of Tyler's plan."

"I don't get you."

"More killing, Stuart. Well, one more killing. Yours."

Stuart half–laughed, then stopped, seeing she was serious. "Why?" he said in a small voice.

Monroe picked up the gun and levelled it at him. "Because dead authors sell an awful lot more books, I'm afraid."

Stuart felt all the energy sap out of him. He sat back heavily on the sofa and closed his eyes. "God," he muttered. "Can things get any worse?"

Monroe put the gun in her lap. "Stuart, for a few days I've been trying to tell you something. I want you to help me."

"Help you to do what?"

"Get out of *pop*CULT!. Get away from Tyler. Leave all this behind."

"Then just go," said Stuart. "Just walk away."

"I can't," said Monroe. "People don't walk away from *pop*CULT!. People don't leave, unless they're scraped off the pavement like The Waif or found floating in the Thames with a bullet in their foreheads, like..."

Stuart opened his eyes. "Like me?"

"That's what Tyler wants."

"And what do you want, Monroe?"

"I want to get out of here. And I want you to help me."

Stuart sat forward. "Look, if you're not going to shoot me, can you put that thing away? It's making me kind of nervous."

Monroe nodded and secreted the gun in her cardigan again. Stuart said, "So what are we going to do?"

"Well, Tyler's expecting me to kill you now and then go and dump the body. He'll be anticipating that we'll at least be having a farewell fuck, but we're going to have to move quickly."

"You mean *now*?" said Stuart.

"Well, yes," said Monroe. "Unless you want... well, you know. Bullet in the forehead. Floating in the Thames and all that."

"Jesus." Stuart stood and started to randomly pick things up and put them down again. "Jesus *Christ*."

"What are you doing?" said Monroe.

"I need to sort stuff out... to pack."

"For fuck's sake," said Monroe. "We're not going on holiday. Let's go."

Stuart reached automatically for the bowl of Copyright pills but Monroe slapped his hand away and the bowl went skittering across the table and spilled over the floor. "And you can knock that on the head, as well. Tyler's got you well drugged up. It's a wonder you can remember your own name."

Just then, Stuart did remember something. "Oh!" he said. "I need to tell you... About the Machine Elves and *pop*CULT!. I know where they're from and what they're doing here."

But Monroe had drawn the gun again and was peering out of his door. "Tell me on the train," she hissed, then grabbed him by the shoulder and hauled him into the dark corridor.

"You're quiet," said Tyler to MacGuffin. Luther and Karen were laughing at some cartoon show; Monty was skateboarding around the empty space at the end of the warehouse.

"I'm not happy, that's all," said MacGuffin quietly.

"About what? Balfour?"

"About Stuart," said MacGuffin pointedly, staring at his computer monitor. "I don't think it's fair."

"Fair?" mused Tyler. "It's not about *fair*, Mac. It's about *pop*CULT!. Have you forgotten?"

MacGuffin sighed. "Tyler, don't you think this has gone—"

Tyler held up his hand. "What was that?"

MacGuffin cocked his head. "I didn't—"

"Ssh!" said Tyler. "Luther, turn down the fucking volume!"

They all listened to the distant hum and rattle echoing from the gloomy corridor.

"Shit," said Tyler. "The lift. They're making a run for it."

Twenty Nine

"**S**o where are we going to go?" said Stuart as they seated themselves in the carriage of the train waiting for them at Hemp–Weft and the Velvet Underground whispered into life. Monroe had sent one of the carriages eastwards and they had climbed into the other one, heading in the opposite direction.

"I don't know," muttered Monroe, glancing at the receding station behind them. "Just away."

"It doesn't sound much of a plan."

"I wasn't expecting to have to move so soon!" snapped Monroe. "I didn't think you were going to finish the book so quickly."

They continued in silence for a while, then Stuart said, "Well, what exactly are we going to do short–term? The Underground only goes so far."

"We'll ride to Void then get the hell out of here," said Monroe. "We need to get to street level."

"You mean we'll have to go to through the sewers? Past *pop*CULT!?" said Stuart, aghast.

Monroe nodded, but said nothing.

"Do you think they'll be following us?" said Stuart.

Monroe closed her eyes and took a breath. "Yes, they'll be following us. Probably with guns. Now can you just be quiet for a minute, Stuart? I'm trying to think."

Stuart sulked for the rest of the journey. It was him who they wanted to kill, after all. It was his friend who had been murdered. It was him who was on the run deep underground. All he had wanted to do was write a book. Who would have thought it would have caused so much trouble?

"We could go to the police," he said.

Monroe looked at him. "Yes, that would be a good idea. And when we've finished explaining about our involvement in a major civil disturbance at Big Ben, we can spend the rest of the time having the shit kicked out of us by the friends of the bent coppers that Tyler blew up at the Flock warehouse. Excellent plan."

Stuart decided to keep any more suggestions to himself until they were at ground level.

Back at the warehouse, Tyler was handing out guns and Copyright to Luther, Monty and Karen. "They'll either have gone back towards Makhmal or Broccade or forward to Corduroy or Void. There's no upward access at Corduroy or Broccade. I can't really see them heading towards Void, not so close to *pop*CULT!, so the smart money's on Makhmal. Luther, you go to Void just in case. Get some dampener plugs from Mac in case you need to go too near to *pop*CULT!. Karen come with me on the Underground to Makhmal; Monty you go overground to where the tunnel comes up. I think it's at a manhole outside a Burger King; Mac'll draw you up a schematic."

"And what when we find them, what then?" said Karen.

Tyler said nothing. MacGuffin turned from his computer screen and raised an eyebrow. "Girl asked you a question, Tyler. What then?"

"Why do you think we've got guns?" said Tyler.

"We waste them?" said Luther doubtfully. "Monroe too?"

"Nobody leaves *pop*CULT!," grinned Tyler ruthlessly. "It's my way or The Waif's way."

MacGuffin stood. "Tyler. Think about this. Just take a moment. Things are getting out of control."

Tyler made a show of ejecting the ammo clip and slamming it back into the handled of his gun. "Like I said, Mac. My way or The Waif's way. Now you be a good soldier and try to get a handle on which way they're headed, and contact us on the short–wave radio when you do. The rest of you, come on."

They left the train at Void, feeling their way through the blackness until they found the ladder leading up to the sewer tunnel. Monroe dug into her pocket and pulled out a pencil–thin

278

flashlight. "Is that all we've got?" said Stuart.

"It's better than nothing," said Monroe, grunting as she pushed open the trap–door. The smell of the sewers assailed them immediately. As she climbed through, Stuart started at a noise behind him. The Velvet Underground was moving quietly out of Void station.

"The train's going back," he hissed.

"Someone must have called it," said Monroe. "That means they're on to us already. Hurry up."

Stuart dragged himself ungraciously into the sewer tunnel. "Jesus," he said, pulling the neck of his T–shirt over his nose and mouth. "This really is foul. Which way?"

Monroe gestured with the torch along the narrow ledge. Ahead, something squealed and plopped into the water. "Rats," she said. "I hate rats. Take my mind off them and this Godawful stench, Stuart. What were you trying to tell me before? About the Machine Elves?"

As they inched along the slimy ledge Stuart said, "It's about *pop*CULT!. It's like a... well, it's like a spaceship. A UFO."

Monroe laughed and the sound ricocheted off the walls. "Is this more of Tyler's bollocks?"

"No, no," insisted Stuart. "The Machine Elves had been trying to tell me, but we couldn't match our languages up sufficiently to find the right feelings. They're from another planet, Monroe. They've been trapped on Earth for hundreds of years. *pop*CULT! is kind of a living spaceship, which runs off an 'ideas drive'. It sucks in ideas, thoughts, feelings, stores up the good ones, and uses the waste to propel itself along to the next planet."

"That," said Monroe, stopping and looking at Stuart in the gloom, "is possibly the most preposterous thing I've ever heard."

"It's true," said Stuart, pushing her along again. "The ship's crippled and growing at an incredible rate. It was only the size of a pin–head when they crashed here. It was never meant to be stuck in one place like this. It's sucking up too much stuff. The Machine Elves are trapped because they're connected to it. They want to go home."

"And they told you all this?"

"Sort of. I think they want me to help free them." Stuart thought about this for a minute. "Monroe, why was I brought to *pop*CULT!? I mean, why me?"

Monroe shrugged. "We needed a seventh member and Tyler asked me to cast about for someone."

"Just like that? Randomly?"

"Well, no. We asked for a bit of guidance. To be pointed in the right direction."

"From..?"

"Well, from *pop*CULT!. From the Machine Elves." Monroe stopped again and looked at him. "They brought you here, didn't they? They pushed us towards you. When we wanted MacGuffin to dream something up to draw you in, they came up with the Carry On movie. It was tailor-made to get you interested."

"But why me?" said Stuart. "Why me?"

"They must have known," said Monroe. "Must have known that you would be the one to... to do whatever they needed doing. To set them free. But how are you going to do it? What have they told you?"

"I don't know," said Stuart, bunching his fists in frustration. "I can't quite pick up what they're telling me. They seem to want me to... to destroy *pop*CULT!. And they think I can send them home. But I don't know how to do either."

"Destroy *pop*CULT!?" said Monroe slowly.

"Do you feel that?" said Stuart.

Monroe nodded. It was an oppressive, overbearing weight pressing down upon them, a dark, moiling, angry storm. "It's *pop*CULT!," she said. "We're practically right outside."

It knew. It knew that the Machine Elves wanted Stuart to kill it. It knew that he was going to. It was wailing at him, sending blocking transmissions to stop him latching on to just how they expected him to do it. He knew they'd given him the answer, knew it was inside him somewhere, but he was casting about and couldn't quite find it.

They were at the rusty metal door, now, and Monroe stopped, putting a hand to his chest. "Listen," she said.

Stuart cocked his head. There was a slight disturbance in the fetid air, a high–pitched sound bouncing off the wet curved walls. It seemed to be coming from behind them. "Rats?" he whimpered.

Monroe listened for a second or two more then her face fell. "Oh, fuck," she whispered. "It's the hogs. Run!"

"They've definitely come this way, Tyler," said Luther, shining his torch up the ladder at Void. "They've left the hatch open."

"Shit," said Tyler, his voice distorted by static over the short–wave radio. "We're not at Makhmal yet; we'll turn around and come back. It's going to be twenty minutes, though, even at full tilt. You'd better get after them."

Luther put the flash–light between his teeth and began to climb the ladder, poking his head out of the trap–door. But which way did they go? And what the hell was that noise..?

Luther ducked down just as the squealing and shrieking reached deafening volume and the first of the stampeding hogs barrelled around the corner, sloshing through the sewage–filled channel.

"Fuck!" exclaimed Luther, slapping at the radio again. "Tyler, there's a hog run!"

"They must have scented Monroe and Balfour," returned Tyler. "Get after the hogs and herd them towards them."

"*Herd* them?" said Luther doubtfully.

"It's okay," said Tyler. "If they're berserking they won't bother you. The hogs won't stop when they're on a run. You just make sure you keep them moving. We're passing back through Hemp–Weft now; we'll be with you in a minute."

Luther frowned then hauled himself back up the ladder just as the last of the herd, the squealing pale farrows at the back, passed by. He got to his feet and set off at a run, shouting uncertainly,

"Shoo! Erm, shoo!"

"How the fuck can we run through a sewer?" gasped Stuart, slipping on the sludge–damp stone and crashing into the brick walls.

"You'd rather get eaten by pigs?" said Monroe through gritted teeth, the flashlight beam careening around the walls as she ran.

There was a bend in the tunnel and abruptly the ledge ran out. "Bollocks," said Monroe. There was some kind of broken sluice gate and another channel forked away from them. She cast the light back at the rising squealing sounds and the first shadows from the hogs were painted crazily up the walls. "Into the water," she said, leaping down.

Stuart groaned and followed. "Eww," he said as the cold water seeped into his trousers. "Eww. There's shit everywhere."

Monroe waded through the calf–deep filth towards where the ledge began again. Stuart was behind her but slipped, thrashing about as his head went under. She hauled him up and he coughed and spat. Monroe pushed him towards the ledge just as the first of the pigs rounded the bend. She estimated there were maybe a dozen of them, three fat boars the size of small horses at the front, almost translucently pale from generations without sunlight, their tusks curling out from their snarling lips. The beasts slowed and regarded them with their black beady eyes, slop and drool spider–webbing their protruding teeth.

Stuart closed his eyes. "Oh, God," he said. "We're going to be eaten by feral pigs. This should sell a few copies of the book."

Monroe squinted into the darkness as the pigs inched forward. There was a figure creeping about at the rear of the herd. She shone the torch at it. "Luther?"

Stuart opened his eyes. "Thank God. They've come to save us."

"I don't think so," said Monroe through gritted teeth as Luther started to wave his arms and whoop. The hogs put their fat heads down and charged.

With a deliberation that seemed to Stuart to be almost insanely irresponsible, Monroe took careful aim with the handgun then let loose three sharp shots that cracked and echoed through the sewer chamber. The lead hog, now just ten feen from them, stopped short and, with a surprised look on its face, keeled over. The other hogs went into a frenzied squealing, climbing over themselves and turning in the shit. The boars pushed the sows and farrows out of the way and began to reverse and turn in the narrow channel, sighting Luther behind them and forgetting, for the moment, their original quarry.

Monroe gave Luther a salute as he realised what was happening. "Oh, shit," he said, and began to run back the way he came.

"Come on," said Monroe, dragging Stuart by the arm to the far ledge.

Luther set off at a sliding run back along the ledge, turning the bend and running into Tyler and Karen. "Hogs," he wheezed, pushing them backwards. Tyler set off at a run, hauling out the key to the *pop*CULT! room as he sprinted towards the metal door.

"In here," he said, unlocking it quickly and ushering Luther and Karen inside. He hauled the door shut behind him and they listened in a silence punctuated only by the faint fizzing and popping of *pop*CULT! as the hogs charged past outside.

Tyler risked opening the door a crack. "They've gone. Come on. Luther, how far ahead were they?"

"Thank fuck," said Stuart shakily as Monroe stopped and pointed at a rusting ladder set into the stone wall. She shone the torch up a dark cavity that stretched upwards for some way.

"Get climbing," said Monroe.

Stuart tried to count the rungs as he climbed, trying to get some kind of handle on how near the surface the ladder would bring them. He lost it at forty but figured that was enough; this must be some kind of old maintenance tunnel or something. He carried on climbing until his head banged against a metal hatch.

"Thank God," he whimpered. "Monroe, there's a hatch."

"Well open it, then."

Stuart pushed feebly at it. "It's locked."

"Well, put a bit of backbone into it, Stuart," grimaced Monroe. "And hurry up; you're dripping shit all over my hair."

As Sam clocked off she felt the stress of a ten–hour shift at Elysian Fields palpabaly lift from her shoulders. There was just the drive home to Stepney to negotiate, then the delights of a frozen pizza and two bottles of Tesco Pinot Grigio and her bed. And a whole day off tomorrow.

The residents were in the day room where Mrs P was holding another writers' workshop. Sam had flicked through the stories they had been polishing off for the anthology which Mrs P had now secured Arts Council funding for. She had to admit, they were pretty good. Who would have thought a home full of people who, frankly, spent most of their time dribbling into their custard, could be so consistently talented? Where did they get their inspiration, their creativity? It wasn't as though it even made them happy, thought Sam as she collected her coat and her bag from her locker. Mrs Trevor had been complaining that the stories "made her head ache" and more than usual had been waking with night terrors since the writing workshops began. As for Mrs P's almost hysterical schemes to get some of the more lucid residents on TV talk shows... Sam shuddered at the thought of it. Someone at Elysian Fields should be asking questions about whether this was the right sort of thing to be encouraging elderly people suffering from Alzheimer's and all sorts to get into, in Sam's opinion, but all there seemed to be at management level was a growing excitement that the home might be "put on the map" and "have its profile raised". Which, presumably, would mean TV and newspaper interviews for the forward–thinking members of the board who had agreed the project.

Sam was almost out of the door when she heard a muffled banging from the far end of the main corridor. She sighed. It was probably Mr Stevens, got himself locked in the cellar again. She wondered whose underwear he had stolen this time, whose surgical stockings he'd be wearing when they got him, shamefaced and weeping, out. Sam picked up the phone by the door and pressed eight. "Bob, I think Mr Stevens is in the cellar. Can you take a look? He gets awfully embarrassed if a female member of staff answers the door."

Then she was out into the darkening afternoon, fishing in her bag for her keys.

"Come the fuck on," hissed Monroe. "I can hear them."

"Monroe? Baby, it's Tyler. Let's not be rash about this." The voice floated up from the service chute. It sounded half-way up, at least.

Stuart rattled the door again. "It's locked," he said for the umpteenth time. The hatch, when it eventually gave way, had led to some kind of storage room piled high with boxes of bedding and broken easy chairs. A rickety wooden stairway led to the door Stuart was trying to tease open.

"Jesus," said Monroe. She pushed Stuart out of the way then began to kick and punch at the wooden door.

Bob the Elysian Fields handyman listened to the beating on the door as he sorted through his key–chain trying to locate the right key to the cellar store. That Mr Stevens. He was a right one. There was a surprisingly forceful kick to the door and the panel cracked down the middle. Bob blinked in surprise; who'd have thought it from Mr Stevens? He was about to slide the key in the lock when the door jamb splintered and the door was wrenched open from inside. "Blimey," said Bob.

Monroe took hold of his arms and eased him to one side. "Stuart, come on," she said. Stuart climbed through the shattered door behind her, nodding apologetically at Bob. He'd taken just two steps into the corridor when he stopped, tripping over his feet.

"Good God, we're in Elysian Fields."

"You know this place?" said Monroe, giving a coquettish smile at Bob, who was staring unabashedly at her. She looked just like the topless model he'd been studying in the Daily Star just before he got the call to see to the door.

"It's the home my mum's in," said Stuart. "It's practically on top of *pop*CULT!"

"Speaking of which," said Monroe. Tyler had appeared at the door, grinning insanely.

"Heeeeere's Johnny," he said.

Just then, Mrs P emerged from the dayroom, between the cellar door and Stuart and Monroe. "I must say," she began stridently. "All this disturbance is really not conducive to... oh! Mr Balfour! We were just having a reading from your mother."

Mrs P looked at Stuart's stinking, wet clothes and wrinkled her nose. "Oh, have you had some kind of... accident?"

The residents of Elysian Fields blossomed out into the corridor around Mrs P. Stuart's mother was among them. She blinked at Stuart. "Is it Saturday?"

"No, mum," said Stuart. "Look, I'm sorry I haven't been for a couple of weeks, but..."

Tyler sighed, stepping through the wrecked door. "As sorry as I am to break up this little family reunion – which, as far as it goes, is not sorry at all – I must insist that you two come with me, back the way we came. Wouldn't want to cause a scene here in front of your mother, would you, Stuart?"

Tyler held his gun loosely behind his back. The fight seemed to have gone out of Monroe. She took half a step towards the cellar.

"Mr Balfour, who are these people?" said Mrs P, annoyed.

Stuart thought about this. "Actually," he said, "actually, this is my literary agent."

Tyler looked at him, nonplussed.

"Yes," said Stuart, smiling. "This is my literary agent. I was telling him about the work you've been doing Mrs P, and he was most impressed. He said he wanted to read some of the stories, and indicated he was quite keen on actually taking on some of the residents as clients."

Stuart had never seen the inmates of Elysian Fields move so quickly. They looked at Stuart, at Tyler, at each other, then rose up as one, each brandishing a sheaf of printed A4 paper, clamouring and shouting, waving their stories, engulfing Tyler, who put up an involuntary arm to fend them off and found himself forced back through the door. As Mrs P began to call for calm and exhorted her charges to remember her five important points for submitting work to a professional publisher or literary agent, Stuart put his hand in the small of Monroe's back and propelled her down the corridor towards the front door.

"How do you know he won't hurt them?" said Monroe.

"He won't," said Stuart. "Not a bunch of old ladies. Surely not even Tyler's that far gone."

"We're thinking of calling the anthology *Have I Had My Tea Yet?*," Mrs P was saying. "But we are open to suggestions..."

As they ran out into the street, Stuart took a deep breath of air. "Christ, I thought I'd never see the sky again," he said.

On the street outside Elysian Fields was parked a battered orange Ford Fiesta. As Stuart cast up and down the street, wondering what they hell they were going to do next, and Monroe glanced back behind them towards the home, a window squeakily wound down on the car.

"Mr Balfour," said Sam coolly. "I wasn't aware it was visiting hours yet. Have you brought your girlfriend to meet your mother?"

"Oh, thank God," breathed Stuart raggedly. "Sam, you've got to help us. You've got to get us away from here."

Sam sat back in the vinyl seat, the engine idling roughly. "I've got to help you, have I? Do tell me why. And this better be good."

Stuart took a deep breath. "We're being chased by gun–toting underground pop culture revolutionaries who have a crippled

287

alien spaceship in the sewers under London and they're using it to give people ideas and encourage them to become celebrities and writers and pop stars to initiate a modern day peasants' revolt. And they're going to kill us."

Monroe gave him a sidelong look. "Stuart, you're trying to get us out of here, not pitch a movie."

Stuart looked pleadingly at Sam. "Please?"

"Actually," she said, "that was pretty good. Get in."

Thirty

Sam laid the tray of tea down on the coffee table in her living room. Stuart had wanted something stronger but Monroe had advised against it. He poured himself a cup and added two spoonfuls of sugar, standing by the window that looked down on to the bustle of late evening Stepney from Sam's third–floor apartment. He was feeling a little light–headed, a bit jumpy.

"That's the Copyright withdrawal," said Monroe, sipping her tea.

"You haven't got any, have you?" said Stuart in a small voice.

"It's the last thing you need. Between us we've probably got enough in our systems to lead Tyler right to us."

Sam contemplated a Custard Cream and considered what Stuart had just spent the best part of two hours telling her, which was pretty much everything from the moment he'd walked out of Bar Eschaton with Monroe to the minute they'd burst through the cellar door at Elysian Fields.

"Say I believed you," she said through a mouthful of biscuit. "Say it isn't the most bonkers thing I've ever heard. What are you going to do now?"

"Get away from here," said Monroe. "Abroad, preferably."

"What?" said Stuart, alarmed. "I can't flee the country. There's my mum to think about, for one thing. And besides, I've got to stop *pop*CULT!."

"Just remind me, how you were going to do that, again?" said Sam.

"I don't know," said Stuart miserably. "Well, the Machine Elves reckon I know, that they've told me, but I don't have the toolbox to dig out what's inside my head."

Sam sighed. "Look, I don't pretend to know what's going on here. But you're obviously in some kind of trouble, Stuart. You can both stay here overnight if you need to. You and Monroe can take my bed, I'll have the sofa."

"That won't be necessary," said Monroe. "We're not an item, Sam."

"In that case..." began Stuart.

Monroe gave him a look. "If you're about to suggest that Sam and I take the bed, you'd better keep it to yourself, Stuart."

"What is this thing with you?" said Sam curiously. "I mean this looking like you do. Different to different people."

"I'm a walking wank fantasy," said Monroe. "That's what *pop*CULT! does to me."

"And that's why we've got to kill it," said Stuart. "Otherwise, you'll never be free."

"How are you doing, Mac?" said Tyler impatiently.

MacGuffin tapped at his keyboard. "This isn't an exact science, Tyler. I can only crunch the numbers the Machine Elves suggest. They're being quite reticent about this. It's a bit of a struggle."

"I need to know where they are, Mac."

MacGuffin sighed and continued to sift through the data he'd managed to extract from communing with the Machine Elves. It was true what he'd said; they'd become very resistant to helping him recently. They certainly didn't want to give up the location where Monroe and Stuart had fled to. Theoretically, it was a fairly simple job to trace them, especially Monroe, given her long exposure to the Machine Elves and *pop*CULT! He would do it eventually; the Machine Elves could make things more difficult but ultimately they couldn't refuse him.

"How are you doing, Luther?" asked Tyler.

Luther looked up from where Karen was bandaging his leg. One of the straggling hogs had caught him on his calf with its tusk. "Not too bad, just a scratch, really."

"Good, because we need to get on the road again as soon as Mac's done the business. Everyone take five and get freshened up."

Tyler picked up a mobile phone from the desk near MacGuffin and punched in a number. "Monty?"

"No sign yet, Tyler," said Monty. "I did some road–kill

divination on a dead rat I found; somewhere central or the East End is likely. Has Mac got a handle on them yet?"

Tyler put his hand over the phone. "Mac?"

MacGuffin frowned. "Tell him Stepney's a possibility."

"Stepney," said Tyler into the phone. "Go and tag some of the main streets. We might not be able to pin–point them directly, but at least we can let them know we're closing in."

"Look, if that offer for the bed's still available, I'm beat..." said Monroe, stretching.

"Of course," said Sam. "I'll take one sofa and Stuart can have the other."

For some minutes after Monroe had retired, Stuart and Sam sat in an uncomfortable silence, in the cosy, lamp–lit living room. Stuart watched the watching the muted TV and glanced at the Indian knick–knacks dotted around the flat.

"So," said Sam.

"So," agreed Stuart.

"That was really shit, you know, just walking out of that bar with her and leaving me."

"I know. I'm sorry."

"I felt bloody humiliated. There we were, having a great time, or so I thought–"

"We were. Having a great time, I mean. At least I was."

"–and then she comes in and plucks you off my table and you just waltz out with her. And I'm left on my own and everyone's looking at me with this really pitying look in their eyes."

"I know," said Stuart wretchedly. "I'm sorry. Did you get home okay? I mean, well, obviously you got home okay, but–"

"Actually, some guy came and bought me a drink. He felt sorry for me, but what the hell. I brought him home and he fucked my brains out. He was amazing."

At first Stuart thought he was merely embarrassed but then he realised he actually felt quite forlorn at the thought of it. "Oh," was all he could think to say.

"Actually, I didn't really," said Sam, an inscrutable half–smile on her face. "I just got a taxi home, opened a bottle of wine, and wished a thousand Valerie Solanases on you."

"Valerie who?"

"You know, the woman who shot Andy Warhol. The Society for Cutting Up Men and all that."

"Right," said Stuart. "Well, in the circumstances, I can't say I blame you. That sounds fairly reasonable."

Sam laughed. "You know, you looked quite put–out when I told you I'd brought someone back. You've no right to, you know."

"No," said Stuart.

"Anyway," said Sam. "I'll go and get some blankets and pillows. It's probably time we had some sleep."

"Yes," said Stuart, and when Sam had arranged makeshift beds for them on the two facing sofas, he settled down. Long after she'd switched the light off, he stared at the dim, lightly–breathing outline of her, not quite knowing what to think. Then he drifted off to sleep.

Sam was already pottering about in the kitchen when Stuart awoke. He could hear the shower hissing and presumed it was Monroe. His neck was stiff and his feet were cold where they blanket had slipped off them, but other than that he felt a lot better.

Sam came in with a tray of tea and toast and placed it on the table. "I threw your clothes in the waste disposal chute," she said. "Sorry, but they stunk."

"They're the only ones I had," said Stuart.

"I found some old ones that Kev, my ex who I was in the band with, left here. I've put them on the dining table," said Sam as she threw open the curtains. It seemed a bright morning. Stuart looked at the clock on the DVD player; a little after nine.

"Oh," said Sam. "I didn't notice that yesterday."

Stuart rolled his legs off the sofa and wrapped the blanket

around him. He joined Sam at the window just as Monroe emerged from the shower, towels around her hair and her middle. Stuart didn't look at her. Instead, he was looking at the spray–painted letters on the wall opposite.

"*pop*CULT!," said Sam. "That's a pretty cool name, actually."

"They've found us," said Stuart.

"If they'd found us we'd probably already be dead," said Monroe. "They're probably just casting around, trying to flush us out."

"Well, we can't stay here," decided Stuart. "It's not safe for Sam. We're going to have to get moving."

"But where?" said Monroe.

"Tell me again," said Stuart, "about this Grundy character."

"No," said Monroe. "Definitely, absolutely, no."

"But what else are we going to do? Where are we going to be safe?" said Stuart.

"Anywhere. The Maldives. Peru. The North fucking Pole. But not with Grundy."

"But why?" persisted Stuart. "What do we really know about him, other than what Tyler's told us?"

Monroe opened her mouth and then shut it again. She had to grudgingly admit that Stuart had a point.

"Look," he said. "You don't have to do anything. You can go where you want. But I'm sort of stuck with this; the Machine Elves are relying on me to kill *pop*CULT!. I'm not really sure why, but it's something I have to do. I can do this on my own. And I think I need to visit Grundy, because he's probably the only person in the world not under Tyler's spell who might listen to me."

"If I've got this right about *pop*CULT!," said Sam, "then it's the reason that whenever you switch on the TV there's always a hundred programmes about interior design or slimming or making it in the music business. Whenever a book hits the best–seller list there are always dozens of imitators. Whenever a band comes out with a really good song, it kicks off a whole new genre. Is that it?"

"Pretty much," said Monroe. "It feeds popular culture back into itself and replicates until it can't go any further."

"So..." said Sam thoughtfully. "What would happen if it didn't do that? If it was no longer there."

Monroe and Stuart looked at each other. Monroe shrugged. "No more reality TV, maybe. No more tribute bands. No more kids wanting to be pop stars from the age of three. I don't know."

"Not much call for your book, then," said Sam.

Stuart looked at her. A shiver ran up his spine. He was about to say something but didn't know what.

"You can't go to Grundy on your own," decided Monroe. "I'll come with you."

"Me too," said Sam.

"No," said Stuart firmly. "You can't, Sam. I don't know how dangerous this is going to be. I'm not having you hurt."

Sam gave that half–smile again. "At least let me take you," she said. "Where does this Grundy live?"

Seven Canada Square was a slim, shining needle towering over the HSBC building on the next block and was almost as tall as the landmark, pyramid–topped flagship building at the centre of the Canary Wharf development.

"Wow," said Sam, idling the Fiesta. "He lives in that?"

"He owns that," said Monroe tightly.

Stuart peered up from the passenger seat. He was wearing a pair of skinny jeans that he couldn't fasten at the waist and a *Dead Kennedys* T–shirt with the sleeves ripped off. The battered trainers weren't a bad fit, however, and he'd manage to borrow a unisex denim jacket from Sam. Monroe had also raided Sam's wardrobe; when she'd slung on the velour jogging pants, sweatshirt and gym shoes, Sam had breathed, "Wow. I couldn't look half as good as that in my best stuff."

"So what do we do now?" he said.

"This is your call, Stuart," said Monroe.

"Right," said Stuart, unclipping his seatbelt and opening his door. "Sam, give me your mobile. Go home and keep your head down. Monroe, come with me. We're going to pay Mr Grundy a visit."

Monroe laughed humourlessly. "What, we're just going to walk in there?"

Stuart shrugged. "Pretty much," he said.

Sam handed him her phone and said, "My landline's down under 'home'." She gave him a quick kiss on the cheek and whispered, "Good luck."

As Sam drove off, Monroe pointed towards One Canada Square. "That's where The Waif died," she said. "I'm not really sure now that Tyler didn't plan it all along. Looking back, I'm almost surprised he didn't do the same to you at Big Ben. There would have been a certain symmetry to it."

"Don't worry," said Stuart, setting off towards Grundy's building. "Despite Tyler's penchant for high places, I don't think he'll be able to get at us once we're in there."

The lobby to Seven Canada Square was wide and airy and pretty much empty apart from some ergonomically–designed seating areas and a wide reception desk. Above the desk was a sign saying GNOSYSTEM SOLUTIONS. The centre of the glass–walled lobby held a circular lift shaft disappearing up into the next floor, some two hundred feet above. There was no–one in sight apart from a lone woman in severely bobbed hair and metal–rimmed spectacles, sitting patiently behind the reception desk.

Stuart strode up to the desk, Monroe casting glances all around in his wake. She put a hand on the reassuring bulge of the handgun in the waistband at the rear of her jogging pants.

"Hello!" said Stuart brightly. The receptionist glanced at him over the rim of her glasses. "We're here to see Mr Grundy."

She looked down a printed list on her desk and then frowned.

"Can you tell me what department he's in?"

"Mr Grundy," said Stuart again. "He, uh, owns this place, doesn't he?"

"This is the offices of Gnosystem Solutions," said the woman patiently. "It is owned by the company, whose main commercial office is in Geneva. I could check there to see if we employ a Mr Grundy, if you like?"

Monroe sighed and pulled out the gun, placing it on the desk. The woman, to her credit, barely blinked.

"Tell Grundy that *pop*CULT! is here," said Monroe. "Tell him that if he doesn't come down to see us, we're going to start shooting things. And smashing things. Writing our name everywhere. And probably pissing on stuff. And then we're going to get really obnoxious."

Keeping her eye on the gun, the woman pressed a button on the switchboard console. "George?" she said. "I think there's something here that needs your attention..."

"Tyler," said MacGuffin. "No. No, I won't do it. I've had enough."

"Yes, you will, Mac," said Tyler levelly.

"No, I won't."

Tyler hit him. Once, hard, to the stomach. MacGuffin doubled over, sitting heavily on the sofa in the central area of the warehouse, coughing and spitting.

"Do it."

MacGuffin looked up at Tyler. "Please, Tommy," he said. "Just cool your jets and think about this for a moment. You're not only asking the impossible, you're getting totally out of control. Forget about Stuart and Monroe; they don't really matter. Let them go. We can just carry on as we were. We don't need them."

Tyler squatted beside him, placing a hand almost tenderly on his shoulder. "Mac, come on, guy. This is everything we've been working towards for thirty fucking years. We can't give up now.

We're so close. So close."

Tyler helped MacGuffin to his feet. "Come on, let's do this. I've been to see *pop*CULT!. I've tossed a load of old American comic books into it. It should be ready now."

"I really don't know if I can do this, Tyler," said MacGuffin in a small voice. "I don't know if what you're asking is possible."

"It is," insisted Tyler. "Trust me. I just need you to distil what *pop*CULT!'s thinking about into one handy pill. Then I'll do the rest."

Tyler hobbled to his computer station and began to talk to the Machine Elves. After a minute, with Tyler hanging on his shoulder, he said, "They can't do it, Tyler. I knew they couldn't."

"They can," said Tyler. "They will."

MacGuffin worked for a little while longer. "It *might* be possible," he mused. "But it's going to put a lot of strain on *pop*CULT!."

"I know, I know, and I'll make it all right," said Tyler soothingly.

MacGuffin got to work and within half an hour he had a pill the size of a small table tennis ball in the palm of his hand.

"Fucking hell, Mac," said Tyler, plucking it from his grasp. "How the hell am I supposed to take this?"

MacGuffin shrugged. "It was a big ask, Tyler. It needs a big kick. You'll have to break it up."

As Tyler began to crush the pill with his thumb, MacGuffin said, "Tyler, I'm going to ask you one last time to reconsider. You're pushing *pop*CULT! too far, too fast. We don't know what might happen. What you're about to do is unlike anything we've asked it to do before."

"Not really," said Tyler, washing the fragments of the pill down with a bottle of water. "I'm only embracing humanity's post–human destiny. We're all going to be Superman one day, Mac. I'm just bringing it forward."

As Tyler swallowed the last of the pill, MacGuffin took an involuntary step back. Fairy dust crackled on Tyler's bare skin, his hair writhed with static. He grinned. "It's starting," he said.

Tyler looked down at his hands. Tiny golden sparks ran over them like maggots. His fingernails hardened to diamond. "Such power," he said wonderingly.

MacGuffin backed right up against the wall. Tyler's hair was flying around his head now like a fuzzy halo. Electrical impulses played around the fillings in his teeth. His skin had acquired a sheen, like the fuzz of a peach catching a lancing beam of sunlight. Tyler closed his eyes. When he opened them again, there was nothing but a swirling golden–brown mass there.

"Good God," breathed MacGuffin. "Tyler. You've become... I don't know."

"I am *pop*CULT!" said Tyler, his voice honeyed and oozing. "I am *pop*CULT! and *pop*CULT! is me. We are intertwined. We are as one."

"You've never taken so much before, Tyler. It can't be safe..."

Tyler looked at the ceiling. It rippled and dust fell down upon him. "Safe," he said. "I am beyond safe. I am beyond danger. I am beyond human."

"What are you going to do?" whispered MacGuffin.

"Taking care of business..." smiled Tyler, his lip curling. His eyes splitting light, he glanced at the ceiling again. It disappeared, covering him and MacGuffin with more dust and debris. He said, "...in a flash."

MacGuffin reached down, his hand clasping a screwdriver on his desk. This was wrong. Tyler had gone too far. Palming the screwdriver, he leapt towards him.

Tyler looked at him, at the old man rushing towards him with a piece of metal and plastic in his hand. Tyler flicked his wrist and MacGuffin was gone, a wet red smear across the brick wall. He shook his hand and droplets of blood and skin fell from him. The ceiling rumbled and warped again. Then he took one foot off the floor, and then the other. The roof of the warehouse parted for him and he rose to meet the sky, held aloft by eighty–odd years of four–colour fantasies and the deepest hopes ingrained in humanity that when their backs were to the wall, all they would have to do is look up and there it would be. Not a bird. Not a plane. He embraced the cold air, climbed the pollution, ascended above the city.

"My city," Tyler whispered. He continued to climb, a gold and brown fireball, a supernova in the London sky. A storm was gathering, attracted to Tyler's electric glow, and as he levelled out he felt the rain sluicing him, cleansing him. When the city was thrown below him like a shattered jigsaw, he began to rotate, casting his mind out, until he found what he was looking for, shining like a beacon. He pointed himself in the direction of the Docklands, and began to swim through the air.

Mr Grundy paused by the big window overlooking Canary Wharf, swirling the brandy in his glass. "I love London at night," he said.

Monroe and Stuart were perched uncomfortably on a leather sofa in the expansively lush living quarters at the top of the tower. The apartment was moodily lit and light music tinkled from somewhere. There was no–one else in the room.

Mr Grundy turned, fiddling absent–mindedly with his cuff–links. "Mr Balfour," he said. "Miss Monroe. You have no idea of the trouble I have gone to in order to find you. And now you turn up on my doorstep. How very, very odd."

Stuart said nothing. He was beginning to think that this had been a huge mistake. He could feel Monroe bristling at the side of him. George, the big, bald henchman who had come to reception to collect them, had taken the gun from her and Escobar, his sneaky–looking sidekick, had frisked them both, taking great care and pleasure over searching Monroe.

"So," said Mr Grundy. "As you have not touched your brandy, I shall assume that this is not a social visit. Would you care, in that case, to tell me what you are doing here?"

"We're on the run," said Stuart. "From *pop*CULT!. From Tyler. We didn't know where to go."

Mr Grundy nodded, thinking about this. "So you thought you would take refuge with Tyler's hated enemy Grundy," he said. "In the manner of some action–adventure movie, I imagine. But what happens now? Do we perhaps 'join forces' to fight Tyler, now that you have decided that he is evil?"

"We just want to be protected," said Stuart weakly, looking to Monroe for help. She avoided his gaze and stared at the carpet.

"Perhaps you could begin," suggested Mr Grundy, "by giving me the exact location of the entity which Tyler insists on referring to as *pop*CULT!."

Monroe sensed a bargain approaching. "And then what?"

Mr Grundy shrugged. "You shall be protected. In any way you see fit. This is a large organisation with incredible resources, Miss Monroe. I am sure you can be accommodated."

"Maybe first you tell us what you intend to do with *pop*CULT!," said Stuart, sticking his chest out in what he hoped was a show of fearlessness.

"Ah," said Mr Grundy, pouring himself another shot of brandy. "Perhaps this is not a plea for help at all, eh? Perhaps this is a spying mission. Perhaps you have been sent by Tyler to find out my nefarious plans. And once I have told you, you will effect a dramatic escape, no doubt, returning to Tyler's lair and continuing his childish war against me. How awfully exciting."

"This isn't a trick, Mr Grundy," said Stuart.

"Of course not, Mr Balfour," said Mr Grundy. "You wouldn't be so stupid."

Mr Grundy returned to the window, contemplating London. He said, "The entity that Tyler has control of is, by rights, mine, Mr Balfour. It is my property, my legacy. Or rather it would be, if the very laws of nature themselves had not been bent out of shape.

"The thing below London is an object of immense power. Its provenance may be unknown, but its abilities are not."

Stuart opened his mouth to say that, actually, he had solved the mystery of *pop*CULT!, but Monroe stepped on his toe and he stayed quiet. Mr Grundy went on, "Allowing Tyler custody of it is akin to giving the atom bomb to savages. To putting children in control of a passenger jet. He either has little idea of the capabilities of the thing, or he chooses not to care and treats it not with the reverence it deserves, but with utter contempt."

"And you would utilise it how?" said Stuart. "You would rule the world?"

Mr Grundy turned to them once more. "More infantilism, Mr Balfour. No, I would not rule the world. I would make a better world."

"So... how?" said Stuart.

"People do not always know what is best for them. Sometimes they rail against authority, not realising it is only acting in their best interests. Decisions must sometimes be taken that may seem unpalatable, but they are the right ones, nevertheless. Try to tackle crime, and there is talk of *rights*. Try to protect the country from terror and there is whining about *civil liberties*. Time is wasted on trying to convince the populace that they should do this, or that, or not do this, or not do that. With this tool, any government could find its people much more pliable. The possibilities are, quite frankly, limitless, Mr Balfour. And I should imagine those in power will pay a great deal of money for what I shall be offering."

Stuart sighed. He had brought Monroe and himself into the lion's den, or the spider's web, perhaps. Maybe the rat's nest. Whatever animal analogy he chose, it didn't quite come close to doing justice to that sly grin on Grundy's face, a grin that put Stuart in mind of someone else entirely.

"Well, thank you for your time Mr Grundy," he said, standing stiffly. "But if it's all the same to you, we don't really see the point of taking *pop*CULT! out of the hands of one megalomaniac and putting it into the hands of another. We'll see ourselves out."

Mr Grundy calmly walked to his desk, poured another brandy, and pressed the button in his intercom. "George?" he said.

Within seconds George had let himself into the room,

accompanied by the small, wiry Latin American. For one crazy moment, Stuart thought Mr Grundy was going to let them go.

"George," said Mr Grundy. "Please take Miss Monroe into the next room. Mr Balfour is going to give me the location of the thing he so charmingly insists on calling *pop*CULT!. We shall send some gentlemen to check the veracity of his information. If they report that he is lying, you have my permission to hold down Miss Monroe and allow Escobar to brutalise her in any way he feels necessary until Mr Balfour gives us the correct location."

"Oh, God," said Stuart in a small voice. Could things possibly get any worse? As Mr Grundy turned back to his window, which was now streaked with rivulets of rain, he started to plead. "No, look, this has all been a terrible mistake. Look, I think you should–"

"Shut up, Stuart," said Monroe. "Look."

Stuart looked. Mr Grundy was standing with his arms loosely by his side, the brandy glass rolling about on the carpet beside him. Monroe, George and Escobar were all transfixed, staring in the same direction. Beyond the window, in the night sky over Canary Wharf, a ball of golden flames was rising, a halo of buzzing fireflies, a swirling yellow and brown comet moving slowly yet inexorably into their view.

And at its centre was Tyler.

Thirty One

Tyler gestured and the window exploded inwards in a shower of tiny, needle–sharp shards. Stuart bent forward and covered his face with his arms, wincing as the glass embedded itself in the exposed flesh of his hands and wrists. When he opened his eyes again, Tyler was stepping lightly through the window, the golden flames around him dulling and fading as he touched the carpet.

"I would say this was impossible," whispered Stuart urgently to Monroe. "But I should probably know better."

Tyler regarded each of them with an impassive stare, finally alighting on Mr Grundy. A small smile played around his lips. "Thomas," he said. "I told you I would come."

Mr Grundy looked at him, his face pale. "Father," he said.

"What?" hissed Stuart to Monroe. "Tyler is Grundy's dad? How is this possible?"

Tyler laughed. "Stuart," he said. "I'm older than I look, you know. And I must say, I'm disappointed that you came running here with your tails between your legs. And I'm most upset with you, Monroe. Most upset. I presume they are under your protection now, Thomas?"

Mr Grundy waved airily. "Not really. I was going to have them both killed as soon as I had secured the location of your secret."

Tyler picked up the brandy decanter and studied it. "You really are desperate for it, aren't you, Thomas? That kind of obsession can destroy a man, you know. Tear him apart from the inside."

"It's mine!" shouted Mr Grundy, his control evaporating. "It's my birthright. You have no place clinging on to life unnaturally. It's time for the old order to make way for the new."

Tyler guffawed. "You are telling me to make way? You're an old man, Thomas. You're in your fifties."

"You're nearly two hundred years old!" screamed Mr Grundy.

Stuart goggled. "Two hundred years old?" he mouthed at Monroe. She shrugged.

"I have learned a lot in my centuries," said Tyler.

"Not how to hold on to your humanity, evidently," said Grundy.

"Oh, I'm human enough, Thomas. I do everything a human does. I eat and shit and fight and cry and hate and love. I'm just taking it one step further."

"Love?" sneered Grundy. "*Love?* Mother would have liked to hear that. Perhaps in nineteen seventy–eight, when she was breathing her last, when the cancer finally took her."

Tyler faltered momentarily. "I did love her, Thomas. Your mother. Joy."

"You didn't show you loved her," said Mr Grundy in a small voice. "You didn't show you loved me."

"Ah, but you made up for it, didn't you, Thomas? Taking half my fortune from my bank accounts?" Tyler swept his hands around him. "And this is the empire you built with it."

"Enough of this," decided Mr Grundy, regaining his composure and twisting his cuff–link furiously. "Escobar, the woman."

Monroe was grabbed from behind by Escobar as he withdrew a large, curved blade from within his jacket.

"If my fa– if Mr Tyler does not leave within fifteen seconds, open her throat," said Mr Grundy.

Tyler shrugged, and Escobar's head exploded in a mess of blood, bone and fat. "Ew," said Stuart as he was splattered with gore. Monroe gagged and spat a stream of vomit on Mr Grundy's expensive carpet.

"As you said," smiled Tyler, "enough of this. You want to see *pop*CULT!? Then come with me."

"Ah," said Stuart, then more loudly, "Tyler? Are you, uh, still going to kill me?"

"Perhaps," said Tyler. "Perhaps not."

"What about the book? Don't I need to die for that any more?"

Tyler considered this, then waved his arm. The golden–brown

flames around him ignited again and he began to rise. Stuart, Monroe and Mr Grundy felt themselves lifted along with him.

"The book is redundant, Stuart. The game has changed."

There was a noise from the back of the room and Stuart turned to see George fleeing. He didn't know what was going to happen next, but he suddenly knew what he had to do. He delved into his pocket and pulled out Sam's mobile. He jabbed her home number and she answered after one ring. "Sam," he said. "Things have gone arse up here. Listen very carefully..."

"Oh God," said Stuart. The ball of fire that surrounded Tyler had expanded to engulf them all, and now Tyler was stepping back out of the shattered window, taking them with him. *Don't look down, don't look down, don't look down,* Stuart told himself, then as he was gingerly eased through the broken glass he immediately looked past his feet. The ground was so far away as to be negligible. He very much wished for the solidity of the Big Ben clocktower against his back. He blanched and looked at Monroe, who had her eyes closed. They moved off through the air, the rain and wind battering them.

"I could, if I liked, just let go," said Tyler, almost conversationally. "You could fall, Stuart, and die. If that's what you want."

"Not really!" shouted Stuart, trying not to sound hysterical. *You're flying,* a tiny voice insisted at the back of his head. He told it to shut up.

"I have moved on," said Tyler. "Mankind's future no longer rests in the pursuit of celebrity. We have much higher goals now."

They followed the Thames for a while, the lights of London twinkling far below. "People will look up and see me," said Tyler. "Tonight they will dream of me. Tomorrow everyone in London will want to be me. Will want to embrace their super–human destiny. And *pop*CULT! will make it happen. We shall become supermen. We shall be unstoppable. It will be the dawn of a new age."

They hovered over Whitehall for a long moment. "We shall smash Parliament and dance in its smoking remains," said Tyler.

Then he pointed them in the direction of Putney. Stuart looked at Mr Grundy, whose mouth had set in a bloodless line. Then they began to descend, and beneath them the blasted roof of the warehouse beckoned. Tyler floated them through the fissure and into the rain–slick headquarters of *pop*CULT!. As he brought them down to the concrete floor the halo of fireflies dissipated and Tyler looked almost normal.

"Home," he said.

"Where's Luther and the rest?" asked Monroe.

"*pop*CULT! couldn't maintain the multiple–persona projects, not with the energy I needed. They've gone."

"Gone?"

"Yes," said Tyler. "Gone. They don't exist any more. They've been cancelled."

"And MacGuffin?" said Stuart.

Tyler gestured towards the wet, blackening smear across the wall. "MacGuffin got in my way," he said simply.

"So this is where you hide yourself," said Mr Grundy, regaining his bearing now he was back on solid ground. He smoothed down his rain–wet hair. "Like rats."

"Yes," said Tyler. "Like rats. Rats are very adaptable, you know, Thomas. They say they could survive a nuclear war."

"What now?" asked Monroe edgily.

Tyler smiled brightly. "Let's go see *pop*CULT!" he said.

Professor Garrett was less than happy to receive a telephone call from Sam. "We're just going out," he complained. "What did you want again?"

"Stuart Balfour's book," she said. "It's very urgent, Professor. Stuart needs a printed copy of it immediately. It's a matter of life and death."

"And who did you say you were?"

"Sam," she said. "His friend. It really is very urgent."

"You could be anyone," said Garrett. "Look, I'm afraid I have to go. I can't see what Balfour would want with a copy of his book on Saturday night anyway."

"He told me to tell you that Miss Monroe..."

Professor Garrett paused. "Yes..?" he said cautiously.

"...would be *very* grateful if you could organise this," said Sam. "Extremely grateful."

Professor Garrett looked at his watch. "All right," he sighed. "It will take me about half an hour. Here's the address."

Mr Grundy found it impossible to hide his amazement at the Velvet Underground. "Its capabilities are incredible," he whispered, visibly impressed. "It made this from thin air?"

"Not just like that," said Tyler. "The energy needs shaping. Moulding. It takes time and forethought."

"Incredible," said Mr Grundy again, brushing the velveteen seating of the carriage.

"You ain't seen nothing yet, Thomas," grinned Tyler.

"They're getting on like a fucking house on fire," hissed Stuart to Monroe.

"I know. Christ, I don't know if it's a good thing or a bad thing. Imagine the two of them together..."

The carriage slowed and halted in silence. "Void," said Tyler. "Please take all your belongings with you."

"What now?" said Mr Grundy.

Tyler indicated the black velvet ladder set in the wall. "I'm afraid it gets rather messy from here on in, Thomas. Were those shoes expensive?"

"They're Italian."

Tyler pulled a face. "Ah well."

With the sheaf of printed white A4 sheets on her passenger seat, Sam squealed along Professor Garrett's drive and into the labyrinth of his quiet residential estate. Now she had to find her way back to Elysian Fields. As she pulled out on to the main road and tried to figure out her best route, she took pause to wonder what in hell she was doing, and why. She couldn't think of any real reasons for helping Stuart Balfour out. He'd never done her any favours. But she couldn't help liking him. And she had to admit, all this was pretty exciting.

It had taken Professor Garrett a little longer than expected to print out Stuart's book because of an ink cartridge failure. Sam had waited impatiently in his hallway, avoiding the suspicious gaze of Garrett's wife. She put her foot down and ran a red light. Stuart had sounded pretty frazzled on the phone. Afraid, even. She bumped across a mini roundabout and ignored the chorus of horns.

It was six–thirty by the time she pulled up outside Elysian Fields. Gathering the manuscript and the torch she'd been told to bring, she ran to the door, swiping her security card and heading straight for the smashed–up door to the cellar, just as Stuart had said she should.

Another nurse stepped back in surprise as Sam ran by. "Oh. I thought you were on day off."

"I am," shouted Sam over her shoulder. "Just called in to save the world."

Bob the handyman had put yellow–and–black tape across the broken door, and she pushed it to one side and stepped through. At the bottom of the stairs was the hatch cover, loosely fitted. She pushed it to one side and shone the torch down the black hole. "Okay," she said. Stuffing the manuscript into her jeans waistband, she put the torch between her teeth and swung her legs over the side.

By the time she reached the bottom, Sam was having severe misgivings about the enterprise. "Oh, gross," she muttered. It stunk. She edged along the ledge, shining the torch ahead of her. A rat bounced off the ledge and into the water with a light splash. "Oh, double gross," she said.

"I must say," said Mr Grundy in distaste, "that this does not raise my opinion of you or your group in any way."

"We are all of us in the gutter, but some of us are looking at the stars," said Tyler. He seemed to Stuart to be much more like his old self, much less... *other* than he had appeared earlier.

"I don't care if I never see the inside of a sewer again in my life," muttered Stuart.

"That," said Tyler, "is entirely possible."

"You are going to kill us, then?" said Mr Grundy calmly.

Tyler shrugged. "To be honest, I'm not sure. I just want to show you *pop*CULT!."

As they neared the hidden room, Stuart felt a tingle at his spine. It was the Machine Elves, hiding in the shadows behind them, in the spaces between worlds. Perhaps it was them who were bringing Tyler here. They gave Stuart's brain an exploratory touch, and recoiled with something approaching delight.

"Soon," whispered Stuart. "Soon. It's all right. I know what to do now."

Tyler looked at him, shining his torch in his face. "What was that?" He was feeling the presences as well.

"Nothing," said Stuart. "I'm merely talking to myself. It's anxiety at my impending death."

Tyler narrowed his eyes and then turned again. A little way later he stopped, fishing out his keys. "We're here."

Mr Grundy could not have prepared himself for *pop*CULT!. He stared wide-eyed at its glowing magnificence, his jaw slack. "Oh. My. God," he breathed. "I never dreamed... I could not have imagined."

Tyler bounded up on to one of the rickety walkways which spider-webbed the huge cavern. At his approach, *pop*CULT! seemed to roll like a huge, beached leviathan, its surface fizzing and raging and its pseudopodal limbs reaching up to him.

"It's in pain," said Stuart. "You've pushed it too far, Tyler."

Tyler looked at him. "Don't think to speak to me of *pop*CULT!, Stuart Balfour. It is a thing beyond your ken."

"You might be surprised," said Stuart calmly.

"Stuart, what are you planning?" murmured Monroe.

Mr Grundy had collected himself. "Tyler. You know not what you have here. It is not a plaything. It can change worlds. You must give it to me."

Tyler laughed. "It is a thing for fathers, Thomas. Not sons."

Mr Grundy took a step on to the gantry. "Listen to me," he hissed. "This is the most important discovery in the history of the world. You are wasting it."

"I am celebrating it!" laughed Tyler. "I am revelling in it!"

Grundy was on the walkway now. He held out a hand. "Then let me join you. Let us use this thing together."

Tyler opened his arms wide. "Thomas. I thought you were lost to me. Come here."

Mr Grundy rushed forward, embracing Tyler. For a moment they stood there, still and silent, then Tyler grunted and his grip around Mr Grundy's shoulders slackened. He staggered back and Stuart and Monroe gasped; there was the black handle of a knife protruding from his gut, a slick of dark blood colouring his clothing.

"How... very Oedipal of you... Thomas," gasped Tyler, pulling out the blood–slicked knife. He looked down at the wound, which closed and knitted before his eyes with the faintest of glows. Tyler grinned then growled and launched himself at Mr Grundy.

Sam had considered giving up at the point where she was supposed to climb into the sluggish flow of raw sewage. This had simply ceased to be an adventure. But then, from ahead, she heard sounds, and a dull gold and brown glow emanated from beyond the bend of the tunnel, giving her hope. Wincing, she splashed into the dark water and waded to the far ledge, hauling herself out and slopping in wet trainers along to where a metal door set in the brick wall hung open, the same sickly from within painting shadows on the curved sewer tunnel brickwork.

Sam popped her head around the door. "Thank Christ," she said, seeing Stuart. Then she looked beyond him, at the seething mass of god–knows–what, and her brain decided to close down all extraneous activity. "Oh," she said.

Stuart was immediately at her side, easing the copy of his book out of her jeans. "You're a star," he whispered, kissing her on the cheek.

Monroe was at his side. "This better be good," she said.

"It will be," said Stuart.

Tyler had his hands wrapped around Mr Grundy's neck, but his strength was failing, and Mr Grundy was pummelling his wounded mid–section with his fists. "It's over, Tyler," grunted Mr Grundy.

"Never," said Tyler grimly through gritted teeth.

"No, he's right," shouted Stuart, standing at the edge of the abyss that contained *pop*CULT!, the sheaf of papers in his hand. "It really is over."

There was a pause, as though no–one could really believe what Stuart was doing. He couldn't believe it himself, but he knew it was right.

"*pop*CULT! is alive," he said. "But not in the way we think. It's the things you call Machine Elves who are the real entities, Tyler. They're wondrous beings from another place who came to Earth to preserve for eternity the fruits of human creativity. And what did you do, Tyler? You enslaved them."

Tyler and Mr Grundy had dropped their hands now, and were standing on the gantry, listening to Stuart. He went on, "And you're no better, Grundy. If it isn't a peasants' revolt and everybody becoming a TV star or super–hero, it's making the country a paradise for *Daily Mail* readers. You've both got the chance to do something special, something lasting, and you throw it away on your petty little concerns."

Stuart waved his free hand at the amorphous mass, which seemed to have quieted and calmed as he spoke. "Do you know what this is? It's mankind's first encounter with extra–terrestrial intelligences. And what have the fruits of Mother Earth's loins done to it? Locked it in a sewer."

311

Stuart barked a laugh which echoed around the hall. "A fucking sewer! Priceless. It's an example of unknown, unguessable alien technology, and you've locked it in a sewer and made it turn party tricks, pushed it and pushed it until it's in agony and near death and its crew – yes, Tyler, it's fucking crew – have been trapped here for centuries forced to pander to your every single whim."

Stuart stared at them for a long time. "It's obscene," he whispered. "You might as well have put a neon sign on the moon saying 'Earth – please do not approach'. You've set humanity back centuries, Tyler. And you would have done the same, Grundy. Well, like I said, it ends here."

Tyler finally found his voice. "And just what do you propose to do about it, Stuart? A little socially inept writer like you?"

Stuart simply smiled and picked up the first page of his manuscript. "*pop*CULT!: *The definitive history of recent popular culture*," he read. "*By Stuart Balfour.*"

Then he dropped it into *pop*CULT!.

Stuart peeled off another page and let it go. Then another. And another. A whole chapter.

Tyler snorted. "What's this? Some grand gesture? Some symbolic act before I come down there and fucking tear you apart with my bare hands?"

"No," said Stuart, picking up another chapter's worth and flinging it into the air so it confetti'd down and was swallowed up by the swirling mass. "Look what I'm doing, Tyler. Look what *pop*CULT!'s doing. Think how important this book was to you a few days ago."

Another chapter. *pop*CULT! opened to receive it, swallowing it up. Deep down beneath their feet, everyone in the room felt a shudder.

"Page by page I'm putting my treatise of popular culture into *pop*CULT!. I'm feeding it with the history of everything I hold dear. Everything you hate, Grundy. Everything you imagine can free mankind from its self–imposed shackles, Tyler," said Stuart, tossing another fistful of pages.

He held up a chapter. "See this? It's all about reality TV." He tossed it in. The gantry on which Grundy and Tyler were standing swayed slightly. The pages fluttered on to the twinkling plastic surface of *pop*CULT! and were absorbed into it.

Then something happened.

*pop*CULT! belched.

The shockwave reverberated around the room. Tyler and Grundy had to hang on to the walkway as it rippled and tried to tear free from its moorings. Monroe stumbled and held on to Sam for support.

Stuart held up the remaining pages. "You know what's going to happen when I throw the rest of this in, Tyler? You know what'll happen, Grundy?"

He smiled at their frozen faces, then whispered, "Pop will eat itself."

With that, he flung the last of his book – his book that had been read by no other living soul – into *pop*CULT!. The entity, at last understanding that Stuart was freeing it from its unwilling service, reached up a dozen pseudopodal tentacles to receive the pages. As it drew them into its core, *pop*CULT! finally consumed the very essence of itself, and then spectacularly died.

"Holy fuck," screamed Tyler as *pop*CULT! began to come apart, first in pin–pricks then in a storm of globules, a nuclear–powered lava lamp gone into meltdown. The walls were shaking and first dust, then masonry, began to crumble from above.

"Let's get the fuck out of here," shouted Monroe, pushing Sam out of the door. Stuart was right behind them, turning once to see the gantry collapse and Tyler and Grundy locked in each others' arms falling towards the haemorrhaging *pop*CULT!. Whether they were still fighting or finally at peace with each other, he wouldn't have liked to say.

Stuart never knew what made him put his hand in the pocket of his borrowed jeans at that moment, but he felt suddenly compelled to. His fingers closed around a piece of folded, worn

313

paper. As Monroe tried to pull him out, he examined it curiously. It was an old, faded lottery ticket. With a smile, Stuart tossed it into the raging mass of *pop*CULT!.

The channel of sewage was violently choppy as they half–ran, half–waded through it, dragging themselves up the ladder and into the cellar of Elysian Fields. "Get everyone out," Stuart told Sam. "Tell them there's subsidence or something. Just get them out."

As Sam organised the bemused staff and residents, Stuart ran into the street. Further along the road, pretty much where *pop*CULT! lay just below the surface, the Tarmac had buckled and there was a huge dent in the street. There were already people peering into it and on the wind Stuart could hear sirens.

"Is that it, then? Is it done?"

Stuart turned and at first thought someone had wandered out of a nearby house and was talking to him. There was an eminently plain young woman there, the kind your eyes would skim over if you saw her in a pub, the sort of person you might forget to hold a shop door open for, no matter how courteous you were normally. An invisible, innocuous, nobody sort of person.

"Monroe?" said Stuart, aghast.

"Not any more," she said. "The glamour's gone. *pop*CULT! really must be dead. Thank God."

Stuart embraced her awkwardly. Was it really over? He felt a prickle at the nape of his neck, and could sense them crowding around him. The Machine Elves. If *pop*CULT! was really dead, what of them? They were no longer chained to it, but what happened to them now? They were convinced he knew the answer, but he couldn't for the life of him know what it was.

"Hey, look," said the woman who was Monroe.

Just across the street in the shadow of a shop was a bulky, pale figure. The Urban Spaceman. It waved a padded hand at them.

"Of course," said Stuart. "What was it MacGuffin said? 'Mankind's wonder at the mysteries of outer space made flesh'.

It's perfect."

One second the Machine Elves where there, clustered around him, the next they were gone. He saw the Urban Spaceman stiffen slightly, and then a faint glow of golden fairy dust played around him. He began to lope along the street. Then he turned, raised one hand, and touched the thumb and forefinger of his glove together, the other fingers held stiffly aloft. He cast the sign at Stuart, then leapt into the air. And kept leaping. Up, up, up. Stuart put his arm around the woman who was Monroe, just as Sam joined them and looked up at the disappearing white dot as it gathered speed and was swallowed by the night clouds. Stuart waved. The Machine Elves were going home.

"Sam, have you got a pen?" said Stuart suddenly as the final psychic echo of *pop*CULT!'s death throes hit him square in the cerebral cortex. She nodded. "Write these numbers down," he said.

One Year Later

Stuart pointed out his name on the guest–list and the bouncer waved him through the doors into the dark, smoky club. It was already heaving with bodies, and he had to push his way through the throng to the bar. As he waved his ten pound note at the girl, he caught sight of the woman who was Monroe, standing off to one side, alone. She waved at him and he mimed a drinking motion at her. She nodded and mouthed what looked like "lager" at him.

When he'd extricated himself from the crush he handed her a bottle of beer and gave her a kiss on the cheek.

"Good crowd in tonight," she said.

He nodded. "Lots of industry people here, apparently."

The woman who used to be Monroe had barely been given a second glance since she walked into the club. It was a novelty that still delighted her. "So, how was it today?" she said.

"Not bad, as far as these things go," said Stuart, taking a swig of his beer. "It was quite a good turn–out. A lot of Mrs Zygmundewicz's friends were there. They're quite sprightly for their age, even if most of the conversation at the Polish Club afterwards was about who was going to go next."

"At least you gave her a good send–off."

"Least I could do," said Stuart. "I've paid for two funerals this year, Mrs Zed's and Walter's. At least I know Mrs Zed died happy; she reckons that on that night, the night we killed *pop*CULT!, her dead husband Lech came back and they danced to Strauss waltzes until dawn."

The woman who was Monroe shrugged. "A lot of strange stuff happened that night. It was the *pop*CULT! fall–out. Ghosts, UFOs, lights in the sky. That's why we've had all these paranormal shows on the telly, I reckon. At least that super–hero craze fizzled out."

"Well, it was bound to after that bloke dressed as Batman got shot raiding that crack–house," agreed Stuart. "Although I think there's a guy calling himself The Magnificent Trevor still helping old ladies across the road." He paused, then said, "Do you think we did the right thing, in the end? Do you think it made any difference?"

She sighed. "Who's to know, really? I don't think many people will have noticed one way or the other. I read a story in the paper the other day saying that fewer kids want to be celebrities, these days. More students are taking plumbing courses than media degrees."

Stuart nodded. "I saw Professor Garrett a couple of weeks ago. He's hardly had any applications this year. He's worried they're going to close down his department. And I went to see Jane and Quentin's new baby as well. It looks like Quentin might be made redundant; the production company he works for's in a bit of trouble. Seems no–one wants reality TV shows about slimming much any more."

"Oh dear," said the woman who was Monroe.

"I bunged them a few grand in an envelope, stuck it through the door after I'd left. They'd never have taken it. Too proud. But I don't like to think of them struggling, not with the new baby."

"How's the money going?"

"Pretty much gone, to be honest. I bought the flat and I've got my mum in a much nicer residential place with one–on–one care. Gave Sam some to kick–start the band. A million doesn't go very far these days, you know."

"And how is your mum?"

"Not great," said Stuart tightly. "Going further downhill every day. At least that book thing never got off the ground; I don't think she could have handled that. The money does help, though. She's as happy as she can be."

"Pity you had to share the jackpot," said the woman.

Stuart shrugged. "I should have realised I wasn't the only one who'd pick up the numbers when *pop*CULT! broadcast them. Biggest Lotto jackpot ever, highest number of people to share it. Still, no point being greedy, is there? I still wish you'd let me give you some."

"I don't need it, Stuart, honestly. I'm having a lovely time at the moment. I've got a little flat, doing a bit of temping work, pleasing myself. I'm just enjoying being me, for a change."

"And, uh, the other thing?"

"Celibate and loving it," said the woman who was no longer Monroe. "Although..."

"Although?"

"There is a nice boy at work who's been asking me to go for a coffee."

"Do you think you will?"

"Well, he *is* a nice boy. Perhaps. Anyway, what about you? You're looking good, Stuart. Did you buy those clothes yourself?"

Stuart looked at the stage where the band was setting up. Sam was speaking into a microphone, one finger in her ear, waving at the sound man to reduce the levels.

"Uh, no. Sam's influence. But I'm doing great. Better than great, in fact. She's brilliant. I think I might be helplessly in love, actually."

The woman who was Monroe pointed with her bottle at the banner strung behind the stage. "Good name for a band."

Stuart nodded. The banner said *pop*CULT!. "Sam thought it was a shame to waste it."

"So you've abandoned all plans for your book, then?"

"For the pop culture thing, yeah. Thought it had served its purpose. Didn't seem right to resurrect it. I have been doing some scribbling on another project, though."

"Do tell."

"It's about everything that went on. The whole *pop*CULT! thing."

The woman who was Monroe gave a rueful little laugh. "It might be a bit far-fetched for most people."

"That's why I'm writing it as a novel. A science fiction thing."

"We were all just fictions to Tyler," she said, a little distantly.

"Good luck with it. I'll have to come to the book launch."

"No stunts like climbing Big Ben this time though," laughed Stuart. "The police didn't press charges but I think I'd better keep my nose clean for a bit." He paused for a moment, then said, "Hey, you'll never guess who's also on the books of my literary agent. George. You know, Grundy's right–hand man?"

"Really?"

"Yeah, he's a bit of a reformed character these days. It's supposed to be pretty good, his book. A good old fashioned story. An original, says my agent."

"That does seem to be the watchword these days. Original. Hey, speaking of which, Sam's on."

The band struck up. Later, reviews in the magazines and newspapers would identify the gig as one of the most important ones of the decade, the event that kicked off a whole new scene in music, a scene that smashed apart the old order, that disbanded the musical tribes, that paved the way for a golden age in pop music. For the moment, though, Stuart just really enjoyed it.

Afterwards, there was an after–show party planned at another club down the road. "Are you coming?" Stuart asked the woman formerly called Monroe.

She shook her head. "Early night for me. Great gig, Sam. You two take care."

Stuart, his arm draped around Sam, led the way out of the club and down the street. She looked up at him and gave him a wrinkle–nosed smile. "Did you really enjoy it?"

"Fantastic," said Stuart truthfully. As they passed a beggar, hunched with his knees drawn against his chest, a tatty blanket around his shoulders, Stuart paused and dug into his pocket, dropping a tenner at his feet.

"You're going to run out of money, soon," admonished Sam playfully.

"Practically already have," he sniffed. "But with your pop career and my writing, I should think we'll be okay."

Sam dug into her pocket and dropped a flyer for the next

*pop*CULT! show in front of the beggar as well. Stuart gave her a quizzical look. She laughed lightly. "Well, he's obviously a fan if he's outside the gig at this time of night."

They moved on and it wasn't until they were some distance away that the beggar raised his head. If Stuart had thought to glance back, he might have considered there to be something familiar about the grimy, lined face, the greasy hair hanging in hanks around his shoulders, the wiry, muscular frame beneath the filthy clothes. But what he would have found most familiar were the beggar's eyes, which followed Stuart and Sam down the street until they had become lost in the crowds of night–time people. They weren't eyes in the normal sense, but glowing translucent orbs, brown shapes writhing within a faintly golden phosphorescence. The beggar snatched the ten pound note from the ground and secreted it within his clothes. He vaguely remembered a time when he had money, when he had more money than he could count. But for a year or more he hadn't known where it was, couldn't imagine a life that didn't involve wandering from doorway to doorway, sleeping rough in bus shelters, scraping food from takeaway containers in bins. He couldn't imagine a life where he even knew his own name.

He picked up the flyer and studied it. *pop*CULT!, it said. His lips moved silently as he mouthed the word. He tried it again, louder, the voice he hadn't heard for so long sounding alien and rasping to him.

"*pop*CULT!."

Then he broke into a wide smile.

David Barnett is an award-winning journalist based in the North of England. He is the author of the novels *Hinterland* and *Angelglass,* and the collection *The Janus House and Other Two-Faced Tales.* He is represented by the John Jarrold Literary Agency, and can be found at www.davidbarnett.org.uk and on Twitter @davidmbarnett. He is married to Claire, and they have two children, Charlie and Alice, and two cats, Kali and Shiva.